I0629645

Copyright © 2019 by Jevasia Stephenson

Printed in Canada

Library of Congress Cataloging-in-Publication Data on file.

ISBN: 979-8-89778-469-1

Also by **LISA K. STEPHENSON**

The Snows of Khione: Book 1

Borderline

The Yellow Brownstone

Even My Hair Is Mad

Late Bloomer

To my family.

Suspended in a world filled with lust, anger, resentment, and hatred, we can only look to the Almighty for eternal guidance. Who is your Almighty? Have you opened your heart to receive Him?

Lisa K. Stephenson

ASIAS BRANDS

New York

Green Trees

PART I.

ROOTS

HER laughter was a celestial melody, like moonlight cascading through a symphony of wind chimes—sweet, enchanting, and utterly otherworldly. She was a vision of beauty, possessing a power almost divine. And I, the Eve to her Adam, despite the reversal of our creation. My baby sister was as unique as they came, for without her, I would be nothing more than a rib within a chest. Yet, no words, no thoughts, no expressions of devotion will ever be enough to truly capture her essence.

SITTING ON MY PORCH, rocking in my chair on this hot summer day, I am reminded of the good ol' days—the ones filled with laughter and commotion as children frolicked outside, climbing trees in search of new adventures. Nevertheless, we were the owners of the newly renovated cottage, purchased for a chance to start anew, to escape the outside world long enough to find ourselves. It became my biggest regret. Peter and I had been searching for a reason to love each other again after all we had endured.

My cottage remains partially unchanged from how it stood fifteen years ago—a large, yellow brick home with an extended fireplace, four bedrooms, and two full bathrooms. Through my illness, I have spent months working tirelessly to bring this cottage up to modern standards, and now, it is finally there. Despite all the pain and hardships that took place here, I am proud to call it home. The crimson tiles, the marble-like counters, the fresh scent of oak that graces my nostrils each morning— these are the things that endure.

The view from the porch is nothing fancy: three oak trees stand tall and wide, their branches stretching over the long, desolate road that extends about two miles down to the neighbors. Each time a car drives by, the dirt kicks up, stinging your eyes and coating the air with dust. During the on-season, customers would drive up, and the children would yell, "Auntie, Auntie! Someone's here to buy from you!"

I would rush outside, leaving my pot on the stove— damn near burning the place down—elated that someone had come by to buy the fresh vegetation I had worked so hard to grow. But with each visitor came the familiar sting of disappointment when they left. I would think to myself, *When will another come? How much of my harvest will go to waste before then?* Business was slow, and more than anything, I resented that man for convincing me to grow vegetation and sell produce. That was all I had become—a fat, ugly, produce-selling woman, all alone, raising children that weren't even mine.

Each day, I sank deeper into my depression, feeling unwanted and unloved. Feeling the urge to take my own life but reminding myself that doing so was a sin. If I ended the one life the Almighty had given me, heaven would no longer be an option. I had so much to complain about, yet so much to be grateful for. Some days were rough and miserable, but they were still good—because God made them good.

It was a time when my faith was tested and restored so often that I knew there had to be a God. Each time I cried out and questioned him, His Almighty would show me a sign or speak to my spirit, assuring me that better days were ahead. Hearing his voice and the laughter of those children made those the good ol' days.

Despite my failing eyesight, I can see the man treading through the heat, his briefcase swinging as he steps lightly past the overgrown cornfield. The South Carolina sun is always one to reckon with, climbing to one hundred and five degrees today. I fan myself profusely, watching as the stiff trees stand motionless against the road, the sand and dust shimmering in the heat. The man, growing weary, no doubt regretting his decision to wear a three-piece suit and such an ornate necktie on a day like this.

Folding his handkerchief and slipping it back into his pocket, I can tell he's a traveler. Must be from the East. He treads forward in disbelief, unsure if it's the heat pressing down on him or his own exhaustion. He had no idea the sun could be so cruel, shining without remorse—not a single cloud in sight to offer relief.

Biting my lip, I watch as he becomes more pronounced with each step, drawing closer and closer. Now stepping firmly onto my land, he slows, his breath coming in short gasps. Five feet from my porch steps, he comes to a halt. A tall, dark-skinned African-American man with squinting eyes looks at me and says,

"Morning, ma'am. My name—eh—Washington Clarke, and I'm looking for a woman by the name of, uh, Ms. Vernette Robinson."

Fidgety little guy—he can't stay still. He rubs his eyes, twitches his fingers, swats at the pesky bees, and wipes at the tears flowing freely down his cheeks, no doubt caused by the merciless heat. I resist the urge to scream, *Stay still, young man, stay still!* Instead, I observe him, realizing that despite having raised plenty of children in my lifetime, he was not one of them.

I hold my head high, glancing at this ol' Washington, thinking to myself, *What could a man this handsome want with an old gal like me?* But I need not worry—he seems harmless.

"I am Ms. Vernette. Now, what do you want? No produce be sold on this land no mo'."

He smiles—a beautiful smile, undoubtedly handsome—then pulls out his handkerchief once more, this time from his back pocket, wiping his cheeks, lips, neck, and eyelids.

"Hello, Ms. Vernette, the pleasure is all mine. You are truly much more beautiful in person."

I lower my eyes, trying to remain discreet so as not to betray the fact that I am flattered, though no doubt bewildered. I continue to fan myself, feeling my shoulder-length gray hair lift and fall against the nape of my neck. I am intrigued. I haven't had a visitor in years—just been living here, day to day, waiting for the good Lord to call me home.

And now here he comes. A visitor. A beautifully sculpted stranger, here inquiring about me.

What a dream I must be having. Could be the sun, playing tricks on me. Or maybe—just maybe—it's the Lord answering my prayers, delivering me a man. But what a long time coming, and this poor man—he can't do nothing for me now.

I chuckle at the absurd thoughts running through my head, and he shoots me a look of fear. "C'mon, poor child, let Vern get you something to drink. You thirsty?"

He continued smiling and panting, still trying to regain his strength, his vitality.

"Yes, ma'am. Some water, please, if you'd be so kind."

I hesitated no more. The last thing I need is a dead body on this here porch. Living out in the middle of nowhere, with my neighbors two miles up the block, this little cottage is all I got. Don't need it becoming no funeral home now. Only person finna die here is Ms. Vern. Yep, that's right—Ms. Vern. And that be me.

"Now, what brings you to this side of town?" I asked, my curiosity at its peak.

"I came across your photo in *The New York Times*, dated August 18, 1968. If my math serves me correctly, you were forty at the time—birthday having recently passed. After reading that article, I realized you had a truly interesting life. I was wondering if you would allow me to write about it. I think your story would sell; people would love you."

Crossing my arms, I shot up from my chair, anger rising in my chest. *Irate* doesn't even begin to cover it. Is my past as a small-time criminal still being broadcast across New York City, when I no longer even reside there? Ain't no way. That crime wasn't even my idea. I repented, and God forgave me. And now here comes this man, wanting to drag me back to a life of sin? I ain't havin' it.

"Look here, pretty boy, that part of my life been gone and *ova wit'*. I'm a new woman—been a new woman ever since them prick cops let me walk free that Thursday morning. You can't come 'round here expectin' me to go back to that place. I left them dark days for the light. Jesus is my light, and I promised Him I would never go back. So help me, God."

I dropped back into my rocker, ignoring Mr. Clarke entirely—forgetting the water I promised him.

"Ms. Vernette, if I may?" He motioned toward the porch step, asking permission to sit.

I sighed, nodding my head up and down.

He settled himself, then leaned forward, resting his elbows on his knees. "I've spent so many days dreaming of the moment we would meet. My father was a journalist before me—read so many books, wrote so many stories— but none like the one he wished he could have written about you. I found newspaper clippings all throughout my home as a boy, and you were the topic of each one."

I narrowed my eyes, listening despite myself.

"A woman with a story like yours," he continued, "should not go unheard. My daddy was convinced the tabloids told nothing but lies. He wanted so badly to write the truth—the truth only *you* can tell."

I stiffened, gripping the arms of my chair.

"I understand you are a woman of age, but please believe me when I say this: your life is truly inspirational. People have found their calling because of you. They've come to believe there is a God. The points you made, the speeches you gave on being a victim of police brutal—"

"Stop!"

I can't hear anymore. My mind begins swirling with thoughts as my life suddenly flashes before my eyes. I knew of the horrible things written about me in those posts, but I had no idea anyone had listened when I spoke my truth in front of the police station all them years ago.

A woman of God, I cannot allow myself to be taken back to that place—the place Clarke is asking of me. That place of darkness.

My eyes fill with tears as memories of the hurt I endured and the pain I caused—both to myself and those who loved me—rush back. But then another thought creeps in. *What if I die, and no one ever knows the truth?*

If I leave this world without telling my side, I will forever be the woman the newspapers portrayed me to be. I will never have given people the chance to see who I really am. I've been exploited, dragged through the mud, and all for nothing. My good name, tainted.

I take a long look at Washington, searching his face, then ask,

"How does this work exactly?"

His eyes light up with glee as he inches a little closer, carefully placing a tape recorder atop my mantle. He reaches into his briefcase and pulls out four legal pads, three blue ballpoint pens, a pencil, a highlighter, and a few thick textbooks on journalism to press on.

A little *too* overzealous for my taste—I ain't even agreed yet.

"I thank you so much for being willing to do this," he says, voice full of energy. "I promise you won't regret it! First, I'll begin by reading you a disclosure. This ensures your legal protection, as well as my own. This is an interview where I will obtain information on your behalf for a biographical novel. In turn, I will write and complete this novel myself."

He pauses, watching for my reaction before continuing.

"Depending on how much detail you'd like to include, this meeting could take anywhere from four hours to four days. Ultimately, it's up to you. But I encourage you to go all the way—of course, the more details, the better. We can take as many breaks as you need. Just let me know. And if at any point you mention something you'd like retracted, simply say 'disregard,' and I promise it will not be used."

I shift in my chair, unsure.

"I'm only here to ascertain the facts, gather information, and reproduce accordingly," he assures me. "I understand this may be difficult, but I want you to know—I'm not just here as a reporter, Ms. Vern. I'm here as a friend."

Then, leaning forward, he asks,

"Do you wish to continue?"

He speaks with speed and sincerity, his words hanging in the air between us. The look in his eyes is praying I say *yes*. The feeling in my gut is telling me to say *yes*.

Then, as if on cue, the sun shifts, and the clouds emerge from their hiding place, bringing with them a cool breeze. A breeze I have not felt in days. The tree leaves rustle, whispering in the wind. I hear the voices telling me *yes*. I feel the presence of the Lord telling me *yes*.

This is my time.

At eighty-six years of age, I wake up each day grateful for another blessing. But maybe—just maybe—the reason I'm still here is because my purpose is not yet fulfilled.

And maybe, just maybe, Washington *is* my purpose.

So, I refuse to hesitate any further.

"Yes, I do wish to continue."

The wind picks up as if to celebrate my decision, carrying Washington into the long day ahead with me, Ms. Vern.

"Do you have a place to stay?" I ask, knowing this will take longer than a day.

He nods. "Yes, but it's quite a distance into town."

I don't even have to think twice. "Then you'll stay here in my cottage."

There is no way I'm letting this young man walk back and forth down this long road every day. I have the extra space, so why not?

His eyes widen in disbelief. "Wow, thank you so much! I am beyond grateful. Believe me, this is going to be great, and I promise your story will change lives. I'll make sure of it!"

His assurance does my heart wonders, but nothing like the whispers in the wind, the chills in the air, filling the atmosphere with a sense of purpose. Telling me that I am making the right choice. That this is where I am meant to be.

And so, it begins.

Washington turns on the tape recorder and proceeds with the disclosure. I listen carefully, understanding and agreeing to the terms.

I am ready.

He clears his throat and speaks into the recorder.

"Good afternoon. Today is August 19, 2014, and we are here to begin the biographical interview with Ms. Vernette Robinson, who has knowingly agreed to our terms and conditions. I, Washington Clarke, a freelance journalist, will begin by asking: Ms. Robinson, how was life growing up with your younger sibling, Veronica Robinson?"

Hearing her name sends shivers down my spine.

—

REMINISCING about my life always brings tears to my eyes. The hurt and hardships that fell upon me and my family make me question: *How is it that I am still alive?*

Growing up in the streets of Harlem, New York, was nothing short of exciting—but at the same time, terrifying.

My father, a police officer who eventually worked his way up to Captain, left every night for his overnight shift. For many long years, he returned in the mornings with a loathsome look, as if the weight of the city's darkness clung to him.

My mother was a housewife, and although we lived on a single income, we never went without.

Our three-story brownstone was located on the west side of the village, close to Manhattan. It was huge—so large, in fact, that our small family couldn't possibly fill it. My mother spent years trying to convince my father to rent out the extra space we had no use for, but she was never successful.

The house even had a spacious basement. With a little effort, it could have been turned into a livable space.

The layout was unique. The first floor featured a mini foyer, while the second floor held two bedrooms. The master bedroom, located on the left, had a full bathroom. The second bedroom, positioned to the right near the staircase, was incredibly spacious but had no windows.

The entry floor housed another full bathroom along the left wall, just beneath the staircase, with an additional closet near the front door specifically used for coats during the harsh winters. A long hallway led to the kitchen in the rear. To the right of the kitchen was the dining area, and just beside that was the living room. To enter either room, you had to pass through the kitchen.

Veronica and I agreed to share the downstairs bedroom as soon as we were old enough to make the request without being reprimanded or considered "spoiled children." We figured we'd have more privacy—and, more importantly, the room had windows.

We *loved* windows.

Living in Harlem, there was always something happening. Never a dull moment.

As I mentioned before, our basement was completely livable—an apartment in its own right, with a bathroom tucked into the back left corner of the lower-level staircase. The large open space, visible from the bottom of the stairs, consisted of a kitchen, dining area, and living space, with a bedroom in the rear.

Despite my mother's constant complaints that the house was too much for her to manage alone, my father refused to consider renting out the extra space. Daddy's pride would not allow him to rely on anyone else, especially when it came to providing for his family.

Over time, my sister and I came to enjoy the vastness of our home—especially when we had it all to ourselves. Our parents spent most of their leisure time upstairs in the master bedroom, leaving Veronica and me free to do as we pleased. They preferred for us to play inside, fearing the dangers lurking outside our door.

Nights felt long, but the days felt even longer as my sister and I found new ways to entertain ourselves during our teenage years. Bored with our usual indoor activities, Veronica sought excitement elsewhere. Staying late after school to chat with friends became one of our favorite pastimes.

As soon as puberty hit, our mother became even more cautious.

"You're both becoming ladies—developing young ladies. You have to think wiser these days," she would say, her voice still echoing in my memory.

By then, my father had been promoted to Deputy Chief, which only heightened his suspicion of us. We couldn't get anything past him. Our mother, on the other hand, remained as naïve as ever.

Barbara Anne-Marie Martin-Robinson, our mother, was a Creole woman from Baton Rouge—or *Red Stick*, as she fondly called it. She had the softest gray eyes and spoke fluent English and French. With her light brown, fair skin and a beauty mark above her upper right lip, she bore a striking resemblance to singer and actress Dorothy Dandridge. Her dark, curly, brunette hair cascaded down to the center of her back, untouched by straighteners.

She grew up in an affluent but eerily quiet neighborhood, where her father, Garrett Anthony Martin, worked as a mortician. He dedicated his life—and every waking moment—to his deceased clients, perfecting the art of making the dead look as though they were merely sleeping. Using natural, nude tones, he meticulously softened their skin, erasing blemishes and scars with precision.

Despite his undeniable talent, my grandfather was a frugal man. Rather than splurging on a business location, he conducted his mortuary services right in the basement of their Baton Rouge home. As a child, my mother often witnessed corpses being carried in and out of their house, leaving her deeply unsettled.

It was no surprise that, as we grew up, we noticed she never attended funerals—not even those of her own parents.

Her mother—my grandmother—was a Caucasian seamstress, renowned for her exceptional craftsmanship. She created some of the most beautiful clothing styles one could ever imagine. Bethany Anne-Marie Martin was particularly famous for her scarf collection and intricately designed winter tribal-print sweaters.

Over time, however, my mother grew to resent her parents. She despised them for denying her the opportunity to pursue higher education. Instead of attending college, she was forced to take care of the household while her parents worked. She had to grow up fast, assuming responsibility not only for the home but also for raising her younger brother—my uncle, Aitkin Donovan Martin.

On his twenty-first birthday, Uncle Aitkin took his own life, overdosing on prescription antidepressants after years of battling a severe drinking problem. My mother did not mourn him. Instead, she was furious—resentful of the years she had spent caring for him, believing she had devoted her life to a lost cause. It was then that she turned to Catholicism, seeking solace and purpose in her newfound faith.

A year later, on her twentieth birthday, my mother met my father, Clive O'Neal Robinson. Fresh out of community college with an associate's degree, my father was instantly captivated by my mother's rare yet profound beauty. He aspired to become a law enforcement officer but had no idea where his career would take him. After searching fruitlessly for a position in Louisiana, he decided to look elsewhere—specifically, in New York City.

It was there, in the big city, that he found life, happiness, excitement, and a joy he couldn't quite put into words. Rather than trying to explain it, he insisted on showing my mother. After just seven months of dating, he convinced her to marry him.

According to my mother, they had a small wedding with only seventeen guests, choosing to celebrate with close friends and family. However, the Martins had other plans—plans that did not include nuptials. They disapproved of my parents' relationship from the very beginning, believing my father was "too controlling." They couldn't understand why he would take their daughter so far away, especially after all they had endured with the loss of their son.

But my mother refused to let them dictate her future. In the end, she chose my father.

Nine months later, on July 23, 1928, my parents welcomed their firstborn. They named me Vernette Ellie Robinson.

My father, Clive, was an orphan. He knew little about his biological parents, having been adopted and raised by a Jamaican-American couple. Immersed in their culture, he spoke with a strong accent, yet his words were always eloquent—delivered with such confidence that even the bravest would cower before him.

I knew he would make a great police officer one day.

At first, he worked as a correctional officer in an upstate prison, but he quickly grew weary of the job. He longed for action, for the opportunity to make a real difference.

When my sister and I finished celebrating our birthdays—I had just turned nine, and Veronica was now seven—he made the announcement. He had been accepted into the police academy.

I remember the way the room erupted in applause. Our new friends and cousins who had migrated to the city shook hands, exchanged smiles, and gathered around to congratulate him. The excitement of his achievement overshadowed our birthday celebration, stealing the spotlight from my sister and me.

At the time, we had no idea what it all meant. But I suppose that didn't matter.

My father was happy, and so were we.

After years of living in Harlem, my mother decided it would be a good idea for us to visit our grandparents—both sets—now that she had reconciled with her parents, years after my sister's birth.

My father, however, refused to go. He claimed he couldn't take time off work, but my mother knew better. The truth was, he simply didn't want to see his parents, though he never disclosed why. As always, my passive mother didn't press him for an explanation. Instead, she suggested that she stay back as well, leaving just my sister and me to make the trip.

The plan was set. We would divide our vacation—three days with our maternal grandparents and three days with our paternal grandparents. On the seventh day, we would return to the big city to reunite with our parents.

The first three days passed in a blur. Our maternal grandparents paid us little to no attention. Veronica and I spent most of our time locked away in the bedroom, pressing our ears against the door as clients came and went from our grandfather's mortuary, sobbing over their lost loved ones. Years had passed, yet my grandfather still ran his business successfully, just as he always had.

It wasn't until our last day with the Martins that Grandma Martin finally acknowledged us. She stopped assisting her husband long enough to take us out, as though making a reluctant, last-minute effort to spend time with her granddaughters. I couldn't shake the feeling that she resented us but was making a conscious effort not to make it obvious. Still, she showed a particular fondness for my baby sister. The resemblance between Veronica and my mother was uncanny, and it was clear that my grandmother favored her because of it.

Veronica and my mother were the spitting image of each other, while I took after my father. His dark skin, large full eyes, high cheekbones, and hardened exterior were all traits we shared. I was also the bigger of the two of us—heavyset, compared to Veronica's petite frame.

That day, as we ventured into New Orleans, the streets were alive. Even in the daytime, the French Quarter pulsed with energy, people swarming every corner, despite it being only two o'clock in the afternoon. As we walked, I could feel eyes burning into us with every step. My sister, frightened, clung to our grandmother's large, black knitted spaghetti-strap dress.

"Get a hold of yourself, child. No one here gon' hurt chu," Grandma Martin chided.

That day was one I vowed never to forget.

We entered a salon called *Allery Hair Dimension Studio*. Its awning was black and red, and the moment we stepped inside, an overpowering stench filled my nostrils. It smelled putrid, as if something had recently died. I instinctively covered my nose, but my grandmother slapped my hand away.

"Don't be rude," she scolded.

She made her way to an empty salon chair and motioned to one of the women in the back.

A tall Indian-American woman with long braids down to her hips emerged. I watched her in the mirror as she sauntered toward us, her expression unreadable—no, not unreadable. Angry. My sister and I instinctively tightened our grip on each other's hands.

I remember Veronica whispering, "Close your eyes."
But I didn't listen.

I kept them wide open, fearfully tracking the stranger's every move as she neared us.

Meanwhile, my grandmother settled into the chair, preparing to have her waist-length brunette hair curled.

The woman's first order of business was prying my sister and me apart, forcing our hands to separate. Then, without a word, she led us toward the back of the salon—past the main floor, past the customers, into a space where, I quickly realized, no one else was allowed.

The room we were instructed to wait in was, without a doubt, a shrine of some sort. Red curtains hung from the ceiling, patched dolls were scattered across the floor, and jars filled with what appeared to be rotting flesh lined the counters, accompanied by flickering candles. The candles burned in perfect alignment with a large statue of a kneeling woman, the ends of her dress clasped between her praying hands.

Although small, the room pulsed with an undeniable power. I could hear faint ruptures within the walls and feel the presence of something unnatural pressing against my skin.

Unlike Veronica, I refused to step inside. Snatching my hand away from the stranger, I lingered at the threshold, suddenly feeling unbearably heavy, as though a shadow had wrapped itself around me. It was an instant reaction—an overwhelming sense of darkness settling over me. I wasn't sure how the stranger perceived my hesitation, but my focus remained locked on the eerie space before me. Slowly, almost in a trance, I backed away.

Veronica, however, entered without hesitation.

The stranger paid me no further mind, closing the curtain behind them. For what felt like hours, they remained inside.

I had no idea what took place in that room, but after that day, Veronica was different. The quiet, timid girl I once knew was gone. She had become restless—almost too energetic. Where she had once been reserved, she was now wild and unpredictable. That day, my sister became an entirely different person.

When the three of us returned to the main area, Grandma Martin fixed me with an eerie stare. She must have known I had refused to enter the room. Releasing her grip on our hands, the stranger spoke, eyes lingering on my sister.

"Une seule a été levée."

Only one has been lifted.

Grandma Martin immediately shot me a look of disdain. Then, still holding both our hands, she bowed her head slightly, her curls falling forward as she murmured,

"Merci."

Just like that, we left, making our way down to the pier, where Grandma and Grandpa Robinson awaited us.

Before we knew it, it was time to visit our paternal grandparents.

My father's adoptive family was warm and kindhearted—an entirely different world from what we had just experienced. They drove down to pick us up, and as we dozed during the journey, we could sense when we had arrived. The very air was different here—cleaner, lighter, more tranquil.

Our grandfather, Roger Angelo Robinson, was an architect—a brilliant one at that. He had designed the very home in which they lived, a grand estate in the wealthy town of Alexandria, Louisiana. Situated on the south bank of the Red River, Alexandria was another affluent city, and our grandparents' nine-bedroom home reflected that status. Surrounded by a high fence and a lush garden that led to the bayou, the house towered three stories high.

We had servants and housekeepers, all of whom were polite and well-mannered. We called our grandfather *Papa,* and our grandmother *Mama*—terms of endearment that made their love for us feel even more genuine.

Papa was originally from Kingston, Jamaica, where he was born and raised before migrating to the United States with his parents. Their first stop had been Columbus, Ohio, but financial struggles soon pushed the family to relocate once again. His father found work as a senior healthcare administrator at a mental institution in Louisiana, prompting them to settle there permanently.

Papa earned a soccer scholarship to Louisiana State University at Alexandria, where he studied architectural design. Straight out of college, he landed his first job with *The Williams Architectural Group*, setting the foundation for a successful career.

Our mama, Sonia Elise Robinson, was a college graduate with a master's degree in business accounting. However, after just four months of working in her field, she decided to pursue something a little more unconventional—fruit smoothies.

Mama had a gift for blending the most delicious smoothies anyone had ever tasted. They were even calorie-friendly for those who cared. With Papa's support, she launched her own business, *Smooth Island Beverage*. It quickly became a hit, and within a few months, her store was invited to participate as a street vendor at the Mardi Gras festival. I heard she was elated when she received the opportunity, and from there, the sky was the limit. In just six months, she turned a profit.

With her business thriving, Mama decided it was time to start a family. However, it was during this time that she learned she was unable to have children. After she and Papa chose adoption, business began to slow down once Daddy entered their lives. Realizing she wanted to devote all her time to raising him, Mama decided to sell *Smooth Island Beverage*. She sold full ownership to Richard Jag Manning, a wealthy business tycoon known for acquiring small businesses. But Mama wasn't sad at all—she sold the company for $750, which was a significant amount of money at the time. From that moment on, she dedicated her life to raising our father, Clive.

Visiting our father's parents was a breath of fresh air. Every morning, Veronica and I enjoyed the luxury of our spacious bedroom, and every night, we stayed up playing pillow fights and telling scary stories. Her stories were always the scariest, in my opinion. The moment I began talking, she would yawn—clear indications that I needed to shut up. But the sound of our laughter echoed through the house, making it feel alive.

Mama was thrilled to have us there. She went out of her way to have the chefs prepare anything our hearts desired. Everything was perfect—until one night.

At around 3 AM, Veronica whispered to me that she couldn't sleep. Everyone else was fast asleep, but I climbed down from the queen-sized mattress and made my way to her bedside. She sat upright, rubbing her eyes until they turned bloodshot. Seconds later, they began to bleed.

Terrified, I instinctively backed away, pulling the sheets over my head.

"What's wrong with your eyes, Veronica?" I asked, trying my best to hold back tears.

"I don't know," she replied, her voice trembling. "But they burn."

I told her to go back to sleep. "Maybe Mama will figure it out in the morning."

But less than thirty minutes later, Veronica let out a scream so piercing it made my ears ring.

I shot up in the darkness, fumbling for the lamp by my bedside. As soon as I lit it, I froze, a warm sensation spreading across my sheets as fear overtook me.

Veronica sat in the center of her bed, staring straight ahead—unblinking. Her head and eyes were locked in place, fixed on nothing.

The shriek had stopped, but the eerie silence that followed was even worse. I dropped the lamp and scrambled out of bed, bolting toward the hallway. My heart pounded as I ran to my grandparents' room, glancing over my shoulder every few steps, terrified that something was chasing me.

Then—bam!

I slammed straight into the legs of one of the servants, Holly.

Holly knelt and began wiping my tears.

"Oh, honey, is everything okay?"

She was a Caucasian woman with the most beautiful smile, her hair wrapped into a neat bun. Dressed in a long, sheer nightgown and bed slippers, she reached over and kissed my forehead.

"Did you have a nightmare?" she asked.

I nodded.

"Well, I have just the thing for nightmares." Her voice was soft and tender.

Reaching behind her neck, she unhooked a small gold-plated Christian cross. She smiled as she gently placed it around my neck, carefully lifting my ponytail.

"Jesus is your protector, okay? He won't let anything happen to you, I promise."

I struggled to smile but still reached in and hugged her as tightly as I could. I knew she hadn't expected it, but there was absolutely no way I was going back into that room with Veronica. It was like she had been possessed.

Refusing to return down the hall, I asked, "Holly, may I please spend the night with you?"

I bit my bottom lip profusely—I always did that when I was afraid—hoping she would say yes. And she did.

"Of course you can, honey. Let's go."

She grabbed my hand, and we walked side by side down the long corridor to the servants' quarters. For a brief moment, I wondered if I should mention what had happened to Veronica but decided against it. What could Holly possibly do anyway? Besides, by then, Veronica was probably fast asleep.

That morning at breakfast, Veronica didn't seem strange at all. It was as though nothing had happened. But I knew I hadn't imagined that night—Holly's necklace was still around my neck.

From that early age, I knew something was wrong with my sister. I just didn't know *what*, so I never pushed the issue.

The next three days came and went, and before I knew it, we were on a plane back to the Big Apple, reuniting with our parents. I really did miss them.

The entire flight, I kept staring at Veronica, wondering if she was okay.

Once we arrived home, our parents bombarded us with a million questions—how their parents were doing, how they were living, and what strange experiences we had endured.

I had nothing to say. Neither did Veronica.

We exchanged glances, chuckling and grinning— expressions that read as guilty, but still, neither of us spoke.

That's when my dad said it.

"Oh, so no one is going to say anything? I like that— one team, one fight, huh?"

And just like that, the tandem punishments began.

PART II.

TRUNK

GROWING UP, VERONICA was my best friend. She and I were inseparable—until the year I turned seventeen, eagerly awaiting my eighteenth birthday, while she was sixteen.

We attended the same high school, shared the same friends, and even had the same taste in guys. People often thought we were twins, just non-identical, as I began growing into my looks.

I was the voice of reason in our relationship, constantly trying to get Veronica to do the right thing. If she got punished, I got punished. Each day after school, we lingered, chatting or just hanging out, much to our dad's dismay—he *hated* when we were late.

Our routine never changed. The final bell would ring, and as I started walking home, Veronica would run off in the opposite direction, leaving me no choice but to follow.

Every day we got in trouble.

Every day, for months, we both received a beating from our dad right before supper.

After a while, I became so accustomed to it that I stopped caring. Breaking the rules was *fun*.

At night, we would snicker in our beds, whispering to each other like mischievous little kids. When our mother made her rounds to ensure we were asleep, we would pretend—just for a little while. Before long, though, we'd both be snoring.

After a while, despite always being together, I was clearly the outcast. Veronica had developed far faster than I had—her breasts fuller, her hips wider. I envied my baby sister.

Men would practically break their necks to watch her walk, and she *knew* they were watching. Every time, she put on a show. She'd drop her books on purpose, bending over slowly to pick them up, making sure her long, jet-black hair blew in the wind. She'd hike up her uniform skirt just enough to show a little more thigh.

Back then, that kind of behavior was considered *whorish,* but I would never label my baby sister.

I was the brain—straight A's, top of my class. By the time I reached the eleventh grade, colleges and universities were already offering me scholarships.

My parents were *proud.* So proud, in fact, that sometimes they made Veronica feel like an absolute failure. A bad influence. Our father made it clear every day just how proud he was of me, always bragging, always singing my praises.

He knew Veronica didn't take school seriously, so he never even bothered asking her to.

He had other plans for my baby sister.

Soon, Veronica became more and more stressed over her failing academics. She put in the effort, but no one wanted to come to terms with the possibility that she might have had an intellectual disability—dyslexia.

It wasn't ignored, just misunderstood. After all, it wasn't until the 1970s that dyslexia became a recognized diagnosis, and even then, it was said to be hereditary.

Frustrated and overwhelmed, Veronica began to rebel, lashing out and finding pleasure in reckless behavior. Her destructive ways finally caught up to her one night.

I was sitting on my bed, studying my chemistry book, when I heard her sobbing. Curious and slightly concerned, I left my room and walked to the dining area.

What I saw nearly sent me into a nervous breakdown. Veronica was sitting by the back door, covered in blood. Our parents had gone to a vineyard for the weekend, leaving us alone.

I approached cautiously, my heart pounding.

Without saying a word, she jumped up, ran to the refrigerator, and grabbed a bottle of water. She chugged it in desperate gulps, water spilling down her chin.

Then, she spoke.

"I hit him… and I think he's dead."

A cold chill ran through my body, goosebumps prickling up my arms.

"Dead?" I echoed in confusion, needing to make sure I had heard her correctly.

"Yes, Vern. *Dead!* I think I killed a man. I was on my way to see Kevin, and this man—he just appeared out of nowhere on the highway."

Neither of us had a driver's license. Hell, we didn't even have *permits*.

Our parents hadn't driven themselves to the vineyard—they were picked up by a carpool—so both of their cars were still in the community garage.

A sinking feeling settled in my gut. Whose car had she taken? I prayed it was our mother's 1940 Chevrolet and *not* our father's 1946 Cadillac. But knowing my baby sister, I already knew the answer. We sprinted to the garage, and my worst fears were confirmed.

The Cadillac.

The front fender was crumpled, the windshield completely shattered. I clutched my head, panic settling deep in my chest. We were just *teenagers*. We had no idea what the hell we were doing. But my father? He wouldn't care. He would *kill* us. I turned to Veronica, voice trembling.

"Where's the body?"

Her answer made me lose control, and I pissed my pajamas slightly.

"I put him in the trunk!" she blurted out. "I mean... what was I supposed to do? Leave him on the side of the road?"

I grabbed her by the shoulders, shaking her, my breath ragged.

"What the hell, Nica? Are you crazy?! You should have called the police!"

Her eyes filled with tears as she collapsed against me, burying her head into my shoulder. And for the first time that night... I realized just how deep we were in.

"Vern, I need you."

Her tender voice made my heart melt.

"Okay," I said, steadying my breath. "Let's see if Dad has something we can use to cover the body."

We searched tirelessly through our side of the garage, our hands fumbling through shelves and bins, until we found some large black garbage bags, a shovel, and a bag of gravel.

I hesitated before opening the trunk.

The moment I did, bile rose in my throat. I turned away and vomited all over the garage floor, my body convulsing from the sheer horror.

Veronica stood still, trembling, despite the suffocating summer humidity. The man's body was mangled—unnaturally deformed, as though his head had been bashed in.

"Are you sure he died on impact?" I asked, my voice barely above a whisper.

This didn't look like someone who had just been hit by a car. His body was stiff—too stiff for a fresh accident. There was dried blood everywhere, too much of it, and deep gashes slashed across his face. I wasn't a detective, but something about this wasn't right.

"Veronica…" I turned to her, demanding the truth. "Are you *sure* you hit this man?"

She looked at me with disdain.

A chill ran through me.

Her eyes told me everything I needed to know.

Without a word, she tore open the garbage bags and slipped on a pair of gloves.

"We need to move quickly."

The next few days passed in a blur.

By the time our parents returned home, we had scrubbed the Cadillac from top to bottom, disposing of rags, buckets, and bloodstained tissues across our neighbors' trash bins. Our hands were raw, our bodies aching, but we had no choice.

But none of it mattered when Daddy got home. He gave us both an ass whooping worth remembering—not for what we had done, but for getting into an accident with his car.

He didn't care that I wasn't the one who snuck out and stole it. He never did. In his eyes, we were a team—one fight, one punishment. No exceptions. He grounded us for almost two months, taking away our record players and banning us from watching television.

Honestly? It felt like a *reasonable* punishment.

But my mind wasn't on the grounding.

Each day, I obsessed over where we had buried the body. Would the police find him? Were they already looking? I felt the weight of unseen eyes everywhere I went—burning into my skin, dissecting my every move.

But not Veronica. She went about her days as if nothing had happened. It hadn't even been two full weeks, and already, she was back to her perky self—laughing, flirting, living.

One afternoon, after English class, I rushed to my locker, determined to go straight home.

Veronica, of course, had other plans.

I spotted her in the main yard, running off into the woods with a boy.

Kevin Landkamp.

A senior like me. Caucasian.

He had always had a thing for my sister, but publicly dating Blacks was not allowed.

Against my better judgment, I followed them.

Accidentally snapping branches as I tried to step carefully, I winced at the noise, hoping they wouldn't hear me. From behind a tree, I watched Veronica and Kevin lying on the grass, tangled together—kissing, groping.

A strange heat spread through me.

Moisture pooled between my legs, and I quickly turned away, pressing my back against the tree trunk, my breath uneven.

I heard Kevin's voice, low and casual.

"So, how did it go the other night? I've been by your house to see you, but your windows are always closed."

"My dad took away everything, and I'm on punishment, remember? I told you that."

I stiffened.

"Oh," Kevin said. "Thanks for covering for me. You know my parents have a good reputation—I can't afford to go to jail."

My stomach twisted.

I had been lied to. Used.

To protect *him*.

I wanted to storm out of my hiding place and scream at them both—expose them, make them feel the same betrayal I did. But I didn't.

Instead, I turned and walked away, my fists clenched, my heart hammering. The walk home felt longer and lonelier without Nica by my side. When I stepped through the front door, I heard my mother humming a church tune from the kitchen.

I tried to slip past unnoticed, but she caught me.

"Girls, come here, please," she called.

I exhaled sharply, dragging my feet toward the kitchen table and taking a seat.

"Where is Nica?"

I wanted to tell her.

I wanted to say exactly where Nica was and *who* she was under. But I didn't.

"Not sure, Mom. I left right after my last class."

My mother barely spoke after that. A God-fearing woman, she firmly believed in *not sparing the rod*, though she never laid a hand on us herself—that was always my father's duty.

I knew what was coming.

Before she could press further, I got up from the table and slipped away, heading to the bedroom my sister and I shared.

I pulled out my chemistry book, forcing myself to focus. It was my worst subject, the one class where my teacher always threatened to fail me.

I lost myself in equations and formulas, not realizing how much time had passed until I glanced at the clock.

5:25 PM.

Still, no Veronica.

I heard the front door swing open. My father's heavy footsteps echoed through the house, followed by my mother's soft voice greeting him.

And then—

"She's not home."

She wasted no time telling on us.

A sharp knock pounded against my bedroom door, making my breath catch in my throat. I swallowed hard, knowing exactly what was waiting for me on the other side.

And when I opened it, my heart dropped.

"Where is Veronica?" My father's deep voice sent a chill through me.

He was an imposing man—6'4", broad-shouldered, and effortlessly commanding. My mother, delicate in comparison at 5'5", stood behind him with her arms folded, her expression unreadable.

I hesitated.

Saying I didn't know would make me look like a liar. They knew how close Nica and I were. But admitting that I *did* know would make me a snitch. Either way, this was going to end badly.

So, I lied.

"I'm not sure, Dad."

Both of them stared at me, their eyes narrowing in disbelief. My father folded his arms.

"When she walks in here, you send her to me. You understand?"

I nodded quickly, bracing myself for a blow.

But it didn't come.

For almost seventeen years, Veronica and I had been inseparable. Without her, I felt unsteady—like a missing piece had been ripped away. We ate supper in tense silence. When my father finished his meal and stood to take his dishes to the sink, the front door slammed open.

All heads turned.

It was 7:45 PM when Veronica stumbled in, reeking of alcohol. Her hair disheveled, and her face was a wreck—bruised, her lower lip split, her right eye swollen and blackened. Her clothes ripped. She looked like death.

I had never seen her like this.

My father stood motionless; his jaw tight. My mother gasped, covering her mouth as tears welled in her eyes. I watched in stunned silence, my stomach twisting.

What happened to her?

Veronica swayed on her feet, eyes glassy and unfocused. Then, without warning, she collapsed.

We all moved at the same time—too late.

Her head struck the wooden table in the hallway with a sickening thud.

And just like that, she was unconscious.

—

"What was it like for you, seeing your sister like that?" Washington asked politely, removing his blazer. He took a sip from the tall glass of water I had managed to fetch him.

"I felt responsible," I admitted, my voice quieter than before. "She began to hate me."

—

FOR DAYS, VERONICA and I hadn't spoken. Once she returned home from the hospital after spending several nights there, our parents had a long talk with us. My dad made it clear that he was not pleased with me for leaving Veronica the way I did.

"You must protect one another, love one another, because you all've got in this life," he said. "It's a cold world out there, and no one's gonna love you like your sister loves you."

Those words resonated deeply within me as I took a long, hard look at my sister, whose wounds were now slowly healing. She looked vengeful. To me, she seemed ready for war—war against me, war against herself, and war to the death. No matter how many times I apologized, I knew she wasn't receptive. My dad noticed the tension, which was why he decided to have the conversation with us in the first place.

School was no better. Nica and I didn't spend as much time together anymore. Slowly, our friends began to separate. I had my crew, and she had hers. Despite us sharing friends at one point, they obviously had their preferences when it came to choosing sides. I had my two friends, Warren and Courtney, and Nica had her posse: Carl, Lorraine, Whitney, Melissa, and Ty. They were very popular, and even those who hadn't been friends with us before suddenly started to gravitate toward Veronica once they noticed she and I weren't inseparable anymore.

I continued to feel exiled—left out and misplaced in the world. I had begun searching for colleges and universities to attend with my guidance counselor one evening when I started noticing the confrontational atmosphere hanging around me. Day after day, I was followed, discussed, and mocked until one afternoon, after gym class, I noticed a new group of seniors idling by the doorway. As I made my way past the girls, I felt a nudge from the one standing on my right. After that, my books hit the ground, and I blacked out.

I only remember falling to the ground and being kicked in my stomach repeatedly, in unison, by about seven girls. I raised my arms to protect my face, but realized it wasn't a good idea when one girl kneeled, struggled with me to remove my arms, and then instructed one of my attackers,

"Get that Negro bitch in the face!"

What felt like hours, but was really only four minutes, went on until one of the teachers finally raced down the hall and began flinging the girls aside to get a visual on me. I was taken to the nurse's office, where I was treated.

For a week, my parents kept me home. On the day of the incident, after being picked up by my father from the nurse's office, we drove in silence. I had this awful feeling in the pit of my stomach. I still hadn't seen my face. He didn't talk about what happened, and neither did I. All I kept wondering was, *Where could Veronica have been?* To my surprise, my father didn't even wonder that. Had he wondered, he would have asked—though, not that I would have known the answer.

When we arrived home, my mother quickly fell to her knees, began anointing my head with olive oil, and prayed while speaking in tongues. She demanded all demons flee from her home and prayed for covering over both my sister and me, from Our Lord Almighty. She instructed me to take a cool shower and go straight to bed. I entered the bathroom, and that's when I saw the horror.

My left eye was completely swollen shut. I felt it, but had no idea it was that bad. I had bandages around my head, and you could see the blood seeping through where the gash had been left. My arms felt weak; I could barely lift them. I noticed the black-and-blue bruises on my shoulders, my right and left sides, thighs, and a bite mark on my neck. I was a mess. They really got me good.

Later that night, after my nap, I noticed Veronica laying in her bed, her back to me. I hoped that she hadn't been asleep, as I really needed to speak to her. I struggled upright in my twin bed and sat cross-legged, suffering through the pain.

"Veronica, are we even?" My eyes to the hardwood floor as I spoke, almost whispering, watching her lie there, pretending to be asleep with her pillow cradled between her legs. Her hair had just been washed; I could tell by the way it curled up and shone. I knew she was responsible for having me jumped, but I just couldn't prove it. I only hoped this would be the end of our feud and her growing to hate me so much.

Finally, she started whispering.

"You know that day after I snuck out with Daddy's car? I went to see Kevin, and I made it there perfectly fine. It wasn't until I was making my exit that he persuaded me we should go to this party. I told him it was late, and I refused. He begged and begged until I said yes. Once we got on the interstate, he told me I should let him drive because he had more experience. So, I let him. Ten minutes later, I felt my whole body plunge forward, and my head slammed against the dashboard. He had hit a man, knocking him down into the gorge."

I listened as she started to cry, sniffling and wiping away her tears, still making no eye contact, with her back turned. I wanted to get up and hug her, but I figured maybe it would be too soon. So, I let her continue.

"I panicked, Vern. I had no idea what had happened. It all went by so fast. There was no light, nothing—so he kept on driving. I kept screaming, 'We have to go back!' He rambled on about his reputation and not wanting to go to jail, and then he mentioned you. He said, 'I bet if it were that ape-looking sister of yours, she would know what to do.' I told him to take me back, and I'd think of something. Vernette isn't the only smart one. I'm smart too! So, we went back, and that's when we slid down into the gorge and lifted that man, throwing him into the truck. I told Kevin to leave and let me handle it. So, he did. He ran in the opposite direction, back home, but not before he kissed me and told me he loved me. For the first time, he told me he loved me. I then came here and let you handle it."

I was confused. Was she angry with me because her crush thought I was smarter than her? I mean, granted, many people thought that, and she knew it, but hearing it from him must've triggered something in her. I was at a loss for words. I couldn't reply. I had no idea what to say. She had dragged me into her web of lies and convinced me to commit a crime that could have potentially gotten us both locked away for life. But she was my sister, and no matter how much hurt she caused me, I still loved her.

I decided to walk over and console her. By then, she was drenched in tears. As soon as I touched her, I felt her body pull away, and then she screamed, "Do not touch me!" Her hands were shaking, and her eyes pierced a hole in my heart.

"Daddy said we're supposed to protect one another, Vern, but you didn't protect me! You left me that day after school. You left me for no reason, but how many times do I hear about how perfect you are and how wonderful you are, and I still continue to love you? I gave you friends, and you left me so those guys could hurt me."

I started to cry. I had no idea Veronica felt that way, and she was finally letting it all out. What she revealed to me that night was something I was nowhere near prepared for.

"They raped me, Vern. Four of them…and his father. Kevin took me to his house after I couldn't find you anywhere, he promised to take me home. But not before bringing me back to his house, where his friends were all drinking and playing video games. I thought it was okay. After I searched for you and everyone told me you had left, I was angry. I wanted to drink and smoke to get you off my mind. But then I had too much. By the time I was ready to go, they were all just standing there, and all the girls had left. I was the only one. I was all by myself for the first time in sixteen years. I was all alone!''

Veronica slouched back down, wiped her face, and whispered, "So no, we're not even."

I was too afraid to sleep that night. I stayed up until the sun began to rise, thinking to myself what a horrible person I was and how I could have been so selfish toward my one and only baby sister. Raped. We were both virgins, so the mere thought of being forcefully raped by four boys and a grown man made me sob. I wailed into my pillow, feeling her pain and praying, asking God to please forgive me for abandoning my sister.

Needless to say, the rest of my senior year became a nightmare, a living, breathing nightmare. I had absolutely no friends. Veronica had power—due to her fair skin, her proximity to whiteness was closer than mine, and because of that, she made me public enemy number one. Sometimes, I was too embarrassed to even enter the cafeteria because of the hurtful things people would say. I was called a Nigger, an ape, fat, ugly, jealous, and hateful. Some were empathetic, while others simply laughed.

I never found those jokes to be comical, only hurtful. But with each passing day, my mother reminded me how beautiful I was. She loved us both, no matter how much we hated one another; there was no doubt about it.

Veronica fed her friends my insecurities, and I had the displeasure of facing them every day. I knew she was prettier, skinnier, her hair longer, her skin lighter, and all I had was the ability to multiply fractions in my head at warp speed and score really well on aptitude tests. Once graduation came around, I was ready to leave her behind.

After my first two years at the University of Albany, I made some great friends, built beneficial relationships, and, for a time, felt superior in our sibling dynamic. Then Veronica graduated from high school, and it was her turn to start college. Just when I thought I had successfully eluded Veronica's shadow, she managed to outshine me there as well. I was infuriated. We had to share the same dorm, the same space, the same everything—just like when we were at home. All because I had been coerced into transferring schools at the last minute, as Veronica had not been accepted into the institution I was already attending.

I had big dreams of heading off to New York University or even Columbia University for medical school, and an undergraduate degree from Albany would have surely secured that for me. African American female medical practitioners were definitely scarce at that time.

But Veronica and our dad had other plans. He knew Veronica wasn't much of an intellect but possessed exceptional beauty, so he ensured we both went to the same school to avoid any tension between us. He was completely oblivious to the fact that there already was tension. Our father knew I would excel intellectually, so he figured if Veronica were around me more, I'd have a positive influence on her. But nothing could influence

Veronica—not me, not our parents, and sometimes, not even herself.

She lived each day like it was her last, never fretting over the future or what it might hold. She believed that worrying caused wrinkles, and, like our mother always said, "Leave your burdens at the altar." Apparently, that's where Veronica left everything: her morals, values, self-worth, and trust.

All of it was left at the Catholic Roman altar. Despite being an obvious atheist, Veronica never spoke of such things. She knew how much our mother leaned on God, and she could never gather the courage to tell her she simply didn't believe there was one.

From the time we were younger, after visiting our grandparents, Veronica never even liked the mere utterance of the name Jesus. She cringed each time. Luckily for her, I was the only one who ever paid attention. Days later, after we visited Louisiana, the only other person who began to notice the change in Veronica was our father.

The moment we arrived at the airport that beloved Sunday evening, I witnessed my father give a look I had never seen before—a look of brokenness. He looked hurt, disheartened even. He knew he had lost one of his girls to the evil he dared not speak of, nor return to. He knew what awaited us in Louisiana once we arrived under the care of our maternal grandparents. Daddy was well aware of the hatred they had for both him and our mother, reconciling only as a means to lure us in and hurt us. But our dear mother, as naïve as she was, could never be convinced, so he hadn't even tried.

The ride home that evening was quiet. Veronica and I sat in the back of the vehicle, seatbelts tightly fastened, listening to the reggae music resonating from the Cadillac stereo. I watched in the rearview mirror as my dad stole glances at my sister, his eyebrows knit. I knew he felt it. He felt what I had felt. He sensed there was something different about her; I just know he did.

Moving forward, our father made sure that Veronica and I remained as close as ever. I'm sure his intentions were for her to emulate my actions since I was the older sibling. He made several attempts to make it clear that the two of us were to move as one, think as one, and react in unison, never allowing either of us to feel defenseless.

Years later, he still hadn't stopped, as he drove us both to our new home. Our community college campus, where I would be continuing my higher education while Veronica began hers with intermittent visits to our parents. My dad was elated, telling everyone on the force that his daughters had been accepted into the same institution. Which, ultimately, was true—but not quite.

To get Veronica enrolled, our dad did pull a few strings, as the daughter of his ex-colleague had recently been appointed Dean of Students. Caroline Blake Anderson expected nothing but the best from the Robinson girls. I'm not sure what our dad had said about our decorum, but my academics spoke for itself. Veronica, on the other hand, had to take placement exams, starting the year with intermediate-level courses—courses she barely attended. Most of her time was spent in the dining facilities, where she hung out with boys and homosexual females, after toying with the thought.

Veronica's features hadn't changed much. She still had the face of innocence and retained many of our mother's traits. Her body was now curvaceous, and her hair had grown longer, thicker, and full of attitude, swinging effortlessly as she walked. To my knowledge, Veronica showed no imperfections—except for her disinterest in getting an education. It was a wonder she graduated from middle school.

After months of living on campus, I had fully adapted to this new college life, reassured that transferring from a university to a community college would not hinder my chances of attending a prestigious medical school. With my father having a badge, there would always be favors he could call in, in exchange for making something go away.

Sometime later, the parties, the drinking, and the late-night group chats were becoming a regular part of my routine. I was doing everything except studying, and it was bringing my sister and me closer together. I was failing my History course and had no idea how to change that. Veronica, on the other hand, was simply breezing through everything. I wondered what her trick was until she told me she wasn't doing so well in Geometry.

So, one night while sitting in our dormitory, we made a deal. I would assist her in math, and she would assist me in History, but, as always, Veronica took the easy way out.

"Professor Donovan keeps failing me on these exams. He says I'm not being descriptive enough in my open-ended responses."

"Well, Vern, maybe you aren't. Maybe you need to explore your creative mind. Let it run deep and stop being so afraid to release your inner craft whore."

"A craft whore?" I chuckled.

"Yes, the craft whore. You're smart enough to know what that means, big sis. Now, what time does Donovan take his lunch break?" I knitted my eyebrows, perturbed.

"That's Professor Donovan and Um… after our 12:45 class. Why?" Veronica began braiding her hair into two sections, just as she did every night before bed.

"So, about 1:50 then, in Bernadine Hall?" I had no idea what she was up to.

"Yes, that sounds about right."

"Okay, Vern, I'll just find him tomorrow. Too bad he isn't cute like Mr. Jackson. It would've made things more fun," she said, her laugh sounding sinister.

I rotated my desk chair so that I could face her. "Veronica, what are you going to do?" I asked, placing my left arm around the back of the chair for support. Veronica always tended to surprise me.

"Well, I was planning on blackmailing him. After I seduce him and we have sex, I'm going to threaten to tell Caroline. Now, depending on how good of a boy Professor Donovan is, this could either be blackmail or a fling. Totally depends on him, you know?" She said that with such confidence and contentment. I couldn't believe my ears. I was disgusted, and I knew it showed all over my face.

"Listen, you asked me for help, okay? Don't look at me like you're judging me. I didn't ask for this crap; Daddy put me here. Now I have to do what I have to do to get by so he can be proud of me, too. Sorry we weren't all blessed with the smart gene, Vern," she spoke sarcastically. I stood in anger, feeling like once again Veronica was using her looks to get by.

"So, you have sex with your professors!? Really, Nica? Don't you have female professors? I mean, for goodness' sake, the sex must not be that good because Professor Jackson still seems to be failing your ass!" Veronica began to move with haste as she struggled to get dressed, her eyes now wide. As usual, my guess was that she was heading to the pub. Then she stopped midway, slamming her right palm onto the doorway and started laughing hysterically.

"My female professors, Vern, enjoy me very, very much. Professor Jackson is just really loyal to his wife, so he doesn't even know what I taste like. So as far as math goes, I just fucking suck at it!"

As she made her way through the door, I screamed as loud as I could, nearly rupturing my vocal cords, "Maybe that's because there's no lesson on leg division!"

I was pissed. She always managed to win. People like Veronica got whatever they wanted, even if it was at the expense of someone else's happiness. I bolted through the door and decided to get some fresh air myself. After what I had just heard, why not? I walked across the campus until I saw twenty-four students vertically aligned—twelve on the right and twelve on the left—all rallying and marching with signs in the air: *End Segregation. Free Minorities. Racism is still alive.*

They wore all-black outfits, and I was confused. I had no idea who they were or what they were doing, but I knew they were marching for a cause—a significant one at that. They were eager, angry, and most definitely loud. A young man with bravado caught my attention, stumbling later like a fool while waving his fist in the air, careful to speak only when he knew someone was watching. I approached him swiftly as he began to fall behind the rest of the group.

"Hey!" As soon as he heard my voice, he flew backward, stumbling over a nearby tree stump. I chuckled almost instantly—the boy was clearly frightened. "Are you alright?" I had to ask. It looked like he had knocked himself pretty hard.

"I'm fine. You know it's after hours, gal. What are you doing out here? Don't you women watch the news? Better get back inside." Just like that, he took off running to catch up with the members of his organization. In an instant, the alarms sounded all over the campus.

—

"Wow, Ms. Vern, this is great! How are you feeling?"

"I'm feeling fine. The sun's leaving us, so maybe we should go to bed and continue tomorrow. That's when the fun stuff starts!" I smile with enthusiasm because the reason this man has traveled all this way is that he wants to hear more than just an educational background on me and my baby sister, I'm sure. Sauntering into my cottage, I continue to feel the cool breeze. Tonight, I think I'll leave the windows open; the night air will do us both some good.

The way Mr. Clarke looks at me makes me wonder if maybe he is a reporter. As I speak, his eyes burn with a look of admiration, rather than intrigue. I wonder if he is who he says he is. Otherwise, I may have a deceptive con-man in my home, and I do not do well with those.

"Ms. Vern, I just want to say before we both go to bed how thankful I am, once again, that you're allowing me the opportunity to stay here. If you don't mind, I would love to cook you breakfast in the morning. You know, as a sign of my gratitude."

I flash him a quick smile. No one has cooked Ms. Vern a breakfast meal in years. I chuckle as I say, "Of course, son, I would love that."

Smiling, Mr. Clarke retires to his room located at the top of the stairs on the far right. That room used to belong to one of them boys—he's changed his name, and now I forget. And he's all grown up but doesn't even visit. However, I never make it up to the second level anymore. My feeble legs can go only so far these days.

I take my night's rest right here, down in the living room area on the sofa bed, which I've never stuffed back in ever since that blessed day all them years ago when Peter and the boys quarreled. They left the place in shambles, and my back never felt the same. Having learned my lesson the hard way, I never intervene when the young boys get to fighting.

Each time I close my eyes, I dream of my interpretation of heaven: the pearly white gates, the long corridor filled with clouds, and angels singing. Then I reach Him, and once I stretch my hands to touch His— Beep, beep, beep, beep. I don't understand why I still have an alarm clock set to 6 AM, not like I have anything to do or anywhere to go these days.

I stretch my weary arms and extend my pudgy legs, watching my feet in disgust, adorned with corns, calluses, and bunions from my long marches. I glance over into the kitchen where I see Mr. Clarke standing innocently with the skillet, engaging me with the wonderful smell of something well prepared.

"Good morning, Ms. Vern. I made some bacon with scrambled eggs, just waiting on these waffles to cook."

Morning always comes to greet me.

One hour and a stomach filled with delicious food later, I'm licking my lips, placing my dish atop the coffee table.

"Washington, my oh my, you cook like a man I once knew. Breakfast was amazing!" I have to express my satisfaction—a meal this good should never be eaten without praise.

"Well, thank you. My mother was never around, so my father pretty much taught me everything I needed to know. He taught me never to depend on anyone—not for food, not for money, and sometimes not even for love. So, I love my work and remain loyal to it. May I ask, Ms. Vern, how do you afford to buy your groceries and other supplies? You seem very well stocked."

I answer him with glee, "Well, son, I raised about nine children, and some of the grandnieces and nephews still come by once in a blue. Hell, you might meet one today. So, they always bring me food, some money, and restock the kitchen and my medicine. They take care of me, just like I did them. I am blessed."

"I'm so happy to hear that, Ms. Vern. Glad to know you have people around you who love you."

He sounds a bit disappointed, sad even, as he speaks with disinclination. But quickly, he regains composure as he retrieves the tape recorder, placing it adjacent to my sofa bed.

"We've really covered a lot, Ms. Vern, but you and I both know we have to talk more about your sister. She's done some horrible things to you, no doubt, but there's a story beyond what you're telling me. If you don't feel comfortable sharing, then by all means, you can simply say so."

I've already begun, figuring there's no use stopping now. With the winds speeding up, I have no choice but to maintain. So, I decided to waste no more time and go on with my story.

—

MY MYSTERY MAN was an African-American activist, a member of a group educating African-Americans about our history across the campus, created by Rosie McArnold, a senior at the college, looking to go into politics. David Matthew Harrington and I began dating shortly after our abrupt meeting that night.

My first boyfriend, David, and I were wonderful together! He was a junior, just like me, looking to join the military post-graduation. His major was criminal justice; he hated school but managed to get good grades and participated in just about every protest around. I idolized him. He became my best friend and, eventually, the love of my life. He decided to attend college because his mother begged him to after his father was slain by government administrators during a three-hour-long protest. She wanted a different life for him, especially since he now had the opportunity.

For months, David and I were always together, but he never saw the inside of my dormitory. I feared him meeting my sister. My insecurities caused this fear, and it was a full-time job keeping them apart from one another. Each time he asked if he could visit me, I always had an excuse. I avoided the conversation about me even having a sister completely.

I simply enjoyed him. He was adorable. A dark-skinned gentleman with grey eyes, he had a dark brown, medium-length afro with deep sideburns. His birthmark, in the shape of Texas, was located on his lower left cheekbone. I would watch it move each time he chewed. I had an infatuation, and he loved me for it.

Winter caught us in the snow, playing around as he threw me from one end of the field to the next. We constantly kissed and touched one another in the beginning. I knew eventually we would make love, but I hoped for marriage first. With him, I wanted to know he was all mine and would forever be mine, creating unforgettable memories on our wedding night.

David went to the gym every night, so his body was almost perfect; he was a work of art. I enjoyed watching him undress once he returned from working out in his dorm, lying on his bed. After he showered, he always smelled masculine. He slept on his back every night so I could comfortably sleep on his chest, feeling it rise and fall over and over again while listening to his heart pounding—a lullaby to me. Our love knew no boundaries. I felt so comfortable around him; everything became easy: our relationship, and our friendship—both became my most prized possessions.

"David, are we going to grow old together?"

I hated being so emotional, but found that it was inevitable after I had fallen madly in love. He constantly reassured me of our happiness, always complimented me, and remained a consistent hopeless romantic. Whenever he was stressed with classes or received disturbing news from home, I always made sure to keep his mind occupied.

I reminded him of my love for him. I did things for him as well, and it felt great. Exchanging gifts, shopping for one another, lighting candles for movie night, having picnics on campus, and taking long strolls and bike rides—our love was a fairytale. I had met my prince. I looked forward to meeting his mother, and after about three months of being together, I was asked to speak with her over the phone.

David was a very private person, so when he asked me to speak with his mother and his little sister, Denise, I felt honored. His mother, Aurora, told me of all the wonderful things she had heard about me from her son and thanked me for keeping him grounded and focused on his academics. Veronica became a distant memory to me, and before I knew it, David and I were preparing for graduation, studying for finals during our last semester, when Caroline approached me.

"Hey, Vern, I haven't seen you in a while. I must say, though, your grades are quite impressive. Keep up the good work." But just before taking off, she turned back and added, "Your sister—I do hope everything works out with her."

I nodded, closing my textbook, suddenly realizing that I hadn't seen my baby sister in weeks. Quickly, I ran to our dormitory—at a quick glance, her things were still there. Afterward, I walked over to student services and asked to use a landline to phone my parents. The moment my father answered, my heart began to race.

"Yes, hello?"

"Daddy, it's me, Vern. How are you guys? I haven't heard from anyone. Is everything okay with Veronica?"

He took a deep breath before answering.

"Vern, Nica has been gone for quite some time. She, um… she needed some time away, but, uh, she'll be back soon. Just continue to focus and do well. Caroline says you're on your way to accomplishing wonderful things. I'll call you later, okay? We have some things to discuss."

Hearing those words made me feel like I was in the Twilight Zone. I ran back to my dorm room without stopping to catch my breath. If Veronica was gone, then whose things were in my room? I rustled through papers, photos, clothes, books—just about everything—before realizing they weren't Veronica's. They belonged to a stranger.

I had spent so much time wrapped up in my relationship and avoiding my sister that I hadn't even realized she was gone. I hadn't even known she was no longer attending school. I didn't know whether to cry or laugh. I was emancipated.

For days, I pondered. Where could Veronica have gone, and why did she leave? Questions that required answers—but there was no one to give them to me. My mother rarely called, and when she did, our conversations were curt.

"How are classes? How are your friends? And I hope you are reading the Bible I mailed you."

That was it. My answers were always: "Good," "Fine," and "Yes."

Graduation was fast approaching, and with Veronica no longer around, I finally began to find myself. I had friends, a boyfriend, and some great role models in my life. Mom and Dad soon began visiting more often. My father had become the Chief of Police—which for a Black man seemed almost unheard of in those times—and my mother had started her own tailoring business.

With Veronica now a pariah—and later learning that she was pregnant—she had gone her own way, leaving our parents completely in the dark about her whereabouts. My father had his suspicions about where she was headed in life, but he never discussed them with me—only with my mother.

My mom had never wanted Veronica to suffer the same fate she had as a child—shunned by her own parents over a simple mistake or even for love. So, she never gave up on my baby sister. In an effort to locate her youngest child, she handed out missing person flyers and inquired with close friends, all of whom had no idea where Veronica had gone.

The day finally arrived, graduation. Family and friends had all gathered for this joyous occasion. David and I were ecstatic, making plans about where we would move after leaving Cambridge and how many children we would have. So many plans!

My mother and father both arrived, and it felt so good to hug them. My father squeezed me so tightly that I knew he was proud of me—it showed all over his face. I introduced David as a friend, but even so, my father still looked displeased. His mustache had thickened, his upper body had grown more muscular, and his complexion had darkened. He looked intimidating. David definitely felt slightly uncomfortable.

So, we exited the parking lot and walked toward the main lobby, where David's mother and sister were waving us down. I was then formally introduced to his mother, Aurora Dina Harrington, and his younger sister, Denise Candace Harrington. His mother was polite, and she and David were practically twins. I knew his father would have been proud of him.

David came from a rough household, which later prompted him to become a member of the Black Panther movement. He marched with its members and fully understood their cause, but he remained frightened. He had seen what the police had done to his father—how they had brutally bludgeoned him during a confrontation while he was simply trying to order food from a Caucasian-owned dining facility. In an attempt to defend himself, his father had tussled with one of the four men beating him, accidentally breaking his neck.

But David did not let that stop him. Watching his mother hold him close, teary-eyed, and seeing his sister witness that tender moment made me truly appreciate my family and all they had done to keep us healthy and safe.

Once the ceremony began, it took about an hour and a half before my name was called. The moment "Vernette Robinson" was announced, I heard the crowd go crazy—my parents screaming at the top of their lungs. As I walked across the stage, I caught a glimpse of Grandma and

Grandpa Robinson arriving. They were scooting across the aisles to where my parents were seated. They both looked so proud, and I felt a surge of happiness rush through me.

I was pretty sure my mother had invited her parents as well, but they had chosen not to attend—at least for the graduation portion. There were no arguments or disagreements, just love in a room filled with happiness.

When the ceremony concluded, the graduates exited single file toward the parking lot, where we would all meet our loved ones. Just as I stepped outside, I noticed them from across the highway walking toward the massive parking lot—my sister, along with both Grandma and Grandpa Martin.

It was a complete shock to see them approaching; it felt as though I were seeing ghosts. Veronica looked amazing. Her skin was clear, her hair well-maintained, cascading down to the middle of her back, her seductive almond-shaped eyes rested, and her makeup was natural, making her look unnaturally flawless. Supposedly months pregnant, she didn't appear to be. Her stomach was small and tight, her curves accentuated by the fitted jeans that hugged her frame, and her gluteus was noticeably rounder. She parted her lips to congratulate me, but all I could do was cry. Once again, she had managed to take the spotlight from me.

I had hoped no one else would notice her arrival, but they did.

My mother ran right past me, and I stood in stunned silence, watching as everyone else took photos with their graduates. Instead of celebrating my moment, my family was more interested in Veronica—how beautiful she was and how she was doing physically. Grandma Martin took little to no interest in me as I stood there helplessly, rage building inside me as everyone ignored my very existence. Even David, who had now made his way over, was fixated on my sister.

Everyone spoke, but I had nothing to say.

Grandpa Robinson and Grandpa Martin stood off to the left, engaged in their own conversation. Veronica, my parents, Grandma Robinson, and Grandma Martin gathered to the right. And I stood in the middle—alone.

Then, I watched in disbelief as my father motioned David over to introduce him to Veronica. And then he said something that made my body quiver.

"You two should go out sometime. Get to know one another."

David smiled and complied. "I would really love that."

I stared in shock as they shook hands and she flashed that devilish smile. Then David turned to walk away, not even joining us for the celebratory dinner. He stepped backward, still smiling, his gaze locked onto her, while I stood there watching—despairingly.

I kept staring, thinking to myself, *How could my father betray me like that?* Then it hit me—I had introduced David as a friend, fearing he wouldn't be good enough in my father's eyes. But I had been wrong. My father approved of him—just not for me. And David... how could he? I felt lost for several long minutes until someone called my name. Then, we all gathered to take a family photo.

Grandma Martin insisted on taking the picture and made sure to place Veronica right next to me. She looked stunning, and no matter how hard I tried, I couldn't measure up. As she wrapped an arm around my waist, pulling me closer, I felt inferior.

My hair was much shorter than hers, barely reaching my shoulders, and dark brown. I had to plaster my face with makeup to conceal my mild acne. I was darker than she was and taller. For years, Veronica had been the slender, semi-thick one while I had been the heavy-set, curvier one—but now, that had changed. She had filled out far more than I had in all the right places. Her breasts were fuller, her waistline was smaller, and her hips and ass were larger. Meanwhile, I had gained a few pounds living on campus.

I felt insecure.

That evening, Veronica was the hot topic. Once everyone returned to the hotel for dinner, my parents were fixated on her. Granted, she had disappeared for a while to stay with our mother's parents, but she hadn't called or spoken to anyone.

Then, the discussion finally came up about the baby.

Before Veronica could even respond, Grandma Martin intervened, simply stating, "The baby is in a better place."

Veronica lowered her head, avoiding eye contact with anyone. My mother suddenly stood up and asked my grandparents to leave. I had never seen her so bold. She knew something was wrong. Everyone stared at her in disbelief. She thanked them for coming but insisted that she wanted to be alone with her children and husband.

Just then, my father reached for her arm, motioning for her to sit down—she was embarrassing herself. But she stood again, her voice louder this time, demanding that the grandparents leave.

Everyone hesitated for a moment.

Then, Veronica turned toward Grandma Martin, who discreetly reassured her that it was okay and to remain seated. It was as if there was some unspoken control between them. I made sure to sit on the opposite side of the dinner table.

My mother waited patiently until we were completely alone before she began.

"Veronica, honey, you have to tell me everything that's happened. You're not yourself. Your father and I can see that. What happened to your baby?"

I wanted to scream. For God's sake, this was supposed to be *my* day—a day of happiness and accomplishment! I had just completed my undergraduate studies and was now planning to pursue medicine, yet here we were, making this day about Veronica.

A part of me wanted to stay, but another part of me wanted to leave. Deep down, I, too, was concerned for my sister. But why did I always have to live in her shadow? Unhappy, lost, forgotten—every time she entered a room.

She began to sob, motioning to my mother that she didn't want to have this conversation. My mother knew something was wrong and made it her duty not to force her. My father, on the other hand, felt differently.

"Veronica, if they did something to you, you have to tell us!"

My mother quickly gestured for my father to stop. It was painfully clear that Grandma Martin had some unnatural hold over Veronica, and it was strong.

"We can't force her hand—my mother already has that control. Veronica just has to find herself," my mother said.

She looked saddened, my father appeared confused, and I sat there, indifferent. We remained in silence for another ten minutes before my father finally broke it. He turned to Veronica and instructed her that she would be returning to New York with us once I finished packing the remainder of my things. My graduation day had been a complete disappointment.

When I returned to my dorm, I packed slowly, weighed down by frustration. Veronica begged to accompany me. As we walked toward the dormitories, she took trips down memory lane, reminiscing about old times. But I wasn't interested in anything she had to say—especially since she had stolen the one thing I had worked so hard for—*my* moment of recognition.

To my surprise, as I carried my boxes downstairs, I noticed David approaching the doors. My heart lifted, and I smiled with relief, no longer resenting him for accepting my father's suggestion to get to know Veronica better.

But then he asked, "Hey, where's your sister? Can't find her anywhere. Did they leave already?"

I was flabbergasted. The shock was so overwhelming that I dropped the box I was carrying, spilling its contents onto the floor.

David noticed my reaction and quickly tried to do damage control.

"No, I was only asking because a group of us were going to hang out, and I know she's your sister, so I figured maybe you'd want her to come. That's all, babe."

A wave of relief washed over me.

I quickly kneeled, gathering my belongings and stuffing them back into the box.

I felt embarrassed—my insecurities were showing. And as if her timing couldn't have been any worse, Veronica came strolling down the hallway just as she stepped off the elevator. She was rolling my two large suitcases behind her, and as quickly as I spotted her, so did David.

He motioned past me, speed-walking toward her, then insisted on helping with the suitcases.

My mouth dropped.

Seeing the fury in my eyes, Veronica, surprisingly, refused his help. But I knew such an act would not be without consequence. I braced myself for what would undoubtedly come next.

Again, David stood there, watching her walk away.

And I stood there, watching him.

By now, it was official—David liked my sister, definitely more than he liked me.

I fought the tears, shaking my head in disgust.

Two years—gone, just like that.

That day came and went. I packed, loaded the car, and sat silently in the back seat as we drove out of Cambridge. I had the chance to say goodbye to everyone, even David, who made it his mission to hunt me down—not for me, but for Veronica.

Out of respect for me, though, she never spoke to him. She did her best to ignore the little mule.

How could I hate her when she was just so lovable?

She hadn't asked to take the spotlight away from me. She had even tried to congratulate me when we made eye contact that morning, but she got distracted by everyone else. And later, she helped me pack up my things and carry them down to the car.

Veronica wasn't a bad person.

I was just so blinded by my jealousy and self-hatred that I found every excuse to loathe her. I leaned over and gave her the tightest hug I could muster.

I even cried.

I loved Veronica with everything in me.

Like a good sister, she felt my pain and knew I was simply coming to my senses when I leaned in to hug her. I had created the tension, and being who she was, she had tried her best to diffuse it. She held me back just as tightly, pressing a tear-soaked kiss to my cheek.

I couldn't let go.

I had missed her so much.

Not a word, not a peep for months, and then she just popped back up—more beautiful than ever.

My heart ached.

In that moment, I realized I didn't want to live without my sister. Our parents watched us through the rearview mirror. My father said nothing, simply leaning over to take my mother's hand, interlocking his fingers with hers as he continued driving.

Both sets of grandparents had left earlier, having been rudely dismissed by my mother during dinner. Neither of them tolerated disrespect, and they had made their feelings clear. They felt my mother had spoken to them unfairly, especially in front of Veronica and me.

But my mother didn't care.

Her children came first.

And with Grandma Martin keeping Veronica and not telling my mother about it, she wasn't pleased about that, either.

"She had no right," my mother had said. "Veronica and Vern are *my* children."

When we arrived home, I noticed that nothing had changed.

Back to Harlem.

Back to the brownstone.

Back to our bedroom.

Apparently, my father had finally decided to rent out the basement to a man named Peter Orlando Moore, someone he described as very discreet.

Inside our room, everything was untouched—our beds still made, our dressers immaculate, and whatever we had left behind still in place.

Veronica and I quickly agreed it was time to get rid of some things. Our Barbie dolls, for example, relics of a childhood long gone. Our father even suggested that one of us take the second-floor bedroom. He offered to clean it out, moving his office to the back den we had always used for storage.

Our parents worked diligently to accommodate Veronica and me. Overall, it took about four days to settle in. Once we were adjusted, Veronica and I began job searching—well, I searched for jobs while Veronica accompanied me.

I knew I wanted a profession in the medical field, hoping to gain experience and start saving for medical school. My parents offered to help pay for my classes, but I quickly refused. I wanted to feel independent. After four years of living without them, I had grown accustomed to fending for myself.

Veronica, on the other hand, had different thoughts and plans. She wanted to work at a nightclub as a bartender or burlesque dancer, white passing her way into a job. She was convinced the tips would be great, that she could network, and that—eventually—she would find her way into the arms of a wealthy man.

I commended her for having such a positive outlook on what I considered an unpromising career. But who was I to judge? For days, I searched and applied for jobs, praying for someone to call me. Yet, no one did. I got leads, but they all required internships, or I was just too dark to qualify.

One day, while sulking, I toyed with the idea of contacting David, knowing he was home now, too. I wondered whether a letter would suffice—something to express my disappointment in how he had treated my baby sister, while also admitting the lingering nature of my feelings for him.

A weak moment on my part.

A week later, David stopped by while Veronica was out on an interview for a part-time waitress position at a gentlemen's club. During that time, he and I spent hours watching movies, baking cookies, and hanging out just like we used to in college.

By the time Veronica returned home, David and I were snuggled up in the living room, watching *It Happens Every Spring,* my absolute favorite film.

She looked drained, as though they had already put her to work.

David was fast asleep on my arm. I gently pushed his head away and made my way down the corridor to her bedroom. She had decided to stay downstairs, while I had moved up to the second floor.

Our parents spent little time at home, always traveling and seeing the world, just as they had always said they would once we got older.

I noticed Veronica had run a hot bath and was slowly submerging herself inside.

"How did the interview go?" I asked, hesitating slightly, unsure of how she would react.

I sat on the edge of the bathtub, watching her. Her naked breasts stood firm on her chest; her hair twisted into a messy bun. With her head tilted back and her eyes shut, as though she were sleeping, she finally responded.

"I suppose I should be grateful." Her voice was laced with bitterness. "I didn't have an interview. They took one look at me and... I had my first session."

Her lips moved, but the words that came out were hateful, angry, and full of regret.

I knew what she meant.

No need to act coy.

"So, what did they make you do?" I asked, scratching my head. Pulling my hair back, I rolled up the sleeves of my housedress, preparing to wash her down.

Taking a washcloth and bar of soap, I reached for her. My right hand glided over her naked body, dipping into the water as the soap trickled down my arm. Kneeling beside the porcelain tub, I reached further, making sure to cleanse every part of her.

She let out a sigh—one I had never heard from her before.

Then, she began to speak again.

"I was tipped seventy-five dollars after being requested for a private meeting. I couldn't dance in heels, so I had to dance barefoot. Seven men watched as I removed my clothes and shook my backside, having no rhythm. But still, Vern, they enjoyed me—the view at least. Then I noticed six of the men getting up and walking out the door, while the seventh just sat there, stroking his penis in the red room. With each stroke, I knew what was coming..." Her voice began to shake as she struggled to utter her last sentence.

Veronica's eyes suddenly darted over my shoulder, locking onto David, who had walked straight into the bathroom—the bathroom inside her bedroom. I thought to myself, *What nerve he must have!* No knocking, no warning, nothing. As he stood by the threshold, staring at my sister's naked body and my right hand now submerged below the water's surface, I knew exactly what he was thinking.

He whispered, "I was going to head home." He motioned toward the door with his right hand as he spoke.

The sound of his baritone startled us both. Veronica shifted her eyes, propping herself up out of the water. My boyfriend's lingering gaze had aroused him; I threw my arms around her, screaming for him to get out. He complied, rushing toward the front door in a frantic state.

I was jealous, and this time, not of Veronica, but *over* Veronica. At that moment, I realized I wanted her all to myself. Veronica looked pleased by my reaction and, very unexpectedly, leaned in and began to kiss me. For a brief moment, I reciprocated. Water dripped from her wet body, and I felt a surge run through me, paralyzing my mind. My thoughts were on *her*, just her—her walk, her voice, her laughter.

And then, I lost myself.

I reached between her legs, massaging her soaking clitoris, palming her breasts—when a force tore through me. I was pushed away so hard that I slid to the rear of the room, my back slamming against the white tiles. I let out a sharp cry and watched as Veronica stood there, sobbing. She stepped out of the tub, clutching her breasts in her hands, scurrying past me in her naked state, water dripping all over the floor as she fled into her bedroom.

I remained on the ground, trying to gather my thoughts and rub the lower part of my back, which now ached from the impact. I had no idea how to react—I didn't know whether to cry, become angry, or remain in my perturbed state of mind.

That night, as I slept, many thoughts filled my head. My parents had no idea what had taken place. The events of that evening were never disclosed—neither by me nor

Veronica—like many others. Of course, we did not want our parents thinking we were attracted to one another. Our mother alone would have called down the angels, gathered the priests, and prepared our home for an exorcism to cast out any unwanted demons or spirits provoking her children. So, Veronica and I remained discreet, never uttering a word about what had happened in that bathroom.

Years later, twenty-four years old, I continued my diligent quest for full-time employment, while Veronica maintained her job as a private dancer and bartender at Nick's Gentlemen's Club down on 128th Street.

One night, I decided to visit the club in hopes of seeing Veronica. I had been out wandering, window shopping, when I came across the club and remembered that she had mentioned the street it was on. The exterior was painted a dirty, dark navy blue, covered in graffiti—images of women cupping their breasts and licking their lips. I could never forget that mural; I thought it was demeaning.

Outside, the parking lot was filled with cars and drunkards. Some men were tussling or rolling dice along the concrete, while others were receiving fellatio in their backseats. I prayed none of those women was my sister.

As I made my way past the parking lot toward the doors, I noticed two large men standing guard—bouncers for the club, no doubt. They were well-built, maintaining an intimidating posture as they watched the inebriated men and women who populated the lot. I kept walking until I reached the end of the ropes. I noticed I was the only one outside waiting to get in.

At first, neither man paid me any mind. I stood patiently, hoping one of them would acknowledge me, and when no one did, I finally spoke.

"Hello, is there an entrance fee?"

The first bouncer took one look at me, then glanced at his colleague, who chuckled. They both shot me a look of bewilderment.

"Listen, girl, this here place ain't no place for kids. Take ya fat ass home."

Admittedly, by the age of twenty-four, I weighed about 167 pounds, but given the nature of my hourglass shape, it didn't show anywhere besides my lower stomach, hips, and thighs. Despite Veronica being the more petite of us two, we shared the same body structure—only my weight was distributed differently. Thick girls were not a cultural favorite—that much was obvious. So, I decided on a different approach.

"Look, I had a long day at work, and all I wanna do is unwind, see some bitches, some nice asses, and some good dancing. So, what is it—fiddy for a stamp?"

I pretended to speak flawless Ebonics despite having never spoken that way a day in my life, believing the dialect, along with a touch of homosexual flair, would be enough to grant me admittance.

"I mean, she look like she stacked," the first bouncer said to his colleague again.

I thought I looked like an average college dork, but to them, I must have smelled of money. My hair was thrown into a messy ponytail, barely touching my shoulders. I had a slight tan, an over-the-shoulder tassel handbag, a red sleeveless mini dress, silver-studded earrings, and open-toed gladiator sandals. My getup was nothing short of ordinary.

"Alright, Ray, let her in. Listen, you don't touch the women, and you don't talk to the women. You understand? They dance, you pay, and that's it!"

I had to tilt my head back to look at him speaking—he was about 6'4" in height compared to my 5'8". He spoke with anger, over-enunciating each word as he motioned with his hands, pounding his right fist into the palm of his left.

I mean, what type of lesbian chick did they think I was? What harm could a little thing like me really do? But I complied, and the next thing I knew, I was walking into what I could only imagine was hell.

The bouncers removed the velvet rope, and after passing through two bolted doors, I finally reached the main room. There were women everywhere! On the bars, in cages, on the stage, in front of men, on top of men, in a back room with slightly tinted windows, and even standing by the doors waiting for new faces.

Once the DJ started spinning records again, I felt a little relieved. Just then, a white-passing African American woman with blonde hair cascading down the center of her torso approached me. She leaned down in front of me, gripping both sides of the armchair, then whispered in my ear,

"My name is Latisha, baby. I'm gonna take care of you tonight."

My eyes widened as I tried to protest that I wasn't interested, but before I knew it, she was slamming her butt on and off my lap to the rambunctious sounds of the blaring music.

The room was still dark, but the lights began to brighten as the DJ made an announcement.

"Next, we have coming to the stage a Creole, exotic little thing. Family straight from the Bayou, newest and sexiest addition to the floor. Fellas, get your money ready—set and throw!"

On cue, the music dropped, and Veronica made her appearance. I sat in shock, clenching my handbag as I watched her walk onto the stage wearing nothing but a pink thong, what appeared to be six-inch fuchsia heels, and pasties over her nipples. She rocked her hips to the right, then to the left, slowly dragging her feet. I watched as she moved closer to the center pole, then took one leap, wrapping her legs firmly around the top, extending her torso backward, and dangling. Her hair flowed wildly as she whipped it back and forth, attempting to catch the rhythm.

She was successful.

The white men were going wild—whistling, standing, clapping—dollar bills raining onto the stage. I tried to remain hidden behind my dancer for the night, but she kept looking back at me. Mistaking my attempt to hide as a desire to see more of her, she obliged.

"Oh, you like that, huh?"

She stood and began removing articles of clothing one by one.

First, her bra—her bare breasts now dangling in front of me. I struggled to look past her. By now, Veronica was at the edge of the stage, spreading her legs wide for all her fans.

She removed her panties, her vagina lips now exposed, as she reached over to tease the men throwing bills from their mouths.

I watched as she grabbed a drink from a gentleman holding a twenty in his hand. She chugged half, then poured the remainder down from the top of her neck, letting it trickle over her body.

She reached for his neck in a coerced manner.

Once he realized what she wanted him to do, he began licking the liquor from the center of her torso, tracing his tongue back up to the depths of her collarbone.

Just then, I noticed a man tackle him from behind, causing an uproar in the club. I assumed it was a bouncer since it was against the rules to touch the women, but it wasn't.

After a closer look, something about this man seemed familiar—his height, his complexion, and the Texas-shaped birthmark on his lower left cheekbone, briefly illuminated by the neon lights.

Blinded by drinks flying in every direction, I managed to shove Latisha aside. She let out a holler.

"This bitch just pushed me, and she ain't paid me, Kenny!"

Fear struck me.

"I'm so sorry! Here, here's five dollars. I'm sorry, it's all I have." I yanked the freshly printed five-dollar bill from my purse—the one I'd gotten from the bank earlier that day—and forced it into her hands. By the time she realized it wasn't a handful of singles, she immediately stopped screaming. Instead, she climbed to her feet and strutted toward the back, disappearing into the dressing room.

Seconds later, the club descended into complete chaos. The DJ ducked behind his equipment, belligerent men hurled their glasses at the panel windows, and the air reeked of sweat and liquor.

Frantic, I searched for Veronica—lifting chairs, looking under tables where women cowered, even sneaking into the VIP room for a peek. She was nowhere to be found. Either she had retreated to the back, or she had already been taken out.

My baby sister.

I couldn't find her anywhere.

Panic rising in my chest, I bolted for the front door.

Struggling to squeeze through the thick crowd of drunken guests, I heard the first gunshots ring out. Now everyone was moving, clawing, trampling over bodies— some who had fallen, others who would never get back up.

And then, for the first time in my life, I saw a dead body. A man crumpled beneath the weight of heels and boots, stomped over in the desperate rush for the exit.

Outside, the bouncers barked at the crowd to calm down before they opened the doors, but it was too late. Sirens wailed in the distance, and at that moment, I knew—either I was going to be arrested, or I was going to be killed. The last thing you wanted was for the police to break up a chaotic, predominantly-Black crowd.

They were going to use force.

And many of us would become victims of police brutality that night.

This club had been hiring more and more African American women who were white-passing, along with Black male bouncers—stronger, faster, and more threatening. But of course, in those times, that was unacceptable. We were still fighting racism and segregation. As soon as the bouncers opened the doors under the officers' orders, the batons came down.

People dropped unconscious, one by one.

I fought my way through, clawing my way outside, squinting against the blinding police lights.

At least fifteen squad cars lined the street, their flashing reds and blues painting the night.

I knew I couldn't ask for help.

So, I ran.

I ran as fast as I could for four blocks, then darted down into the train station.

Panting, I leaned against the token booth, fumbling for money I no longer had—money I'd spent on a stripper only moments before.

Before I could speak, I turned.

And there she was.

Through the turnstiles, Veronica stood parallel to David, his all-black hoodie shrouding her.

She was shivering, crying, her hair a tangled mess.

And before I could muster a word, I watched as he leaned in—

And they kissed.

—

"You know, Ms. Vern, we've covered a lot today; we can stop here if you want to." I know I'm crying, but it's only because of the pain I'm feeling. There is nothing more agonizing than betrayal. That day is one I will never forget. And poor Washington—coming here just to reopen all my wounds, cuts I merely bandaged but never truly healed.

But I love that I can finally share my story.

"I'm so sorry, Washington, honey. Ms. Vern just got a little emotional. But no, son, unless you're tired, I would very much like to continue."

Smiling, I know—this is my time.

My time is now.

No matter how much they've hurt me in the past, I am a new woman. I am a woman of God, and it is through Him and all His grace that I have made it to this point in my life.

—

THAT NIGHT, I LEFT the train station, making my way back home. As I stepped outside, I could still hear the yelling from the gentlemen's club—four blocks away, the same four blocks I had just run. I knew the police would be patrolling the area, but I didn't care. My mind had gone blank, completely empty, as I walked in the direction of my house. I knew it was a forty-five-minute walk, but what I didn't know was how little I would notice along the way.

When I reached my doorstep, I peered inside to see if Veronica had made it home. Of course, she had. She had already showered, her hair still glistening, and was dressed for bed in her boy shorts and a cropped tee. Sitting cross-legged on the floor, she was counting the money I assumed she had managed to grab before being hauled off by my boyfriend. Five years, gone.

I wanted to approach her and ask why.

I wanted to hit her and tell her she deserved it.

But most of all, I wanted to ask God—why did you have to make Veronica so much better than me?

And then, I did.

Standing outside our brownstone, I asked God what did she have that I didn't. Why was it that now, the one man—the only man I had ever loved—had chosen her? I knew Veronica possessed many likable, even lovable, qualities. Hell, even I loved her. But David—I thought he would be the one man, the only man in my life who would actually be for me. All for me. I thought God had sent him to me.

David was everything I could want in a man.

I hesitated no more. I put my key in the door, unlocked it, and stomped inside. After a brief pause in the foyer, I saw my mother walking toward me. She smiled, grabbed my hand, and led me into the kitchen.

"Hi, baby, have a seat."

My beautiful mother, with her benevolent smile, softened my heart. At that moment, I felt relief. I knew tonight was not the right night to confront my sister. I let out a huge sigh and asked,

"Where's Daddy?"

My mother reached across the countertop, grabbed her Bible, and set her glasses over her eyes before removing a notepad.

"Oh, he's at the station, baby. Hired a new boy today, so lots of training. But enough about us—how have you been? I know looking for a job hasn't been easy."

She cradled my hands in hers, placing one gently on top. I knew how much my mother wanted to talk, but my mind was elsewhere. It was after midnight, and I was growing tired.

"Mom, I'm sorry. Can we talk about this tomorrow?"

Not being able to find a job was stressful enough. Talking to my mother about it would only make it harder.

"I understand, sweetheart," she said. "But before you go, I want to read you something I found in the Bible."

She began flipping through the pages, and I put my head down, grinning uncomfortably. The last thing I wanted to hear about was the Bible. I believed in God, but never had any interest in the Good Book—it wasn't entertaining to me.

Sensing my lack of enthusiasm, she smiled—a nurturing, knowing smile.

"Vern, can I ask you a question?"

I laughed. "Of course, Mom, you can ask me anything."

She placed her hands directly atop her Bible. "Why do you resist the Lord?"

I had no idea what she was talking about, but for the sake of being respectful, I continued to listen.

"I was praying tonight for my children. A spirit told me that I needed to pray for my children. Now, granted, your Daddy and I aren't home as much as we used to be, so we don't have the same eyes and ears we once had. So, you know I have to pray. But when the Spirit told me, 'Pray for your children, Vern,' I had to listen."

There was no doubt now—my mother had my undivided attention. I stared into her eyes as she continued to speak.

"So, I began to pray. I began to weep as my stomach twisted at the visions coming before my eyes. Vernette, as I sit here before you, I know I am losing my children. I cannot lose my children. You are my heart and my bellyache. You and your baby sister, Nica, are mine. You are both mine.

"There is a battle raging within Nica that I cannot fight. But when that battle presented itself to you, you fled from it and became exposed to a Higher Power. You were so young, I know you have no idea what I speak of. But Vern, the Lord has a hold on you, and all you have to do is accept Him."

A part of me was done listening to the shenanigans about holds, spells, and rituals. I had had enough.

"Mom, okay, I hear you. But can I please go to bed now?"

My mother was pouring her heart out, but like every selfish young adult, all I could think about was David and Veronica and how they had betrayed me.

"Before you go—" she said, her eyes dropping to my chest. "That necklace?"

I stood, preparing to leave.

"Mommy, I love you."

She slammed her hand on the table.

"Vernette, don't you dare walk away from me. The necklace you're wearing—where did you get it?"

I looked down to see the cross pendant dangling from the sterling silver chain. I had received it from Holly all those years ago while visiting Grandma and Grandpa Robinson.

"I got it from Holly... I think."

She reached down into her blouse, pulling out the same necklace.

Before I could speak, I stood frozen in silence.

"Holly gave you that necklace, and you've worn it faithfully around your neck for seventeen years. How could I have missed that?" Her voice was steady, certain. "Little girl, take up your Bible and read it."

Just like that, she turned away and proceeded to read on her own. I was free to leave the room.

The next morning at breakfast, my mother cooked, our father ate, and Veronica and I suffered in silence. Despite being young adults, our parents demanded our attendance at the breakfast table whenever they were home. If we couldn't make it to one of the three necessary meals of the day, we were required to notify them in advance.

Days passed. I hoped that one day, I would be able to move out and become financially independent, but the job market for African American women was a complete catastrophe. Working for the white man meant grueling hours for minimum wage. Even if I found a job, there was no way I would be able to support myself on my own.

I envied Veronica once again. Although her profession was distasteful and kept close to her heart in secrecy, she still made ends meet.

Taking my mother's advice, I began praying. It led me to leave Veronica alone and not inquire about her relationship with David. He still called and still came by in an attempt to see me, but I made it my business to ignore him.

Night after night, I crept past Veronica's bedroom door, listening as she whispered into the phone. There was no doubt in my mind—she was speaking to David.

She would say things like, "Thank you for being there when I needed you," or "Sleep tight, baby. I love you."

The *love* part caught me off guard.

Who was in love here?

How could love even be a factor?

To my knowledge, they had only been sneaking around for a short while.

But due to my resistance in asking Nica about what took place between her and David, I told myself, *Vern, you will simply never know.* What happened between them stayed between them—as if anyone cared how I felt anyway.

Months went by, and we were now entering the fall season when Veronica announced one evening during dinner that she was quitting her current job—which she had led our parents to believe was a cashier position in retail—and moving out.

Veronica unloaded so much news with such short notice, while I, on the other hand, was still unemployed. I resented her for being the first one to break free and head out into the world. I did everything right.

Went to school.

Got good grades.

Graduated college, and yet, it was her progressing in life, not me. How?

But I did not show my jealousy.

I remained emotionally cached, never mentioning to anyone how I felt. Instead, I smiled, offered my congratulations, and even joked about moving in and demanding a key. Normally, Veronica would laugh at my failed attempts at humor, but for once, she didn't.

I knew something wasn't right.

As an unemployed woman, where could she possibly be moving to? My parents didn't ask that question, though it was clear they were thinking it—or so I assumed.

Moments later, I asked the forbidden question.

"Where are you moving to, Nica?"

Everyone in the room froze.

My father looked away almost immediately as if he and my mother both knew something I didn't. I turned to face Veronica, waiting for her response.

"I'm moving in with David," she said, taking a bite of her meal.

My patience had run out; I had no more desire to remain amicable. I locked eyes with my mother, who, by now, knew I was beyond pissed. I felt my knees buckle as I began to raise my right hand. I had never struck anyone a day in my life.

Veronica would be the first.

Just as I swung, my father reached over, grabbing me by the forearm.

He instructed Veronica to leave.

Her eyes widened in shock as he assured her that he would take care of things. She left.

I had never told my father how serious David and I had been due to my own insecurities. I was just never able to be so bold. So, when he began explaining what was going on, I realized—I could only be upset with myself.

"Sweetheart, why are you so angry? It's not just about your sister—you seem like you're mad at the world!" My father threw his hands in the air, exasperated.

The tears came as I struggled to form sentences, trying to explain my position while also attempting to defend myself.

"Veronica? Dad, she knew how much David meant to me!" I wept as both he and my mother continued to listen, but not with interest—more like confusion.

"What do you mean, 'meant to you?'" My father now stood with his arms folded, his expression growing more displeased. His brows knitted.

"David and I were together, Daddy. He was in a relationship with me ever since we were away at school. We weren't just friends."

He unfolded his arms, his expression shifting from confusion to sadness.

"Oh, Vern, you should have told me. I had no idea— that's why I put in a good word for your sister. I guess I'm just old. I involved myself in something that wasn't my business. For that, I'm sorry." He pressed his hands together and placed them over his chest as he asked for my forgiveness.

I knew my dad loved me and would never intentionally hurt me.

My mother interjected. "Surely, Clive, you're not going to allow this boy to continue seeing Veronica—let alone have her move in with him?"

My father threw his hands up in frustration.

"I just can't seem to win. She loves him, and he loves her. The most I can do is have a talk with the boy. I got involved once, and you see how that turned out, so I just want to do the right thing."

My mother scoffed. "The right thing? Allowing a disloyal young man to take advantage of your daughters? Surely, you must feel there's better for them both out there."

She made some very good points, but my father remained firm in his position. He refused to get involved any further.

I'm not sure what conversation took place between my father and David regarding Veronica, but whatever David said, it must have worked—because despite knowing the truth, my father still wasn't willing to turn him away. He viewed David as the son he never had, and with David growing up without a father, I suppose he had come to respect mine.

But then, why deceive both of his daughters? To me, it was a contradiction.

Weeks later, Veronica began packing her things, although it wasn't much.

I decided to help her.

As I watched her fold clothes and tuck away her belongings, I had to ask:

"Nica, do you hate me?"

I regretted the words the moment they left my mouth, but I couldn't stop myself. I needed to know.

I felt victimized by my own sister—constantly mistreated, constantly betrayed. Intentional or not, she was still the common denominator of all my hurt.

"Vern, of course, I don't hate you! You're my big sister, for crying out loud. You've always been there for me." She kept packing as she spoke, her tone rehearsed, her words hollow. It was as if she had practiced them a thousand times—like she had known my question was coming.

I shrugged and continued helping her pack.

As I sorted through her things, I came across some of the lingerie she had worn during her time at the club. A few back seam stockings and girdles. She caught me staring at the garments, then stepped toward me and snatched one from my hands.

"This one here—this is the one I wore the first time David and I, you know." She smirked. "I mean, he absolutely went crazy."

My heart sank as I watched her admire the red see-through negligee, holding it ever so gently. I knew she wasn't genuine—she felt no remorse for stealing the man I loved right out from under me.

I wanted to ask. I needed to know. Had they been together while David and I were still dating?

The thought repulsed me.

David was a sick man. I had no love left for him. By the end of the day, I had made up my mind—she could have him.

The next day, the moving trucks arrived. My father was at work, and my mother was in the kitchen preparing supper.

When David arrived, I saw the kiss he and Veronica exchanged. My stomach turned.

I motioned for my mother to come to the door so she could speak with the movers. Wearing her apron and cooking gloves, she approached. But the moment she stepped outside and saw what I had seen from the top of the steps, she reached for me in an attempt to console me.

I pulled away.

The last thing I needed was for anyone to feel sorry for me. Veronica had won—again—and I had to do what I did best: move on and let it go.

Once all of her things were out of the house, I did a quick walk-through of her now desolate bedroom. My parents let her take the furniture as well. Veronica was gone, and I remained.

Outside, my mother and Veronica exchanged a few words—brief and straight to the point. I hadn't walked out to greet anyone, so I had no idea what was said between them. Soon after, Veronica climbed into David's pickup truck, and the two sped off.

After walking through her empty room, I noticed markings carved into the floorboards—like someone had tried to pry them open.

Curious, I bent down and began searching frantically for an opening.

After about five minutes, I found it.

The board was so heavy that I nearly cracked a nail trying to lift it, losing my footing in the process. But eventually, I got it open.

I stretched my hand inside and felt a box. Carefully, I pulled it to the surface.

A small black box with a straw sticking out from the lid.

My pulse quickened.

I jumped up and ran to push the bedroom door shut.

I had no idea what was inside, but I didn't want my mother walking by and seeing something that might upset her.

Opening the box, I found a bloodstained homemade washcloth—the kind Grandma Martin used to stitch.

And just like that, I knew.

The baby must have died.

The one Veronica had been pregnant with before she ran away.

I had known something wasn't right. She left home pregnant and returned without any sign of ever giving birth. But now, staring at the bloodied fabric in my hands, the truth became undeniable.

I kept searching.

Buried beneath the cloth embroidered in great detail was a small brown photo album, stuffed to capacity with disturbing images.

Photo after photo of people sleeping, each wearing tiny voodoo doll necklaces. Hundreds of them.

My heart pounded.

What kind of sick shit was Veronica into?

Just then, the door creaked open.

I froze.

In the doorway stood my sister.

The room, once illuminated, was now cloaked in shadow. Darkness settled over us like a heavy veil, and that same eerie pull I had felt in the bathroom that night returned, wrapping itself around me.

Something was wrong.

She looked furious.

Her eyes burned as she stared at me, unmoving. I gripped the book tighter, holding it against my chest as if it could protect me.

"Veronica, what is this stuff?"

I felt like I was face-to-face with an enemy.

She didn't respond. She just stood there, watching me.

And then—

With two long strides, she closed the distance between us. Using her left hand, she reached up and backhanded me across the mouth.

Hard.

I hit the ground instantly. The book flew from my hands, skidding to the corner by the window.

Veronica lunged for it, scooping it up before standing over me.

She sneered, her lip curled, her eyes filled with something I didn't recognize—something dark.

I touched my lip and felt warm blood gushing from the fresh cut.

"Veronica, what the hell?! Why did you hit me?"

We had never fought before. Never.

Her slap caught me completely off guard.

A commotion in the kitchen.

Footsteps.

My mother rushed in, still wearing her apron, her eyes wide with alarm. She looked like the perfect, polite homemaker. Sunlight streamed through the window again, cutting through the darkness, bathing the room in warmth. Veronica recovered quickly.

"I just forgot something," she said smoothly, tucking the book against her side. "Vern slipped over the broken board. Sorry, Mom. Didn't mean to scare you."

Then, she shot me a look of death.

A silent command.

Stay quiet.

But I didn't.

Veronica didn't scare me.

"She's lying!" I shouted, pushing myself up from the floor. "She hit me because I found that voodoo book under the floorboards!"

My mother's head snapped toward Veronica.

Her eyes roamed over my sister, confusion and suspicion creeping into her expression.

Veronica's grip tightened on the book.

For the first time, she looked nervous.

"What kind of book is that, Veronica?"

My mother held out her hand, expecting her to pass it over. But Nica did no such thing. She pushed past my mother. Despite her usually tranquil nature, my mom would not tolerate that kind of behavior, no matter what the age. "Young lady, don't you dare push me in my house! Give me the book, Veronica!"

She now stood directly parallel to my sister, her right hand extended, palm facing upward. For a moment, Veronica hesitated. Then, with a sharp exhale, she surrendered the book. My mother began flipping through the pages.

Her breath hitched.

Her eyes welled with tears.

"Did my mother give this to you?"

Veronica stood in silence; her arms now folded. I lingered by the doorframe, my gaze low. I wanted no part in this. My mother's grip on the book tightened. Her voice rose. "Did my mother give this to you!?"

Never in all our years had we heard her speak in such a tone. Veronica decided now was the time to answer.

"Yes," she said. "She gave it to me."

Tears came instantly.

My mother pressed her fingers to her bottom lip as if trying to hold something in. Then, with sudden force, she burst into prayer—her words slipping into tongues, her only means of reaching the Lord.

She balled her fist and waved it from right to left before turning and walking straight to the kitchen. With steady hands, she lit the stove pilot. She held the book over the flame. The fire caught the bottom left corner.

"No!" Veronica shrieked and lunged toward her, clawing at my mother's right arm. I jumped between them, but Veronica was relentless. She shoved past us both, ripping open the utensil drawer.

Her hands fumbled, searching desperately.

Then she found what she was looking for.

The blade glinted under the kitchen light as she pulled out a knife.

"If you don't give me that book," she seethed, "I'll slice both your throats."

I stood frozen in disbelief.

Veronica's face was changing.

Her eyes dulled, sinking into shadow. Her lips twisted into something unnatural. Her skin, once smooth, now surfaced with blemishes.

She was transforming before our eyes.

My mother saw it too.

She released me and took a step forward, stripping off her apron. Giant strides carried her toward my sister, unwavering.

Behind her, the book burned atop the stove.

A sound tore through the air.

A shriek—piercing, inhuman.

It came from the book.

The very same sound Veronica had made that night.

I clamped my hands over my ears.

Blood still dripped from my split lip, but I could barely feel it. My mother's voice rose, thick with power. She spoke louder in tongues, her body trembling as she gripped a chair for balance. She fell slowly to her knees, pressing her hand to her stomach as if something inside her was waging war.

I watched in awe.

She had power. The kind of power I suddenly found myself yearning for. Minutes passed. She continued speaking, her voice commanding, unrelenting.

Then, she called out.

"Jesus."

Again.

"Jesus."

Again.

"Jesus!"

Veronica screamed, her hands flying to her ears, her fingers digging into her scalp as though trying to keep something from escaping.

Then, with one final cry, she dropped the knife.

She turned and ran.

Bolting out of the kitchen.

Past the dining room.

Through the front door.

And then she was gone.

My mother remained on the ground, curled in the fetal position, crying, praying, pleading.

"Why, God? Why my children? Why Veronica?"

I stood there, unmoving.

I had witnessed it all.

The power of God.

Even if just for a moment.

Something had taken hold of my sister.

And something had taken hold of my mother in return.

I didn't understand it.

Not yet.

But I could feel it.

Something was happening.

Something far beyond what my mind could comprehend.

The next day, my mother changed the locks on Veronica's old bedroom door. She never wanted anyone in there again. She never explained why. Not to me. Not to my father. We just watched in silence as she closed the door, slipped the key into her pocket, and hid it away.

From that Sunday on, my mother never missed church. For the first time in a long time, I decided to join her. Every week, I sat beside her at Holy Hands of Mary Catholic Church, seeking something I didn't yet understand.

Knowledge.

Wisdom.

Answers.

I wanted to know what was going on in the world.

I wanted to know how the spiritual realm differed from the natural.

And my mother noticed. For months, she made it her duty to keep me close—to make sure I never missed a Sunday.

And I didn't.

Because after what I had seen…

I needed to know the truth.

I was glad to be doing something with my mother; she was such a wonderful person. The lives she touched, the people she knew, and the stories she heard were all wonders. She introduced me to everyone—men and women alike—they all knew my name. Before long, I started seeing Peter there frequently as well. Peter was the gentleman my parents rented the basement to—a very nice man. He was a few years older than I was, but undoubtedly a man of God. He spoke the Word, recited passages from memory, and even accompanied my mother on trips to feed the homeless. These were things I never knew my mother took part in. It was as if I were meeting her for the first time.

Every day, my father would come home and tell me to call my sister, but after a while, it wasn't just me refusing—it was the Spirit telling me not to. Maybe she wasn't ready yet, or maybe I wasn't. A couple of months passed, and I decided to get baptized. The day of my baptism, I received a call from my sister. I purposely ignored it. I listened to her voicemail over and over again—her voice was calm, almost pleading, as she asked me to call her when I got the chance. Ever since the confrontation between Nica and our mother, she hadn't spoken to her again. My mother made several attempts to reach out, but there was no response.

Day after day, Veronica continued to call for me. I knew she and our dad still kept in touch, so I figured that was why she thought to reach out to me. But I chose not to respond. I remained steadfast on my path with the Lord, and after several more months of unemployment—relying on financial help from my parents—I finally received a call back for a job I had applied to after church one afternoon.

The position was for a nursing assistant. It was full-time, with full benefits, and the starting salary was $1,643.20 per year. Back then, 1950s, an African American making that kind of money was only a dream. I prayed every day, worshipped every Sunday, and thanked the Lord for every opportunity He had given me.

One evening, I headed out for a walk to the grocery store when I saw a pickup truck parked outside a medical clinic not far from the hospital where I now worked. It looked just like David's truck, though I wasn't entirely sure. That evening, upon returning home, I finally decided to call Veronica.

She answered on the second ring.

"Hello?"

I hesitated, questioning whether I had made the right decision. But then, I spoke.

"Hey, it's Vern."

The tone in my sister's voice changed immediately—from slightly indifferent to completely excited.

"Oh my goodness, Vern! Sissy, I miss you so much! Did Dad tell you to call me? I've been calling you for weeks! How are you?"

I struggled to smile but realized that I was now at peace with myself. Veronica and I both had to move on from the drama in our lives. It had been four months since we last spoke. I was a different person now. She spoke so fast, asking so many questions.

"I'm good, thanks for asking. I finally found a job and have just been going to church, doing the Lord's work alongside Mommy. How about you?"

Veronica fell silent for a moment before she finally spoke.

"I'm pregnant, Vern. David and I have been planning our wedding and just taking things easy. He makes so much money, so I don't have to work."

I scoffed. Here she was again, trying to flaunt her perfect life in front of me. But this time, I told myself not to let it get to me. One day, I, too, would have those things.

She spoke again. "We have a nice little place—maybe you should come by sometime. When are you off from work?"

My eyes widened. Was I truly ready to see David and Veronica now boldly parading their love in front of me?

But then, I reminded myself to do what I had been doing all along.

I decided to trust God.

"Sure," I replied. "I can come tomorrow. I'm not working."

Veronica laughed so hard that her cackle was deafening. "Great, so it's settled. I'll cook, we'll eat, and we can all catch up! Vern, I miss you so much! I can't wait to see you! Do you have a pen and paper to write down the address?"

I didn't have a pen and paper, but I lied anyway. I knew our dad had the address; I could simply get it from him. My curiosity was at its peak, and I was eager to hear where they lived. At least then, I could have an idea about the neighborhood.

"Sure, go ahead." I held the phone tightly, hoping for an address in the slums. She said:

"The address is 4356 Millerton Rd, Riverbank, Long Island. Zip code 14589. We're in the third house on the left. Our street is one-way. Okay?"

A small chill ran down my spine the moment she said "house." She was living the life I had always imagined for myself. Still, I had no idea what kind of work David was doing, considering he too was unemployed post-graduation. But whatever it was, it was good enough to take her from the strip club and make her into a housewife.

Veronica even talked about cooking. Living at home, she didn't know the difference between a deep dish and a frying pan. I felt envious once again. My life had been going well before I called her, but now, here I was, standing there, jealous of my sister. I was a living example of how blissful ignorance truly is. She always won. I faked an ecstatic reply:

"Okay, great. I can't wait either! See you tomorrow."

After ending our call, I placed the phone back down on the receiver, which occupied a small space on the mantle in the hallway. I walked past Veronica's old bedroom. Her door remained a clear memory of what she had become and the beginning of my newfound journey with the Lord.

I struggled with the thought of actually visiting her because of all the memories that would surface once we laid eyes on each other. I'd spent a huge chunk of my life learning how to forgive my sister, but at that point, I wondered why it was still so hard. I walked slowly to my upstairs bedroom, where I heard my parents speaking to each other behind their closed door. They were laughing, giggling, and running around. The sound of love and happiness was all I could hear, but despair and loneliness were all I felt.

I decided against showering that night. I fell into my bed with my arms folded across my chest, as one would lie inside a coffin. I began to pray, asking God to please kill me. I was not happy. My life was miserable, and everyone around me seemed to be living ideally, except for me. So, I began to question: what was my purpose? Why was I born? Was I placed on Earth to be a mere spectator? To simply witness the development and greatness of everyone around me? I thought so much until eventually, I fell into a deep sleep.

The smell of my mother's fresh turkey omelet awakened me. I turned to my side and noticed the clock reading 9:27 AM. What a perfect time to head downstairs and speak to my mom. I dreaded getting out of bed because I knew I would be visiting Veronica.

I dragged myself down the stairs, making my way into the kitchen where, as usual, I saw my mother by the stove. For the first time, Peter was sitting by the dining table, his legs crossed sophisticatedly, reading the paper. He turned to face me, smiling. I had come to know Peter from the church and all he had done with the missionaries, but he and I never actually spoke longer than a *hi* or *hello*. I never thought he would make it to the upper level of our home.

"Good morning, Ms. Vern. Nice to see you finally joining us."

I shot him a look of confusion.

"Good morning to you too. Mom, where's Dad?" I spoke while rubbing my face and yawning. My mother gave me the "don't you start that" look, which consisted of a head roll, head slightly tilted to the side, pursed lips, and squinting eyes. Yes, I nailed it.

"He went to work, Vern. You know this."

I did know that, but you couldn't blame a girl for asking. By now, I had taken a seat. My mother slammed my omelet in front of me, but placed Peter's nicely in front of him.

"So, Peter, what exactly is it you do for a living again?" she asked him.

My mother now sat at the head of the table. I pushed my hair away from my face as I placed my elbow on the table and began to slice into my omelet. As Peter spoke, I continued to keep my head down, and then I felt my mother kick me under the table. Once I lifted my head, she motioned for me to listen to Peter, now giving me that "you need a man, I like him for you, so listen to how great he is" look. That look consisted of another kick to me, a quick head nod in his direction, her fork waving back and forth between him and me, lips pressed together, eyes wide open with an instant vertical nod. Peter, completely oblivious to this, moaned in satisfaction with every bite.

I chuckled to myself, thinking how adorable my mother was trying to play matchmaker. I didn't fight her on this. Peter was, no doubt, a good-looking guy. His eyes were green, very rare for a Black man. Peter's skin was light and fair, with no signs of piercings. He was very well-built, with a beauty mark on his lower left lip. He was handsome, no doubt, but I never made it my priority to view him that way—until now. I listened as he spoke.

"I'm a senior journalist now for the *New York Times*. Been there going on about two years now. I love it. You know, I stay pretty busy. When I'm not at church, I'm at work. Just life, right?"

My mother smiled at me as though she already knew the answer, just asking for the sake of me knowing. I then realized I looked disgusting. I had just woken up, my hair uncombed, and I was wearing a nightdress two sizes too big that I had changed into in the middle of the night. I had the worst morning breath, and once I became aware of the matchmaking situation, I quickly excused myself to go freshen up.

Peter was, no doubt, the perfect man. He was taller than me and had a great job, but he was well into his thirties. The age difference was uncanny. What could a man his age want with a girl like me? I mean, yes, I was in my twenties, but still a child nonetheless—I lived with my parents.

After about fifteen minutes of brushing my teeth, combing my hair, and running some water over my unclean body, I changed into some tan trousers and a much-fitted bib collar shirt. I had a pretty decent figure, to my knowledge, so why not let him know it? I ran back downstairs, where I heard Peter and my mother now discussing the importance of marriage and sustaining a happy home. My mother was making it her duty to get to know this man, something my father thought he was doing when he got to know David for Veronica. I was so elated—my mother was trying to find me a husband. How cute was that?

—

"Sounds to me like the Lord spoke to your mother's heart. She acted accordingly, Ms. Vern."

Thinking of my mother brings tears to my eyes, and with Washington consoling me by rubbing my back, I can feel the love.

—

EVERY RESPONSE, EVERY answer, sounded perfect. He spoke of not having found the right woman for him, how he wasn't big on perfection, and that it was about the heart of the woman. He couldn't see himself marrying someone who didn't know the Lord. My mother looked mesmerized.

Once I emerged, I noticed the look my mother gave me. She chuckled because she no doubt noticed the significant changes I had made to myself. I decided to clean up the kitchen, so I grabbed all the dishes and began to wash them. That's when I heard my mother ask, "Peter, you never mentioned how important it is for a woman to be tidy."

Peter then laughed; we all did. He finally got wind of what was going on, and my mother very politely excused herself. I stopped washing the plates and turned to face him. He swung around in his chair, watching me ever so stylishly.

"So, Miss Vern, I've spoken my life story. Why don't you come, have a seat, and tell me a little about yourself?" I obliged.

Peter and I sat, speaking for hours, and before I knew it, the clock read 3:40 PM. I knew I had to leave soon if I wanted to make it to Nica's in time for supper. Although I dreaded having to end my conversation with Peter, I knew Veronica would be disappointed if I canceled. So, I asked Peter for his number, and he asked me on a date. Of course, I said yes. I was feeling great!

Once I arrived to the station on the Long Island Railroad, I made my way through the thick crowds until I reached the upper level where I whistled for a taxi. I changed before leaving into a baby pink plaid and dot swing tea dress with a pair of tan Bettie Page pumps. The sinister part of me dressed up for David. I wanted him to notice me and feel guilty for leaving the way he did. I had lost a tremendous amount of weight since taking the job at the hospital, and with my sister now pregnant, I knew she would be a lot thicker than when we last saw one another. It was wrong of me to have had such thoughts, I know it, but I couldn't help myself.

Arriving at their neighborhood, my heart began racing. I instantly grew nervous, realizing that I remained unaware of what I could be walking into. But once outside the home, I was mesmerized—jaw dropped. I was blown away by how outstanding their house was. I noticed the huge two-car garage, the healthy green grass that was trimmed really low, and the little white picket fence separating their home from the neighbors. I was in absolute shock.

The neighborhood was no doubt upper-middle-class, with police cars guarding both ends of the entrances and exits. They even asked for identification from both the driver and me before allowing either of us to enter the street. I paid the taxi driver seven dollars for the thirty-four-minute ride and then proceeded to walk up the driveway. Standing outside, I could hear Veronica in the dining area speaking on the phone. She was discussing how thrilled she was that her older sister would be joining her for dinner—I blushed at the timing of it all. I was unsure of whom she was speaking to, but she sure sounded happy.

I trod lightly as I was very uneasy. I wanted to spend as much time outside as I possibly could. The outside of the house was built with red stone bricks, and the front door sat neatly under an overpass shaped like an upside-down V. The lights were bright on the outside, almost blinding. Once I stepped on the porch, the lights came on instantly, sensing my approach—it felt futuristic in a way. Once spotted, I heard the garage doors lifting to my right. Veronica then showed her face through the dining room glass, motioning for me to enter.

I mouthed, "Over there?"

Once she responded "yes," I proceeded to make my way in that direction.

I paced through the immaculate space, large enough to hold three Thunderbirds amongst other things. Once inside, I removed my cardigan and my shoes as the throw rug beneath my feet read:

In this home, we show our toes.
At the table, no elbows.
Eat your meals three times a day,
Then before bed we all must pray.
Welcome

As I made my way inside the home, I realized just how beautiful it truly was. The décor exuded opulence. The long white hallway that led to the garage was where I began my tour. I paced slowly, making sure to catch the amazing view. Once we entered the home, passing through the garage door, I began to take notice of absolutely everything. Her home looked very well put together, as if a designer had taken part in the decorating.

The sitting room had three square black-and-white couches, ornate with white and red throw pillows—two of which seated one person, and the other, a large three-piece sofa at the rear of the room. The three-piece sofa was accompanied by a glass table stand to the right of it, holding a small vase with flowers as the centerpiece.

The all-white-painted room held about six glass overhead lights, a large widescreen television set, and a view to the outside from the sliding doors on both the right and left sides of the room. The tall sliding doors each had sheer curtains hanging from iron rods, and the door handles were made of steel. Forged into them were the letters D and V.

The couch I sat on was the one to the far right, turned slightly facing away from the television set, looking more towards the left corner of the room. The footstools were also amazing—about two in total, both with red top cushions. One was to the left of the chair I sat in, and another was to the far right by an exceedingly large window.

The large centered table looked more like an oversized futon holding a tray of wonderfully placed fruit. There were watermelons, kiwi, grapes, and cantaloupes. Veronica even added some cheese with crackers; she was fancy. She had yet to make her appearance, so I simply sat patiently, munching on the fruits and enjoying the other finger foods.

The throw rug beneath my feet felt soft; it was large enough to cover a significant portion of the room, everywhere the furniture was. The outskirts of the room were covered in grey wooden flooring. I looked to the back where I noticed the pink floral chair, also part of the main room.

I finally decided to get up and walk around as I continued to wait for my baby sister. I could hear her in the kitchen speaking to herself, through one of the two open door frames at the rear, which transitioned into the dining room area. Walking towards the back, I had to watch my step as I inched up on the platform, placing my hands gently onto the glass dining room table and the white-cushioned top chairs.

Just above the table were two wall lights, and one large overhead lamp illuminated the entire room. I wanted so badly to step past the door frames and enter the next portion of the house when Veronica finally made her appearance.

She looked every bit elegant in her youthful, maternal state. She wore a casual red pencil skirt with an all-white button-down blouse, not tucked in, and a yellow-and-white polka-dotted large waist belt. I saw no signs of pregnancy, but I simply continued to observe. I watched her strut across the room in her yellow four-inch heels, smiling gracefully as she pulled the curtains shut, blocking out the sunlight.

Once she turned to the right, I could see the baby bump far more visibly. But her outfit looked great. The colors complemented her skin tone, and she moved with poise. Her hair parted on the left, giving her a right-side sweep, allowing it to fall gracefully down her spine. The tips stopped by her lower back, a deep black.

Veronica looked stunning; she had that pregnancy glow. Her skin was radiant, her eyelashes amplified, and her makeup looked flawless. She now favored actress Lena Horne, whom she admired, with her favorite film being *Cabin in the Sky*. There was no doubt now—Veronica was the spitting image of our mother and Grandma Martin. No wonder Grandma Martin was always so smitten by her. She walked over to me, smiling, and grabbed me.

"Come here, Vern, give me a hug. I missed you so much!" she said. I walked over with a leisurely gait as I reached out, and we both exchanged hugs. The hug she gave me felt so genuine and loving; it was as though she was squeezing into my soul. I was slightly embarrassed as I now realized that once again, Veronica had beaten me at my own game. I came with the intention to outshine her, but even in her delicate state, she still managed to win one over on me.

Once she decided to let me go, she grabbed my hand and walked me over to the three-piece sofa set, where we sat and conversed. I watched her every move as she reached for the cantaloupe to relish. Mindful of her lipstick, she made every attempt not to mess up her makeup.

"So, Vern, tell me everything. How have you been? Who is the lucky guy? Don't be modest."

I was quiet. I said we conversed, but what I really meant was that I listened. I listened to her go on and on about her cravings and how much her appetite had changed since becoming pregnant. David had several talks with her about hiring a nutritionist. She spoke as though they were celebrities. Living in this wonderful world, she was completely insensible. I simply nodded my head in agreement, not wanting to raise any suspicions. I finally decided to speak.

"I have been great, actually. Mommy and I have been spending a lot of time together. We go to church every Sunday, and she's been teaching me how to cook some things. I know you mentioned you were going to be cooking dinner, so I take it you've learned some recipes as well."

Veronica chuckled sarcastically. This came as no surprise to me, knowing just how much she despised our mother. My mention of her did not go over well—her facial expression said it all.

"How is Daddy?" she asked, reaching for more fruit.

Just then, I heard a woman enter from the right.

"Hello, Miss. I have prepped the chicken. Would you like me to begin baking it now?"

This woman was elderly, standing about five feet tall with her fingers intertwined, hanging low in front of her. She wore a long, ankle-length, black short-sleeved dress with black loafers and a large black and gray apron covering her. Her hair was covered with gray, and her eyes were lazy, as though she had not slept in days.

"Oh yes, Lucinda, please. That would be great, thank you," Veronica said. Once she finished her sentence, she continued looking into my eyes, awaiting my response.

But I could not respond. I could only remain confused as I asked, "You have a Black housemaid?"

I was disgusted.

Lucinda took her leave, and I could not believe what my eyes had beheld. One of the many things our race had been fighting for—equality, respect, freedom—and she had the nerve to have her own kind here, working as a glorified slave.

"Look, it wasn't my idea. Once I became pregnant, Lucinda was a gift from Grandma and Grandpa Martin. They thought it only appropriate to send her to me."

I wanted to cover my ears. As a young child growing up, I knew Grandma and Grandpa—or Mama and Papa Robinson, as we called them—had housemaids, but they weren't African American, nor were they actual maids, more like grounds keepers and house managers. Our grandparents still did everything on their own and maintained their home themselves.

"Is Lucinda your maid, Veronica?"

She shot me a look of disdain.

"Listen, we aren't going to sit here and discuss my housemaid, understand? She was a gift to me, and she does a great job around here. I usually don't lift a finger, and David seems perfectly fine with it. So, I honestly do not see a problem, Vernette."

I could no longer hold my tongue.

"David is a hypocrite—" I began.

"Excuse me, there will be no slandering of my man in my house. Oh, my goodness, Vern, it's been so long. When are you going to let David go?"

I was instantly appalled, but I maintained my composure. I just could not understand how a man could go from marching for civil rights to now upholding the act of having an African American housemaid. The thought repulsed me.

"How about we just not discuss it?" I asked, deciding the best thing to do was to agree, move on, and change the subject.

"I would like that. Are you not hungry? You aren't having any fruit?" Veronica asked, watching as I sat with my arms folded, facing forward, continuing our conversation without making eye contact. I was still agitated, but after a slight pause, I responded.

"I think I lost my appetite. So, when are you due?"

I stared through the glass doors, peering atop the hills, noticing the birds as they flew with haste. Veronica smiled.

"In the spring. I don't know what I'm having yet, though. It's too early to tell."

"Are you afraid?" I asked as I finally decided to look into her eyes. I looked forward to her response. I even uncrossed my arms.

"Of course, I am. I'm terrified. I've never been a mother before, and when I told David about my doubts, he assured me everything was going to be okay. I mean, I watch some baby shows, but they just don't do it for me. I still feel uneasy, and with David and me not being married yet, I have my doubts there as well. Grandma Martin and I speak all the time, though. She should be up here by the time the baby is due. She says she's going to help me with the preparations. She's been great."

I just didn't understand why Veronica was being so stubborn toward our mother. How could she not want to include her in all of this?

"Why haven't you called Mommy?"

She reached for some cheese and crackers before answering.

"Grandma Martin has told me not to. She says Mommy isn't a part of me anymore, which I believe. I mean, Mommy and I have always clashed, and I never understood why. But then Grandma Martin said she isn't her daughter anymore—that I am her daughter. So, to remain a part of her, I need to have no affiliations with Mommy."

I couldn't believe what I was hearing.

"Wait, and you agreed!?"

She nodded.

"Of course I did. Grandma Martin has introduced me to a world where I can get absolutely anything I want. I mean, ever since the sacrifice, I've been unstop—"

She caught herself mid-sentence, pausing, looking around, and then quickly trying to change the subject. "I think David should be on his way home now so we can eat."

The clock read 5:58 PM. I wasn't letting this go—I refused to.

"What sacrifice, Veronica? What did she sacrifice? Did she hurt you or someone else?"

I searched my mind until it hit me. I sat staring into Veronica's almond-shaped eyes, trying to search for anything—any sign of life left within her.

"Did she sacrifice your baby?"

As soon as the words left my mouth, Veronica's head snapped in my direction as though I had just uncovered her most hidden, darkest secret.

Then, in walked David through the left doorframe.

"Hi, sweetheart."

Veronica shot out of her seat, running over to him, where she planted a big, wet kiss on his lips. I sat with my back turned. I could not bring myself to face them yet.

I heard him speak my name, and my entire body quivered.

"Hello, Vernette, how are you?"

I continued to sit with my back turned, massaging my temples with my index finger. I closed my eyes before answering.

"I am just fine, David. Thank you for asking."

My mind was racing. The bloody cloth under the floorboards, my mother praying...it was then that I decided to utter a quick prayer. I spoke to God as fast as I could muster, slowly drowning out the sounds of everything around me. With my eyes closed, I felt it. I felt the darkness I had felt that day in the bathroom.

Just then, Grandma Martin appeared before my eyes. Her mouth was wide open as she let out a shriek, and I screamed, falling off the sofa, landing firmly on my butt.

I turned quickly to see Veronica, Lucinda, and now David all staring at me in complete shock. Veronica was being protected by David, her arms wrapped around his torso.

Something was not right; I felt it, and I continued to feel it throughout the evening. I wanted to leave, but I forced myself to stay. I knew I was in no condition to travel home—growing lightheaded since my only meal that day had been breakfast. And so, I remained there and ate the dinner that had been prepared.

As the sun began to set, we all sat at the dining table, Lucinda began bringing out the dishes one by one. She placed our cutlery neatly in front of us—everyone except for David. I watched as David and Lucinda patrolled around one another, moving in and out of the kitchen and dining room. He brought out his own cutlery, dishes, and even his food. Observing their behavior, I realized that David did not allow Lucinda to serve him.

Once he sat at the table, everyone began to eat, including Lucinda, who sat inside the kitchen on a stool by the counter. I could not bring myself to lift my fork until I prayed. I interjected, asking everyone if we could say a quick prayer before eating. Veronica immediately declined.

"Not to be rude, sis, but we don't do that here."

"You don't pray over food, or you don't pray at all?" I asked.

David kept his head down but stopped eating for a moment to listen.

"Vern, what difference does it make? The dinner looks great. I know David is hungry—how about we just eat?"

The dinner did look great; Lucinda was most definitely a wonderful cook. She had prepared a baked whole chicken with red beans and rice, along with bread pudding. She brought that Louisiana fire to the kitchen. But I had to ask,

"If you don't pray, why is there a prayer mat by the garage door entrance?"

Veronica smiled. "Oh, that was a gift from David's mother. I wasn't putting that by the front door, so he and I agreed to place it by the garage instead. Can we eat now, Vern, please?"

I scoffed; David was not wearing the pants in this relationship.

"Whatever. I'll just pray over my own food."

Veronica chuckled. "Yes, that works."

Almost half an hour later, I reflected on how delicious dinner had been. But once again, I noticed something strange. Immediately after eating, Veronica and I remained seated at the table, while David removed himself. He went into the kitchen, cleaned his dishes, and tidied up his mess. Then he exited, but not before his cologne lingered in the air.

Veronica looked embarrassed, though I couldn't tell why. I could only speculate that she hadn't expected me to witness David's behavior toward Lucinda, making it evident that he, too, did not approve of having an African-American housemaid.

But her discomfiture was short-lived. She handed Lucinda her dishes and left the table, leaving Lucinda to do her bidding. I followed Veronica, and we both sat once again in the sitting area. Moments later, David joined us, a glass of grape wine in his left hand.

"Would you like a glass, Vern?"

I immediately said, "Yes," despite the fact that I was not a drinker. I figured, why not have one glass?

One glass turned into several, and before I knew it, I was inebriated, slurring my words. I even distinctly remember laughing so hard that I stumbled onto the floor. Veronica drank only water, but David was feeling the same way I was—there was no doubt. We all continued to relax in the sitting area, entertaining ourselves. David began telling jokes about work, and I started joking about my life because that's all my life was—one big joke.

Suddenly, I felt my ponytail being tugged. I reached up to see who it was, but I only felt Veronica's hands pulling my hair farther and farther back, exposing my face as she brought hers closer and closer to mine. She leaned in so far that she kissed me gently on the lips. My eyes closed, immersed in the moment.

David continued to watch us both as Veronica slid down to the floor, lying atop the throw rug where I was. She unbuckled her belt from around her waist, continuing to kiss me over and over again. I wanted so badly to pull away, so badly to tell her to stop, but while my mind was thinking one thing, my body was feeling another—her tongue deep in my throat.

Eventually, I felt Veronica's hand moving up and down my thigh, her right hand tickling and massaging my clitoris while her left hand held my head in place. I jolted up and pushed her away, sliding myself back until I hit David's legs. He, too, reached down, pulling my hair and kissing my neck gently. Veronica suckled on my breasts as she pulled my dress down, exposing my bare chest. I tilted my head back, allowing them the chance to take advantage of me.

Just then, I heard my name being called.

"Vern, hey, Vern, wake up!"

I snapped out of a deep slumber, my eyes opening to see Veronica standing above me in her pajamas. It was undoubtedly nighttime. The shades were all closed, the room dark and chilling. My bag lay on the floor next to me.

"There's a room upstairs I've prepared for you. You can shower and feel better, okay?"

I agreed, carefully standing. Placing my hands on my head, I thought to myself, *Why would I dream about having sex with my sister?* Things were getting out of hand.

The next morning, I awoke to the sweet aroma of freshly boiled eggs, pancakes, and turkey bacon strips, all piled onto the dining room table, laid out buffet-style. Still wearing my dress from the day before, I brushed my hair into an unstable ponytail and brushed my teeth using a toothbrush left on top of the bathroom sink, still wrapped in its original packaging.

Standing alone in the kitchen, I removed a dish from the cupboard and made my way into the dining area, where breakfast had been placed. As I began adding food to my plate, I noticed Lucinda walking in from what appeared to be the laundry room area.

I heard giggling and laughter. Approaching Lucinda carefully, I asked,

"Good morning. Where is Veronica?"

She looked irritated—angry that I was speaking to her, angry at her job, angry in general. As I listened more closely, I realized she had the thickest Louisiana accent I had ever heard, similar to that of our Mama Robinson.

"They gone to the doctor for a checkup."

I knew she was lying because why would she have cooked so much food? She avoided eye contact, moving quickly as she frantically wiped down the counters and chairs…

—

Knock, knock, knock…

"Auntie! Auntie, are you home?"

Now, who on Earth could this be so late? Washington looks just as perturbed as I am. He stops the taping and walks with me over to the door. Peering through the right window curtains, my eyes behold my beautiful grandniece.

I open the door, limping quickly, bypassing the discomfort in my legs to give her the tightest hug.

"Oh, my word, baby, have you grown! C'mon in here. How have you been? How is work?"

As she walks inside, a suitcase behind her, an uneasy feeling takes hold of me. Washington, ever polite, steps forward, and as he introduces himself, I notice the look on her face—she appears peeved.

"Hello, sir. It is very nice to meet you. My name is Emily Harrington," she says, turning to face him. Shortly thereafter, she and I lock eyes again. "Everything is fine, Auntie."

"The pleasure is most certainly mine. Washington Clarke here."

They shake hands. Laughing to myself, I notice an immediate attraction between them once Emily decides to let her guard down. But Washington changes that—looking away almost immediately once he notices her lustful gaze.

"Auntie, may I please speak with you alone?"

Washington catches the hint and dismisses himself to the upstairs bedroom.

"What is it, baby?"

Emily is beautiful—the second youngest of my grandnieces and nephews. She now resides in California, working as an accountant for those big ol' movie stars. She is always well-groomed, dressed in pantsuits or skirts with tall heels. Her long, curly hair has never been straightened at the roots, just like my mother's. She stands about 5'8", slim and slender, with clear skin and a natural tan. Her eyes remind me of her grandmother, my baby sister—narrow and dark brown.

"I came across an article about you the other day while shopping with one of my clients. You never told us you were arrested before."

I lower my head in shame.

"That young man you see here is here for that exact same reason, Emily."

Grabbing hold of her left hand, I walk her over to the dining room, where we both sit at the kitchen table. For a moment, I shake my head, displeased with myself. *Why is my past coming back to haunt me? Why now?*

"I just don't understand, Auntie. It's obvious you were much younger, but what about my grandma? Where was she? What really happened?"

My Emily is so innocent—I cannot continue to lie to her. I beg Washington to join us.

She possesses some traits not of our family—clearly inherited from her dear mother, Tippy Maria Douglas, now the ex-wife of my late nephew Jordan. Her inquisitive nature sets her apart. Due to our abundance of undisclosed information, everyone in the family knows never to ask questions. Perhaps that is why she has remained so oblivious until now—protected, in a way, from the heinous acts our family has partaken in.

After Jordan's death, Emily spent some time in foster care until her mother once again proved herself capable of raising her only child.

"How is your mother?" My curiosity peaks, knowing full well that her mother would never have approved of this visit.

"She is well. I recently got her a condo out in San Francisco so I can keep an eye on her. Alana-Lynn and I want to move you, too, Auntie Vern. I don't understand why you insist on staying so far away. There is nothing for you here."

Shaking my head, I remind her—copiously—that I am here, that I am someone, and that this home is where I have consciously spent many years raising Veronica's children, Emily, and her wonderful cousins. There is life here—blood, history—rooted deep into those large trees standing firmly outside my home. Generations have come and gone through these cabin doors. This is where my last days will be spent, a request the Lord and I have unanimously agreed upon.

"Sweetheart, thank you, but I am fine. I love living here, and now Washington is here to keep me company."

She shoots him a look of contempt.

"Auntie, who is this man?" she asks quickly, no longer blinded by his beauty. She needs answers—he is a stranger, after all.

Washington interjects. "I am a reporter from New York. I meant to clarify earlier, but you seemed determined to speak with your aunt. But, um, basically, I'm here inquiring about the same article you're holding in your hand."

She holds up the newspaper clipping, a photo of me being carried away in handcuffs, staring back at me.

"So, you're a reporter who, from the looks of it, has been staying here with my aunt? Shacking up with your stories seems a bit unprofessional to me."

I can't listen to this anymore.

"I am the one who suggested he stay. He's traveled such a long way."

"Auntie Vern, no. He is here to capitalize off you. I know men like him all too well. My clients and I have the displeasure of meeting and arguing with reporters all day long. Please do not trust this man—especially not with your story, our story. This is our life, Auntie. Why does he deserve to be a part of it?"

Smiling, I grab her manicured fingers, twirling them gently as I lean in and kiss her cheek. Despite her soft-spoken nature, she ensures that her voice is heard and her words are understood.

Washington intercedes once again. "No, please, I am nothing like that. I have always been infatuated with your aunt's story ever since I was a child. Day after day, I watched my father pick his brain, trying to figure out her story until it drove him to an early grave. I assure you, my presence here is nothing short of genuine."

"Washington, please, let us continue," I say, releasing my grip on Emily and reclining into my dining room chair. Closing my eyes, I hear Washington pulling out a seat. Emily now sits still, ready to be a part of my legacy. As the tape recorder clicks on, I continue to speak.

—

THAT AFTERNOON, WHEN I returned home, my mother and father were away. I hadn't heard from Veronica for the rest of the evening and decided to spend some time with Peter. I gave him a call, and we spoke for hours until he invited me down to his place for dinner.

When I arrived, I noticed his apartment was still very much a bachelor's pad. Not much had changed since Veronica and I were children playing down there. A small storage closet had been added to the immediate right of the bathroom—no decorations, just simple. As I made my way toward the kitchen area to grab a seat, I noticed there was barely any furniture. A small, tan loveseat graced the center of the living room, and adjacent to it was a glass coffee table cluttered with magazines, *New York Times* papers, rubber bands, and more. Peter was sloppy. Old chip bags floated across the floor. The carpet was beige and, by the looks of it, had never been vacuumed.

But when I reached the kitchen counter, I realized that was where he took the most pride. His countertops smelled of fresh lavender, his sink glistened, and his refrigerator was packed with all kinds of fresh food. He had always told my mother how much he loved cooking, but I was impressed.

He asked me what I was in the mood for. I smiled, whispering, "Surprise me," to which he responded,

"Oh, I have just the thing."

Just then, he reached for the skillet and began throwing in diced chicken breasts. He grabbed a chopping board, mincing peppers, onions, tomatoes—so many fresh, colorful ingredients. I waited patiently as he prepared dinner, even wandering into the bedroom.

Peter's bedroom was small—the smallest part of the apartment. It had one dresser large enough to fit a body, a full-size mattress, and a small television set in the corner.

After taking my own brief tour, I had to ask, "Peter, where are all your things? It's practically empty down here."

He smiled as I reached for a can of Pepsi from the corner of the counter. I sat down, sipping slowly, listening as he spoke.

"Sweetheart, I have what I need. Why splurge on all the wrong things? Why do I need three sofas when I am one man? Why do I need decorations when I know no one in town? The big question here is, who would I be impressing with all my materials, with all my wants?"

I smiled. Peter was adorable. He chopped up the chicken and began stirring everything in the skillet, adding a hint of red wine. The gravy started to boil, and I couldn't wait to taste his creation. He moved swiftly, gently, and knowingly around the kitchen.

Just then, I heard footsteps above our heads. We both looked up, wondering who it could be. My parents weren't around. I placed my Pepsi down and told Peter I'd be right back.

I stepped slowly up the stairs, opening the door leading to the first floor of my home. More noises came from the kitchen—a chair dragging across the hardwood floor. All the lights were out, so I could barely see a thing. Just then, Veronica appeared, standing in front of me with her arms folded.

"Nica, what are you doing here?"

I searched the wall for the light switch. She wore an all-black sleeveless jumpsuit, a navy blue blazer with the sleeves slightly rolled up, and navy blue flats. She carried a small yellow clutch and wore yellow studded earrings. She looked well-dressed, as though she had just left an important function. Her hair was tightly pulled back into a bun resting at the rear of her head.

"Lucinda drove me here because I needed to get out of the house. David and I had an awful fight. He wants Lucinda gone. He feels like she doesn't respect him and despises the idea of having an African-American housemaid. Do not say I told you so, please. But I told him no—she was a gift to me, just like everything else."

Veronica leaned against the kitchen counter before taking a seat in the chair I assumed I had heard dragging earlier. I leaned against the wall, relieved. Now that Peter and I were getting closer, I cared less and less about David and Veronica. What I didn't want, though, was for Veronica to ever meet Peter. There was no telling how that would go, and I refused to take any more chances. Very discreetly, I shut the basement door behind me.

"Look, you have to understand where he's coming from with this. David was once an active member of a society whose primary goal was to assist in the eradication of segregation and equal rights for our people."

Veronica rolled her eyes.

"English, Vern, English. What the hell does that entire—whatever you just said—even mean? Look, I understand his position. I just don't care. I think he should stop being such a brat. She cooks wonderful food, she's a nice woman, and she does all the little things around the house so that I don't have to. I mean, in my state, I can't do much anyway."

"Yes, Nica, but she's Black!"

"Oh, so if it were a white housemaid, things would be okay?" she said sarcastically.

"No, but I guess he wouldn't be this reluctant toward the idea."

She started getting comfortable, removing her blazer and kicking off her shoes to the corner.

"Anyway, I don't want to talk about it anymore. You left in quite a hurry this morning."

I decided to take a seat too. I felt bad—I knew Peter was still waiting for me.

"That's because you left to go to your doctor's appointment and didn't even have the decency to tell me anything."

She began removing the pins from her bun, letting her hair fall freely.

"What doctor's appointment? David and I were home all day. We were in the laundry room practicing my breathing. I heard when you got up and came down for breakfast, but I couldn't break the exercise. I told Lucinda to fetch you."

I was appalled. That bitch had lied to me.

"Not according to Lucinda. She told me you and David had left. I knew I heard laughter in there—I just didn't want to be rude and call her a liar."

Veronica laughed hysterically, clutching her stomach.

"That Lucinda is a trip. I can't believe she did that."

Just then, I noticed the bruises on her right upper arm—two, to be exact. They were fading, but I could still see the remnants of what they once were.

"Veronica, did someone hit you?"

I reached over, pressing on her arm. She immediately pulled away.

"No, I fell. Anyway, is there anything to eat in this place?"

She got up quickly.

"Nope. Mommy and Daddy left, and I've been busy. Speaking of Mommy, I'm surprised you came here. What if she were home?"

I watched as Veronica searched the cabinets for food.

"I knew they weren't here. Daddy told me they were going to Florida to look at houses."

I was shocked. "What? House hunting? Mommy didn't say anything to me about that."

Veronica laughed.

"Duh, of course, she didn't. Yet you're Team Mommy. Maybe you should consider switching, like I did," she said with a shriek. "Vern, dammit, there's no food."

I couldn't speak; all I kept thinking about was—what if they really did move? Where would I live? My salary wasn't nearly enough to afford an apartment on my own. The abrupt news left me unable to carry on a conversation. All I wanted to do was lie down.

"Don't look so suicidal, Vern, my goodness. They're only house hunting, and I doubt they're moving anytime soon. Now, are you going to help me find some food?"

As Veronica spoke, I continued to stare off into space, only snapping out of my trance when the doorbell rang. I had no idea who it could be. Veronica stepped past me and casually made her way to the front door. The bell rang again—and then once more.

"Okay, I'm coming!"

Three clicks later, I heard a loud slap. I turned suddenly to see David standing by the doorframe while Veronica clutched her right cheek with both hands.

I bolted out of my seat, racing down the hallway. Without thinking, I stepped around her and shoved him with all my might. He tilted backward, barely keeping his balance as he almost went flying down the stoop steps. I knew he wanted to hit me back, but he just stood in silence as I began to interrogate him.

"What the fuck! Did you just slap my sister? What the hell were you thinking!?" I yelled, knowing I would need to repent that night for my foul language.

"Vern, it's okay. Stop, please."

I couldn't believe my ears. "No. David, you need to leave before I call the police."

He stood there in complete shock.

"Vernette, this is none of your business. You have no idea what your sister did to me!"

Veronica suddenly started laughing uncontrollably. Strands of her hair covered her face as David and I watched in bewilderment. Then she lifted her head, opened her eyes, faced me, and said,

"Vern, please don't get involved. I'm going home now. I love you, okay?"

She sauntered into the kitchen, reached for her blazer, placed it neatly around her shoulders, grabbed her clutch, slid her feet into her shoes, and then walked back toward us. She kissed me gently on the cheek.

"Good night, big sis."

As she climbed into David's pickup truck, I could hear him muttering indistinctly.

"Once we get back home, I want that bitch gone! Do you hear me?"

Veronica sat in absolute silence, staring straight ahead. She never once looked back as they drove off.

I stood by the door, gathering my thoughts, when I realized Peter was still waiting for me. I had wasted almost an hour upstairs.

I rushed down to the basement, greeted by the smell of something amazing. Smooth jazz played softly as Peter stood in the kitchen, setting dishes on the countertop.

"Hey, how did everything go up there?"

I felt a wave of happiness wash over me and smiled from ear to ear as if I hadn't just experienced that ordeal. He had just finished cooking dinner and was plating our meals. I wanted so badly to kiss him—he looked charming.

I climbed atop the counter stool and waited patiently until he finished. Once he was done, he reached into the cabinet and placed two small wine glasses beside our dishes.

I remembered what had happened the night before, when I drank at Veronica's and refused the alcohol before he even had a chance to present it. He chuckled at my forwardness and then broke out the sparkling cider.

"Sorry to disappoint, but I'm not a drinker. The only use I have for wine is in my cooking," Peter said jokingly. We sat and ate. That night, I fell in love with a man.

Every day for weeks, Peter cooked me dinner, until one night, I eventually offered. My parents had taken yet another trip to Florida, Kissimmee to be exact. Still, they had never disclosed the nature of their visits. For days at a time, Peter and I had the house to ourselves. We went on dates to the drive-in theater, sometimes out to restaurants, and even took long walks through the parks when the weather permitted. Before I knew it, two months had passed, and I was ready for more. I saw no flaws in him;

he was intelligent, polite, respectful, and kind—everything I thought of David, but more.

Veronica and I hadn't spoken since the day she left, but I was so busy enjoying my new life and my new relationship that I honestly hadn't minded.

One night, when I returned home from work, Peter and I later met up at a convention center where a rally was being held. Husbands, wives, children, and grandparents all stood outside listening to preachers making speeches about equality and segregation within the Black community. My heart filled with admiration as I witnessed an abundance of African Americans in one building, all coming together for a worthwhile cause. We listened to the protests, and then I looked at him and told myself that it was time. I wanted us to make love.

Peter was very deep into his religion, as I was, but temptation got the best of me. I reached over and whispered in his ear that we should head back to his place. I knew better, and so did he, because he wasted no time giving me a look of disappointment. Quickly, he dismissed the thought by grabbing my hand and remaining firm, listening to the protests and the quarrels taking place on 125th Street in Harlem, NY.

We weren't too far from home. Plus, I noticed he had a tape recorder in his right hand, which I assumed was for a story he would later be putting together for *The New York Times*. He held an excellent position, but there was no doubt that he had earned it. Peter had both a bachelor's and a master's degree in expanded journalism with a minor in sociology. He had worked for almost every paper in town, written exemplary breaking news stories, followed many emerging civil rights activists, and was even mentioned as one of the most influential writers of the generation. He was a very articulate and diligent man, not to mention God-fearing, which was only a plus.

We arrived back at his apartment after listening to the two-hour-long protest. Normally, once we arrived home, Peter and I would part ways—him through the gate, heading straight toward the basement door entrance, and me up the stairs to the main entrance. But this time, I asked for something different.

"Peter, do you mind if I spend the night with you?" His response made me blush.

"Sure!"

His eyebrow raised; eyes dilated—an unmistakable sign of admiration. I knew fornicating was a sin, but I wanted so badly to do it anyway. I kept using cognitive dissonance as a way of talking myself out of the guilt, telling myself things like,

"Peter and I love one another," and "We will one day be married, and by then, sex with him will no longer be a sin."

So many thoughts consumed my mind as I ran like a child on Christmas morning toward him. We both headed downstairs through the basement entrance. I stood by the doorway where I removed my shoes and leather jacket. I pulled my hair into a very messy ponytail and made my way toward the bathroom while Peter sat on the edge of his bed, checking his answering machine.

After about five minutes of using the restroom, checking my makeup, and fixing my hair, I proceeded to make my way out toward the bedroom. On my way, I passed the couch and noticed a small pillow and blankets laid out neatly. I peeked around, looking for Peter until I felt his palms cover my eyes from behind.

"Miss me?" he asked.

But I didn't miss him. I wondered exactly what game he was playing. I removed his hands, turned to face him, and asked,

"Baby, do you want me to sleep on the couch?"

I figured there was no use beating around the bush.

He chuckled and responded, "Well, no, I am. I mean, we certainly can't sleep together, you know that, right?"

I threw my head back in frustration, but he didn't notice. He kissed my cheek and continued smiling as he walked me toward the bedroom.

Once we arrived, he exited, shutting the door behind him. It was me, the dresser, the blank TV, and his bed. I was absolutely livid. With all his schooling, how could he possibly believe I would choose his bed over my perfectly comfortable mattress upstairs in my bedroom? I took a seat on the bed and slouched for a minute, pondering how upset he would be had I simply gone upstairs.

After thirty minutes, I tiptoed toward the staircase. Passing him, I stopped momentarily to stare; he was fast asleep. Once I reached upstairs, I carefully opened the door and made my way to my bedroom. When I arrived, I began to undress, realizing I had forgotten both my jacket and shoes downstairs by Peter's.

It was a long night as I tossed and turned, my mind refusing to let up and allow me the chance to sleep. I was thinking about Veronica, about David, about my family, about where I would live once my parents relocated. So many thoughts plagued me. Finally, I realized I needed to relax. There was no way I was going to get any sleep if I stayed up thinking about all those things.

Eventually, I fell into a deep sleep, but didn't stay that way. I heard crying, like sniffling, throughout the house. It sounded almost like a whisper, maybe even a child. Someone was in my home. I could feel their presence, and eventually, I felt eyes staring at me from the ceiling in my bedroom. I sat up, frightened and mortified, looking around to see if this was some sort of prank being played on me. I was always one to sleep in complete darkness, as any sort of light during bedtime only served as a distraction.

"Vernette."

Once I heard my name whispered, I knew I wasn't imagining things. I removed the covers I was under and proceeded toward my bedroom door. The entire house was in darkness, and the faint whispering continued as I followed the sounds of my name resonating through the halls.

I continued to step lightly until I reached the banister. Once there, I stood perfectly still. I couldn't move. The entire house grew quiet, and I heard absolutely nothing— not even voices from outside. Before I knew it, I went flying down sixteen steps. I felt the push on the back of my neck. Tumbling down, I heard a crack in my wrist. I wailed out a cry. Immediately, I thought it had broken. Despite the pain I was now feeling all over, I curled into the fetal position, holding onto my wrist, rocking back and forth, whispering the name "Jesus." That's when the voice began calling my name again.

"Vernette, this way, Vernette."

I wanted to scream. I wanted so badly to tell whatever it was—or whoever it was—that I was not in the mood for any more shenanigans. I was really hurt. My wrist began to pulsate as the sounds of my name grew louder and louder. Sliding my body back and forth, I was now in clear view of the basement door, leading down to Peter's. The door very slowly creaked open. I stopped crying, my eyes widened as I felt myself wet my panties slightly. My breathing increased. I glanced around quickly at my pitch-black home and saw a light shining in from the glass window above the front door. I figured maybe someone had heard the fall and came by to investigate.

That's when a knock came, and try as I might, I couldn't get up to answer it. It felt as though someone was holding me down, pressing their body heavily atop my abdomen. I attempted to let out another loud cry, but what escaped was something of a shriek. That's when there was another knock on the door.

"It's the police. Is anyone in there?"

I struggled until, finally, I screamed, "Yes!" as loud as I could, and that's when it happened. My first supernatural experience.

Something yanked my now-injured wrist away from my grip and began pulling me forcefully down to the basement. My left hand still free, I clawed my way through the halls when I heard and felt one of my nails break. I could feel the wallpaper tearing beneath my fingers. I became hysterical. I no longer felt the pain in my wrist. I was far too scared, my chest bouncing up and down from my hasty breathing, my eyes darting back and forth.

Once I reached the top of the basement stairs, the grip was released, and the door slammed shut right in my face as I attempted to reach for the doorknob. That's when I heard her...

"Vernette, come down, I'm right down here."

I could no longer help myself. I began to cry. I sobbed like a five-year-old child. The officer's voice became indistinct and eventually non-existent.

I refused to move. The bottom of the stairs remained dark as well. I could see absolutely nothing down there. I was even afraid to think if Peter was down there. As soon as I thought of him, I heard a muffled scream come from his bedroom. I knew he was in trouble. Despite my fearful nature, I marched down those steps so fast to see my sister standing before me.

We were alone in nothingness, surrounded by a black hole behind us. She stood firm, wearing an all-white dress with a hood that she had placed over her head. I took two steps back as I watched her feet lift off the ground, and she began to float toward me. Once we made eye contact, she leaned in and licked my left cheek.

I closed my eyes tightly, praying that this was a dream. Once I opened my eyes, I turned to see the face of evil standing directly before me. I screamed, feeling myself pass out.

"Vern, Vern, wake up!"

I heard Peter's voice hovering over me as I flailed my arms, still gripping my injured wrist. In my dazed state, I started swinging at him, landing weak punches with my eyes still closed.

"Vernette! Please wake up—you were having a nightmare."

Peter grabbed my arms, pinning them gently above my head. I blinked, my breath heavy, searching his face for confirmation that I was no longer trapped in the dream. The moment I realized I was awake, I broke down. Sobs wracked my body, and Peter remained by my side, his presence grounding me.

Apparently, I had fallen asleep downstairs after all. Confusion swirled in my mind. My blackouts… Why were they happening? What did they mean? And why was Veronica always there? Her presence was never comforting—it was dark and unsettling.

Peter suddenly released me, his expression shifting to one of horror—something I had never seen on him before. Without a word, he took my hand, guiding me down onto our knees. I followed his lead, my lips trembling, my heart pounding. I bowed my head as Peter began to pray:

"Jesus, oh mighty Jesus. Lord, Vernette and I, your children, come to you tonight seeking guidance and protection. There is an evil presence among us, dear God, and we ask that you cast it away. This is a Christian home, where only your spirit and that of your angels shall dwell. These nightmares, these shadows—I bind them in your name, Lord, for you are great and all-powerful. No enemy that rises against you shall prosper, no demon, no unclean spirit.

Lord, we ask for forgiveness—for our sins, both known and unknown. Do not forsake us. Cast out impure thoughts and keep us under your covenant, dear God.

Cleanse our hearts and minds, and grant us the strength to walk righteously. Give us your daily bread, that we may be nourished by your word. Lord, I bless your name. I love you, Lord. Together, we say: Amen."

The room fell into silence.

Peter and I sat together on the edge of the bed, his arm wrapping around my shoulders as he gently pulled me into his chest. His heartbeat was steady, protecting me in a way I hadn't realized I needed.

"Did you have a bad dream too?" I asked, absentmindedly twisting the ends of my hair.

He exhaled deeply. "No, I had a wonderful dream. But I watched you for about five minutes before waking you up. What I saw put the fear of God in me. Are you praying on your own, Vern?"

I swallowed hard. The truth was, no, I wasn't. I muttered a quick prayer before bed, but it wasn't nearly enough. I spent little time with God outside of church. But I couldn't bring myself to admit that to Peter. The last thing I needed was a scripture lecture.

"Of course I do. Why do you ask?"

Peter placed his hand on top of my head, his touch warm and gentle as he stroked my hair.

"Lying to me won't help you. You are in a battle against darkness. I watched you tonight—fighting, as if you were up against a real, physical being. Whatever you're dealing with… it's not something you can face alone. Find your Bible, baby. And find God."

I sat in silence as tears rolled down my face; I had absolutely nothing to say. I had never mentioned to Peter the things Veronica and I witnessed as children or the events that took place that day in the salon during our visit with Grandma and Grandpa Martin. I was at a total loss for words. Staring down at the unclean beige carpet, I felt my eyelids grow heavy until, eventually, I fell asleep.

The next morning, I woke up neatly tucked under the blankets in Peter's bedroom. I stumbled outside and found him sleeping peacefully on the sofa. Not wanting to wake him, I quietly gathered my things and began making my way up the stairs.

Despite the sunlight beaming through the windows, illuminating the house, I was afraid to enter my home. About ten minutes later, I heard keys jingling at the front door—my parents had returned, laughing and exchanging jokes as they stepped inside.

I stood in the kitchen, preparing breakfast before heading off to work, when I overheard my father flirting with my mother. "See now, I keep telling you…that flight attendant was checking you out! I was like, 'Watch out now, this little lady is taken—so taken!'"

My mother giggled, responding playfully, "That's right, all this body here—we both know who it belongs to, Daddy."

I cringed as I listened to their exchange, disgusted by their attempt at flirtation. They hadn't even realized I was home. Purposefully, I slammed the skillet into the sink and turned on the faucet. The kitchen fell silent.

"Vern, darling, is that you?"

"Yes, Mom, I'm in the kitchen," I called back.

I waited as my mother made her appearance. She looked stunning—her curls loosely dangling past her shoulders, a red rose pinned to the left side of her head. She wore a long sunflower maxi dress that swept the floor as she walked. Her skin was flawless, and she looked refreshed, smiling from ear to ear. I knew she couldn't wait to show me pictures of her and Daddy on the beach in Orlando.

I was happy that she was happy, but inside, I was burning. Dying to know if they were moving—or worse, if they weren't moving at all.

"Mom, can I ask you something?"

"Sure, baby, of course, you can ask me anything."

She took a seat at the table just as Daddy walked in. He and I exchanged hugs, but he remained silent, reaching into the refrigerator to grab a Pop. Smiling, he kissed my mother on the cheek before exiting the kitchen, leaving us to talk.

"Okay, so what is it you wanted to ask me?"

I hesitated, but only briefly, "Mom, are you and Dad moving to Florida?"

My voice cracked slightly. I was on the verge of tears, thinking about how close I was to becoming homeless. My mother, sensing my distress, shot up from her chair and chuckled. She grabbed my shoulders and pulled me into a hug.

"Oh, Vern, you and Peter are going to be so happy here. I know the news must have come as a shock, but I promise it's all in good faith. We just wanted to surprise you!"

I pulled away from her grip, now morbidly intrigued.

"What news, Mom? What are you talking about?"

Her expression shifted to one of shock.

"Um… did Peter not… tell you… the news?"

Frustrated, I threw my hands up.

"No, Mother! Peter has not told me anything! What is going on?"

"Is he home?"

That was when I lost all interest in the conversation. I slammed my plate onto the table and began wolfing down my breakfast. The faster I ate, the sooner I could leave for work.

"Vernette, answer me. Please don't be angry, baby. I had no idea he hadn't mentioned anything to you. It was his idea to be the one to give you the good news."

I set my fork down, rubbed my temples, and looked up at my mother.

"Mommy, what news?"

She took a deep breath before responding.

"Okay… the answer is yes; your Daddy and I are moving to Florida. We put a down payment on a home in Kissimmee. But… we received our down payment from Peter. He's buying this house from us."

I froze.

"You see, sweetheart," she continued, "your father and I… well, we're getting older. Florida is warm and lovely, and the house we found is everything we've ever dreamed of. But we wanted this home to stay in the family—it's the first home we've ever purchased. With the money Peter paid us, we were able to find our dream house. And, Vern… he has agreed not to sell this house. One day, he wants to turn it into a rental property, but more importantly, he wants to eventually move you and him out to Florida as well."

She smiled, reaching for my hand.

"He's going to marry you, Vern!"

I felt nauseous. My eyes widened. The thought of my mother and Peter planning my future behind my back was sickening. I couldn't even get the man to have sex with me—so how on earth did I manage to get him to buy me a house? My own house, at that. Peter had some nerve keeping this from me.

I continued to converse with my mother, assuring her that it was okay that she had told me what was going on. She felt horrible, but I told her I would act surprised when Peter announced the news to me. I still wasn't happy about her and my dad moving to Florida. How could they just abandon everything we had come to know like that? I was, no doubt, being selfish. I knew my parents had done a wonderful job raising us, but truthfully, I was just afraid. With everything happening with Veronica and David, not to mention my sexless relationship, I had a growing sense of anxiety.

"What convinced you and Dad to sell the house to Peter, Mom?"

What she said next took me by complete surprise. She shrugged.

"Well, Vern, we needed to make sure you would be taken care of. Plus, your dad and I think Peter is a great man for the job."

I was bewildered by this and urged her to elaborate.

"Vernette, baby, let's face it—you're only getting older, and things aren't as easy for you. I honestly don't know why you're struggling so much. You haven't gotten a vehicle, no new clothes, no friends, and you're in your mid-twenties."

Admittedly, my mother was right. I was at a dead-end job, making little to no money. I had no idea how I was going to piece my life together. But I had hoped that, of all people, my mother would have had enough faith in me—or even in God—to trust that things would turn around.

"Now, honey, I don't want you to go thinking I don't believe in you, for the Lord has blessed me with not one, but two beautiful green trees. But we all need a little help sometimes, and let's face it, as women, we can't really do too much."

My mother was stuck in an era where women indeed lived in a man's world, but I was determined to prove her wrong. Still, I couldn't help but blush at her comment about Veronica and me being green trees. I always overheard my mother and her friends refer to their children and grandchildren that way. If your trees were green, it meant they were healthy, strong, and protected by the love of God to reproduce those of the same kind.

"Mom, why do you so heavily believe that a woman cannot be successful without a man? I mean, you have two daughters, for crying out loud! Do you honestly believe that, on our own, we can accomplish nothing?"

I looked up at my mother, who remained standing by the kitchen doorway, her arms now folded. She looked away momentarily before returning her gaze to me, her expression filled with dissatisfaction.

"How could I not believe such a thing when it was your father who saved me from an unhappy life? He was well-educated, successful, and hardworking—he still is to this day. He is the reason I am where I am now. But I don't believe that success is completely unattainable for a woman; I do believe that assistance is necessary. We were given two legs to stand on, Vern, not one. Think about it, baby."

Just like that, she left me with my thoughts. I was not happy. I remained seated, pondering my next move. I couldn't even fathom seeing Peter at this point. I was still furious that he had kept something so significant from me—my parents moving, him buying my home, renting my home!

Quickly, I jumped up, slightly dizzy, and threw my dishes into the sink, realizing I was going to be late for work. From the top of the stairs, I heard my mother call out,

"Vern, I love you."

I smiled slightly as I uttered, "I love you too, Mom."

Her words, though minimal, were enough to keep my lips curled into a smile the entire day. I truly did love my mother and knew she meant well.

As I worked my eight-hour shift, I dreaded the thought of returning home. I knew my parents would have either left or gone to bed, but I also knew I would have to face Peter—and I just wasn't ready.

How could I marry a man when I had absolutely nothing to offer him besides my body and good looks? What if we hit hard times? How would we survive? How would our children be fed if he were the sole breadwinner? I wanted more out of life, and after years of daydreaming, I had finally woken up to see the world for what it really was. With segregation and destitution on the rise, African Americans were becoming more marginalized.

Once my shift ended, I returned home where I left a note saying that I would be staying at a nearby motel.

I paid for a two-week stay.

By day three, Peter called. But our conversation was short. He could tell I was not interested in speaking at the moment.

As the days passed, I went shopping for new clothes, undergarments, and even food. I found myself becoming content—until I realized I was running out of money. I was barely making ends meet; in fact, my ends were nowhere near each other.

It wasn't until Thursday evening, while reading in my room, that I received a call from Veronica. Thinking it was Peter again, I answered without questioning how she had found out where I was.

"Hello?"

"Hey! I miss you to pieces!"

I was too embarrassed to explain to my baby sister that I had been living out of a motel for the past few days. Ever since she had learned the news from our father, Veronica had become incredibly inquisitive. She absolutely needed to know everything, and no amount of detail was enough to satisfy her hunger for gossip. I hesitated, not responding quickly enough.

"Vern, can you hear me? Are you there?"

"Yeah, Nica, I'm here. How's the pregnancy going? You're due pretty soon, huh?"

By now, I was just trying to make small talk. The truth was, I had no longer cared for Nica and her Cinderella story. To make matters worse, despite them not speaking, I knew our mother fully approved of her life—the whole saved-by-a-man narrative. And here I was, supposedly being saved by a man, yet I just couldn't accept it. I yearned for more.

"The pregnancy is wonderful, Vern! I can feel my body changing, and my breasts have even gotten larger. David loves that!" She giggled before continuing. "By the way, Grandma Martin is going to be here in a couple of days. I'm sure she'd love to see you! Will you be able to stop by?"

Veronica sounded so upbeat and excited. But seeing Grandma Martin was nowhere on my to-do list. That woman hated me—every inch of me—and Veronica, being so young and naïve, still hadn't noticed. But I did what any big sister would do. I agreed, even against my better judgment.

"Sure, I'll come by."

I glanced down at my toes, curling them back and forth as I struggled to pick up a piece of tissue from the floor.

"I think this is going to be so great! I cannot wait to see you. And Vernette, please come. I need you, okay?"

In an instant, her tone shifted from whimsical to tense.

The following Friday, without fully realizing it, I had made up my mind. Before I knew it, I was on the Long Island Rail Road express, heading to her home. I still hadn't gone back to my own house, so the few clothes I had fit perfectly into my over-the-shoulder bag.

It was morning—9:24 AM—when I arrived at Nica's home. As I made my way through the garage entrance, the first thing I noticed, aside from the door being unlocked, was that the doormat had been removed. Suddenly, an uneasy feeling surged through my body. Goosebumps rose on my arms. Something about the atmosphere had changed—even the smell.

I stepped cautiously through the long hallway until I reached the living room, the same place I had been the last time I visited. And there she was.

—

The kettle begins to whistle, and despite hearing it every day, I still dread the sound.

"Emily, please, do you mind turning that bothersome thing off?"

"Auntie, why do you have packed boxes in the corner?"

Medium-sized boxes, packing tape, figurines, and countless other objects reside in a small area nearest the stove. Once I started feeling the signs of illness, I packed up my life—or at least what remained of it—bringing things down from the upstairs to the ground floor for easier access. Living alone is nothing short of depressing, and those who enter my home can often sense just how unhappy I truly am. It is lonely, and with my ailments, many wonder how a woman my age, my stature, and my condition manages to keep such an immaculate home. But I always tell them, it is the Lord who lends me His strength day by day, as I am on borrowed time.

"Are you chilly? I can grab a blanket from upstairs."

Emily remains close to my side, doing her best to ignore Washington. She has no interest in getting to know him any longer. For the past two days, she has prepared my meals, cleaned my home, and even gone out to buy my medicine. I knew she would—these are things she always does when she visits.

"By the way, Auntie, how long is this Clarke guy going to be here? He's getting a little too comfortable."

Washington has gone to shower in one of the upstairs bathrooms. I wait until I hear the water running before I respond.

"Sweetheart, I know this is all new to you, and I'm sure you know far more than lil' ol' me when it comes to reporters and such. But I have a calling placed on my life. The truth—my truth—it needs to be told."

Emily's eyes begin to well.

"So, are you going to tell him about my father and me?"

Her tears soften my heart. Her story is one of great pain. Seeing how deeply she is hurting, I feel it too. Tears well in my own eyes as I reach for her, pulling her into an embrace, letting her rest her head on my shoulder.

Just then, the shower pipes go still.

I kiss Emily on the forehead, knowing this will be hard for her to accept. Telling her story—a story she isn't ready for others to hear—will change everything.

"Good morning, ladies!"

Washington makes his way down the creaking stairs wearing a red, bleached-out short-sleeved top paired with knee-length shorts. By the fourth day, he had gone shopping in town after realizing he would be staying for a while. Now, on day six, we have only just begun to scratch the surface.

As soon as he enters the room, Emily quickly regains her composure and saunters off into the kitchen, where she insists I try her delicious banana oatmeal biscuit recipe made from scratch. A delightful breakfast can change even the worst of moods.

It is time for me to shower and prepare for another day. Before heading to the bathroom, I ask Emily how long she plans to stay, knowing her career is demanding.

"However long it takes for you to finish, Auntie," she replies, her warm smile filling my heart.

I walk toward the downstairs bathroom, a space personally rebuilt to accommodate my elderly state. As I step inside and close the door behind me, I pause, listening for any sign of an amicable conversation between Washington and Emily. After a few moments of silence, I hear Washington speak.

"So, what exactly do you do for a living?" he asks, his voice slightly hesitant.

"I work hard for a living. Do you?" Emily replies, her tone sharp. "I mean, you travel hundreds of miles to stalk people, but realistically, do you call that work?"

Her condescending tone catches Washington off guard, and he does not immediately respond. Eventually, Emily lets up, shifting her approach. "I'm a celebrity accountant for a reputable agency in San Francisco. I landed the position straight out of college after interning there for two years as an undergrad. Where did you go to school?"

Washington pauses before answering.

"NYU. I studied journalism with a minor in public relations and graduated at the top of my class. My father would have been proud of me. All those late nights studying, working my ass off for this very moment—to do what I love. So, to answer your earlier question, no, I do not consider this work. I worked to get here, to earn an honest living doing something I'm completely passionate about. Can you say the same? Oh no, I forgot—you're still working."

Sarcasm at its finest. A long pause follows.

"I-I-I didn't mean to insult you," Emily stammers. "Obviously, you're an intelligent man, and only a few can accomplish that, it would seem. I'm impressed."

Washington then replies, "The last thing I want to do is impress you. Rather, I want to teach you something."

Emily scoffs.

Finally, I step into the shower and begin to scrub my aching body. I feel my limbs growing fatigued the longer I stand, and the longer I sit, it feels like I am dying. Four minutes later, as I step out of the shower, I can faintly hear Emily and Washington conversing once again.

"...the thought of my aunt telling you everything about our family is really discomforting. I mean, who are you? Aside from a college graduate doing what he loves to do," she sounds as though she is mocking him. "Is that to capture the lives of others in ways they could only dream of? You never quite explained."

"Nor do I intend to," Washington responds. "I am an honest man doing an honest job. I understand you're afraid, but as I've explained to your Grand-aunt, there is so much more to her. So much that could change the life of someone else—someone facing similar, if not the exact same, challenges. That's what her biography is all about. It's about giving her the voice and the spotlight she lost while being a shadow to her younger sister—"

Her voice slightly elevates, now barking with rage.

"How dare you make such a statement! You know nothing about my grandmother! You know nothing about my Auntie Vern! Nothing about us. Shadows? What are you even talking about? You say you studied the news—well, exactly which part? Because I was all up in there at eight years old, with cameras shoved in my face as reporters questioned me about being a victim of rape! The media slandered our names while populating their magazines and papers with lies and horror stories! You are a phony, and I refuse to stay here and allow you to continue trying to expose us for your own monetary gain."

"You think I don't know who you are, Emily? I know all about you—front page news, from what I recall. But why would I even begin to interpret or build upon the lies of someone else? I'm all about the facts, and goddamn it, sue me. Sue me for thinking I can come here and make a difference in the lives of those who need it. The famous Harringtons, your father, uncles, and aunts, were headline news for years, and this is the moment to get the clarification you need. The public deserves—"

"Why does the public deserve anything? Just because the papers re-ran a forty-year-old story to sell more copies? Oh, the true crime bait." Emily interrupts. "The media single-handedly destroyed us, forcing us to move out into the middle of nowhere. Now, to even have a possible chance at leading a normal life, we have to bury our family name, and yet here you are with your shovel, disguised as an outdated tape recorder."

Stumbling my way out of the bathroom, I immediately scream,

"Stop it! Both of you!" I enter into a twilight zone, witnessing my grandniece and a reporter bickering in my home. "I will not tolerate this now. This here is a peaceful home, and I am a peaceful woman. Don't bring that ruckus in here. Fetch me a chair, please, would you?"

Emily and Washington both run to my side, each attempting to grab a dining room chair for me to rest on. I exit the bathroom wearing nothing but a large black robe, carrying my cane. Emily runs to the living room, searching through the boxes for the one marked "**CLOTHING**."

Quickly, Washington proceeds to leave us, walking out onto the patio. Emily and I remain inside, where she assists me in dressing myself in a blue and green box-patterned linen top and a pair of old trousers, which still fit me quite snugly.

I've been living on my own for decades. The help was never a necessity until now. As the days drag on, so do I. My feet struggle to lift from the ground, and I've lost my liveliness.

"Auntie Vern, are you okay?"

"Yes, baby, please pass me my medicine box." I was diagnosed with terminal pancreatic cancer two years ago, though I have yet to disclose this to anyone. I was told I only had another eight months to live, but here I am. I pray I have a relaxing death, painless and without regret.

Washington is a blessing in disguise; I have to convince Emily of this as well. The nine pills I take daily all need to be consumed with food. After Emily made such a wonderful breakfast, it's time to take my medicine. I beg her to take me outside.

Sitting on the patio stoop is Washington, who stands quickly to hold the mesh doors open as we approach. Both he and Emily avoid any kind of eye contact, which doesn't sit well with me. I take a seat on the rocking swing, placing my cane to my immediate left. I begin rubbing my right thigh as the breeze starts to blow me away. Closing my eyes, I envision her face. Veronica.

"Auntie Vern, I am deeply sorry. I am only trying my best to understand what's going on here. The last thing I want to do is hurt you in any way." Emily sounds very sincere. Washington then begins to speak.

"Ms. Vernette, I apologize as well. I acted unprofessionally, and I assure you that won't happen again." I honestly hadn't wanted an apology from either of them. I know they meant no harm, and poor little Emily is just trying to protect me and herself. Who can blame her? This book will not only affect my life, but it may very well impact hers as well. She most definitely has a right to her feelings.

"Washington, Emily, both of you are simply a blessing to me. Please, let us not allow the devil to provoke any malevolent thoughts into our minds or corrupt our actions. The outcome of our hard work, I have faith, will turn out well. Emily, Washington must be just as timid and skeptical as you are. I mean, here he is, out on a limb with a story he believes is worth something. He may have a family he's missing or even a wife. We must be mindful of these things and be a little more cooperative. Is that okay, baby?"

Washington steps back down onto the stoop, letting his right foot hang as he prepares his tape recorder while chewing on the tip of a toothpick, which hangs conspicuously outside his mouth. Emily sits alongside me on the swing set, gripping my right hand as she holds it to her lips and kisses it ever so gently, gracing me with a smile—a clear indication that she's ready for me to continue.

"Ms. Vern, I'm ready when you are," Washington says.

—

WALKING INTO THE LIVING room where we had all gathered once before, I saw Grandma Martin staring outside through the patio's sliding doors, positioned next to the EKCO nineteen-inch black-and-white television set on the floor. A sudden chill ran through me, and I shivered slightly. My entire body went cold.

She was absolute perfection. The only signs of her aging were the laugh lines along her lips and lower jaw. The resemblance between her, Veronica, and my mother was simply remarkable. To the untrained eye, one might mistake them for triplets, at least until getting a closer look to notice the age gap between them.

She stood there, smoking a cigarette through her pipe, her fingernails freshly manicured and painted a haunting black. Her dark hair was pulled back tightly into a secured low bun, without a single strand of gray. The lipstick she wore was a deep, bloody red—a striking shade.

Her caramel complexion was free from imperfections, as though she had never aged a day. In fact, her age remained a mystery to me. Growing up, she never disclosed it—not even her birthday, at least not to me. Maybe Veronica knew. After all, she had lived with her for a long time.

She was dressed in a monochrome ensemble, her top and bottom in two shades of gray, with a black-and-white poncho draped down to her knees. The bristles brushed lightly against the glass door each time she took a drag from her cigarette. Her hands were adorned with fine jewelry, the same pieces she had worn faithfully every day since we were children. The fourteen-karat gold-plated diamond ring on her left ring finger was a clear indication that she and Grandfather Martin were still very much married—and that ring looked brand new.

As her poncho slipped off her shoulder, I watched as she gracefully tossed it back into place with a swift, practiced motion. The bangles on her wrist jingled loudly, clanking against each other. She took one more puff before speaking.

"Asseyez-fille."

I always dreaded the sound of her voice, not because it was harsh, but because every word she directed at me carried an unsettling weight. Her tone was always so cold. I had no idea what she had just said, so I remained standing—until I heard a voice call out from the kitchen.

"She means sit down, Vern!" Veronica shouted from afar.

Even with the translation, I still felt more comfortable standing. Just then, Veronica made a very pregnant appearance, looking as though she could give birth at any moment. She wore an all-white, lace see-through negligee with a black bra and panties underneath. Hobbled slightly, she made her way over to me and leaned in to give me a hug, whispering in my ear, "Don't be nervous." As she pulled away, she smiled. She could probably hear the rapid thumping of my heartbeat.

Grandma Martin pressed her lips together and, without another word, made her way to the odd pink chair positioned to the right of the black-and-white square-patterned sofa. Crossing her legs, she continued to puff on her cigarette.

"It is a shame you do not know French, gal. It is as though you have abandoned a part of your heritage."

The last words she spoke ended with a roll of her tongue. Yet, she spoke eloquently, with such elegance. Despite her loathsome attitude toward me, I always enjoyed listening to her—so long as her sentences were not directed at me, which was seldom the case when we were children.

As I watched Veronica pace back and forth, bringing out the finger foods, I finally decided to take a seat on the loveseat. I sat nearest to the right armrest, as far away from Grandma Martin as possible. Placing my over-the-shoulder bag by my feet, I curled my toes together, ashamed of my appearance. I knew I looked nothing short of destitute. Discreetly, I tried to unravel my unkempt ponytail, hoping to make myself look at least somewhat presentable.

Finally, Veronica joined us, settling into the single black-and-white square-patterned chair closest to Grandma Martin. Moments later, Grandma Martin stopped smoking her cigarette to stare at me, obviously bewildered. I shifted uncomfortably under her gaze. The silence became unbearable, and at last, Veronica spoke.

"Vern, sis, how have you been?"

She knew how I had been. The question was just a way to get me talking, but I played along. As I began to speak, Grandma Martin took another long drag of her cigarette before burning the bud into an ashtray Veronica had placed on the center table alongside the finger foods.

"I've been good, actually. Um… just getting ready to, you know, branch out on my own."

I spoke nervously, forcing an awkward smirk to cover the lie. I prayed to God no one noticed. I knew damn well I was going nowhere. I just couldn't bear the thought of exposing my dull life in front of my compulsively judgmental grandmother.

"Branching out? What does your husband do for work?"

Grandma Martin suddenly seemed interested as she pulled another cigarette from her Lucky Strike pack, lit it, and crossed her legs, throwing her poncho over her left shoulder once more.

"No husband…I am a nursing assistant at a hospital not too far from—"

Before I could finish, she burst into hysterical laughter. Veronica and I exchanged a perplexed look.

"Oh my! You? Helping people? To what—live? Sometimes, I bet you don't even know how."

I wanted to cry.

My knees buckled as Veronica looked at me with sorrow. Almost instantly, her expression changed. With forced cheerfulness, she sought to change the subject.

"Vern, tell us about your love life. I bet you've found a special guy by now, huh?"

By now, the only thing I had found was that my self-confidence had been completely dismantled. I had nothing left to say. I was sure Veronica meant no harm, but what a question to ask at such a time. It felt malicious, like a calculated attempt to break me down—a nefarious plot between the two of them.

As I unconsciously lowered my head, offering no response, I heard Grandma Martin announce that she was heading to the restroom. The moment she exited the living room, I felt Veronica's hand gently touch my left knee. She almost leaped from her seat to join me on the loveseat.

For what felt like minutes but was merely seconds, she reached out and caressed my chin with her soft hands, gliding them along my cheekbones before trailing back down to my chin, where she tugged lightly. Then, without hesitation, she kissed me—tenderly, deliberately.

I closed my eyes, allowing myself to savor the moment. Just as I began to return the gesture, I opened my eyes, only to find that she had already returned to her seat. Her long ponytail swayed side to side, the only evidence that what had just happened was real and not a figment of my imagination.

Grandma Martin reappeared, now holding a shot of scotch in one hand and a cigarette in the other. As she prepared to sit, I watched as Veronica lifted her left hand, placing her index finger vertically to her lips—a silent command.

Later, Grandma Martin resumed her interrogation, pressing me about my life, our mother's choices, and how long I planned to keep up the pretense of happiness. I answered each question truthfully, reminding myself that I had nothing to fear. She was merely a bitter woman, bewitched by her own demons, and she could do me no harm.

But I was wrong.

When her questioning finally ceased, I decided to ask a few of my own.

"Veronica, is there anything I can get for the baby?"

Before Nica even had the chance to respond, Grandma Martin cut in.

"No, there is nothing the baby needs. I mean, what can you afford anyway?"

That insult was my breaking point.

I knew then that this woman was never going to like me, and there was no use in trying anymore. No matter how accomplished I was, she saw none of it. The only thing she cared about was physical appearance, and it was no secret that I did not meet her approval. Or was it something more?

As I shut my eyes and silently prayed for peace, she spoke again.

"Not to be rude, gal, but you should focus on other things. Veronica and the baby are not your priority."

I knew Veronica and her unborn child were not my first priority, but that did not change the fact that I would soon be an aunt. And as an aunt, I wanted to support my baby sister and her child. Of course, Grandma Martin could never understand the bond between sisters. She had been the only mulatto child—the love child of an unfaithful bloke. Always regarded as superior to her siblings because her blood was intertwined with the Caucasian race.

I simply decided to ignore her.

"Veronica, if you do need something, don't hesitate to ask."

Veronica shook her head in acknowledgment, smiling at me. The evening dragged on as we finally indulged in the delectable finger foods she had so thoughtfully arranged. The cheese and crackers were my favorite; I couldn't help but enjoy them all, completely unaware that Grandma Martin was still keeping a watchful eye.

"Careful now, gal. You eat like you're pregnant, too."

I wiped my fingers with a napkin, deciding that it was time—time to stand up for myself.

Calmly, I responded, "No, you see, that can't be as I am not yet married. My boyfriend, Peter, and I are both children of God, and we are waiting until marriage—"

Once again, Grandma Martin cut me off. She became infuriated, rising abruptly from her seat. Her eyes hung low, the cigarette burning right on cue as she growled at me.

Veronica turned her head toward the double glass patio doors, her body still facing forward. It was almost mechanical, as if she had shut down entirely, her expression no longer visible from where I sat.

Just then, Grandma Martin spoke.

"Mon petit bébé, ne pas écouter ce discours d'un Dieu. Je vais vous conduire."

She didn't finish—at least not aloud. Instead, she stepped away, exiting the living room, her eyes fixed on me, seething with anger. I had no idea what she had said or to whom she had spoken. I only remembered the way she stood, her arms extended toward the floor, speaking sternly.

Veronica remained unresponsive.

I continued speaking to Nica as if nothing had happened, casually reaching for more food from the center table. I felt accomplished. I had won. Grandma Martin was too embarrassed to face me now.

"Can you believe that woman, Nica? She's freaking crazy. I mean, how long did she think I was just going to sit here and take the insults? It's one thing to be an atheist, but she's completely gon—"

As I spoke, I noticed something strange.

Veronica's breathing had stopped. Her chest no longer rose and fell as it should.

I gasped, tossing my food into the air as I rushed to her side. I fell to my knees, staring at her lifeless form—her mouth hanging open, her eyes wide and unblinking.

She looked dead.

Her gaze was fixed past the patio doors, her body utterly still.

Panic surged through me. I began performing CPR, my hands pressing desperately against her chest. The sight of her haunted me, filling the room with an eerie stillness. I wanted to call for someone—Lucinda, anyone—but fear paralyzed me.

And what about the baby? How would it survive?

Laying her flat on the Persian-style rug, I began mouth-to-mouth resuscitation, tasting her saliva—yet feeling no air enter or exit my body.

I checked her pulse.

Nothing.

She was gone.

I stopped, my hands trembling as I frantically searched for any sign of injury—something, anything—to explain what had happened. But there was nothing.

Just as I lifted my hands to check her pulse again, I was suddenly hurled backward. My body slammed against the glass sliding doors, the impact rattling through me.

Then, I felt it.

A force—unseen, yet undeniable—wrapped its hands around my throat, cutting off my airway.

I clawed and scratched at my neck, my feet dangling, my heels scraping against the carpet. My lungs burned as my airways continued to close. My vision blurred, my eyes rolling back into my head.

I was dying.

This force—this thing—was killing me.

My legs fluttered weakly, my body convulsing as the room darkened around me. If this was death, where was the light people always spoke of?

I saw nothing.

Only emptiness.

As life began to slip away, a sharp slap struck my right cheek.

I gasped, snapping back, coughing frantically as air rushed into my lungs. Never in my life had I been so grateful for something as simple as breathing.

As my vision cleared, I saw Grandma Martin standing over me. Her left hand was hidden beneath her poncho, her right gripping her shoulder as she held up the fabric.

She looked down at me with an undeniable hatred.

She scoffed before she spoke.

"This God you speak of—do not mention Him around me, gal. I am no believer, and neither is she."

Just as she uttered the word, *she*, I witnessed something impossible—Veronica awakened from death.

Gripping the wooden armrests so tightly that one snapped under her grasp, her head tilted back slightly before she let out a piercing scream.

She was no longer lying on the ground where I had placed her.

She was back in the chair.

Her scream was deafening, loud enough to crack the window above my head. It was the same scream I had heard when we were children—only this time, her voice more mature—staying with Grandma and Grandpa Robinson.

As the sound died down, she turned to face me, her expression one of pure innocence and confusion.

"Vern, how on Earth did you get over there?"

I didn't answer.

Instead, I felt the world around me tilt, my body giving way as darkness consumed me. The last thing I registered was the loud thud of my head hitting the floor.

Then, silence.

I felt nothing. Heard nothing.

For the first time, I was not afraid.

I stood in the center of an endless black void.

Then the screams began.

They echoed from all directions—bloodcurdling, frantic, and agonizing. I had no idea which way to turn. I only knew I had to find the source.

I told myself to run north, but my body remained frozen.

I *thought* I was moving. I swung my arms as if to take off, but I remained in place.

Panic crept in. The void grew darker. The screams grew louder.

Then, a door appeared before me.

I hesitated, unsure of where it would lead, but something inside me knew I had no choice.

I stepped through.

The moment I crossed the threshold, a wave of dizziness hit me. My head spun. My eyes burned. The world around me shifted.

And then, I saw her.

Veronica lay on her back in the distance, her legs propped up as though she was preparing to give birth.

Her screams no longer echoed—they *throbbed* in my eardrums, a relentless pounding that forced me to clasp my hands over my ears. I had never heard anything like it.

I ran to her side, grabbing her trembling hand.

"Everything is going to be okay," I whispered.

I was lying.

I had no idea what was happening.

The room was still cloaked in darkness. To my knowledge, we were the only ones here.

I bellowed for a nurse, for a doctor, for anyone.

Blood gushed between her legs, pooling beneath her. My hands began to sweat. My mouth hung open in horror as she continued to scream and sob.

I had no clue what to do.

So, I did the only thing that came to mind.

I ran to the foot of the mattress, preparing myself to deliver the baby.

Veronica quieted.

Then she moaned, her body twisting in discomfort, her face buried in the mattress. The darkness around us thickened, my vision blurred, and then—

A sudden, violent surge of blood erupted from between her legs, shooting straight into my face.

I choked.

My mouth filled with the sickening taste of blood and vaginal secretions.

I gagged, spitting onto the ground—only to recoil in horror.

The blood had transformed into *maggots*.

They wriggled toward my bare feet, squirming, multiplying.

That nightmare was the last time I ever felt normal.

Shaking, I grabbed the hem of my shirt and frantically wiped at my face. I wished I could have scrubbed the skin off entirely.

Then—silence.

Veronica lay still.

Afterward, somewhere in the darkness, Grandma Martin's voice murmured, her words indistinct but chilling.

"Maintenant, vous êtes levé."

She appeared before me like an insidious shadow, clothed in a black dress, her hair wrapped in a black turban. She wore no earrings. Swiftly, she stepped forward, raised her left hand, opened her palm, and blew a fine powder into my face.

The particles filled the air, swirling around me. I waved my hands frantically, trying to dust them away. My mind raced—what had she just done to me?

I fought against the nightmare, still battling the invisible particles even as the warmth of the sun beamed against my right cheek, pulling me back to consciousness.

My breath came in sharp gasps. The hairs on my arms stood on end. My vision blurred as tears welled in my eyes. I was terrified.

The next morning, I awoke to sunlight streaming through the patio glass doors, illuminating the entire living room. I sat up abruptly, rubbing my eyes with both hands. As my vision adjusted, I saw Lucinda standing above me.

She wore a yellow apron over blue trousers and a periwinkle short-sleeved blouse.

"I think you had a bad dream, Vernette. Here is your wardrobe for the day. Your sister advised me to leave these for you." Her tone was unsettling, almost malevolent.

I scrambled to my feet, snatching the clothes from her arms without a word. Rushing into the laundry room by the kitchen, I quickly changed. She had left me a pair of black straight-legged pants, a perfect fit, along with a black button-down blouse. After flattening my collar and fastening the buttons, I gathered my previous clothes and shoved them into a plastic grocery bag I found in the detergent basket.

Slipping my feet back into my flats, I stormed into the kitchen, where Lucinda stood at the table, folding a navy-blue men's blouse.

"We are to go to the hospital now. Do you have your things?" she asked, refusing to make eye contact.

I hadn't brushed my teeth or combed my hair, but none of that mattered.

"Why are we going to the hospital?" I asked, my voice uneasy.

She shot me a look of discomfort.

"The Lady of the house has gone into labor."

Her words sent a jolt through me.

Labor.

But Veronica was only seven months pregnant—if that.

Panic surged in my chest. I needed to leave *now*.

Impatiently, I watched as Lucinda took her time, folding each garment with meticulous care. Frustrated, I grabbed my bag from the living room floor and made my way toward the garage door.

Lucinda followed, and together, we drove to the Luther Field Hospital emergency room.

The car ride was silent.

The moment we arrived, I bolted from the car, rushing toward the receptionist's desk.

"Hi, what floor is your maternity ward?"

The security officer directed me to take the visitors' elevator up to the eighth floor.

I followed his instructions.

As I stood inside the elevator, willing the doors to close, Lucinda slipped in just before they shut. I said nothing, only listening to the soft chimes as we ascended.

Finally, the elevator doors slid open. I hurried to the nurses' station, my heart pounding.

"I'm looking for Veronica Robinson," I said breathlessly.

Before the nurse could respond, Lucinda's sharp voice cut through the air.

"She means Harrington. Mrs. Veronica Harrington. Your sister is a *Mrs.* now—have some respect."

Her words were laced with contempt, her eyes boring into me as if daring me to challenge her.

The nurse shook her head. "Yes, she's in room 271. May I ask your relation to the patient?"

"Yes, I'm her sister."

I walked away slowly, scanning the numbers on the walls as I searched for her room. Then, just before reaching it, I passed the newborn nursery.

And that's when I saw him.

A tiny, pink baby boy snuggled in the top right bassinet.

My breath caught in my throat as I read the name on the label.

Matthew Aiden Harrington.

PART III.

BRANCHES

MATTHEW WAS perfect. He cooed softly, smiling as he dreamed his little dreams. His feet were so small, his hands delicate and lovely. He was everything I had imagined and more.

Veronica, my baby sister, had given birth to her first *Green Tree*. I was happy for her—truly—but a quiet envy gnawed at me. My life felt stagnant, as though the train I was on had never left the station. Time kept slipping through my fingers, especially in her presence, while her life seemed to be on cruise control, effortlessly moving forward.

After standing at the glass window for over five minutes, a nurse approached me.

"Which baby are you looking for?" she asked nicely.

I smiled and replied, "I've already found him."

Matthew had the tiniest nose, the fullest lips. He resembled his father, but only slightly—or at least, that's what I thought. Then again, the more I looked around, the more I realized that nearly every baby in the nursery shared similar features. The rooms were segregated at the time.

Sliding my hand gently across the glass, I took a deep breath and turned toward Veronica's room.

When I entered, I saw a doctor, Lucinda, David, and Grandma Martin already inside by her bed—Bed B. The steady beeping of the heart monitor filled the space as nurses and doctors spoke to her about the birth.

Despite Matthew arriving four weeks early, he was healthy. The doctor reassured Veronica that hospital nurses would check on him periodically to ensure he was meeting key developmental milestones.

I leaned against the doorway, arms crossed, waiting patiently for the doctor to finish. My eyes flicked to David, who was listening intently as he provided instructions on newborn care. He and Veronica were both first-time parents, absorbing every word with a mixture of excitement and nervousness.

My heart tightened as I watched them huddled together on the hospital bed—Veronica's arms lined with IV needles, her hospital gown loose beneath three layers of linen. I wasn't surprised. The room was chilly. It was mid-September of 1955, the season where warm days shifted into crisp, cool nights.

When the doctor finished, he asked, "Would you like to spend some time with your newborn?"

"Yes!" Veronica answered immediately, her voice brimming with excitement.

A nurse entered moments later, cradling Matthew securely in her arms, his tiny head resting against her forearm. Carefully, she placed him in Veronica's arms.

I remained by the door, watching.

Grandma Martin, now seated in the chair near the window, observed in silence as well.

The room suddenly felt smaller, almost crowded. And for the first time, Veronica hadn't acknowledged me.

Her entire focus was on Matthew. Her eyes glistened with love, as though no one else in the world existed.

A pang of jealousy twisted inside me, but just as quickly, I felt foolish. I was envious of a child—*her* child. Matthew had all of her attention, while I had none.

I exhaled, letting the feeling pass, and adjusted the strap of my shoulder bag. It was time for me to leave.

I turned toward the door, but just as I reached for the handle, I heard David call my name.

"Hey, Vernette!"

I turned to see him standing about two feet from the door. I moved quickly, eager to head home.

"Hey, where are you running off to? You know Veronica is going to want to see you."

I knew he was right, but I felt like it was time for me to go. So, I lied.

"Oh, I have to work the evening shift," I said, tilting my head slightly, hoping to sound convincing.

"Oh wow, that sucks. I mean, it would have been nice if you could have stayed. Thanks for coming and being a part of this, you know."

He lowered his head, his voice softer now.

"Hey, I know you and I never really had a chance to reconcile or talk about what happened, but I just want you to know I'm truly sorry—for everything. It was really shitty the way I went about things."

His hands were tucked into the pockets of his jeans.

I had my moments when seeing David and Veronica together shattered me, but after meeting Peter—after him and I becoming something—David slowly faded into my past. Or at least, that's what I wanted to believe. But his apology was needed, and for a brief moment, I felt at peace.

"Thank you for that. I appreciate it," I said sincerely. "I really should get going. Tell Veronica I love her, please."

He nodded, pressing his lips together, his brows slightly furrowed. I knew he would. He seemed sincere.

Later that afternoon, when I returned home, I noticed my parents weren't there. I dropped my keys on the hall table, but before I could take another step, a voice shouted,

"Where on earth have you been?!"

I turned to see Peter standing by the basement door, gripping the handle, holding it slightly open.

"I was worried sick. So were your parents. Veronica called last night to let your father know you were with her. But why disappear like that, Vernette? You're not a child anymore."

His tone was scolding. I felt reprimanded. For someone reminding me that I was no longer a child, he sure spoke as though he was speaking to one.

I had no words. I stood still, waiting for my brain to process what I had just heard—waiting for it to craft a response. But after a whole ninety seconds... nothing.

Instead, I shrugged, rolled my eyes, and started up the stairs toward my bedroom. I needed a shower. I wasn't in the mood to argue.

Peter stepped fully into the hallway, standing at the bottom of the staircase. His voice softened.

"Look, Vern, I'm sorry, sweetie. I was just really worried. I had no way of reaching you. What was I supposed to think?"

I stopped midway up the stairs, looking down at him. He was waiting for my reply.

"I'm sorry," I said at last. "I just needed time. And space."

I was still upset with him for going behind my back and propositioning my parents—especially since the proposition involved me.

His voice was gentler now. "Do you mind if I cook you some dinner?"

I couldn't help but chuckle. Peter was a magician in the kitchen, unbelievably talented.

"Of course, you can!"

I dashed to my room like the child I once was, quickly undressed, and stepped into the bathroom for my shower.

Just as I let the water run over me, I heard footsteps approaching. My heart quickened. It couldn't be Peter.

Cautiously, I peeked out from behind the shower curtain—only to see him standing there, undressing himself as well.

Hurriedly, I yanked the curtain shut.

"Peter, are you getting naked?"

Laughing hysterically, he responded jokingly, "Yes. Is that a bad thing? I just realized I need a shower too—I haven't had one since you left me."

Knowing him to be quite sarcastic, I wondered, *Is he actually going to shower with me?*

I refused to ask any more questions as he stepped into the shower behind me. I felt his body brush against mine—his pelvis grazing the curve of my backside. It was the first time I had ever felt him in such an intimate way. The firm muscles of his chest pressed lightly against my back, and then, without warning, his tongue caressed my left shoulder. Despite the hot water streaming over us, a shiver ran through my body. I clenched the washcloth so tightly that soap and water trickled down my thighs.

Seconds later, I felt something small glide up my spine. Just as I turned, my body bathed in water, I opened my eyes to see Peter on one knee inside the bathtub.

My back bore the full pressure of the water, and he, too tall to kneel fully, struggled to balance himself. I watched him wobble for at least ten seconds; his expression determined but undeniably awkward. The sight made me giggle, but before I could laugh outright, a wave of emotion overtook me. Without warning, I began to sob—though with the water streaming down my face, it was nearly impossible to tell.

He was proposing. A ring in hand.

"Vernette—pride-too-big, love of my life, patient, beautiful, and marvelous Robinson—will you do me the honor of marrying me?"

With each word, my tears turned to laughter. Overcome with joy, I grabbed the ring and shouted, "Yes!"

As he jolted up to embrace me, he nearly slipped, making us both laugh through the tears. Our kiss was luscious—wet and lingering. I felt every inch of his body against mine, and in that moment, I couldn't imagine a more perfect way to end my day. My hands roamed his torso, pulling him closer, but my excitement quickly turned to disappointment when he suddenly announced that he had to go.

Once again, I was left longing, saddened by the fact that we wouldn't be making love. And yet, despite the ache of unfulfilled desire, I couldn't help but feel elated. The rock on my finger defied gravity—it was enormous.

Peter, ever the man of God, was simply trying to do the right thing. But a playful, slightly exasperated me couldn't resist asking, "If you still aren't ready for sex, then why are we both naked in the shower?" I smiled, my hands still resting on his torso.

He grinned. "Sweetheart, naked is the way we came into this world. And if we're going to spend the rest of our lives together, we might as well see what the other is getting. I mean… are you satisfied?"

I was. He was hung, and complete perfection.

His large arms wrapped around me so tightly that I felt utterly secure. His body was immaculate—free of blemishes, tattoos, or scars, except for a tiny black beauty mark, no larger than a dime, just above his waistline. His pink lips, slick with water, lightly brushed my neck. Then he kissed me there, suckling the droplets from my skin. My thighs trembled. What a tease he was.

"I have to go," he murmured. "Dinner tonight at seven. And don't be late."

I chuckled, releasing my grip on his torso.

As he stepped out of the bathroom, I turned back to my washcloth, trying to steady myself.

But the moment lingered in my mind. My body still burned with unfulfilled needs.

And so, as the water continued to flow, I let my hand wander—determined to finish what he had so deliberately started.

I would repent later.

—

"Whoa, please, that's one part we may skip."

Poor Washington feels uncomfortable. I can imagine how disturbing it is to listen to the sex stories of an elderly woman, but the story must go on.

—

I STEPPED OUT OF THE shower feeling like a new woman. I dressed in a pastel blue cape collar swing dress after applying my lotion and slipping into my undergarments. I heard my mother and father return home, chuckling from the bottom of the stairs; I rushed out to hear what was so funny.

"Hi, Mommy, hi Daddy. Where have you two been?" My mother's smile quickly turned into a frown once she gazed upon my face. I stood at the top of the stairs, her eyes telling of a baleful, destructive legacy. My father, taking notice, turned to her.

"Sweetheart, is everything all right? It's Vern." She motioned his hand away from her waistline as she began to speak, her eyes widening with each word.

"You are not my Vern. I know my daughter. Each time they leave Clive, they don't come back." I wanted to cry. My father and I both had no idea what she was talking about. I was not her Vern. How could she say that? Clearly, I was very much still myself. I will admit I did feel different, but there was no doubt that I was still me. My father, grabbing her hands, said,

"Baby, listen, we had a long day. We've been packing and things like that. Maybe you just need some sleep." My mother begged my father to listen. They conversed, pointed, and discussed me as though I was not even there. I became a mere shadow.

"Vernette is not at the top of those stairs. Clive, I have been begging you to come to church, begging you. Had you known Jesus, you would know those who are not protected and guided by His light." My father interrupted her.

"Stop it, okay, just stop it. You sound crazy! Vernette is standing right there, and she is simply happy to see us both. Now cut it out. I don't want to hear another word about it." My father turned to face me, but I was busy facing my mother, who was looking at the ground.

"Vernette, baby, don't worry. I think your mother just needs some sleep." I didn't respond; I just continued to watch as my father spoke and my mother now studied everything around her, looking perplexed. She was no doubt thinking to herself: *Where could she have possibly gone wrong? When did she lose me?* The lost soul, who had no idea she was even lost.

Placing her hands on her forehead, a clear sign of a migraine, my father asked if he could walk her to their bedroom. She complied. I moved to the side, allowing them space to walk upstairs. From that day on, my mother never looked at me the same. She and I barely even spoke. Her last sentence to me left me shaken.

"I tried to protect you from that woman, my mother, but still, you let her in. May God have mercy on you both."

"It's okay, sweetheart, she just needs some sleep, that's all." My father held her hand, walking her each step of the way like she was a weakened old woman. He kept trying to console me; he felt the pain I was in. Her words struck me like a knife. I didn't even get the chance to share my good news with them.

Once their bedroom door slammed, I felt chills rise up my arms. If I wasn't Vern anymore, then who was I? What happened to me? Just then, the phone rang, startling me. I ran down to answer it.

We weren't green anymore…

What felt like weeks had been months since Veronica and I had spoken. I never uttered a word, took any of her phone calls, nor did I return them. There was no doubt I was staying away out of fear, but I was also still feeling a little jealous.

Aside from the tip teaser I received from Peter a while ago and his abrupt marriage proposal, he remained sequestered for a while: business trips, traveling with family, volunteering at churches, and even participating in segregation marches throughout the tri-state. Peter and I only saw one another two times a week—once on Sunday immediately following service when he and I would come home, and he would prepare us dinner, and Thursday mornings right before his weekly meeting at work where he would discuss the nature of his business trips, journals, and proposals for more interesting news, which would require him to go away again for the opportunity to interview a source.

Opportunities were beginning to present themselves time and time again for Peter. By mid-December, he was looking to begin his own printing business. Of course, he had now acquired the financial backing, community support, as well as the experience and knowledge needed to start such a business. And of course, I remained optimistic when the idea was first presented to me and looked forward to seeing him make his dream a reality, despite him not having much time for me.

Peter and I remained abstinent—even throughout the holiday season; I assumed his frequent traveling meant he was avoiding the topic and act of sex with me. I did, however, advocate to him that once we were married, the traveling and excess of business trips would have to cease. He complied, making my assumption almost correct.

Three months after the birth of Matthew, my mother and father finally made the big move to Florida. They were ecstatic to be leaving. My mother and I spoke, but only seldom after her encounter with me the day that I was no longer her sweet Vern. She still never discussed with me exactly what she meant, nor why she said what she said. Once she was gone and Peter and I were named the new homeowners of my current home, I began involving myself heavily in interior decorating, starting with the kitchen and working my way around the rest of the house.

—

"Were you at all frightened to be living in that home still? I mean, after all that had taken place here?" Washington asks.

—

INITIALLY, I HAD AN uneasy feeling about remaining in the home, but then the idea began to grow on me. I had no desire to leave my neighborhood, and my job was within walking distance. I also knew pretty much everyone. I felt safe, almost. Aside from the protesting and occasional looting, which took place less than a mile away, it did not involve me, so I did not involve myself.

Once my parents had relocated, the remainder of their belongings were junked and removed from the premises. I missed my mother dearly. She even emptied my bedroom. I was astonished when I saw her do this. For about four days, I resided at Peter's place while he was away on business and heard the noises of the movers rattling above my head. But at no point did I make my way up there to converse with her or debate her decisions to discard or retain items.

I knew our relationship had changed when the Sunday following our minor altercation, I refused to go to church with her—the first time in a long time. I told her I would not be attending. Her facial expression told me all I needed to know. I simply did not attend because I was not up to it, with work, and being newly engaged. I just wanted one Sunday to myself. However, I did continue to go afterward, but that did not matter to her.

My father, on the other hand, remained neutral and knew what he was looking forward to when he and my mother would make their departure, starting a new life.

"Listen, baby, your mother, uh, she's going through some changes. Don't let her get to you, all right? She still loves you, Vern."

My dad and I had a talk one day when he arrived home from work, and I was sitting on the stoop taking in the winter breeze—the cold never bothered me; in fact, I preferred it.

"Hi, Daddy!" I said happily.

"Hi, baby doll, what you doing out here this time of day?"

"Nothing much, just clearing my mind a little bit."

Knitting his eyebrows, he asked,

"Is it that man Peter? I told your mother he was too damn old for you. You need yourself a young one, starting life. That man is already done establishing himself and is buying houses."

Hearing how my father really felt about Peter came as a surprise. I never knew he had such reservations about Peter and me dating. Sternly, he said,

"C'mon, Vern, you're such a bright, beautiful young girl. You have your whole life ahead of you. What that man wants with you is a mystery. Does he treat you well?"

By now, my father had made his way past the little black gate and taken a seat beside me, pulling his pant leg slightly up before sitting down.

"He treats me great, Dad. I mean, he and I have our differences, but who doesn't? And the age gap, I mean, it doesn't bother me too much."

"Okay, as long as you're happy, I'm happy," he said, smiling. "How is your sister? Have you spoken to her?" I knew he would find a way to involve Veronica, and at this time, it had only been about four and a half months since Veronica had given birth, and she and I had not spoken. With my head down, I mumbled,

"No."

"No! What do you mean, no? Well, why the hell not?"

No matter how old I was, whenever my father spoke in a commanding tone, I always trembled, afraid he might begin scolding me just like old times.

But just like old times, my father remained true to his belief that Veronica and I should always remain on good terms. After all, we were, and still are, all that one another have in this world. But quickly, I learned and believed otherwise when she went away after flunking out of university. I never heard from her at all. She disappeared, and no one ever mentioned the importance of our sisterhood then. Of course, I couldn't mention that to my father. He would surely become defensive, thinking I was judging his parental skills or, even worse, accusing him of favoritism. I responded the best way I knew how.

"I've been kind of busy, Dad." I knew he knew I was lying. Placing his right hand on my thigh, he asked me to look him in the eyes. I hesitated at first, but I did what I was told.

"Love your sister, Vern, love her hard. She isn't like you. You're much stronger, and it's your strength that she relies on to get her through the tough times. It's the reassurance of your love, and my love, and your mother's love that keeps her going and keeps her in the right frame of mind. We do not abandon one another in this family. You understand me?" He spoke eloquently, staring ferociously into my eyes; it was almost like he never blinked. I hung on to every word and felt a surge of goosebumps race up my arms.

The wind speeds were beginning to increase as the latter part of the afternoon began to settle in. I was fighting back tears as I knew that my heart was starting to harden and I was becoming less sympathetic toward Veronica. My last experience there had changed me somehow. But not in a good way.

Every time I was around Veronica, I felt fearful of her. My father would never understand, and I was uncertain at the time, but at that moment, I wasn't sure if I loved him for being such a great dad or pitied him for being so oblivious to what was taking place. I just had to remind myself that it wasn't his fault. If anything, he was the victim—a mere pawn to Veronica, calling him daily to taunt my mother when they had their falling out. My father, being the man he was, thought nothing of it. Immediately afterward, I felt the best thing to do was simply change the subject.

"How is Mommy doing, Dad?"

Florida, in my opinion, was a great place for my mother and father to have relocated. Calling every other day to check on me, my father made his usual long-distance calls with loud guitars playing in the background, accompanied by the sound of seagulls bellowing, indicating they were in a home by the beach. My father transferred to the City of Orlando Police Department. He had taken a demotion, but it was only temporary for six months, as he assisted the current chief of police and learned the new laws governing the state. Besides, his retirement was still a long way off. I was happy for them.

Time flew by, and now it had been six months since I last spoke to Veronica. I even contemplated changing the house number. She still called, and for months, had not left a single message until one Tuesday evening.

I listened.

"Vern, hey, it's me, Nica. I've been calling. I sure hope you're doing okay. I wish you would call me, Vern. I miss you so much. Everyone is gone; David included. He's having some trouble adjusting to parenthood, and honestly, so am I. I—I just really hope you're all right. Daddy says you are, but I don't know, I..." She hung up after her voice began to tremble. I could always tell when Veronica was on the brink of tears, and in that moment, she sounded ready to break down. I will admit, I was touched by the message, but once again, I didn't respond.

I had no idea what to say.

On my days off from work, I became heavily infatuated with the idea of designing our home. I tested different paint colors, textures, tiling, and fencing for the outdoors. Our home, Peter's and mine, was a true beauty. I began my renovation from the outside patio all the way up to the attic. I had never noticed how unclean the attic was when my parents resided there. Dust populated more than just the squeaky floorboards. It was on the ceiling, dangling atop unopened boxes, a rusty piano I never knew we had, and some old instruments, which I assumed were for Veronica and me to become musicians—a dream my mother had for us since we were adolescents.

I dusted, waxed, mopped, and began piling old boxes atop new boxes until a booklet of photos came flying from a white box marked "FILMS." There were dozens of them, but no projector. The absence of a projector caused me to quickly lose interest in the box. But just as I attempted to walk away and return to my mopping, I couldn't help but satisfy my curiosity. I went over to the box and began to read aloud the titles written in all white, duct tape placed neatly around the camera film. They were lined up horizontally against one another, appearing to be in alphabetical order.

They read: *Birthing an Angel, Cradle with Vern, Daddy Clive, Green Trees, Hello Nica, Joyful Beginnings, Memories, Riding, Riverside Fishing, Trip to Louisiana, Tuscan Sun,* and *Vernette and Veronica.* When I saw that I had my own video, I became far more intrigued, frantically searching for a projector screen and the equipment to go with the reels.

Sadly, I came up empty-handed.

After hours of searching, cleaning, and rummaging through old boxes, I came across a sapphire-colored pencil pleated button-back Deborah Spring dress just before stepping on the ladder to head downstairs. The gown hung at the rear of the attic on what appeared to be a clothing rod, supported by a wire hanger with its spaghetti straps. Using my flashlight, I shone the light over to the area for a clearer view. Pacing slowly, I stepped across the floorboards, careful not to fall through. Finally, I reached the dress and began to unzip the left zipper, curious as to how I would look in it.

Realizing I was still in the attic, I grabbed the dress off the hanger and proceeded back downstairs to the master bedroom. Once there, I began to undress slowly, admiring my now curvaceous body, no longer saddened or emotionally burdened by my rough exterior. No doubt I had grown into my looks. Taking notice of my soft, blemish-free chocolate brown skin, I began to smile from ear to ear. I even decided to let my hair down; it had been a while since I allowed my hair to touch my shoulders, praying it would even reach that far. To my surprise, it did—longer even. My natural hair was beautiful, not soft to the touch and curled at the roots like my dear mother and baby sister, but coarse. I giggled at myself, laughing at just how beautiful I was.

Finally, I managed to squeeze into the gown, designed by Heimann Carriages—an African American dressmaker making a name for himself in Harlem. It was expensive, no doubt. Handmade and tailored. Surprisingly, the dress fit me almost perfectly, only slightly shorter, since my mother was far shorter than both my sister and me. She had the body of a model, and all I kept imagining was what she could have looked like in it—slim, tall, and slender. The dress straps were tiny, definitely a dress for the new age, modernized. How could my mother have forgotten this beauty when moving?

I flaunted my new dress, twirling, laughing, and being careful enough not to trip over my own feet. Just then, the doorbell rang, interrupting my brief moment of happiness. I scurried down the stairs still in my dress to see the movers from the furniture store standing outside, ready to bring in the new fixtures I had ordered from the store not too far from home.

"Just a minute!" I shouted as I began making my way back up to my bedroom. I maneuvered quickly to get out of the dress, but I ripped it slightly under the zipper. Disappointed in myself, I mourned my new dress for a quick minute, my smile and happiness diminishing as I slid my legs into my capri pants and a blouse.

Racing back down the stairs, I unlocked the front door to see an angry man on my patio, a clipboard in his left hand. Reggie, as his nametag read, was a short Indian-American, his eyes an ocean blue, and his uniform was filthy. The t-shirt he wore on the upper right corner read, *Furniture New York!* The company was new to the neighborhood, and their furniture was imported; I had gravitated toward their store because I craved versatility and distinctiveness. With them, that was exactly what I got.

I signed the papers, scribbling my name as four men began swarming in, asking questions on top of questions about where to put what. Directing those men felt like directing traffic during rush hour. Instead of the sound of horns, came the sounds of complaints, confusion, and bickering among the movers. I prayed they would get it together and not ruin the new furniture before my fiancé or I had a chance to try it out.

For hours, they remained diligent while bringing furniture into our empty home. At that moment, I was experiencing a mix of emotions. I felt like an adult who was now on her own, but saddened that my independence came from dependence. I knew I would have to be mature about the situation, which is why I kept a smile on my face and looked forward to playing the amicable housewife role very well.

Once they concluded, I received a phone call from Peter—the phone from my childhood remained, but the mantle was gone—telling me that he would once again be missing dinner and returning home in the morning. I was agitated and thought maybe I, too, would devote my time to an overnight project of my own: decorating. I spent the remainder of the evening painting, waxing the hardwood floors in the dining room, vacuuming the carpets, and moving the new furniture throughout the home. I put up curtains, fluffed pillows, folded and put away laundry, waxed figurines, and wiped down every inch of our house. I prayed that my body would withstand the punishment I was dealing to it because I so desperately wanted to finish my decorating. Not out of excitement, but out of pure anger, frustration, and annoyance.

Before I knew it, seventeen long hours had passed—the sun beginning to rise. My home was complete, and surprisingly enough, I felt no pain until I went up and ran a hot shower. Washing my hair and massaging my scalp made my entire body tense. My arms ached, my back burned, and my stomach was in knots from not eating anything substantial. Yet still, I was not tired—filled with adrenaline. I felt like a walking zombie, and that was exactly what I was.

Once I finished showering, I still saw no signs of Peter. I slipped into my pink and purple pajamas; the dress now hung safely in my closet. Once I began swooning over my interior decorating, I made my way toward the kitchen. But as soon as I reached the stairs, I was stopped by a feeling of uneasiness. I looked up and to my right, pushing the door to Veronica's old bedroom slightly open. It was empty. I had stayed up all night fixing and decorating, but somehow managed to miss her old bedroom. Just then, I no longer felt the urge to fight anymore. I fell to my knees and began to cry.

Struggling to catch my breath as the tears fell from my eyes, I placed my hands on my neck, feeling the burning sensation, and the pulsation eased me slightly. I caught my breath, continuing to stare bewildered into the empty bedroom. No furniture, no curtains, no cleaning supplies—just an empty room. Just as I managed to catch my breath, I curled into the fetal position, sluggishly lying on the threshold when I heard the sound of keys jingling at the front door. In walked Peter, wearing an all-black tracksuit. Dropping his briefcase, he fell to my side.

"Baby, honey, is everything all right?"

Peter spoke in a panic. I did not respond. Instead, I continued to stare lifelessly into the empty bedroom. Placing my head on his shoulder, I inhaled the sweet aroma of a feminine cologne. I bothered not to ask any questions, as my speculations were simply that—speculations.

Peter threw my body over his shoulder and proceeded to walk me up the stairs to our bedroom. Once there, he leaned over, rolling me onto our mattress, where I immediately turned to look away from him, allowing my tears to flow freely. Still, no words passed between us as he removed his jacket and began to run the water inside our bathroom. My mind was running a marathon as I pondered his infidelity, my unconscious cleaning rampage, and eventually Veronica—the sacredness of her bedroom to me.

As the day pressed on, so did our relationship. I never mentioned the perfume as Peter cooked us a wonderful dinner in our newly decorated home, which he complimented me heavily on. Its perfection, the attention to detail, the patterns, the décor—everything was to his liking. When he, too, noticed the emptiness of one of the bedrooms, he dared not question me why. He simply did as my mother did: grabbed a key and locked it shut. I did not argue, nor did I fuss. Obviously, I was experiencing some trauma, and the last thing I wanted to do was include him in the madness.

That night, I dreamed sweet dreams, walking through my home, the firm arms of my soon-to-be husband providing me with warmth, and my footsteps echoing through the halls. The rich wood-paneled doors remained the same, as did the small front porch, complete with a quaint wrought iron railing and a sturdy wooden swing. The hallway walls were painted a soft pastel mint green, a popular shade of the time, and the original oak flooring gleamed, its natural grain evident. A large round mirror, framed in a thin gold design, hung just to the left at the bottom of the staircase, reflecting the warmth of the room. The simple yet elegant rug, in a muted floral print, stretched from the foyer to the kitchen, neatly sectioning off the space.

Due to the limited space between the front door and the staircase, I had created a subtle division, placing furniture pieces along the front of the house to provide the illusion of a foyer. The rug demarcated the distance between the two main areas: the foyer and the kitchen. As I walked from the foyer to the kitchen, the walls were adorned with a pair of framed prints, both on the right side, spaced about ten feet apart, each showcasing a tasteful landscape.

When I reached the kitchen, the cheerful yellow walls greeted me, with the laminated grey floors beneath reflecting the light that poured through the windows. The kitchen was bright and functional, the classic 1950s style evident in the polished yellow cabinets with chrome handles that lined the upper and lower countertops. A vintage breadbox sat prominently on the counter, its bold "**BREAD**" inscription in block letters. The all-white stove, positioned centrally on the north wall, was a reliable focal point. The sink, pipes, and a small shelf for utensils were located just beside the doorway leading into the dining and living room area.

The kitchen table was set with modest but charming décor: two place settings, a large fruit bowl with bananas, pears, and grapes, all accompanied by green and white linen napkins, forks, and knives that coordinated with the hallway color scheme. Though small, the kitchen held a nostalgic charm, unchanged since my parents had owned the home, with only a few minor touches added to keep it functional.

In the adjoining dining and living room, I aimed for a clean, mid-century modern look. The piano, which had been gathering dust in the attic, was moved by the furniture men who happily assisted. The all-black instrument, though broken, had been polished and cleaned, its glossy surface now a striking visual centerpiece. The hardwood floors, freshly waxed, reflected the bright natural light that streamed in through the windows, making the room feel open and airy. The walls, painted in a warm vanilla, created a neutral backdrop for the bold accents I had added.

In the far corner, next to the piano, I placed small white and yellow throw pillows along the windowsills, which were wide enough to sit on. A tall, vintage floor lamp cast a soft light over the dining table, which comfortably seated six, its wooden chairs simple yet elegant. Above the table, a new light fixture—an economical yet stylish design with a small circular shield—provided additional warmth. I had plans to spend many nights here, savoring the quiet moments in this tranquil space.

The living area also featured five chairs: four single seats and a loveseat with forest green cushions and wooden oak arms. A matching coffee table stood nearby, with a yellow armchair to the right, and a red one beside it, both made from oak with handles on each side. Across from these chairs, two more single seats in deep midnight blue and ocean blue were arranged around a small tan-colored coffee table, its top decorated with a small, unused ashtray—purely for aesthetic purposes, as neither Peter nor I smoked.

To the right of the seating area, a larger heating vent ensured warmth in the room, though it wasn't meant for sitting like the other one. The same economical light fixture cast its glow over this part of the room as well. A large window, the only one in the entire space, sat directly behind the loveseat. I resisted the urge to place any rugs in the room, convinced it would make the space feel cramped. Despite the initial doubts, I convinced myself that the room was perfect just the way it was.

The next morning, the clock read 8:47 AM. I heard noises in the kitchen and wondered why Peter hadn't gone to work by now. Once I made up my mind to go downstairs, the smell wafted up to me, far more arousing now that I was hungry. My stomach growled, officially having gone longer than twenty-four hours without food. Making my way into the kitchen, my eyes beheld an unusual sight.

"Good morning, pumpkin. My omelet isn't as good as moms, but it's something."

My voice was still groggy, and I initially struggled to respond, finally saying, "Daddy!" I was so happy to see him—he had no idea. I ran over, giving him the biggest hug I could, but not before tripping over an abnormally large black bag.

"Dad, what in the world brings you here?" I smiled as he motioned for me to have a seat.

"I don't want to talk about why I'm here just yet; I want to talk about you. I miss you, Vern." He smiled as he sat down, placing our meals in front of us, shuffling around for cutlery.

"Dad, they're in the drawer next to the stove." He appeared surprised that I had obviously renovated.

"I love what you've done with the place. I gave myself a small tour. I hope you don't mind." Of course, I didn't mind. I was glad he felt comfortable enough to take a look around.

I spent the entire day with my father before realizing that Peter had indeed left that morning without saying a word to me. While sitting in the living room area, my father and I continued to converse. That's when things became slightly awkward.

"How is the Peter fellow? I still haven't met him…as your…partner, you know. I was hoping to meet him today, pumpkin." My dad stared into my eyes, as though he knew something I didn't.

"Well, Daddy, Peter is working." In an attempt to digress, I added, "I was thinking of taking some classes at the university to get another degree. They've cut my hours down at the hospital, so…" I smiled, hoping to distract my father from my absent fiancé to avoid an argument.

"Sweetie, how often is Peter here with you?" Now, I wanted answers. It seemed he knew something he wasn't telling me.

"Daddy, he comes and goes. I see him. He's here often." It was as though he knew I was lying. He gave me the "father look"—his left eyebrow raised, his eyes widened, and his smile vanished.

"Vernette, if you need anything, you can let me know, okay? How are things between you and your sister?" Finally, it seemed as though he had given up hope, deciding to focus his attention where he felt most comfortable: talking about Veronica. I despised the thought of discussing Veronica; it seemed like that was all he and I ever talked about.

"Things between Veronica and me are fine, Dad." I lied again, and he knew it.

"Vernette, goddamn it! You've isolated yourself from your family, and you don't even realize it. What are you doing with yourself? It's like you've just given up on life, on your family. You let a man you barely even know trick you into this domesticated lifestyle." I had to interrupt.

"Daddy, please, don't be a hypocrite. Mommy did the same thing. She became a housewife, left her mother and father in a whole other state to be with you!"

Shaking his head, he said, "Yes, your mother did, but the difference is that I remained by her side, supported her through everything, and didn't leave her to make the four walls of our home her new companion. Besides, that was a different time, and things are different now. You have far more opportunities than she did back in our day. Don't waste your life. I have had and still have high hopes and expectations for you. You're so talented, Vern."

I knew my father meant well.

I lost my grip, and that's when the tears came. Sobbing, with my hands firmly gripping the oak handle of the yellow single seat I occupied, I watched as my father disappeared and returned with the large black bag from earlier, packed with items.

"Your mother and I wanted to bring you a few things for your new *home*. She got a little shopping-happy with the décor, but she's pretty confident you'll love them."

Wiping my tears while forcing a smile, I noticed our conversation had left a few loopholes, but nothing a couple of gifts couldn't fill. As the bag approached, I became overjoyed. It was like Christmas morning for grown-ups.

I began pulling things out of the bag.

First came the etched bowl, a chrome metal lamp— perfect for the coffee table between my single sofas—two miniature grey mice figurines, and a Syroco wall plaque, which nearly made me lose my cool.

"Daddy, oh my goodness, I love this! Where did she find it? I thought they weren't going to be available anytime soon."

Laughing, he responded, "Your mother went out of her way to get these things together. She knew you would love them."

The bag began to deflate as I pulled out the last two items: a newly built German alarm clock and two vintage pewter Japanese ashtrays. Chuckling, I said to my now stern-looking father,

"Don't worry, Daddy, I don't smoke, and neither does Peter. Knowing Mommy, she just thought they were cute."

I placed all of my new gifts on the floor near my feet before standing to reach over and give my dad a hug.

"She wished she could have been here, pumpkin. I wish you would call her."

After receiving all of her gifts, I most definitely would. It felt good seeing my dad, and just having him around absolutely made my day.

"Well, Vern, I think I ought to get going now. You know, the older I get, the worse my sight becomes."

As we both stood, I reached in to give my father another hug. I was sure going to miss him. Walking him toward the front door, I noticed my dad placing his hand on his head, as though he had forgotten something.

"Oh, sweetheart, seeing the piano, I know you've been to the attic. Did you happen to find a dress up there?"

I wanted to scream. I had ripped that dress while trying to take it off, and now he was here to collect it. I had no idea what to say.

"Um, Daddy, I kind of ripped the dress yesterday when I found it. I promise I didn't mean to. I swear. You can tell Mommy I'll get it fixed, I promise."

His face lit up. Smiling from ear to ear, he said, "Fixed? Oh, sweetheart, don't worry about it. I'll make up something. She'll just be happy to have it."

I nodded in acceptance. I felt awful.

I went to fetch the dress and then interrogated him about where he would be headed next. He told me he was getting a taxi to Nica's, where he would be seeing her and the baby—he and Mom had gifted her some items a few months back. Then, he would be catching a red-eye flight back to Florida. As he took his leave, I thought long and hard about the things he and I had discussed.

It was time…

Once I arrived at Veronica's house, I entered through the front door, Lucinda releasing the latch to grant me access. I stood in the foyer, glancing around. It had been some time since Veronica and I last spoke, and even longer since I had visited. I expected some changes, but nothing too drastic.

Lucinda still looked the same—mundane and malicious. It was obvious they were in the process of refurbishing or perhaps even moving. Boxes, bubble wrap, and packing tape decorated the foyer, leading up to the staircase. Their home appeared nearly emptied of furniture, aside from a small coat rack. I took advantage of it, placing my coat on one of the hooks. The last few weeks of winter were brutal; I had almost not made it.

It was Valentine's Day, 1956. Around this time, *Look* magazine had published the confessions of J.W. Milam and Roy Bryant regarding the murder of Emmett Till, and just a few days later, Martin Luther King Jr.'s home had been bombed. So, even though I had my suspicions about Peter, I tried to be understanding of his long work hours.

I was beginning to lose my mind in that house, being home every day…alone. I no longer appreciated the roof over my head or the bed I slept in because it wasn't my earnings that provided them. Finally, when my hours dropped drastically at work, Peter begged me to quit entirely. I created the home, but I lost the man.

We set a wedding date, but he was too busy to assist with the preparations. After a while, I buried myself in planning the perfect wedding, drowning in the details as if they could fill the emptiness he left.

I remembered envying Veronica for being a housewife, only to later look down on her for allowing a man to make all the decisions—placing her into a corner as if she were worth nothing more. Yet, in time, I too became a victim. The woman in the corner. The one worth nothing more. The woman with her palm up every payday, waiting for money to be handed to her while doing nothing but spending it.

I despised myself for it.

For being submissive.

For losing my voice.

For losing my fire. Even if he was cheating, I could never confront him. I was a volcano waiting to erupt, my anxiety mounting. And I started to miss *her*.

Crave *her*.

After leaving me that message some time ago, Veronica never called back. So, I took it upon myself to make an abrupt visit, praying for an amiable reunion.

I approached the master bedroom, my toes curling against the soft crème wall-to-wall carpeting. It took her a while to even notice I was there, and as I suspected, they were moving. Boxes were stacked in the hallway—some full, others empty. It was my first time visiting the upstairs portion of her home. I had no idea they were living so lavishly.

Once I reached the top of the staircase leading down to the foyer, the scent of raspberries filled the air—something like cologne. I treaded slowly, turning left, the only direction available. At the far end of the hall, I saw the bathroom and heard the sound of a baby playing, thumping on a mechanical device, singing lullabies and repetitive melodies. It had to be Matthew. He sounded so happy. The sound of his laughter sent chills down my forearms as I suddenly longed for a child of my own.

I passed a large mirror decorating the wall just before the master bedroom door. Could Veronica have been so much of a narcissist that she needed to check her appearance before entering her own room? I couldn't help myself—I quickly glanced at my reflection, searching for any imperfections. I found none.

My hair remained in a simple, unfashionable ponytail. I had never been one to fancy a cut and curl like most women or embrace the beehive hairstyle that became popular after Audrey Hepburn hit the big screen. Still, my insecurities made me tug at my V-neck red-striped blouse and dust off my red straight-legged pants. I patted my hips to ensure they weren't too wide.

Just as I began to feel slightly beautiful, Veronica popped her head out from her room, her eyes widening in amazement as we locked gazes. But just as quickly, she ducked back inside when Matthew started to cough.

Veronica had not aged. She looked exactly the same as she had during our university days. Her long, exotic hair was now styled with a deep center part and loose curls at the bottom.

I wasted no more time in the hallway.

Stepping into the bedroom, I found her sitting on the edge of her bed, legs crossed, holding baby Matthew in her arms as she rocked him while feeding him a bottle of milk. He had grown so much. Dressed in what resembled a sailor's suit, his tiny hands curled slightly, his long hair forming soft ringlets. He closed his eyes.

Once he finished, Veronica placed him meticulously at the center of the mattress, where a baby blanket had been spread out beforehand. Then, she stood.

We remained silent, simply admiring one another. I had yet to cross the threshold.

Veronica was always fashionable. She wore a slim-fitted, navy-blue bow-tie casual swing dress with a pair of white Oxford pumps.

I began the conversation with an apology. I had to apologize for not staying longer the day she gave birth, for being late, and for not being around to help her all that time. She pretended to ignore me completely.

"Can you pass me that packing tape near you?" she said as she walked over to the fireplace, placing a box on the ground beneath it and beginning to wrap figurine statues in newspaper before boxing them.

She paced the room in a tranquil manner, a smirk on her face as I stood there, completely shocked at just how amazing she looked. I rubbed the top of my head, pulling slightly on my ponytail, only to remind myself that my hair was nowhere near as long as hers.

Snapping out of my trance, I made my way over to the packing tape, walking slowly toward her. As I handed it to her, I noticed the dark black nail polish she wore. The color complemented her skin tone beautifully, making her appear even lighter than she actually was.

Veronica paced back and forth, leaving small heel indentations in the carpet, creating a visible trail. Finally, after packing the last fireplace statue, she asked,

"So, what brings you here?"

I was at a loss for words. I was clearly not relaxed—completely on edge and unsettled. It made no sense to me. I didn't even know why I was there, aside from the fact that she was my sister and I wanted to see my nephew. I should have known that seeing her would only make me feel more insecure about myself. It always did.

But I took a deep breath before responding.

"I wanted to see how you and the baby were doing. Um, you didn't sound too good when you left me that message. I—I guess you could say I was worried."

She remained perfectly still after applying the first coat of packing tape over the box holding her statues. Her back was to me as she turned slightly, her expression unreadable. She smiled her beautiful smile, and I anticipated a loving response.

Instead, her smile quickly faded as she spoke.

"You were worried? You're such a fucking liar! You were never worried about me. A worried sister would have been here with me. A worried sister wouldn't have left me to raise a child on my own when I have no clue what the hell I'm doing. You weren't worried—you were jealous, Vern. Admit it!"

She had waited a long time to tell me that. I could feel her anger, see her rage, and even fear what she might say next. I knew I was jealous of my sister, but hearing her say it—hearing the words spoken out loud—put everything into a whole different perspective for me.

Before I knew it, I had broken down.

I didn't want to be strong anymore. I wanted to be vulnerable, so I let myself be that, just for a moment, as I explained my side of the story.

"Veronica, for years—years—I lived in your shadow. Never pretty enough, never good enough. The only thing I had going for me was my education, my intelligence, and even that wasn't enough. I promised myself I would become something—be a doctor, be important, and not end up a goddamn housewife. I did everything by the book. I went to school, graduated, and still—you have everything.

My life, Nica, was never supposed to be like this. You stole the one person who believed in me. You stole the one person who would have probably encouraged me to aim for that doctorate. This is my life… you are living my life—but you poisoned it! How am I supposed to face you every day?"

By now, through all the screaming, Matthew had woken up. Veronica and I stood staring at each other. The look she gave me held no sympathy. Lucinda came rushing in, grabbing Matthew, his bottle, blanket, and some toys, rolling her eyes at me as she made her way out of the room.

"What am I supposed to do about that?"

I hadn't expected a pity party, but some kind of empathy would have been nice. Veronica remained cold; I couldn't remember her ever being this way. She refused to let herself give in emotionally and refused to show any sign of weakness.

I sighed. "Let's just move on."

She responded quickly.

"I've already done that. You haven't. I'm not the one complaining about my life, Vern. You're the one still living in the past."

I felt a wave of agitation wash over me. No one knew what I was going through, what I was feeling, nor did it seem to matter.

I let my guard down completely. If I wanted to mend our relationship, it had to be now.

"You stole the man I once loved, and all I'm asking for, Veronica, is an apology."

"I don't do those. Apologies are foolish. You want a reason to forgive someone, so you ask for an apology? If you really wanted to forgive me, you would—whether I apologized or not. Forgiveness isn't for the other person, Vernette. Forgiveness is for you.

Besides, you never told me about your relationship with David. I had no idea you and he were involved. No freaking idea! When Daddy introduced us, David told him that you and he were just friends. So, if you're looking for someone to hate, hate him. Get an apology from him if you need a reason to forgive. But don't make this about me."

She was right.

I hated myself for trying to make her feel responsible for the fact that I had stayed trapped in the past, no matter how futile it was. I had blamed her this whole time, never once realizing that maybe I was the problem. My jealousy had consumed me. It was far beyond David. I made it about him just to keep things cordial, knowing deep down that I envied her for so much more.

Funny, because David had apologized, and he was no longer my problem.

"Veronica, again, I am sorry."

She shook her head in disappointment.

"That's the difference between us, Vern. I never needed an apology to forgive you."

I sobbed.

I decided it was best to keep my distance. Veronica stood by the fireplace, close to the window. Neither of us moved, but I broke down. I felt horrible. Palming my face, I heard her footsteps approaching. She grabbed me, pressing my face against her left shoulder. She smelled so divine.

Her heels added at least two inches to her height, so I tiptoed slightly, gripping her tightly. I felt her grip me just as firmly. We stood there, holding each other, for at least three minutes.

I thought about everything—leaving her as a child, abandoning her that day in the salon—and then another question dawned on me. But I decided against asking. It would only do more harm than good.

When she finally released me, she smiled.

Joyfully, she rocked my shoulders back and forth and asked, "When is the wedding? You can't possibly think I didn't notice that gorgeous ring on your hand! So, tell me all about him."

Grabbing my hand, she led me over to her mattress. I sat on the edge as she pushed her way to the center, kicking off her heels. With her back against the chestnut headboard, she placed a throw pillow between her legs and another atop her abdomen, clutching it tightly.

I felt awkward discussing Peter with Nica. After David, I always feared she would do the same with Peter. But I decided to take responsibility for what had happened and told her about him. Nica was thrilled to hear about us—how he cooked for me, the way he proposed. She even let a tear fall when I told her about our celibacy. I described how charming he was, how delicate, mature, and kind-hearted. She listened intently, and I talked so much that I didn't even notice when the sun began to set.

"Vern, I'm so happy for you. Sounds like you've found the man of your dreams," she said, her eyebrows knitting together, her smile laced with cynicism.

I had spent practically half the day with Veronica and promised to return the next day. By 7:00 PM, I knew Peter would begin to wonder about my whereabouts. I had no interest in disclosing my every move to him. Spending the day with Nica felt like a weight had been lifted off my shoulders. But as I left, I couldn't shake the feeling that this was just the calm before the storm.

When I arrived home, I noticed the soft glow of candles illuminating the kitchen. I shut the front door loudly to announce my presence. Peter stuck his head out from the kitchen doorway, holding a bowl of salad he was tossing. Smiling, I removed my coat, hung it on the hook, and tossed my keys onto the mantle before making my way down the hall and into the kitchen.

Everything looked and smelled amazing. Peter had been gone for almost three days. I knew his job was demanding, which was why I stayed levelheaded. The way he kissed me as I took my seat at the table made me suspect he wanted to talk. As he placed the dishes on the table—salad, vegetable rice, steamed fish, and carrot cake for dessert—I took a deep breath. He sat down across from me.

Grabbing my hands, he began to pray over our meal. There were about nine candles flickering around us, along with a bottle of cranberry sparkling cider—his favorite, since he didn't drink alcohol. As he started serving our plates, he spoke.

"Vern, how do you feel about children?" He held up a hand before I could react. "Now, before you go freaking out, I've been thinking. I might cut some of my days at *The Times*. As you know, I've been meeting with people to discuss starting my own press group. You've done an amazing job with the decorating. And from what I can see, the wedding planning is going great, too."

I glanced at the photos pinned up around the room—wedding dresses, catering lists, venue locations. Everything was laid out to perfection.

He leaned over to kiss me. "So... how do you feel about starting a family?"

I had no feelings.

Here I was, feeling great that my sister and I had begun mending things, and now Peter was bringing up children.

Smiling, I took Peter's right hand as I spoke. "Peter, there's so much you don't know about me. I was just hoping I'd have more time." I felt my eyes begin to water.

Peter let go of my hand and slid his chair closer, gripping my left shoulder as he pulled me into an embrace. He whispered, "Baby, I'm here now, and I'm sorry I haven't been around as much as I should have. But I'm here now, and I want you to tell me everything—anything you feel comfortable sharing. You have my undivided attention."

I took several deep breaths before speaking.

"I was a junior in college when I met my first boyfriend. He was my first everything. First kiss, first hug, first… everything. When he and I started our relationship, we kept it a secret from almost everyone we knew. Being an African American in college was already a big deal. The last thing our parents wanted to hear about was us being in a relationship—a 'distraction.' So, we kept our distractions to ourselves and shared so many wonderful moments together. I fell in love with him after only a short time. We carried on our relationship for about two years.

Two months before graduation, I was studying for finals and getting noticed by many of my Caucasian professors. They constantly encouraged me, telling me I had the potential to become an outstanding physician. I let the praise go to my head and convinced my boyfriend that we should celebrate. By 'celebrate,' he assumed I meant having sex. But I was a virgin and wanted to wait until marriage—that had always been my belief.

At first, he seemed to accept it, but I could feel him slipping away. Then graduation came, and he saw her—

my sister. 'We were young,' I kept telling myself when I noticed how fixated he had become on her. Eventually, I had to move past it, only to later forgive him and rekindle our love. But I guess he just used that as an excuse to get back into Veronica's orbit. They betrayed me."

Peter pulled me into his arms, pushing us both away from the table.

"I will never leave you. I love you. I'm so sorry you had to go through that. But I'm here now, baby. I'm here, and you never have to see that sick, lying man again."

I sighed. "He's my sister's husband."

Peter pulled away almost immediately, his eyes widening in astonishment. "Huh?"

"...their son is my nephew..."

"Oh..."

—

"I can only imagine the shock on his face when you told him that."

Washington's eyes gleam with something deeper than his words convey. Another story, even. He fidgets strangely between each sentence that spills from my lips, as if the weight of my words unsettles him. I begin to wonder—what is his truth? Is he truly this deeply saddened by the story of a stranger? He paces, weeping and sniffling, moving back and forth from the kitchen to the outside patio where we now gather on another humid, sunny day. A cigarette emerges—the first since his visit days ago. One puff, two puffs—he chokes discreetly, inexperienced, behind my dear Emily and me.

Emily interrupts, "Some journalist you are. What is your problem? She isn't even finished."

Emily has shed a few tears, consoling me as I force myself to relive the past, demanding my mind grant me access to the dark days buried deep within my subconscious. She remains loving and compassionate despite the grim tales unfolding about her grandmother and me, like a premonition before confirmation. She grips my hands as Washington stubs out his unfinished cigarette.

"Auntie Vern, I love you, and I completely understand why you're doing this now." Her smile makes my own tears fall.

Her phone rings. Washington positions himself on the second patio step, regaining his composure—still speechless.

"Auntie Vern, it's my mom. What should I tell her?" Emily's voice trembles as she turns to me, gripping her phone tightly as it vibrates relentlessly.

Smiling, I reply, "Tell her the truth."

Her heart beats rapidly. "But you know she hates when I'm—hello?"

Before the phone stops vibrating, Emily quickly answers, pressing it to her ear as she stomps into my home. Once inside, Tippy's voice becomes unmistakable. Despite Emily's discomfort, she tries to maintain composure.

"Hi, Mom, how is everything?"

"Everything is great. Your boss called me yesterday, Emily. He says you haven't been to work. What's going on, baby? Is everything okay?"

Emily puts her mother on speakerphone. Tippy sounds worried—and so am I. The realization that Emily has cut off communication with everyone back home unsettles me. Angers me, even.

Tippy now lives in Dayton, Ohio, with her husband, Richard Montgomery, and their two sons, Addison and Elijah. She prayed desperately never to have another daughter—the pain she endured while raising Emily remains indescribable.

"Mother, please calm down. I'm perfectly safe. I've been with Grand-Auntie Vern."

Infuriated, she snaps, "With who? Why the hell are you on that demonic farm with that demonic woman? Emily, go home now, or I'll come and get you myself!"

She loathes my family—and for good reason.

Washington and I continue to listen as he readies a fresh tape for yet another segment of my chronicles.

"Mommy, please, you're overreacting. I'm fine, and I'll call you when I have the chance. I promise everything is all right."

Before Emily can hang up, Tippy pleads, "Emily, pl—"

But the line goes dead.

Emily emerges from the cabin. I glance at her before lowering my head.

"Emily, your mother is right. You should go home now."

Immediately, she throws herself into my armchair, startling me. "No, no. Ever since I was seven years old, all the way up until now—twenty-two years later—I've been lied to, dismissed for asking questions, reprimanded for even thinking about my father. Now, I know my answers are here. I am where I need to be. Mr. Montgomery—he is a great man. But he is not my dad.

You know about my father. And if being here is the only way for me to know more about him, too, then here is where I'm going to stay. I was nervous at first. But now... now I'm intrigued. I need to know why he did what he did. Of course, my mother never talks about it, so please don't shut me out, Auntie Vern."

She is so convincing. But the truth she seeks about her father may not be the truth she can handle.

Yet, I cannot force her away.

So, I do the one thing I know I must do.

I continue.

—

TWO WEEKS AND THREE days later, Peter and I were married at the city hall courthouse in The Bronx. It was an amazing day. His co-worker and future business partner, Aaron Donahue, served as his best man and witness to our nuptials. We decided to forgo a wedding because he felt a hint of resentment toward my family—Veronica for marrying my ex, my ex for cheating with my sister, and my father for lacking the backbone to end the relationship.

The next morning, winter remained vicious, but spring was fast approaching as I turned, waking up in the arms of my new husband. I was blissful, kissing Peter on his wet lips, consummating our marriage over and over again as the sun began to rise.

That night, I arrived at Veronica's house, skipping up to her bedroom after being let in by Lucinda and handing her my coat to hang. Veronica and David still appeared to be packing, but once again, David was nowhere in sight.

Their home looked even emptier than before. I ran up the stairs and barged into her bedroom, only to find it empty. Confused, I bellowed for Lucinda. She met me at the bottom of the staircase, standing statuesque, her eyes piercing through me. Timidly, I asked,

"Where is Veronica?"

In a lethargic manner, she responded, "The Mrs. is not here. She and baby Matthew have gone for a regular doctor's visit."

I glanced at my watch. It read 8:49 PM. I wondered to myself—what doctor could they possibly be visiting at such an hour? Seeing my disbelief, Lucinda continued,

"You're more than welcome to wait for her arrival."

Her lips barely moved when she spoke, and her eyes always squinted at me. I became flustered, questioning whether or not I should wait. Before I could conjure a response, Lucinda spoke once more.

"It is settled. I am cleaning, and you cannot be in my way. I suggest you wait upstairs in the master. I will alert you once they arrive."

Just like that, she turned and walked away. Nothing about her had changed—not even her hair.

I did as I was told and waited in the master bedroom. Despite there being nowhere else to sit beside the bed, I refused to sit there. Instead, I curled up on the carpet by the fireplace, placing a throw pillow under my head for support. Before I knew it, I had fallen asleep.

Hours later, I heard Lucinda call my name from the bottom of the staircase. I understood why. The commotion from Veronica's arrival was anything but discreet.

"I refuse to continue living like this! Why are all of these boxes still down here? I specifically told you to put them away immediately. What is it? Why are you not following directions?"

As I gathered my things and prepared myself to witness the wrath of Nica, I couldn't help but feel sorry for Lucinda, who clearly did her job well. I had never once seen an unkempt home when I visited. She did the laundry, cooked, and even became responsible for Matthew, tending to his needs. A few boxes in the foyer should have been no reason for Veronica to act so belligerently.

Moments later, I surfaced, peering down the spiraling staircase to see Veronica, baby Matthew, and Lucinda all huddled near the front door. Lucinda was removing Nica's trailing black cotton cloak, folding it in her arms instead of hanging it on the coat rack. The cloak looked mysterious, haunting, with meticulously stitched hems that matched the one baby Matthew wore.

I thought long and hard about where she could have really gone. She was dressed as though she had just returned from attending a séance. A malevolent look darkened her face as she threw Matthew into Lucinda's arms. I screeched, fearing he would hit the floor.

Fortunately for us all, Lucinda was a good catch. Simultaneously, they both shot me a look. I fidgeted, feeling as though I had just been caught performing an indecent act. I felt embarrassed, completely unsure why, so I let out a nervous chuckle. The room seemed to close in, the walls and mechanics disengaging. Our dialogue slowed, our tones reduced to mere whispers. Suddenly, everything felt normal again once Lucinda took her leave.

"Well, well, well, what brings you here, Vern?" Nica raised her right eyebrow, careful not to frown nor smile, giving me no indication as to whether she was pleased by my visit or completely sickened by my presence.

Stuttering at first, I remained at the top of the staircase, watching as she rustled through the boxes closest to the entrance, kicking them toward the rear, leading to the garage door. I began to speak, my tone slightly elevated since she was no longer visible.

"Nica, I have the best news!"

Despite the fear I felt—both from the eerie stillness of the house and something unsettled within myself—I remained enraptured by the news I had to share. Nica was not herself, and anyone who knew her could testify to that. Her silence and sudden disappearance began to worry me. Slowly, I started descending the stairs, my hands gliding along the banister.

As I reached the middle landing, she reappeared, now holding a coffee mug in her left hand. My palms began to sweat, my forehead pulsating—perhaps from the chandelier's illumination overhead. I couldn't understand why I was so nervous, almost anxious. I wanted so badly to blurt out that I, too, was a married woman—not only out of sheer excitement but also because a small part of me wanted her to see me as an equal.

She stepped lightly toward the doorway, removing her black snow boots by kicking them off one by one with the opposite foot. Then, she slid into a pair of red cotton slippers. Her all-black attire left me dazed, wondering why she was dressed so somberly. She wore a buttoned-up black polyester blouse paired with an ankle-length black skirt. Her hair was wrapped into a tight bun at the back of her head, pulled so tightly that veins protruded from her forehead. There was no way she had been to a doctor's office.

"Sorry, I had to get my tea. Now, what were you saying?"

Still, her tone remained nonchalant as she began making her way up the stairs. Eventually, she passed me and entered her bedroom. I simply followed behind.

"Nica, what is going on? You're obviously not yourself," I said sympathetically as she glided to the center of her mattress, still fully dressed, careful not to spill her tea.

"Vern, I am almost positive that you didn't come here just to ask me about my problems—especially without any warning that you were coming at all. So let's not make this about me."

She wasn't my little sister anymore. She wasn't happy and loving; she was dark and baleful. Even her eyes told me—she wasn't in there. Her pupils were fully dilated, her skin pale, and dark circles were beginning to form under her eyes. Seeing her up close only made me wonder what she wasn't telling me.

Finally, I took a seat at the edge of the bed. Fearfully, I asked, "Where has David been? Has he even been helping you at all? You look exhausted. A stark difference from the last time I saw you."

I scanned the room, searching for something—anything—that could explain what was wrong. On the nightstand to the right, I spotted what appeared to be prescribed sleeping pills. Little pink pills, dozens of them, in a transparent bottle.

"Nica, why do you have those?"

Immediately, she shot me a supercilious look before sliding the bottle into the top dresser drawer. I crawled toward the center of the mattress, where she sat. Still, she said nothing, only taking small, slow sips of her scorching hot tea.

I felt terrible. Why hadn't I seen this coming? She was depressed.

I pressed on, asking the hard questions—I just wanted a reaction, something to let me know she was still in there.

"How long has David not been around? If you aren't happy, then you need to say something. Look, I know it may not be easy, but you shouldn't be dealing with the stress of raising a child alone with just a house nurse. David should be here—he needs to help you."

I hadn't noticed when my voice began to rise, but as I drew closer to the end of my statement, I became angrier. I strongly felt that David was the problem. He was nowhere to be seen during my recent visits. Not to mention the abrupt packing—the boxes everywhere.

She needed to come to terms with what was happening if she had any intention of moving forward. Minutes passed in silence.

Before I knew it, frustration took over.

"Veronica, goddamn it, talk to me!"

"Do not yell at me, Vern! Please!" she snapped. "You think you know everything, don't you? Well, you don't.

David is wonderful—he has been wonderful to Matthew and me. We're packing because we're moving into a bigger house to expand our family. I'm pregnant again, if you must know.

I know you want so badly for him to be the problem, but he isn't the problem at all. You are. And just because he left you to be with me, you still haven't forgiven him. But shit, get over it!"

My body went numb.

She was still hiding something—I could hear it in her voice.

By now, Veronica had finished her tea and placed the mug on the left nightstand closest to her. I remained speechless. She wanted to hurt me with that comment about David, and she succeeded. Truth be told, I would have been over him already if they hadn't been together. No matter who I married or who I slept with, David would always be my first love, and there was no changing that.

To ease the tension, I pushed the issue no further.

"Nica, I'm married. We did it yesterday."

Although my head faced forward, I could feel her eyes burning into me from my left side. Before I could utter another word, she grabbed my shoulders, squeezing them so hard I almost yelped. Then she started laughing.

Nica, obviously, felt relieved.

I hoped I had made her feel better—reassured her that I was no longer interested in her husband.

Even though it was a lie. I did not want David for myself, but I wanted him gone, away from her, away from our family.

I did care about her. I did have her best interests at heart.

She hugged me—not out of excitement, but out of liberation. Our relationship could finally reach new heights.

We gossiped for hours, talking about my first time with Peter—what it felt like, how he made me feel, how he was the man for me.

Chuckling, I said, "Wow, baby number two. You've been busy. So, are you excited?"

Nica and I lay on our backs, staring at the ceiling, our fingers interlocked—her right hand with my left.

"I am, a little," she admitted. "I'm hoping so badly for a daughter. Having a son is great, but David is more involved with Matthew. When he's home, I barely get to touch him.

David really has been wonderful, Vern. He and I have come such a long way, and the only reason he hasn't been around much is that he has been assigned a huge criminal case. With all the child kidnappings happening here on the island, he believes we will be targeted—especially since we're colored. It's for the best that we move. I'm going to miss this house, though. The memories—oh, have you spoken to Mom or Dad? Grandparents?"

Her words were comforting.

Unfortunately, I hadn't been in touch with either of the grandparents. I had been too busy—too consumed with my own life. Selfish, I knew.

As for my parents, my dad and I spoke periodically. But I hadn't yet told him about my marriage.

And my mother? Nothing.

"No, Nica, I haven't. How about you?" In an instant, my mood shifted from excitement to agony.

"Daddy and I speak every day. Grandma and Grandpa Robinson call pretty often to check on the baby. They've both retired. Dad says he's finally going to take a trip there this summer; he would love for all of us to go. Mother still hasn't spoken to me, but I hear she's excited to see Matthew, so I think it would be wonderful if we both went to Louisiana this summer to meet up with Mom and Dad and see the grandparents. Don't you think that would be great?"

That did sound great, but I couldn't help but ask, "What about Grandma and Grandpa Martin?"

Veronica purposely skipped over them. She nodded her head.

"They're all right. Grandma Martin has been pretty sick, though—polio. It just...happened. She looked fine the last time she was here, you know. Grandpa is staying strong. Mom knows, but she isn't going to visit them, Dad said. I asked him—if she doesn't visit them, how will she know when they're dead? He just got all upset and emotional, saying I shouldn't say things like that. But really, Vern, how would she know?"

My father never told me any of this. A part of me was angry, and another part was sad—not just because my grandmother was dying, but because my father had entrusted my baby sister with this information and not me. That jealousy in me began rearing its ugly head once again. I didn't want to ruin the moment, so I responded,

"Money. That's how she'll know. Mom hates funerals anyway. It shouldn't surprise anyone that she prefers to keep her distance."

Veronica shook her head in disappointment.

"That was a long time ago, Vern. She needs to get over that. What if one of us dies before her? Will she not attend our funeral?"

I shot Nica an uneasy look.

"Let's not think like that."

I couldn't believe she said that—with such confidence, as if she weren't a mother herself. Before I knew it, my watch read 2:43 AM. Nica and I had talked the whole night. I felt exhausted and was in no mood to travel back home.

Nica crawled out of bed and began to undress. Her brown panties and brown bullet bra were exposed. Underneath all that black clothing hid a well-sculpted, pregnant stomach. She appeared to be about three months along. Not a stretch mark in sight, her caramel complexion still radiant. I, too, removed my clothing.

My sister and I slid under the blanket.

The HMV Salisbury vintage heater crackled. I feared it would spark, as I had never heard that sound before. Not long after settling in, I turned to face the right, staring out into the dark hallway. The bedroom was now pitch black, and Nica's arms cradled me. I felt her protruding belly button press against the small of my back. Despite the slight discomfort, I managed to drift in and out of consciousness.

While lucid, my thoughts remained my own— drifting to Peter and me after our first moment of pleasure, thinking about how wonderful he was, how sweet his sweat tasted, and how well he knew how to handle my body. He was definitely more experienced than I had anticipated.

Just then, my thoughts were interrupted by a strange noise coming from the hall—the sound of a whisper. I opened my eyes to see nothing but darkness, giving my pupils a few seconds to adjust. As they did, I turned to see that Veronica was still fast asleep, now positioned opposite me.

My mouth felt dry.

I turned onto my back. The whispers grew louder, but I still couldn't make out what was being said. It wasn't until I heard the faint noise right by my face that I shot up. The whisper turned into a screeching voice.

"You have been touched!"

The words bellowed from the left of me. By the time I registered the sound near my ear, I jolted upright—or at least tried—before feeling Veronica's grip on my wrist. She shoved my hand away, and then, suddenly, she began strangling me.

She climbed on top of me, her eyes still closed, her hands wrapped firmly around my throat.

"You have been touched, Vernette. Touched. Touched. Touched."

With each word, she thrust me back and forth, her grip tightening. Air slipped from my lungs. My eyes rolled to the back of my head. I struggled to reach for something—anything—to fight her off. But she was so strong.

Tears streamed from my eyes, surely drenching the pillow beneath me. The only thought that crossed my mind was whether or not my mother would attend my funeral. My limbs weakened; my arms fatigued. And then, as I opened my eyes again, I saw Veronica above me—and above her, a shadowy figure.

It was Grandma Martin.

Veronica's eyes snapped open.

Her pupils were a deep, unnatural red.

I gasped, my throat burning, but no sound came out.

Panicked, I reached blindly until my fingers wrapped around the dresser lamp. With all the strength I had left, I swung it, slamming it into the back of Veronica's head.

She flew off me, bouncing from the right side of the bed onto the floor.

Everything happened so quickly.

As I gasped for air, my hands clutching my bruised neck, I felt a sharp strike across my right cheek. A punch.

The night turned to day.

I propelled to the floor on the opposite side, my forehead slamming against the nightstand. A warm, thick sensation trickled down my face. Blood.

I rocked back and forth, pressing a trembling hand to my forehead, struggling to keep the blood from gushing everywhere.

My vision blurred.

My head spinning.

Somewhere in the distance, I heard sirens.

The piercing cry of an ambulance.

The heavy thud of boots against the floor.

Then a voice.

"You stupid bitch! You hit my wife! I saw everything." He told the police. "She hit her, and my wife is pregnant. I want her charged."

I barely processed the words before another blow struck my face.

The sunlight was blinding as emergency responders lifted me onto a stretcher. I heard a voice instruct me to keep my head back. I obeyed, my gaze shifting to the side.

Veronica lay unconscious on the stretcher beside me.

David was freaking out.

Lucinda stood by the bedroom doorway, baby Matthew in her arms.

Her face was unreadable.

That day, I was left in the emergency room, waiting for a doctor among other patients, having no idea where Veronica had been taken. While I sat there, David suddenly came scurrying in, two officers trailing behind him. Before I had the chance to say a word, he went ballistic.

"I have apologized to you, and I figured by now you would grow the hell up and move the hell on. You hit my wife, and I promise you, Vernette, if you come near her again, I will have you thrown in jail!"

The officers remained observant, keeping David at a safe distance from me, but it was obvious that if they hadn't been there, he would have hit me again. I couldn't help but plead my case.

"David, you are so wrong. I—I don't know what happened! She was trying to kill me!" I began to cry. I knew I wasn't crazy.

Just then, a nurse arrived to check on my stitches.

"She didn't do anything!" David snapped. "I walked into that room, and while trying to be careful not to wake either of you, I saw you reach for a lamp and start attacking her while she slept. You need help, Vern. You're a freaking lunatic! If you come near my wife again, I will have you put away—committed—whatever works. Do you hear me?"

Immediately, I lost whatever sympathy I had tried to maintain and went into defense mode.

"She is my baby sister! I would never hurt her—especially not for you. You are not worth it, David, so please stop acting like this is about you. She tried to strangle me in my sleep! I was defending myself!"

By now, the entire room had taken pleasure in our hostile exchange. One of the officers interjected.

"Ma'am, I'm going to have to ask you to calm down. We'll be taking a statement from you in a minute. Sir, please return to your wife's bedside. My partner and I will handle this."

David's face crumpled, and he began to weep.

"Vernette, I swear, you stay away from my family. You stay away."

My heart felt like it was skipping beats.

"You can't do that! She's my sister, David!"

Walking away, he shouted over his shoulder, "She's my wife. I'll do whatever I have to."

—

"Ms. Vernette—"

"Mrs., I am still a married woman," I tease.

"My apologies. I just assumed, since you haven't mentioned anything before, that—anyway, um, that was great. My one question, though—how did it make you feel? Hearing David say you would never see your sister again?"

"I wondered who would attend my funeral, who would deliver my eulogy. And what frightened me the most was how long it would take before I die. I had a defining moment, Washington—one that made me realize just how worthless I was without my sister. I had no purpose other than her."

—

SPRING CAME, THEN SUMMER, and no trip to see the grandparents was ever mentioned. It was as if my parents had gotten wind of the incident and cut me out of their lives. It may not have been intentional—my father seldom called—but I knew something was different.

Around November, I heard that Veronica had to have an emergency C-section, during which she gave birth to her second child: Ebony Elise Harrington. I heard Ebony was gorgeous. She had inherited many of her mother's features along with her father's complexion. I struggled with the discomfort of not having the opportunity to meet her.

After that, my father started calling frequently again. Peter continued traveling for business, and I, well, I remained a lonely little housewife. I knitted in my spare time, baked endlessly until food became disposable, and eventually started bringing goods to the neighbors. Everyone loved my cherry pies, and more often than not, I was asked to bake for occasions such as wedding receptions, meetings, and even children's birthdays. The thought of turning it into a business crossed my mind, but

I lacked the confidence—especially with Peter constantly discussing the details of his freelance writing and business ventures. I simply didn't want to burden him with more talk of such things.

For weeks upon weeks when he was home, I baked for his meetings. We spent our time in the kitchen—me baking, him discussing matters of importance with his colleagues. Before I knew it, I was waiting on them hand and foot, serving meals, desserts, and then cleaning up afterward. I had gone from being a hardworking nursing assistant to a housewife to a housemaid. I lost myself in it all.

Pretty soon, our marriage had been reduced to nothing more than sex. I cooked, he ate, we had sex, and he left. No conversation, no love, no interest. I was losing him as I continued losing myself.

I made several attempts to reach Veronica via mail. I wrote her letters of endearment, sent packages of children's clothing for my niece and nephew, but after months of doing this, I still didn't hear from her. I wondered if their address had changed or if she truly did hate me.

I became so tired of the life I was living. I wanted change after months of unhappiness and withering away. The first drastic thing I did was cut off my hair—my natural kinky curls are now shorter. For days, Peter didn't notice the change. He didn't even seem to care. Once I had had enough, I cornered him while he showered.

"Peter, you and I should talk."

"Sweetheart, you can talk to me later. I'm showering, can't you see that?"

I hated the way he spoke to me.

"Peter, no, we have to talk now!"

"Okay, Vernette. What is so important?" He was obviously annoyed. We both were.

"Peter, what is going on with you? You're barely ever here, you haven't even noticed that I've cut my hair, and we—we don't even speak to one another anymore. I bet you're heading out once you finish showering, huh?"

He scoffed.

"Good God, you women are just never satisfied. I've been working my ass off so you can continue to have this roof over your head. I am a black man in a white man's country trying to take care of you and me. Excuse me if I don't have time to sit and cuddle you every damn day."

"What did you just say? I was a working woman when you met me. I did not ask for all of this—"

"Whether you asked for it or not, you came in and accepted it. The thought of not having to work any longer, living off of my means, the thought of being a housewife. Don't act all innocent, Vern. You wanted this. Well, this is what it is. It gets boring sometimes. Read a book, watch some old movies, do something, but stop complaining about it."

He was right. I had so many reservations about being a housewife; I thought it was demeaning, but at some point, I had accepted it. I wanted what Veronica had; she made it look so easy, so effortless. I had no more words. Instead, I thought of something interesting. Watch some old movies, he said. I remembered the old films I had found in the attic. All I needed was a projector.

I removed myself from the bathroom, making my way down the staircase into the kitchen, where I began preparing dinner. I suffered in silence. Moments later, I heard Peter making his way toward me.

With my back turned, he began massaging my shoulders as he whispered sweet nothings in my ear. His right hand lifted my dress, exposing my left thigh. He then rubbed his hands up and down my torso. I continued rinsing the dishes as though I felt nothing, all the while thinking of the films I would begin watching as soon as he left.

Once I finished the dishes, his head found its way between my legs, licking my clitoris. I gripped both hands on the kitchen sink, my back still turned, as his tongue rotated between my vagina and anus. I closed my eyes, enjoying him, feeling the tickling sensation until my legs began to clench his face. Immediately, he arose, pushing my body forward—bending me over, my face now in the sink. He lifted my sundress, ripped my underwear, and inserted his penis inside of me.

For the first time, sex with him was painful.

With every thrust, my body ached.

—

"I am sorry, ladies, but may I please be excused? I have to use the restroom. Please, Mrs. Vernette, you may continue, as the tape recorder is still recording."

Emily shoots Washington a look of confusion, as do I. Standing, he begins walking away.

—

AS I WAS SAYING…

He never let up, forcefully thrusting himself into me over and over again before exhaling in excitement. I felt my body run cold as he released himself inside of me. My eyes closed. But what I feared most was that he was not the same man I had married—far more aggressive. This version of Peter no longer attended church and was no longer benevolent. Pulling down my dress, my hands shook. I could not bring myself to face him. I continued gripping the sink, patiently waiting.

While fixing his clothes, pulling up his jogging pants and wiping the sweat from his forehead, Peter exclaimed, grabbing an apple from the fruit dish in the center of the table, "I will be home in the morning."

Those words hummed through me as I heard the front door slam. I slammed a few things of my own. Three of our favorite dishes went flying to the ground, the splinters cutting me slightly. I felt nothing until I felt pain. Grabbing a tablecloth, I wrapped it around my left foot, where blood was gushing from the bottom. I could not locate the wound at first. I hopped over to one of the table chairs, away from the mess I had made. I just sat and squeezed my foot, praying for the blood to stop. Before long, it did, and I rose from my seat to hop back over to the counter drawer nearest the living room entrance, where I kept a small first aid kit. I removed band-aids, gauze, and pads, sat on the threshold between the two rooms, and began patching myself up.

Once I finished, I remembered the videos. I refused to waste my time grabbing them from the attic until I purchased the projector. I grabbed some cash from one of Peter's coat pockets before tossing it around my body, slipped into my sneakers, and began making my way to the corner store—my foot throbbing.

On my way there, I felt saddened by the sounds of children playing in the snow—the holidays were upon us. Finally, I reached the store after about ten minutes of walking; I loved walking, especially on New York City streets. There were always great kinds of people and experiences to witness. Nine dollars bought me a used projector. I whistled for a taxicab, which, back in those days, was called a checkered cab.

Arriving home, I was so excited to begin viewing the films that, at first, I had not noticed the second taxicab across the street from my stoop, idling. Once inside, I raced up to the attic. As soon as I spotted the box, I heard the doorbell ring. This angered me deeply. All I kept wondering was, who on earth could it be? I was not expecting anyone, and I certainly was in no mood to collect catering offers. I left the box at the tip of the attic opening and began hobbling down the stairs to the front door, feeling pain from my wound. Once I opened it, who I saw caused my heart to skip a beat.

It was Veronica.

Seeing her did not excite me; rather, it angered me. She was dressed in a red wool pencil skirt that accentuated her figure, paired with a white cashmere sweater, modestly cut to cover her shoulders and arms. Her undergarments were of a soft ivory hue, the bra well-constructed and neatly supporting her frame. On her feet, she wore classic black leather pumps with a moderate heel, more practical for the winter chill. Her hair was styled in a neat, tight chignon, rolled and pinned at the nape of her neck, with a smooth, flawless finish that complemented her look.

She stood graciously, her stomach flat again. She smiled a warm smile as I stood, staring into her eyes, wanting so badly to dismiss her. She held her clutch tightly in her hands, beige with a zipper on the front for easy access. Her makeup was immaculate, nude with a bold red matte lipstick. She resembled someone preparing for church. The more I stared at her, the more I saw my mother in her.

"What do you want?"

I couldn't help but sound quarrelsome. That day marked ten months since our last encounter. She owed me an explanation—or at least, I thought she did.

She didn't answer me right away. Instead, she smiled and reached down to give me the tightest hug I had ever received—examining my buzz cut. Laughing, I could do nothing but hug her back, my tears flowing freely. "Where are the kids?" I asked.

"Both are with Lucinda today," she replied, her voice light and reassuring. I let her in. I didn't care to ask about David and whether or not he'd granted her permission to come and see me. All that mattered to me was her, and her alone. Once inside, I embraced her again. I had missed her so much. She always looked so ravishing, and she smelled wonderful. I felt alive as I touched her. I felt like I was living again. I needed her.

Sadly, she said, "Vern, how have you been?"

I pulled away, not sure how to answer. Hopelessly, I responded, "I've been missing you." I let out a huge sigh of relief—my sister was my best friend.

Now laughing as our tears began to dry, she said, "Oh my goodness, look at us, we're such a mess!" I agreed, offering her a place to rest her clutch on the mantle by the door. She kicked off her pumps but not before whistling out to her cab driver, motioning for him to come over. I peeked outside and saw him pop open the trunk, bringing out three medium-sized suitcases. Immediately, I shot her a look of bewilderment. Her eyes began to well.

"Vern, please, I need you." I hesitated no more. I slipped into my sneakers and made my way past the little black gate to the curb, where I assisted the cab driver in lifting one of the black leather suitcases.

A few hours passed, and Veronica still refused to tell me why she had left David and their two children, especially so close to the holidays. I didn't want to push the issue, so I didn't ask more than once. Eventually, as she and I were putting away her things in what used to be my old bedroom, upstairs across from our master, she began to speak.

"I am twenty-seven years old, and I am so unhappy. All I've become is a body for babies, bearing child after child, suffering through pregnancy after pregnancy, all by myself. With each additional baby, it feels like more of a strain on me. David is great as a father, but I have no idea how to be a mother, Vern. It's like every time I get pregnant, I hope that the motherly instincts will finally come, but now I'm pregnant again, and I'm just dreading it."

When Veronica told me she was pregnant again for the third time, my heart dropped. It seemed as though she was incredibly fertile. In my mind, I cursed the heavens above, wondering how a woman who was so obviously ungrateful could continue to receive such blessings, while I could not. As Veronica went on, I started to realize, maybe Peter was not a bad man, just a sad one.

That night, just like old times, Nica and I stayed up talking, laughing, and reminiscing about our childhood. We recalled when our father gave us our very first beating, how Nica cried every time I was hit. She begged our father to hit her instead. She always hated seeing me cry, and seeing her sad always broke my heart. The night stretched on as we sat beside the cooling vent in the living room area by the kitchen. She gave me lovely compliments about the house.

By the time we got up to head back upstairs to the bedrooms, I remembered the broken glass all over the kitchen floor. I couldn't forget how Peter had behaved that morning. I helped Nica pass by the mess carefully, and I did the same.

As I reached for the banister to head upstairs, with Nica leading the way, we heard the front door open. I, being closest, called out, "Peter?"

He responded, "Yes."

I was surprised he had returned home.

Once inside, Nica stood by the fifth step, watching. He walked in wearing a tracksuit, though it was completely different from the one he had left the house in. He turned on the hallway light and immediately noticed Veronica standing on the staircase. He remained speechless, and an awkward tension filled the air. Shockingly, Peter and Veronica had never met. Given the circumstances, they could not have met at a worse time. Seeing the anger in my eyes as Peter stood next to me, staring at her with undeniable interest, Veronica extended her right arm, careful not to lose her balance on the stairs, and introduced herself.

He was smitten by her beauty, just like everyone else. I shook my head in disbelief. Even if he had found her attractive, I wished he had been a little more discreet about it.

"Hi, my name is Veronica, Vern's little sister. You must be Peter. Nice to meet you."

He did not extend his hand to meet hers. Instead, he simply said, "It's nice to meet you, too. Vern, can you and I have a word?"

Veronica and I exchanged an awkward glance, both surprised by his sudden request. She continued making her way upstairs while Peter and I headed toward the kitchen. Once again, I had completely forgotten about the broken dishes on the floor. When Peter turned on the light, he momentarily forgot why he had called me back there in the first place. His expression darkened with rage as he took in the mess. He turned to me, his voice sharp.

"What the hell, Vern? What happened in here?"

I remained silent, moving swiftly to the corner where I grabbed the broom and dustpan from the closet. As I made my way toward the sink to start sweeping up the glass, Peter did the unthinkable. He stopped me, placing both of his hands over mine, his head bowed in disappointment. Then, in a remorseful tone, he said, "I'm sorry."

My eyes widened.

"Sorry for what?"

I knew he had every reason to apologize, but I wasn't willing to accept it unless I was sure he knew why.

Looking directly into my eyes, he said, "I'm sorry for everything. For staying out late and not coming home. For treating you like my enemy when you're my wife—my beautiful wife. I love you so much, and I'm sorry. I know you've been trying so hard to make me happy, and I promise I'll make it up to you. Let me clean this up, honey. You go to bed. I'll be up in a minute."

I wasn't sure how to feel—relieved, confused, or even sad. What I did know was that, somehow, God had given me my husband back.

I did as Peter told me and headed upstairs to our bedroom. As I passed the guest room where I had settled Veronica, I noticed her peeking out and whispering for me to come closer.

Once by the doorway, she grinned and whispered, "Vern, you are so lucky! I've seen that man in pictures with David. I had no idea that's who you married."

I furrowed my brows, confused.

"Pictures? David?"

What could David possibly know about my husband?

I wanted to press Nica for answers, but I didn't have time. I heard Peter coming up the stairs, and before I knew it, he and I were both standing outside our bedroom. To avoid raising any suspicions, I simply told Nica,

"Goodnight."

That night, Peter and I made love again.

Over the next two weeks, things between Peter and me were great. He started cooking dinner for me again, just like old times, and even promised me a vacation to visit my parents. It felt good to have my husband back—I hadn't realized just how much I had missed him and his gracious personality. The fear I had of Nica and Peter meeting quickly faded when he treated her as nothing more than a sister-in-law.

He recalled stories my mother had told him about our childhood, often mentioning that she believed I was the wiser of the two of us. According to him, my mother's words reinforced the importance of marrying an ambitious woman—a quality he knew I possessed.

During those two weeks, Nica never mentioned David. He sent letter after letter, none of which she cared to open. She missed the holidays with her children and husband, even ringing in the New Year with Peter, me, and some of his coworkers. I hosted a small gathering, baking treats and singing holiday carols. She and I did the grocery shopping together. Being pregnant, she had quite the appetite, but she contributed financially to many of the household expenses. Because of this, Peter didn't mind her staying with us.

Nica dressed conservatively during her stay—mid-calf skirts, full-length blouses, and her hair always tied neatly in a ponytail, never left to flow freely. I appreciated that. She had always known how to attract the attention of any man, but she respected that Peter was mine. However, despite her conscious efforts to dress modestly, I still worried. I felt slightly intimidated, but I fought to remain confident that Peter would never betray me in such a way.

Aside from her insistence that she wasn't prepared for a family, Nica and I never discussed the real reason she had left her marriage. Instead, we enjoyed each other's company—baking, watching television, modeling old clothes, and my personal favorite, shopping. Nica had expensive taste. I couldn't afford to spend money as freely as she did, but I enjoyed going along for support. She introduced me to new designers, trending styles, and even helped me pick out a negligee.

On Sunday morning, Peter and I went out for lunch at a nearby coffeehouse within walking distance of our home. Nica didn't join us, preferring to have time to herself, which she called "meditating." By the time we returned home, Peter asked if I would mind him going into the office to finish an article for Tuesday's paper. I agreed, appreciating how much he had changed.

When Peter and I decided to work things out, he reduced his work hours, adjusting his schedule to only four days a week. Ultimately, this made me happy, but the reduction in hours also brought changes to our finances.

By the third week, David arrived unexpectedly.

Stepping onto the stoop, an uneasy feeling washed over me. As I turned the key in the lock, I heard my name.

"Vernette!"

Immediately, I froze.

I knew that voice anywhere.

It was David.

When I pushed the door open, I saw Nica standing at the bottom of the staircase—as if expecting us, her left hand resting atop the banister. She wore a tall, solid black dress that reached her ankles, her growing stomach lifting the fabric slightly in the front. Her waist-length hair hung freely around her face, wild and unkempt. Without a word, she pushed me slightly away from the door.

At that moment, David and I stood face to face. He stepped onto the stoop and thrust the front door open.

"Nica, you and I have to talk!" he demanded, his voice sharp and unyielding.

Nonchalantly, she turned to me. "Vern, please give us some privacy." Her eyes then shifted to David, her hands steady and unwavering.

I hesitated but chose to leave the front door area, running up the stairs. Just before reaching the top, I stopped and listened.

David wasted no time pleading with my baby sister, but she remained apathetic.

"Sweetheart, the kids need you home. I need you. Whatever has happened, I promise I'll fix it. I swear, Nica, baby, I'll do anything. I just need you to come home—"

"David, no. You're weak," she interrupted coldly. "Where's the man who defied rules, the man who knew no bounds? You're a simple idiot. I don't need an idiot; I need a man!"

"What the hell are you talking about? I ain't no idiot. Veronica, I told you about talking to me like this!"

"Then do something about it! Hit me! Yell! Get angry! Show me you give a damn when you're not swimming between my legs! All you want to do is hug, laugh, and love. You are weak!"

"Veronica, stop it! For goodness' sake, stop it! We're a family now—there are kids involved—"

"Those things you call children are death! They're sucking me dry. We don't need love—I have enough of it. I don't need it from you, too."

"This isn't you talking. Clearly, you're the one changing. What do you want from me?"

"I want defiance. Freedom. A life without rules. You think you can make me into some loving housewife and mother? David, you don't know me. With each child, I lose myself, and I'm starting to go crazy."

"Lose yourself how? What are you talking about? Please, Veronica, I lo—"

"Don't you dare say it! Don't you dare tell me you love me! It's pathetic."

What happened next made my eyes widen in horror.

David began to bleed from his nose. Blood trickled down from both nostrils as he staggered, grabbing the doorframe for support. His eyes stretched wide in panic, one hand clutching the wood, the other pressed firmly against his face to stop the bleeding.

Veronica remained impassive.

I rushed past her, placing my hands atop David's head, tilting it back, trying to help. But when I turned to look at her, I froze.

Her eyes were blood-red. Veins pulsed along her arms, visible beneath her skin. She looked like a demon standing before me.

Terror gripped me so tightly that I hadn't realized I was squeezing David's head, making his pain even worse.

"Vern, let me go, please!" he begged, his voice muffled. "Please, I can't breathe!"

I remained in a trance until the sound of a police siren snapped me back to reality.

Veronica fled to the kitchen, her gown swaying behind her. From the foyer, I heard her gasping, struggling for air.

David tore himself from my grip. Without looking back, he ran down the stoop steps, past the little black gate, and into his vehicle.

I tried to chase after him, but an unseen force yanked me back inside. Before I could react, the front doors slammed shut on their own.

Above me, the light bulb exploded, plunging the room into darkness.

Night had not yet fallen, and for that, I was grateful. The thought of now being alone in my home with Veronica unsettled me. It was strange—I had long understood that her presence meant spiritual warfare. Yet, some part of me could not bear to be away from her. When things were good, they were great. But when things were bad, they were demonic. Still, it wasn't enough to make me abandon her.

Slowly, she emerged from the kitchen, her eyes downcast.

"Is he gone?" she asked.

As she approached me, I instinctively cowered, creeping back toward the front door, my eyes never leaving her. She now stood in the center of the hallway.

My nose suddenly felt wet. Then, my eyes began to water.

I wiped my nose and froze at the sight of blood smeared across my hands. My body trembled, and a soft whimper escaped my lips. I looked up—Veronica was gone.

"Nica!" I called out.

Silence.

I called her name again and again, my voice growing more desperate, but there was no response. Heart pounding, I ran to the kitchen and turned on the faucet, splashing water onto my face. Still no sign of her. Not a sound, not even a whisper.

I watched as the blood swirled down the drain. I tried to clean my hands, but no matter how much I scrubbed, I kept leaving smudged fingerprints across the counter. Frustrated, I grabbed the kitchen towel and wiped my hands vigorously.

Then, I broke down.

My sister was something beyond my understanding. Something unknown.

I began reciting a quiet prayer in my mind.

Just then, the house trembled slightly. Dust fell from the ceiling. That's when I realized—she had never left.

A shiver ran through me as I turned toward the stairs.

Moving cautiously, I ascended, step by step, my hands empty, my face now clean.

Softly, I called out, "Nica?"

"Yes," she answered, her voice eerily calm.

A chill crept up my spine.

I called her name again. "Nica, where are you?"

I already knew the answer. She could only be in one place—the bedroom she had been occupying for the past three weeks.

But still, I hesitated before entering.

With a trembling hand, I pushed the door open slightly. My breath caught in my throat.

Veronica sat by the closet door, her arms folded, her gaze locked on something unseen.

Her voice, guttural and distant, filled the room.

"She's in me now."

Her eyes snapped to mine.

At that exact moment, the house phone rang, shattering the eerie silence.

I gasped and bolted to my bedroom, snatching up the receiver with shaking hands.

"Hello?"

"Vern, sweetie, hi. It's your father."

His voice was weary.

I took a deep breath, relieved to hear him. Not just because I had missed him—but because his voice grounded me, pulling me away from the terror creeping into my mind. I collapsed onto my mattress, still trembling.

"Hi, Daddy."

"Vern, honey, I have something to tell you."

"Okay, but—I have something to tell you, too. Maybe you should go first."

A heavy pause.

"Your Grandmother Martin passed away yesterday. Polio." His voice cracked. "I've been trying to reach Nica, but I haven't been able to get a hold of her. Have you spoken to her?"

Before I could even respond, Veronica appeared in my bedroom doorway.

Arms folded.

Eyes burning.

She knew.

She knew what our father had just told me.

Her expression told a story. A story filled with rage.

I swallowed hard, my voice barely above a whisper. "I'm sorry."

Grandma Martin had meant more to Veronica than she had to me. And though I hadn't fully processed the news, I knew this loss had shattered her.

On the other end of the line, my father hesitated. "Vern, sweetie, I know you must be sad. Your mother is pretty shaken up, too. We just got the news last night. As for the funeral arrangements—"

"There will be no funeral," Veronica interjected.

Her voice was malevolent.

Her eyes shifted.

Then—she was gone.

Vanished.

"There will be no funeral," he continued.

A single tear slipped down my cheek.

I squeezed my eyes shut.

Something was wrong.

As much as I wanted to tell my father what had happened between Veronica and David, I couldn't. I didn't even know where to begin, or how to explain any of it.

I knew my mother wouldn't be in any state to talk, so I didn't ask to speak with her. As far as I was concerned, the conversation was over.

"I love you, Daddy," I whispered.

"I love you too, sweetie. Please don't forget to let your sister know."

"I will."

And just like that, the call ended.

I crept slowly to my bedroom door, pushing it until I heard a click, ensuring it was locked. Climbing into bed, I curled into the fetal position, forcing myself to sleep.

By three in the morning, I was still awake. My mind raced, Peter once again occupying my thoughts. Amongst everything else, he was out late—again. I sat upright in bed, my room engulfed in darkness. I refused to illuminate anything around me.

Thud. Thud. Thud.

Three loud bangs came from the guestroom. I flinched at each sound, too afraid to investigate. My mind conjured up all sorts of possibilities. Was Nica trying to hurt herself? I shuddered at the thought but remained frozen in place.

Thud. Thud. Thud.

Three more deafening bangs sent a chill down my spine. I finally stood and rushed to the guestroom. The door was locked. Fumbling with the handle, I called out, "Nica, is everything okay?"

Then, I heard it.

A man's voice—deep, groggy, almost demonic.

"Stop it! You are hur-ting- me."

Goosebumps ran up my arms. I pressed my ear to the door, whispering, "Nica?" My heart pounded as I glanced down the staircase. Everything around me was pitch black. I wasn't alone. I could feel it.

THUD!

The final bang sent me stumbling back. Suddenly, the voices multiplied—two, three, all speaking at once.

"You are hurting me."

"The hurt is inevitable."

"Huuurrrtttttt!" one voice shrieked.

Panicked, I banged on the door, my fists relentless, knuckles raw. Finally, the door swung open.

Nica stood before me, rubbing her eyes.

"Hey, Vern… are you okay?" She yawned, confused. It was obvious my banging had woken her.

Stuttering, I asked, "W-were you banging your head against the wall? Was someone in there with you?"

She chuckled. "No, why would I do that? And no, I'm alone."

I scanned her face, her arms, her hands, her knees— searching for bruises. She frowned, watching me. "Vern, what are you looking for?"

I ignored her questions and gently pushed back her hair. That's when I saw it—a large, open gash on the far left of her head. My breath hitched. I reached out, touching it lightly. She winced, grabbing my wrist.

"How did I get that?" she whispered, her voice trembling.

I had no answers. The only logical explanation was that she had been sleepwalking.

Leading her into my room, I retrieved the first aid kit from the bathroom. As I cleaned her wound, she sat silently, her expression distant. I carefully placed gauze over the cut, securing it with surgical tape.

"Do you really think I was sleepwalking?" she asked finally.

"That's the only logical answer, Nica."

Tears welled in her eyes. "What if I hurt the baby, Vern?"

I stiffened, recalling her earlier conversation with David. My stomach twisted. "I thought you weren't too thrilled about the idea of children anymore, Nica?"

Her eyes widened. "What? No! I love my kids... even this one." She placed a hand on her stomach, stroking it tenderly.

I watched her, my own sanity unraveling. Did any of it really happen? The voices, the banging, the wound on her head? As she gazed at her stomach, so full of adoration, I began to doubt myself.

The next few days passed in a blur. Neither Nica nor I mentioned that night again.

My father continued calling about Grandma Martin's funeral arrangements. Grandpa Martin carried on with his business as if her death meant nothing. My mother, exhausted by the constant inquiries into medical histories and illnesses, expedited the cremation. She refused to attend.

Nica didn't feel compelled to go. Neither did I.

Before we knew it, two months had come and gone. The Spring breeze blowing against our skin. Veronica had not experienced any more episodes, and I had managed to avoid any further hallucinations. Her stomach continued to grow, the baby kicking more than ever. This excited us—excited me. Nearing thirty, I had begun to think I would never know what it felt like to witness pregnancy up close, so I cherished those moments.

Sadly, with each of Nica's pregnancies, there had always been tension between us. This time, I was determined to change that. I wanted to be there for her every step of the way.

David continued calling and writing letters, many of which I responded to, assuring him that Nica was safe with Peter and me. He worried constantly, with Lucinda raising the children while he worked. I had even suggested that she bring them by one afternoon. Though hesitant, she eventually agreed. Matthew, now almost two, and Ebony, just six months old, needed their mother. Nica was truly happy, though she remained unsure of the baby's sex. We had no idea what to call it. She loved the names Jordan for a boy and Elise for a girl.

By now, Nica and I had developed a daily routine. Each morning, we woke to the smell of breakfast prepared by Peter before he left for work. Afternoons were spent indulging in trashy talk shows and home cooking networks. By evening, we had napped, refreshed ourselves, and immersed ourselves in domestic activities—knitting, sewing, cleaning, and preparing dinner. Nica handled most of the baking while I prepared the meals this time around. I had grown so accustomed to this life. I loved having her with me. I enjoyed her company, our conversations, and our shared routines.

One morning, while savoring the delicious breakfast Peter had made for us, I suddenly remembered the home videos stored in the attic. I had wanted to watch them for so long. The moment I mentioned them to Veronica, she shoved her plate aside and bolted upstairs toward the attic.

I hadn't planned on watching videos that day. Grocery shopping still needed to be done. But she insisted.

For hours, we struggled to assemble the projector I had purchased, completely clueless about what we were doing. What should have been a simple task took nearly four hours to complete.

By the time we finished, everything else had faded into the background.

We forgot about dinner.

We forgot about everything.

We lost ourselves.

The first video, *Birthing an Angel*, was dedicated to me. By the way my father handled his Rolleiflex classic twin-lens video camcorder, it was clear he was brimming with excitement—though his inexperience was just as evident. He documented everything, from the moment they left the house to their arrival at the segregated hospital's emergency room. My mother practiced her breathing as she was wheeled up to pediatrics.

"Today is the day I become a daddy!" My father turned to face the lens, grinning from ear to ear. Watching him on film, we could feel his excitement. I chuckled—it made me feel so good to see him that happy.

By the time my mother began pushing, she was in immense pain. My father turned the camera toward himself once more. "No cameras allowed in the delivery room. Be back when she's here." The screen went black.

Moments later, the camera switched on again, capturing me inside a bassinet, wrapped in a pink cotton blanket. My name was scribbled on a tag just outside the glass. *Vernette Robinson.* I chuckled again, watching my tiny hands wiggle from side to side, my toes curl, and then—just as I let out a big yawn—my father let out a scream.

"Did you see that, baby doll? My, oh my, we make some pretty babies! She has my eyes."

Both of my parents chuckled before my mother, exhausted, turned over and drifted into a deep sleep. The video ended.

"Vern, you were so cute!" Veronica leaned over, squeezing me tightly.

I was getting thirsty. "Do you want some water?"

Her expression answered before she spoke.

"Do you have any wine?" she asked.

I chuckled. "No, Nica, you're pregnant. No alcohol."

She pouted, sinking into the sofa. "Vern, you have no idea what it's like to have babies back-to-back. It feels like I'm always pregnant—like I've forgotten how to have fun."

Despite her comment stinging a little—I had long since convinced myself that I would never know what it felt like to be pregnant—I tried not to let it get to me. I knew she meant no harm.

Still, I went ahead and poured myself a glass of wine, grabbing a bottle of spring water for Nica. When I returned and tossed the bottle into her lap, she shot me a bewildered look. I chuckled, taking a slow sip—teasing her, almost.

"Hmm, that was good. What's next?"

"I swear, Vern, if you weren't my sister, I'd pour this water all over you. Matter of fact—who cares? We grown now. Daddy ain't here to give us no whopping."

Immediately, she turned, giggling as she emptied the bottle over my head. My hair, face, clothes, and couch were drenched—my wine now completely diluted. We laughed so hard that night; I couldn't believe she had actually done that.

I bolted, running away as she chased me into the kitchen. She turned the faucet on, cupping water in her palms before flinging it at my face. Not wanting to leave a mess trailing through the house, I decided to fight back. We were shouting, laughing, and having an amazing time. I reached into the fridge, grabbed two more water bottles, twisted off the caps, and prepared for my revenge. Moments later, we collapsed in a huge puddle of water—neither of us wanting to clean it up.

I rested my head on Nica's shoulder, still laughing. We were both out of breath.

Just then, Peter arrived home, startling us as he flicked on the kitchen light.

"You two sure know how to make a mess."

Neither of us moved. We sat there, backs pressed against the kitchen cabinet beneath the sink, my clothes still soaking as water continued seeping through them. Peter quickly grabbed some bread, butter, and a knife before exiting just as fast, leaving Nica and me to our chaos.

Finally, I decided to stand. Nica extended both arms, signaling for me to help her up. I pulled and pulled, praying she wouldn't slip in the water. When she was finally on her feet, I told her to go get changed while I cleaned up. She refused, insisting that she had started the mess.

For about a minute, we went back and forth, but she looked exhausted. Cleaning wasn't something I wanted her to worry about, so I insisted. Finally, she relented and disappeared upstairs.

Once I finished mopping, sweeping, and wiping everything down, I rolled my jogging pants up my legs and took long strides toward the stairs, careful not to leave any water trails. Peter was already fast asleep. I showered, then changed into one of his oversized t-shirts, a pair of tennis shorts, and socks. Rubbing some hair oil along my scalp, I tiptoed toward Nica's door and knocked quietly.

She, too, was fast asleep.

I refused to wake her, so I made my way back downstairs to the living room, where I decided to watch the rest of the home videos. Pouring myself another glass of red wine, I settled in, watching in amazement.

Cradle with Vern.

"Clive, honey, if you don't get that camera out of my face…"

My parents had a nursery all set up for me in what appeared to be the bedroom next to theirs. The walls were painted fuchsia pink with an animal-printed border. An all-white changing table stood against the wall, accompanied by a tiny mirror. The table had built-in drawers, and beside it sat a large brown cradle—handcrafted, vintage, of course—along with a wooden rocking horse.

"Baby, you know I gotta capture every moment now. I'm just a man in love with his family," my father said, circling my mother and me. She appeared to be breastfeeding me, a light-yellow towel draped over my face. I guessed he wanted a better shot.

Teasing, she said, "You about confused, that's what you are." She kept rocking back and forth. "One minute, you a cop. Next minute, you Alfred Hitchcock. What you the master of now? Neonatal care?"

I laughed so hard. My mother was quite the joker.

"Now, you go on with all that teasing. I love watching you be a momma. You take beautiful care of just about everything."

"You always know what to say."

"I always save my best for you."

Smiling, my mother pulled my father closer, kissing him tenderly. He placed the camera on the floor, kneeling as he felt around for the power button and shut it off.

I refilled my glass, removed the reel, and loaded another. Although the films were short, they were captivating and emotional. The sound of the projector reel was loud—I prayed I wasn't disturbing them…

The next film was titled *Daddy Clive*.

It opened with my father standing above me, lifting my arms over my head in the park. He looked as though he was trying to teach me how to walk for the first time.

"You have to let her go, baby. How else she gonna learn?"

My father refused. "I don't want her falling now."

"Clive, they're going to fall—only so they can get back up. Let her go, baby, please."

My mother continued filming, while my father hesitated. Then, finally, he let me go.

I took four good steps before falling onto my backside.

My mother became hysterical. The camera lens zoomed in and out, shaking slightly as she laughed and squealed, "My baby walking! Clive, she walking!"

"That's not all our baby girl can do. Say 'Daddy,' Vern. Go on, say 'Daddy.' You said it for me yesterday."

My father sat by a tree trunk, placing me between his legs. He clapped his hands together, pleading, "Go on, baby girl, say 'Daddy'—"

I only laughed, patting my legs. I stared into the camera, then at my mother, then at my father, before finally saying, "Da-Da."

Once again, my parents erupted with joy. They were laughing, kissing, smiling.

"No, no, not fair—you gotta say 'Mommy' now, Vern!"

I had no idea why everyone was so ecstatic, but their excitement made me laugh right along with them.

My mother refused to film any longer. Pouting, she said, "You taught her that, Clive. No fair."

My father pulled her close, kissing her forehead, then kissing me. He held us both under that tree just as the film flickered and shut down.

I refilled my glass, telling myself I would watch only one more before bed. And I did.

I reached for the next video, the one titled *Green Trees*.

"Clive, baby, looks like we're having another girl!"

My mother exited her midwife's office. The year was 1929, holiday season. By then, childbirth had undergone a complete social transformation. It was considered a pathological process, one in which only a small minority of women escaped damage during labor.

Although excited, my father's tone carried a trace of fear for my mother. He also sounded slightly disappointed—clearly, he had hoped for a son. But he remained supportive. After receiving the news, he kissed my mother all over. Her midwife had told them she was five months along and that the baby was healthy and kicking.

"Everything looks great. I'll see you both in about two months for another checkup," the midwife reassured them.

My father kept the camera rolling all the way home. They hollered for a taxicab, and once inside, my mother began rubbing her stomach apprehensively. Her thick winter coat made it almost impossible to see her growing belly, but she was huge.

When they arrived home, my father placed the camera on the kitchen counter nearest the sink, capturing a view of the table closest to the hallway doorframe. My mother took a seat, spreading her legs slightly as she lowered herself slowly. She hadn't turned to face the camera—it seemed as though she had no idea it was even there.

Removing her jacket, sweater, and scarf, she exposed her stomach. Oddly, she glanced around the room, as if making sure no one else was present. Then, lifting her shirt, the scene shifted from affectionate to horrifying.

Her belly was covered in bruises—some fresh, deep blue and black, while others had begun to fade into a dull purple.

I sat upright on the sofa, my breath hitching. I could not believe my eyes. Tears welled as I watched my mother in the film, clearly in pain.

She leaned back in the chair, rubbing her stomach once more. Then, closing her eyes, she whispered,

"My little green tree, if you can hear Mommy, I want you to know that I love you very much. You are going to be healthy, beautiful, and strong. I pray that God continues to watch over you—"

Suddenly, she began to twitch, her pain intensifying. She bellowed for my father. He appeared within seconds, grabbing hold of her right hand as she squeezed it tightly. His sharp cry echoed in the room.

"Clive, Clive! I think I'm having contractions! Clive!"

She kept shouting his name, over and over again. My father quickly reassured her, his voice trembling, that everything would be okay. Amid her agony, she managed to utter,

"Where is Vernette?"

"She's with Nessy," my father answered quickly. That name did not ring a bell.

He dialed the midwife. After a brief conversation, he helped my mother to her feet and guided her out of the kitchen. Their figures disappeared from view, marking the end of the footage.

"Are you watching the videos without me?"

Veronica's voice startled me.

The pitch-black room was no place to see shadows or hear voices without an obvious source. Nica sounded shocked—and angry. I moved quickly, shutting down the reel and returning the films to their boxes.

"No, no. I just couldn't sleep, and I didn't want to wake you."

"But we were supposed to be watching them together, Vern."

She rolled her eyes, clearly bothered that I had gone through our family memories without her. Something weighed heavily on my heart, though—something I wanted to share with her.

"Nica, when Mommy was pregnant with you, she had these weird bruises on her stomach. Did she ever tell you about that?"

Veronica, pretending not to hear me, reached into the refrigerator and pulled out a bottle of water. As she walked away, she responded sternly,

"No, she never told me anything."

Guilt crept in. I felt as if I had betrayed her somehow.

Despite her disinterest, I called after her anyway, "We can re-watch them tomorrow morning!"

Instead of responding, I heard her bedroom door slam shut.

Once upstairs, I noticed Peter wasn't in bed. The clock read 4:54 AM. I had no idea it was so late, and when I heard the shower turn on, I couldn't understand why Peter would be up this early. I decided not to pry; I simply didn't have the energy to. The lights remained off. I began removing my clothing, my shorts falling to the floor, just as a cool breeze blew past my ankles. I knew I had hallucinated—the breeze felt something like a draft. I decided not to dwell on the thought while removing my shirt.

That's when I felt the breeze blow again. This time, it lasted about nine seconds. I stumbled to the left and then to the right, the breeze still blowing.

Without thinking, I fell to my knees, lifting the bed skirt. What I saw caused me to quiver. It appeared to be some kind of black hole. The breeze picked up, now breathing, and then a hand reached out, grabbing my right forearm. The arm was skeletal, with long, pointed fingernails. I tried my best to pull away, but the force holding me retained a firm grip. My arm began to bleed, my eyes watered, and my head was now being pulled.

Multiple arms extended from the black hole. I opened my mouth to scream. My eyes widened with fear, but no words, no sounds, left my mouth. I cried, tugging away, my left arm desperately trying to break free, my head firmly gripped by whatever this thing was—its force trying to rip my body in half.

Just as I managed to pull away, I shouted, "Jesus!" as loud as I could. Peter stood watching me from the bathroom door, a towel wrapped around his lower body and another towel patting his hair dry. He watched in amazement as his paranoid wife patted and banged on the floorboards beneath the bed. The hole simply vanished.

I stood quickly, tears in my eyes.

I put my hands together, praying he didn't think I was crazy. My mouth was moving, but no words escaped. I stood there, stuttering. Peter remained perfectly still, watching me as though he had just seen a ghost. Finally, he shouted,

"Vern! What's gotten into you?"

Goosebumps raced up my arms. I could not speak. Finally, I looked down at my right arm, only to see an imprint of five fingers burned into my flesh. Immediately, I fainted.

"Vern, hey! You're up."

Nica sat by my bedside, her hands rubbing up and down my shoulders. I turned to face the clock. 8:47 AM. I'd barely gotten any sleep. I rubbed my neck and eyes.

"What happened?"

She removed her hands from mine. "I don't know, but when I heard Peter leaving this morning, he asked me to keep an eye on you. He said you fainted earlier."

I remained skeptical. "Fainted? There's no way."

To be honest, I was feeling a bit disoriented and had almost no recollection of what had taken place earlier. Completely unsure of why, I suddenly became agitated. Placing her hand atop mine once more, I sat upright, preparing to get out of bed. Before I knew it, Veronica and I were quarreling.

"No! Don't touch me! Just… God, I can't do this anymore." I felt a rush of emotions run through me. My mind was fueled with anger as Nica went into defense mode.

"Do what, Vern? What's the matter?"

I kept telling myself over and over, I can't deny the strange occurrences, the lying, the pretending, and trying to ignore that everything is all right. Blinded by my own resentment and misunderstanding, I began to shout at my baby sister.

"This, all this pretending. It's like every time I'm around you, I have these terrible nightmares and visions of women blowing dust in my face, or—"

Immediately, Nica interrupted me. It was as though I had triggered her somehow.

"Vern, no, shut up! You don't get to blame me for that. No one does!"

Finally, I stood. "I'm not blaming you, I'm simply stating facts. Every time you come around, Nica, this happens. It can't all be a coincidence."

Nica was now pacing back and forth, her hands caressing her pregnant belly, before she paused. She said,

"You're such a coward and so selfish. All you do is make everything about you. Well, what about me? Don't you think I'm scared too?"

In that moment, I wasn't accepting her attempt to play the victim. I didn't want to. I had a burn on my arm that was hurting all too much from an unknown spirit with no answers as to why. I was in no mood to feel sympathetic.

"How the hell am I supposed to know, Nica? You don't open up to me about anything. About your religion, your beliefs… it's almost as though you don't believe in anything."

"It's not that I don't believe, I just don't know how to. Your *higher power*—He has no control anymore." This was no longer my sister speaking to me. I could feel it.

"Well, you need to control it; it's driving me crazy."

I wanted the conversation to end. I wanted us to go back to being happy. I had vented, so I was no longer angry. Now, I was fearful. She had this look in her eyes— a look I had not come to know.

She continued her rampage, "There you go blaming me! Take some damn responsibility, Vernette! We were supposed to have gone in together, and don't make this all about my presence. I've been here for months now, and you haven't complained about anything unusual—like skeletons coming out of the ground or dust being flicked into your face."

Her words, her tone, were all indications that I was indeed in imminent danger. I hadn't mentioned anything to her about what I believed had tried to grab me into the ground, nor had I mentioned anything to Peter. So I thought—how could she have known what I had seen? I had no intention of setting her off any further. I remained calm, exclaiming,

"Because I've been trying to ignore it. I've been trying to tell myself that maybe I'm imagining things. That is me taking responsibility, but I'm tired of feeling like I'm going through psychosis. Not to mention, you and I, as children, did everything together." Unintentionally, I triggered her again.

"We didn't do that! You let me go by myself, just like the time you left me with those boys. You were—and you are—always leaving me, and then you wonder why we're so distant and so different…ugh."

Abruptly, she stopped speaking and began making her way out of my bedroom. I should have let her go.

Instead, I followed her, angered that she was not willing to let go of the past.

"No, no, you don't get to do that, don't dismiss me. Are you seriously saying that because I didn't protect you, you ended up hurt? Jesus, Nica, give me a break."

She stopped, her head turning slowly. "You think this is still a game, don't you? If you want to survive this, then stop fighting it."

I knew that wasn't my sister talking—her voice had changed, and her tone was sinister. Still, I couldn't help myself. I wanted answers. Whatever was inside of her was also inside of my home.

"Where are you going? Nica, get back here!"

But I was too late. She had already made her way into her bedroom, locking the door behind her. Just then, Peter emerged from the staircase.

"Vern, what's going on? I could hear you both screaming from outside." Deciding to walk away from her door, Peter and I made our way back into our bedroom.

"Veronica and I just had a terrible fight; I honestly don't feel like speaking to anyone right now." So we didn't speak to one another. I proceeded to straighten our bed, first removing the pillows decorating it as Peter made his way into the bathroom.

"I understand, sweetheart, but if you two are going to fight, then just argue—don't let it get physical to the point where you're both breaking things." He pointed to the cabinet mirror hanging above our sink basin. Never once had Nica and I been physical with one another, so I was definitely curious as to what he was referring to. I decided to take a look for myself. What I saw caused me to tremble—a long gash in the center of the cabinet mirror.

"What… what are you talking about? Oh my God. We didn't touch anything in here, let alone break the glass. It didn't even shatter!"

Peter and I exchanged a look of horror. It wasn't long before Nica appeared, smiling from ear to ear, caressing her pregnant stomach, frightening us both.

Cheerfully, she asked, "Peter, do you want to watch some old videos with us?"

My eyes widened. Peter respectfully declined. He mentioned he would be leaving soon for a meeting and that he had only returned briefly to check on me. I did not object. I had no more room in my mind to question his infidelity or even entertain the mere thought of it.

For weeks, I stayed as far away from Nica as I could. When she was upstairs, I would head down to the foyer, kitchen, or dining room. If she came down to the kitchen, I stepped lightly upstairs to my bedroom, where I kept the door closed at all times throughout the day. Things were awkward. I knew she felt it, but had no desire to confront me about it. I had no clue what to say or how to react. I just wanted to understand what was happening to her. Slowly, I felt myself losing interest in prayer, God, or believing that He was my savior, because how could the ones I love be suffering so much around me?

By mid-May, Nica and I were becoming more distant. She visited the doctor without me. Oddly enough, as the weather began to break, David started stopping by far more frequently. Some days, Nica allowed him the chance to sit outside with her on the stoop and speak to their unborn child. I felt bad for David. He looked so wearisome. He was tired of having to act as a single parent to their two children while watching from afar as their third developed into its third trimester. I felt so ashamed. I could not watch any longer as Nica remained nonchalant while he rubbed, cooed, and tickled her pregnant stomach.

She appeared cold and distant. Walking away, I heard David violently shout, "What do you want from me!?" in the distance. I immediately made my way back to the window, but I wasn't quick enough. Nica was already making her way back inside. She and I exchanged a glance before she continued to saunter past me up to her bedroom. As David stepped inside, I confronted him.

"What's going on?"

"Nothing, Vern. This isn't your fight. You shouldn't have been involved in the first place." I could have slapped him for speaking to me as though I were just an intrusive family friend. We were both being affected by Veronica, albeit in different ways, but we had more in common when it came to her than he was willing to admit.

"Sometimes I think you forget my position in her life, David. First, assaulting me, then threatening to have me committed? Has it ever occurred to you that maybe she isn't in love with you anymore—"

"Goddamn it, Vernette, don't feed me that bullshit! You and I both know she has a family to take care of, and yet here you are, lonely and miserable. You keep her harbored up in here, living like a pair of sorority sisters."

"Don't yell at me! David, stop! You have no right. I have no idea why she left, so don't pin that on me. Maybe if you were half a man, she would have more respect for you. Who knows, maybe she left to allow you to actually raise the children you create. Let's face it, you're good at training sperm swimmers, but when they make it to the finish line, you aren't there handing out trophies!"

"Hey, you and your smart mouth! I am not the problem; you would do well to remember that. Granted, I wasn't smart enough to fall for a woman who wasn't your next of kin, but that son of a bitch you went ahead and married, he's just smarter—" I froze. David was not the same person. This was not the gentle man I once knew. This David was far more hostile, arrogant, and patronizing. What was he trying to imply? Did he confirm my suspicions—Peter was having an affair? How would he know?

"Stop it! David, please go," Veronica shouted.

What started as a simple conversation escalated into a screaming match right there in my foyer.

"Nica, no, gosh, I'm so sorry. I need you to come home, baby. I promise things will be different. I'll be home more. The kids miss you. Please!" He pleaded, Veronica, standing atop the stairs.

"Just go. I'll be home in the morning."

I continued to stand by the door, pondering. The feud between David and me came to an abrupt end. He reluctantly gathered his thoughts, his pride bruised, and drifted sadly out the front door. Slamming the door behind him, I turned to face my sister.

"You knew and didn't tell me?" Tears filled my eyes, fighting the urge to scream. Still, I remained composed.

"How could I? Would you really have wanted to hear that from me?"

She was right. The first time I had a man taken from me, Nica was the other woman. At that point, I had no clue how I would have reacted had the other woman told me about there being another woman in the life of a man I was involved with, this time, that man being my husband.

I did the one thing I could think to do: I blamed myself.

"What's wrong with me? Am I not beautiful enough? I mean, why does this keep happening to me? Why would you say I was lucky to be with him? I mean, if he's cheating on me, how is that luck in your eyes?"

She sighed, motioning for us to sit along the staircase. With my arms folded, I walked over, like a pouting child. Placing her head on my shoulder, she said, "Mommy prepared us for this. She spent our entire childhood preparing us for the men we'd encounter in our lives. The cheaters, the abusers, and the liars, all disguised as providers. Traditional modern men we could never escape from."

I disagreed. "She never prepared us for this, Nica. What are you talking about? If I was prepared, then why am I so surprised?"

"Because, Vern, you were always so focused on trying to be an equal that you didn't know when to be submissive. We're women, and women were created to serve their husbands. I said you're lucky because your husband loves you—that's clear to even the blindest of folk. He's just sad."

"You sound like Mom."

"I told you, she prepared us."

Maybe Veronica was right; my mother did show us the warning signs very early on. During this time, nearing the sixties, women still weren't equals, no matter what the law said.

"Hell, we can't even get a credit card without the men in our lives, not even earn decent wages in the workplace," Veronica joked.

But it wasn't a joke. It was just a harsh reality. No one respected us, not even the men we laid with. Veronica and I were beginning to get along again.

"I understand you're frightened as a mother, but why leave him? Why now?"

Veronica sat upright. Looking into my eyes, she responded, "You remember that morning when you and I awoke and he hit you?" I nodded.

"Did you even wonder how it was so easy for him to have done that? I mean, without even an ounce of hesitation. He just...hit you."

I hadn't given that day much thought after everything transpired. But she raised a good point—or was she manipulating me? She didn't know I had heard her speaking to him that day...provoking him.

"Does David hit you?" I humbly asked, nervous about her answer. The second she fixed her lips to speak, I felt my heart skip a beat. She's the division. It was starting to become clear to me.

"We've all made mistakes. Also, I think I will leave in the morning. Let's go watch the rest of the videos!"

I wanted to shout, scream, throw, and destroy things. Seeing the look of anger on my face, Veronica stood, her dress gracefully flowing behind her as she swung around the banister, making her way toward the kitchen, blissfully smiling. Deciding to dismiss my thoughts, I complied.

We began watching the next film, *Hello Nica.*

"Her nose is so tiny, her hands, feet, and uh, she looks just like you, Barb," said a woman wearing a calf-length, pink pastel daytime dress. She didn't look familiar. Her hair was long and dark, her eyes a soft gray, and her features slightly resembled those of our Grandmother Martin.

"Who is that woman?" Veronica asked.

"I have no idea," I replied. We continued watching, hoping that either of our parents would provide some insight. The woman stood over Veronica while gripping my hand firmly.

"What will you call her?" she asked.

My father spoke with glee. "See, Nessy, that's where we're both confused. I like Veronica, but Barb here likes Victoria. Now, what do you say? Don't she look like a Veronica?"

"Oh, no, this is not fair! You both outnumber me," our mother said, chuckling as the woman continued to massage her gently. The delivery room was packed with African American women, and the sounds of women in labor resonated throughout the halls. Every now and then, my father had to place the recorder down, careful not to capture footage of the wrong woman.

"Now, now," said Nessy. "She can pass for a Veronica—call her Nica for short. The Vicky ain't for our color."

My father laughed hysterically, and Nica, sitting beside me, chuckled as well.

"I guess you both win," my mother muttered.

"Now, now, puss, don't be like that. You know me and Ness just pulling ya leg."

"I just gave birth, Clive. To pull my leg now would be a form of torture," my mother teased.

"Oh, Veronica, Veronica, can we hold her once you're done?" my father asked the nurse.

The room was so crowded. The bassinet was close to the bed, and my mother stretched her arm to fix the blankets inside. But the nurses were still working on Nica, tubes running to and from her arms.

"Yes, sir. Once we finish, she'll be all yours."

An anxious toddler, I ripped my hand away from Nessy and ran over to the bassinet to take a look at my baby sister. Afraid I was up to no good, Nessy grabbed me just before I could reach it.

"Oh no, little Vern, you need to keep yourself calm."

My mother insisted that Nessy place me atop her bed, and she did. Holding my hand, my father took several steps back, capturing us in the entire frame. Nessy stood beside the nurse while my mother lay on her cot, cradling me as she fixed the barrettes in my hair.

"My family is beautiful," my father could be heard saying. The video ended soon after.

"Daddy is so silly," Nica said.

I was still curious about our conversation from earlier.

"Nica, are you really going home in the morning?"

"Do you want me to stay?" she asked seductively.

My eyes widened because I knew where this was going. Sinful thoughts entered my mind, and I panicked, quickly pulling myself out of them.

"No, no, it's best that you go home. The kids… they need you. David was right," I said.

I scurried into the kitchen, standing in front of the sink, gathering my thoughts. But the lustful thoughts—the idea of kissing her, palming her breasts, massaging her clitoris—kept weaving in and out of my mind. I could tell she had the same thoughts as she made her way closer, pressing her stomach against my back. Her right palm reached around to caress my belly as she kissed my right ear tenderly.

Just then, Peter walked in.

Noticing the awkward moment between us, he said, "What's for dinner?"

Nica, standing where she was, should have noticed him first, yet she said nothing. She made no attempt to stop her flirting. I, on the other hand, upon hearing his baritone voice, quickly panicked. I had no idea what time it was. Looking up, I saw the clock read 4:54 PM. Peter wasn't due home for another hour.

I turned to face him. I had not prepared dinner—we had other issues to discuss. Peter hadn't seemed to mind before, but now, he did.

Seeing the look on his face—a look of disgust—I whimpered, knowing that Veronica meant me no harm. She stepped lightly past him, dominating the room with her presence. Peter stood still, waiting for her to exit so he could give me a verbal lashing.

"What's going on here?" he asked.

Quickly, I stopped him. "I know, honey. I know what it looks like, but I swear that's not what it is. I just… we just… sometimes… we just—"

I was babbling, confused, no longer able to look him in the eyes.

He turned to me and said, "I'm disappointed in you, Vernette."

Just like that, he walked away.

Biting my bottom lip, I was left standing in the kitchen, alone. Seconds later, I remembered I needed to be cooking. So that's what I did.

—

"Your recollection of the past is impeccable, Mrs. Vern. You've been doing so great. I really want to thank you for truly investing yourself in this project. I know it is going to be amazing."

"Amazing?" Emily asks, shaking her head in disbelief. "It's interesting to hear the story, but the relationship between you and Grandma is borderline incestuous. I mean—" she continues, lowering her head, her voice diminishing. Quietly, she sits, her eyes fixed on the dirt road.

"We definitely could all use some rest. We can resume tomorrow morning."

Nodding, I comply, watching as Emily and Washington both make their way into the cottage. I, on the other hand, remain seated in my rocker on the patio, looking up at the night sky. A blanket of stars glistens above, and the cool South Carolina nights are always something to be grateful for.

"Auntie, are you coming inside?"

Smiling, I take Emily by the hand, kissing her ever so gently. I know she is frightened by my story—our story—but truly, I grieve at the thought of becoming the reason she remains haunted for the rest of her life.

"Emily, sweetheart, do you think it may be time for you to head back to the city? I know your mother has been calling, and what about your job?"

Looking at me with sadness in her eyes, unable to resist her tears, she lets them fall freely down her cheeks.

"I deserve the opportunity to hear it firsthand, right here, from you—rather than pick up a copy from a bookstore one day and have to read it for myself. I am exactly where I want to be. My mother loves me, there's no doubt, and she has done an amazing job raising me. But I am an adult, and I want to learn the truth about my father, about me, Grandma Nica, and you. You raised my father, and partly me too. I want to stay right here. Please."

She places her head on my shoulder, kneeling slightly. How can I deny her this?

"Next time Tippy calls, I'd like a word. I know she has questions and is no doubt worried. She is indeed a good woman. I will explain the nature of your visit and only pray she understands."

"Oh, thank you, Auntie! Thank you, thank you, thank you!"

Emily squeezes my neck tightly as she hugs me with glee. Of all my grand-nieces and nephews, I have always adored the sound of Emily's voice.

—

THE NEXT MORNING, we readied ourselves, and Veronica and I headed off to her home.

"Peter isn't in the best of moods."

Fiddling with my fingers, I tried making small talk with Veronica. We sat next to each other in a checkered taxicab.

"That's because Peter's an idiot. He doesn't realize that you're the best thing that could have happened to him."

She was sweet one day, and evil the next. I felt like she had me trapped in a world of her own, controlling my emotions. Inevitably, she would become the reason for my descent into madness.

Upon arriving at her Long Island residence, Nica and I entered through the garage. Despite her absence, the house remained immaculate. Lucinda, washing dishes in the kitchen, was startled when Veronica made her way past the dining room. With no regard for how heavy her luggage was, Nica immediately demanded that Lucinda carry her bags in from the taxicab.

Veronica had begged me to accompany her on her return home. I did my best to convince her otherwise, arguing that her children needed to spend time with her and her alone. But she wouldn't hear of it. So, there I was.

"Your bags, ma'am."

Lucinda hadn't changed a bit. She looked eerie and dark as usual, her hair pulled into a tight bun that exposed her broad jawline.

Inside, Nica began to tour her home—a home that was supposed to be empty, as she had planned to relocate, only to find that everything remained the same. Nothing had been moved. She did not look pleased.

"Lucinda, where is all the new furniture I purchased for the new house? And where are the children?"

Lucinda stood with her hands intertwined behind her back. I took a seat in the living room on the loveseat nearest the cone fireplace.

"Ma'am, after your sudden leave of absence, your grandmother saw to it that the children were placed in a proper Negro-owned child facility. I remained responsible for the upkeep of the home, and David, well, he was tasked with preparing for your return. Speaking of which, I am sorry for your loss, ma'am."

"And what of the furniture? The house?" Veronica insisted.

"That arrangement was…canceled, ma'am. After your departure, it was no longer an option."

Veronica eyed her with contempt. "What time are the children coming home?"

"A few hours from now, ma'am."

"Did Grandma send anything by mail…before…?"

I interrupted, shocked, my voice rising in sudden panic. "Wait, what? Grandma Martin—"

Nica demanded that I stop speaking. "Vern, shut up!"

Lucinda answered calmly, "Yes, ma'am, in the foyer."

After a long sigh, Veronica asked, finally showing her true emotions—grief, "What time will David be home?"

"Later this afternoon, ma'am. He will be picking up the children beforehand."

"I see. Thank you."

I continued listening as Veronica and Lucinda carried on their conversation—or what seemed to be a conversation. Lucinda spoke discreetly while Veronica projected her voice. It was as if there were things she did not want me to hear. But I pretended as though I heard nothing, glancing every so often through the patio windows, noticing two women jogging along the sidewalk.

Moments later, I decided to join them in the foyer. Veronica removed her tan-colored trailing shawl and threw it toward Lucinda, who inadvertently let it fall behind her, causing Veronica to gasp slightly. Without hesitation, Lucinda picked up the shawl and gently placed it atop the coat hook.

I was appalled.

Veronica shot her a look of disdain. A woman in love with her clothing, she considered treating her garments with anything less than honor a blatant sign of disrespect.

A timid Lucinda said, "My apologies, ma'am. Truly, I thought you were handing it to your sister."

Finding her excuse fictitious, Nica proceeded up the staircase, her eyebrows knitted in frustration.

I remained downstairs, pacing aimlessly. In an attempt to make small talk, I asked, "So, how are the kids?"

Lucinda responded reluctantly. "They are well."

"And David?"

Her eyes shifted. "With all due respect, I must tend to my duties."

Just like that, she disappeared.

Seconds later, Nica bellowed from her bedroom for me to join her. Grateful for something to do, I ran upstairs to the master bedroom.

I arrived and was instantly confused.

"Are you packing?"

Nica and I exchanged opposite expressions—I was bewildered, while she was elated.

"Of course I'm packing. Why do you think I came here?"

Noticing multiple pieces of clothing being propelled from her wardrobe, I hurried to keep them from landing on the floor. I was growing exhausted from running back and forth, trying to catch each item as she tossed them out one by one. She stepped quickly, pressing dresses against her body to determine the fit. Once she was satisfied, I attempted to catch my breath.

"For starters, I thought you came home to be with your kids, your family," I said, breathing heavily.

"No, I came home for new clothes. The ones I had were dirty, and the laundry machine at our house hasn't been replaced since we were green. Jeez, Vern, get Peter to step into the '60s."

"What? No—your kids. What about your kids?" I felt horrible, like I was complicit in breaking up her family.

"Everything is under control here. Why are you panicking, Vern? My goodness, relax."

She was so calm, so happy. She continued trying on clothes, tossing aside old ones—many of which I wanted to keep for myself. But Nica and I were different sizes. Even pregnant, she weighed only about one hundred and thirty pounds at five feet six inches. Still, I refused to let the conversation slide.

"I'm panicking because you haven't been home in months, and your children are probably wondering what happened to you."

Back in those days, there were none of the fancy gadgets you all have now. When she was gone, that meant no phone calls, no texts, and no emails.

"No one is thinking about me. You and I have more videos to watch, and everything is fine here. If I'm not worried, you shouldn't be either," she said, folding her cashmere sweater tops and placing them neatly atop one another in her Hartmann belting suitcase.

I became agitated. Unless I knew the truth, I couldn't allow her to keep running from her responsibilities.

"I can't let you continue doing this, Nica. We weren't abandoned as children, and I can't let you do that to yours."

"Vernette, c'mon, no one is abandoning anything. I'll come home—just when I'm ready. It's really not a big deal. Don't you like having me around?"

The truth was, I feared having her around. Although Nica and I were building a strong bond and her presence kept my mind occupied, I couldn't shake the feeling that she was partially responsible for my nightmares. But, of course, I could never tell her that again—at least not now.

"I love having you around, but the same person I love having around—your children would love her too if given the chance to be with you."

Despite her frustration, she never once stopped packing.

"Vern, stop acting like that, okay? How about this—we take them to the park, they do all the things children do, I do what housewives do, watch them play, and you and I can complain? Then I'll come back, finish packing, and we'll leave."

I knew my facial expressions were giving me away. I was growing increasingly perturbed by her persistence and complete reluctance to actually stay home.

"What are you running away from?"

I shot her a look of compassion, my willingness to understand her pain, her fears, and everything else she might have been experiencing. Motherhood could be a terrifying thing, and maybe—just maybe—she wasn't as ready as she had thought. I begged for the truth. I begged for absolution.

"I am not running away. The kids are fine," she continued to insist.

Her demeanor shifted. She rolled her eyes, paced frantically, and avoided eye contact.

"They're being raised without their mother—that doesn't make them fine!" I shouted.

"Vernette, you were always so overly dramatic."

Finally, she did it. Amid her frustration, she threw her arms in the air. Running her hands through her soft, jet-black hair that cascaded down her back, she folded her arms tightly. After several deep breaths, the tears began to fall. She turned away, hoping I wouldn't notice, but I did.

The packing came to a halt.

She took a seat on the far-left corner of her queen-sized mattress. There was no doubt in my mind that I was being manipulated again, but I couldn't help myself. I stepped closer, standing before her, and asked softly,

"Is he really beating you?"

My voice barely rose above a whisper.

She said nothing.

As her weeping became more pronounced, my stomach twisted.

"Oh my God, he's been beating you," I whispered again. "Did Grandma Martin know about this?"

Drying her tears, she replied, "Glad to know you went to college for a reason. And no, she didn't."

"How long?" I scoffed.

Veronica resumed packing—quickly now, without caring that her clothes weren't folded and might not fit properly in her suitcase.

"Vern, you don't have to do this. We don't have to do this. I am fine, the kids are fine, and that's what matters most."

She wanted to be a good mother.

She wanted to raise her babies.

There was a look in her eyes—remorse.

Sadness.

Emptiness.

She wanted the best for her children, yet there was no way to describe what she was going through. Everything appeared so simple despite its intricacy.

"So why haven't you brought the children to stay with us? I'm sure Peter wouldn't mind."

I remained completely oblivious.

Frightened, she responded, "Because that's not how this works. Besides, David is a great father."

Nonchalantly, I spoke while assisting Veronica with her packing and folding. "I always assumed he wasn't because he was always working and—" I began to ramble, but Nica immediately interrupted me.

"No, no, he's great. He and I just don't see eye to eye on a lot of things."

Her tears had dried, and her tone was now confident. Her attitude had once again turned authoritative. I felt swindled—like I had been given a performance momentarily. Nica had only needed to convince me just enough, using her deceptive ways. But I refused to let the conversation simply end.

"How long has this been going on, Nica? Have you told Daddy? And what about Mom? Does she know? Do they know?"

"Vern, stop making this a big deal, okay? It's under control."

I could tell she was becoming annoyed. Her tricks worked wonders on me. How could anyone deny that beautiful face, that tender voice, or that act of purity? Psychologically disturbed—that was how I would describe her uncanny ability to convince anyone of just about anything, regardless of the truth.

"There is no control when you're not here to raise your children!"

The words escaped my lips before I could stop them. Though they weren't directed at Nica, I had spoken out of pure frustration.

Choosing to respond, Nica snapped, "You don't know because you're not a parent! Stop worrying about it!" she bellowed.

Before she could say anything else, I dropped the clothing in my hands, took two deep breaths, and prepared to leave. Irritated, I stepped toward the bedroom door with force. As I reached for the handle, I heard Nica call after me.

"Vern, I'm sorry. You know I didn't mean that."

Just as I exited, David entered.

So upset by her comment, I didn't even think to turn back and stay by my sister's side after everything she had just told me. I just wanted to be alone. I wanted to be selfish. I wanted to feel my anger. I needed space.

Not long after, I heard David's voice booming from down the hall.

"Now you come home after all this time? Huh? And what's this? You're leaving again!? What is she doing to you? What kind of nonsense has Vernette put in your head? Look at me!"

"David, let me go! Don't get all angry. You and I both know why I'm not here," Nica shouted back.

I couldn't take it anymore—the constant scrutiny of my inability to bear children, watching my youngest sister and the man I had once loved engage in their lovers' quarrel, and feeling completely out of place in my own life. I wanted to protect Veronica, but then it hit me—who was going to protect me?

I ran down the staircase, past Lucinda, who was mopping the foyer, and bolted for the door. Looking back every few seconds to see if anyone was following me, I realized no one had even noticed my absence.

Moving swiftly, the spring breeze made my body quiver. When I reached the corner, I whistled for a taxi. One pulled up just in time, and within a minute, I was on my way home.

Slamming the door behind me, I was met with the sound of Tommy Edwards' *Morning Side of the Mountain* echoing through the house.

I hung my cardigan on the hook before making my way down the long corridor. I felt lightheaded. As the record continued to spin, an overwhelming sense of dread washed over me. Something bad was going to happen—I could feel it. My left eye twitching.

Then, as my nostrils caught the savory scent of sweet potato pie, I quickened my pace—only to come to a sharp halt.

There was a woman.

In my kitchen.

With my husband.

A woman with blonde hair.

"Hey, sweetheart," Peter said cheerfully. "How were things with Veronica? Surprised you're home so soon."

Still listening to the soft croon of Tommy Edwards, Peter danced his way to the kitchen threshold where I stood. He gave me a soft kiss on my left cheek, but my eyes remained locked on the woman sitting at my table.

She was eating from my dishes.

Licking my silverware. And making no attempt to acknowledge my presence.

So I decided to introduce myself.

"Hi, my name is Vernette. And you are?"

I pranced over to the sink, angling myself for a better look. Now fully inhaling the scent of Peter's homemade pie, I stole a glance at the woman, who still refused to make eye contact.

"Elizabeth," she said flatly, stuffing another bite of pie into her mouth as Peter walked over to serve her another slice.

"Oh my goodness, Peter, you're quite the cook!" she gushed.

Peter, oven mitts on, pulled another pan from the oven. He looked at me and asked, "You hungry, honey?"

Throwing my hands up, I exclaimed, "Peter, what is this?"

They were both acting as if this were normal. As if what they were doing was okay.

"This is my sister," Peter said.

"Sister?" I turned to face her, stuttering. I had never met Peter's parents, but this woman was Caucasian—anyone could have attested to that. She extended her hand for me to shake. I obliged, still reluctant.

"Sister?" I repeated.

They both chuckled.

"Yes, Peter is my younger brother."

I couldn't believe my ears, though my eyes were another story. There was no way to argue what was clearly in front of me. They continued to laugh, she continued to enjoy her pie, and Peter began to roast a chicken, preparing to place it inside the oven. His apron read **KISS THE COOK**, but at that moment, all I wanted to do was slap the cook.

"Peter, may you and I have a word, please?" I asked.

Removing his apron, Peter joined me in the hallway for a conversation.

"Sister?" I asked again, bewildered.

"Yes, Elizabeth is my sister. I told you, I was adopted. Our parents died when I was eighteen, and she's been taking care of me ever since. My, my, Vern, what else will you claim to not have known about me? I'm pretty sure I've told you just about everything," he said.

Sadly enough, he was right. I remember him telling me he was adopted by a Caucasian family when his mother passed away. Instead of being orphaned, they took him from the church they all attended. That's how he grew up in Christianity. I guess I had been so consumed with my own problems that I had unintentionally blocked out all outside information.

I became instantly apologetic. "I'm so sorry, things have just been so crazy lately with Veronica and the baby—."

"No, no, I get it. I just figured, since your sister was practically living here, I would at least invite mine to come out for a day or two."

I thought that was a great idea. Peter was truly a great man. He had gone through all the trouble of preparing a great meal for everyone, and here I was, thinking I had just come face to face with his paramour. I felt like a complete idiot. After regaining my composure, I planted a nice, wet kiss on his lips. However, I did find it strange that after over a year of marriage, he had only now found it profoundly fitting for me to meet his sister.

After intrinsically punishing myself for coming off impolitely, I went back inside the kitchen. Instead of a handshake, I demanded a hug from my sister-in-law. She and I had never met, and I was sure Peter had a good reason. On the other hand, Elizabeth was beautiful. She had ocean-blue eyes and shoulder-length blonde hair pinned neatly to her scalp. Her rosy red knee-length dress looked expensive—a Christian Dior design, to be exact. I couldn't wear such clothes, but women of wealth and a lighter skin tone most certainly could. I only admired her from afar.

She smiled a lot, more than the average person. For hours, we talked and laughed as Peter and Elizabeth became nostalgic, reminiscing about the good old days.

They talked of their late parents, their pet dog Max, and the little house by the farm they'd always sneak off to, to watch the herd sleep. But something was odd—Peter speaking, Elizabeth voluntarily finishing his sentences. Initially, I thought she might have had an inflated ego, eager to talk. But, unfortunately, I later learned that wasn't the case.

Before I knew it, the whole day had passed. I was exhausted. Kindly, I excused myself, leaving Peter and his sister to catch up some more. I begged Peter to clean the kitchen. He kissed me gently on my right cheek once again after convincing me that the kitchen would be spotless by morning. Believing him, I took my leave.

Walking out of the kitchen, I could feel the eyes of both Peter and Elizabeth monitoring my every step. Once I reached the bottom of the banister, I turned to wave goodnight to them both. They were both staring at me, and I felt awkward.

That night, as I climbed into bed, my thoughts prevented me from immediately dozing off. Eventually, I fell asleep, but a feeling of discomfort woke me. I thought Peter had climbed into bed, and I was not wrong, apparently. I decided to step out of bed, looking up into the shadowy darkness. I noticed the time read 4:34 AM. I began making my way toward the bedroom door, the door I had not shut behind me. Once in the hallway, I heard noises coming from the guest bedroom—moaning.

After taking several steps to the right, I pushed the door open. Under the covers was a woman atop a man. They were fucking, screaming, and now banging the headboard against the wall. I wanted to yell! Peter was having sex, right next to our bedroom. How could he do that? Tears began to fall from my eyes, my heart pounding, my palms sweating.

"Peter!" I shouted.

Both of them stopped—turning slowly to face me. It was Veronica. Peter, underneath her, thrusting his penis into her vagina. I watched as she moaned and moaned. Her eyes settled on me.

Something in me wanted to join them.

Just before I could walk away from the door, a naked Elizabeth came up from behind me, gripping my breasts. I let out a small shriek. Closing my eyes, I embraced her, rubbing my hands between her legs. I fondled her clitoris as I continued to listen to Veronica moaning.

"I love you, Vern," a soft voice whispered in my ear as the penetration went deep between my legs.

"I love you too, Nica!" I said, my eyes still closed. Then it stopped. The pleasure I had been feeling now felt like eyes burning through my flesh. Moaning, I yearned for more. But I got nothing. Opening my eyes, I watched as Peter climbed off of me, curling under the blankets, his back turned. Gripping the sheets, I could do nothing but sob silently. What's happening to me? I thought.

The next morning, I visited Elizabeth in the kitchen, pouring herself a cup of coffee. I entered after her and began to pour mine as well. Holding her cup close, she turned to face me, unbothered, silent. Then she said, "What does he see in you?"

Thinking I might have heard her wrong, I begged her to repeat herself. "I'm sorry, what?" Clearing her throat, she took another long gulp before answering.

"My brother—what does he see in you? I mean, you aren't the most attractive woman, you haven't given him a family, and you do nothing with your life. You're a misfortunate, ugly, bloated carnie."

Before I could respond, the room went black. Grandma Martin appeared where Elizabeth had been standing, her black shawl covering her face. She reached out her hands, attempting to grab my head. Before I could move, I thought of throwing my coffee into her face.

"Vernette, Jesus Christ, that thing is hot!"

Before I knew it, I had splashed a mug full of hot coffee into the face of my sister-in-law. Listening to her bellow in pain, Peter made his appearance. I held a cloth filled with ice, pressing it against her forehead.

"What did you do?" he shouted.

"She threw the coffee in my face! Peter, oh my God, it burns!" Elizabeth sobbed.

I stood in shock before I made my way out of the kitchen and up to my bedroom, where I changed into a pair of jeans and a cotton blue top. Racing down the stairs, I noticed Peter shooting me a loathsome look. Grabbing my jacket, I attempted to make my way out of the house. I felt so confused, afraid of what I might do next, unable to distinguish reality from fantasy. My hallucinations were growing worse.

—

"Maybe Veronica isn't the reason after all,"

Washington says with confidence. Deciding not to entertain his presumptuous remark, I continue looking at the sky, pregnant with rain, as I remain motionless.

—

UPON OPENING MY FRONT DOOR, I froze as Veronica stood opposite me, holding her leather suitcase in her right hand. Her hair was uncombed, stuffed into an uncomfortable ponytail, and her left eye was battered shut. A pregnant Nica fainted in my arms. Before I had the chance to scream, I slid to the floor, holding her as she sobbed. After that, the day went dark.

I awoke the next day tucked between my sheets. Turning to face the clock, I saw it read 6:47 AM. I pinched myself. Feeling the pain, I realized this was not a dream. I sat upright, placing my hand across my forehead—my temperature felt normal. Then, the doorbell rang.

I struggled for a moment to get up, feeling slightly dizzy as I turned to plant my feet on the hardwood floor. I reached for my silk housedress, slipped into it, and pranced down to the foyer. I gave no thought to anything around me—my husband, my estranged sister-in-law, or even my baby sister. My world felt empty, and I didn't mind it. I was in a trance.

Opening the door felt like déjà vu, only this time, Nica stood opposite me, dressed as if she were attending Sunday morning service. She wore a mid-calf indigo pencil skirt accompanied by an off-white, military-breasted blazer, a belt loosely knotted at her waist. She smelled of fresh peppermints. White, delicate gloves covered her hands, and white two-inch kitten heels completed her look. The blazer embraced her pregnancy, creating a look that was both classy and subtle. The high-top ponytail she wore was a bit more unusual; however, it only complemented her features.

Her red lipstick stained my cheek as she leaned over to kiss me—right before slapping me out of my daze.

"What did you do that for?" I asked, holding my face. My cheek burned.

The world around me resumed: the cars honking loudly, the neighbors screaming at one another, and the couples speaking animatedly as they strolled down the block holding hands.

Nica removed her gloves. Gripping her suitcase, she took small steps past the threshold.

"That was for leaving me," she said, cutting her eyes away from me.

What happened next unfolded in a matter of seconds. Before the door could click into place, I heard the suitcase drop to the ground. Nica was gripping the banister, her thighs leaking fluid. She was going into labor.

Panicking, I ran to the kitchen to grab towels, the sound of children playing outside distracting me. Their laughter sounded like cackling and grated on my nerves.

Her screams frightened me—I was completely overstimulated.

I sat her down on the bottom step.

Veronica began undressing, ripping off her blazer to reveal a sleeveless white silk undergarment.

Following her usual breathing technique, she remained calm. Unable to speak, she motioned for me to follow her silent instructions: grab the towels, place them between her legs, lock the door—the noise was agitating her. All of her directions were simple.

I admired my baby sister. Despite the pain she was experiencing, she remained patient with me. I moved as quickly as I could.

The screaming grew louder. Just as I was losing all hope, Elizabeth walked in and immediately recognized the situation. She took control. Throwing her chestnut-colored hair into a quick bun, she reached into her bag and pulled out two pairs of latex gloves.

"Put these on," she demanded, then flew to her knees. Asking Veronica to sit back, she placed her left hand between her legs.

"You're almost fully dilated. Vernette, go upstairs and fill the master tub with lukewarm water—now!"

At first, I hesitated, insisting that Veronica needed a hospital and that there was no way we were prepared to deliver a baby.

Infuriated, Elizabeth repeated, "Go fill that tub now! This baby is coming whether we go to a hospital or not!"

Her shouting didn't help. Still unable to speak, Nica shot me a look of compliance.

Nodding, I ran as fast as I could to my bedroom. I turned on all the pipes, found a bucket, and began filling the tub manually when the water wasn't flowing fast enough.

Done.

The tub water reached its maximum capacity. Still in my housedress, I ran to the bottom of the stairs, where Elizabeth had gone into full nurse mode. A stethoscope hung around her neck, her gloved hands positioned carefully between my sister's legs, making sure not to apply pressure. Veronica was still panting, her breathing excessive.

"Stay with me, Veronica. You and your baby are both going to be fine, understand? Just keep breathing—you're doing great."

Just as I thought things were beginning to stabilize, a shriek tore from Veronica's throat, followed by a gush of blood spilling from between her legs. Still, Elizabeth did not seem fazed. Instead, she kept Veronica focused on breathing while proceeding to instruct me further.

"Vernette, I need you to help me carry her up to the bathtub. Quickly—this baby is coming."

"I-I-I ca-can't do this... it hurts s-so-so bad."

Finally, Veronica spoke, stuttering through her breath. I felt helpless. I wished we could switch places. Her petite body was fragile, her pregnant belly weighing her down. I sobbed as I watched my sister in pain. Closing her eyes, I saw a tear slip down her cheek.

"Sweetie, my name is Elizabeth—Elizabeth Dawson, okay? I've been a nurse for seventeen years. My specialty is neonatal care. I promise you are in good hands.

My brother invited me here so that I could look after you. I do this for a living."

I had suspected she had some experience, but Peter barely discussed his family with me—not their professions, not even that he planned to bring his sister along to care for mine. The nerve of him. The disclosure left me stupefied. How had I not known this? Why would he keep it from me? I felt myself slipping back into that trance, only to be jolted awake by the sudden blow of Elizabeth's heel colliding with my ankle as she kicked off her shoe.

"Wake up! This is no time to be daydreaming. Help me get her upstairs!"

I did as I was told. I held Nica by the arms while Elizabeth grabbed her from the waist. We lifted on the count of three. Veronica provided little to no assistance, her blood trailing along the staircase. Her screaming grew more intense once she was lifted. She began to fidget in our arms, causing us—twice—to nearly lose our grip on her. I prayed she would stay still, finally resorting to begging as I realized we might not make it to the bathtub if she didn't stop moving.

"Nica, Nica—Jesus! Please, you have to stop moving! I'm very scared as it is, and you are not helping. Stop moving!" I cried.

Taking my words into consideration, she placed her hand atop her belly and, for approximately twenty seconds, stayed still—just long enough for Elizabeth and me to place her into the tub.

At the time, I didn't realize the water was too high. The moment she went in, a surge of water overflowed, drenching us all. Elizabeth lost her footing, slipping and losing her position between Veronica's legs. Once again, Nica let out a sharp cry.

"Vernette, the baby is coming now—we have to deliver! Veronica, listen to my voice. You are in the water. The baby is going to be fine. Now, I need you to push," Elizabeth coached.

I stood there, my slip clinging to my body, blood dripping from my hands. I watched in amazement as Veronica pushed, screaming as she gripped the sides of the mint-green bathtub. Her hair was now in disarray. We were all completely soaked.

Minutes later, as I sat in a puddle of water near the bathroom door, I realized I had no more use. Elizabeth coached, Veronica pushed, and by eight, we were all smiling at a healthy baby boy.

Jordan Shane Harrington was born four weeks premature.

The date: May 27, 1957.

—

A trip to the market today will do me some good, I think, as I gather my purse and food stamps. Running low on food, I am finally seeing that I need Emily more than I like to admit.

As usual, the South Carolina sun greets us warmly. A smiling Washington hands both Emily and me steaming hot plates of his specially seasoned omelets. Quite the chef he is—he reminds me a lot of Peter. Grateful for the company, I can't sing their praises enough. Both Emily and Washington are a godsend.

"Mrs. Vernette, I hope that dish isn't too hot. If so, I can always wait until it cools," Washington exclaims. Modest little thing, always concerned for my safety and well-being. In just a few days, we have all begun to feel like the center of an everyday family.

Our routines are set—Washington and I wake before the sun, Emily later in the afternoon. By the time she wakes, I am already halfway through a day's dictation. Washington and I seem to be making great progress. Excited about our trip to the market today, he prepares to restock cassettes for the tape recorder, pens, and additional legal pads.

Taking a seat across the table, Washington, Emily, and I sit quietly, enjoying our meals as the tree leaves rustle outside.

Moments later, Washington asks, "Ma'am, exactly how far is the market?"

"About where you had walked from, son?" I reply. Distance shouldn't be an issue—he trod all of five miles from town just a few days ago.

Chuckling, he responds, "No, I only ask because I want to make sure you're able to travel that far."

I sneer. "Whatchu tryna say? You think I'm too old to walk?"

Still laughing, he says, "C'mon, Mrs. Vernette, you know me better than that—I'd never pin you against a wall. I know you're strong, strong-willed, and strong-boned. I'm just looking out for your safety, that's all."

Shaking my head, I glance at Emily, watching her take large bites. I have to remind her that eating so fast will only do her more harm than good.

"Take your time, Emily."

Laughing as bits of pork bacon escape her lips, she muffles, "Auntie, I'm just so hungry!"

Staring into Emily's eyes, I notice a look on her face I have come to know all too well.

"Are you pregnant?" I ask without a bit of hesitation.

Shying away from me, she nods yes. We all exchange a look of excitement and joy.

God is so wonderful to me, I think.

Many generations, many children, so much laughter and love all within one lifetime. I cannot possibly ask for anything more.

"Have you told your mother?" I ask happily. Knowing how much Tippy despises both my family and me, it is no wonder she will be quite disheartened to know that I have the pleasure of hearing such news before her.

"No, I haven't. I honestly just found out two days ago. I've had the pregnancy test in my purse for weeks—just been too afraid to take it. Then, hearing all of this talk about children and babies, I just had to know."

Placing my forehead into my palm, I feel lightheaded. Emily is not to blame, but news like this—no matter how soon—still comes as a shock to a woman my age.

"Who is the father? I haven't heard you mention anyone of interest."

Washington pays neither of us any mind as he clears the table of our used dishes.

"He's a man, Auntie. He works in the finance department. We've been together for quite some time, but Mother isn't fond of him."

Nodding my head in disbelief, I continue my inquiry. "Why is that? Does he not treat you well?"

Surprised, she says, "No, no—he treats me well!"

"So, what is the problem?"

"He's married," she shrugs.

A glass slips from Washington's eavesdropping hands, inadvertently drawing attention to him. Glancing at him briefly, I notice an abhorrent look on his face.

Catching my breath before responding, I say, "Married? Why on Earth would you be dating a married man—sleeping with him—and now carrying his child?"

Walking away, Emily brushes off the conversation.

"Auntie, please. Now is not the time. I have always hated lying to you, which is why I didn't want to. But you seem to be asking all the right—and wrong—questions. Elliott and I have a rather unique relationship. I'm okay with our arrangement."

I cannot believe my ears. For clarification, I have to reiterate.

"You are okay with sleeping with a married man—the father of your child? Are you now all right with being a single mother?"

Waving her hands, motioning for me to change the subject, her eyes dart toward Washington, who now occupies the dining room, setting up his recording station.

"Please, I'd rather not talk about this. I could have sworn we were going to the market," she says softly.

I am no longer in any mood to go to a market, although the thought of squeezing a fresh, ripe cantaloupe would be nice right about now.

"No market today," I say, making my way toward Washington, who does his best to pretend he hasn't heard the conversation between Emily and me.

I want to continue my story. Just as I open my mouth and Emily begins making her way upstairs, isolating herself from us, there is a knock at the cottage door.

"Oh, Ms. Vernette!" a voice calls—a man's voice, to be exact.

I know who this is. Why, it's ol' Albert Miller.

Albert is a short, pudgy thing with a beer belly wide enough to replace a drum, and he always reeks of whiskey. A functioning alcoholic, through and through.

"What brings you here?" I ask, making my way to the squeaking cottage screen door, my cane supporting me with each step.

"Don't be silly, Vernette. You know me and the fellas like to come by once in a while, make sure your fridge is stocked. You need anything, love?"

Albert sure is a kind man. For years, he's been delivering me food, eliminating my need to go to the market sometimes. Still, I enjoy the time spent there—not always trying to be cooped up in this here cottage.

"Well, Albert, now that you mention it, we could use a few things, but only if you don't mind. I have some young ones here who are willing to travel."

His decorum makes me feel like I am the one being intrusive.

"No, no, you keep them young visitors on in here. Chile, stop it now. You acting like you a stranger. I'm gonna wait on out here while you get that list together. We'll be back with a full truck of fresh vegetables and some groceries for you before the sun goes down. Understand?"

Laughing discreetly, I know Albert to always be dependable. For years, he has delivered me goods, but this time around, I honestly thought he had forgotten me.

Standing by the screen door, Washington listens as Albert and I discuss the groceries we need. Adding his own request, he says, "Uh, Sir, we need some nutrition bars—the good kind, preferably from Nature Valley. Also, some peanut butter, regular lightly salted cashews, oh, and some ice cream—cookies and cream, specifically."

Surprised by his extensive appetite, ol' Albert whistles for his truck driver to come over with a pen and pad. His commercial truck, marked **INDUSTRIOUS TOWN MARKET**, is the only market within a five-mile radius that all the townspeople frequent. He makes deliveries but only to his special customers. I happen to be one of them, due to my condition—and the eight dollars I usually tip him in addition to the cost of my grocery bill.

I have no use for cash anymore, a mattress full of money awaiting the day it is there no more. I cannot take the money to the grave, as I now breathe on borrowed time.

My body aching from standing too long, I motion for a seat. Albert quickly obliges, brushing the pollen from my patio chair. He anchors my arm, helping me step over gently.

Whispering, Washington asks, "Mrs. Vernette, do you think we should place an order for prenatal vitamins? You know, for, um, Emily?"

Albert and I exchange a look of bewilderment. Washington smiles at Albert despite his embarrassment.

"Of course not!" I bellow, a sharp pain in my right hip now agonizing. Seconds later, after deciding to change my mind, I motioned once again to Albert, this time to add the vitamins to his list.

Interrupting, Washington says, "Oh, sir, the good kind—not the cheap stuff."

A prissy little thing, this ol' Washington. A man of expensive taste. If given the chance, Veronica would have loved him.

With an obvious knack for fashion, surely, he does not want for anything—his Givenchy wallet populated with two American Express credit cards and nothing but large bills to fill it. This becomes apparent once Albert, preparing to take his leave, is called over by Washington, who hands him two crisp hundred-dollar bills—well over the amount needed for our well-being.

Albert, smiling from ear to ear, rushes to his vehicle, assuring both me and Washington of his immediate return.

"Oh, oh, wait a minute, Albert! May you please fetch me some white undershirts? Size medium, if you may?" Washington asks.

With no hesitation or objection, Albert agrees. "Why, yes, son, absolutely. Anything else you think of, let me know once I get on back, and I'll get it for ya, no charge."

Missing his two front teeth, Albert grins before slamming the passenger seat door once firmly seated, continuously smiling at Washington and me—a clear indication that he is pleased with today's transaction.

The South Carolina sun begins to show its true talents, beaming relentlessly out of the sky onto my darkened skin. Closing my eyes for a quick nap on the patio, I cannot help but notice how relaxed Washington is. Normally, he is prepared with his recorder, pen, and pad before noon hits. Today, he is out collecting the sun alongside me.

"No interest in my story anymore?" I ask, continuing to relax with my eyes closed.

"Of course, I'm still interested. I just want to know, off the record, why did you settle for second place?"

A question like this—the one question I fear I do not have an answer to. But I will try anyway.

"Second place was never my choice. I just didn't have what the world wanted at the time. I thought I did, which made finding out that I didn't all the more devastating. I became comfortable living in the shadows. No one had expectations of me anymore—only to be there for her. And I was okay with that. A part of me still is."

"Hmm, I understand."

Quietly, Washington disappears.

An hour or so later, the weather begins to shift, and my heart races. Opening my eyes, I see Emily and Washington standing out by the oak trees, conversing happily.

How long have I been asleep? I wonder.

Hearing my grunting, Emily makes her way over. Without a word, she reaches down and gives me a tight hug.

"Thank you for my vitamins," she whispers.

As I pat her back, I watch Washington sporting a brand-new white undershirt, accompanied by a pair of calf-cut suit pants. I suppose the delivery was a success.

NICA, ELIZABETH, PETER, and I cared for baby Jordan. His presence in the home consumed us—morning, noon, and night. Many nights, he kept us up with his screaming, but we took turns prepping, feeding, and changing his diapers.

Day after day, Peter and Elizabeth would leave, stating they had errands to run. Peter permitted me to use his finances on Nica, insisting that we buy anything the baby needed.

David came by almost daily, whenever work permitted. Nica was still not ready to return home, despite my desperate pleas for her to do so. It had been three weeks, and Matthew and Ebony still had no knowledge of their newborn baby brother. Hospital visits with Nica to get Jordan examined were both tiring and strenuous—making sure the stroller was set up properly, always having to remove and readjust the car seat each time we entered a new taxicab.

I held all of the baby's belongings, feeling like the nanny almost. Not only did I accompany them on hospital visits, but I also woke up for the 5 AM feedings. Veronica pumped every hour on the hour, filling our fridge with small bottles of breast milk. I will admit, at first, I was slightly disgusted. I had no children of my own, but no matter how tired, stressed, or confused I was, I still envied the fact that Jordan was not mine.

I held him in my arms as he cooed, burped, smiled for the first time, and grabbed my index finger, shoving it into his mouth. Jordan was a fair-skinned baby with the most adorable soft gray eyes. He was perfect.

David loved that boy. He loved the fact that child after child, he and Nica kept producing the most magnificent and conventionally attractive offspring. Their genes meshed perfectly.

Although his visits were sometimes long, other times they were cut short when Peter arrived home at night. As observant as I was, I noticed that the two never made eye contact, and David was always adamant about Nica living off the salary of another man. In those days, it was considered a sign of disrespect—the thought of another man taking care of your family.

David and I no longer exchanged words, only awkward, silent looks as we transferred baby Jordan from his arms to mine. We remained cordial, both for the sake of Nica and the baby.

Our home was filled with laughter and joy, and peace reigned. Finally, I was not having any nightmares, and things were going great. A baby around the house, keeping us all occupied, was exactly what we needed.

Did Peter seem happier? Of course, he did. Peter began spending more time at home than he had in years—minus his errand runs with Elizabeth. Jordan may have been a handful, but he kept my mind engaged.

As the weeks pressed on, I began to notice the chemistry between Elizabeth and Peter dwindling, but no doubt still there, which ultimately became quite questionable to both Nica and me—only she seemed a little less surprised.

"Why does it seem like all you've done lately is keep an eye on those two?" she asked, dipping her body into the mint-colored bathtub filled with bubbles and lukewarm water. She began massaging her inner thighs.

Down in the kitchen, Jordan was asleep in his bassinet while Peter and Elizabeth prepared dinner. I wondered when Elizabeth would be leaving, but Peter's response was vague.

"Soon, I guess."

There was no way I was going to discuss my discomfort about another woman living in my home, claiming to be related to my husband. If I did, I would have been a hypocrite. After all, Veronica had spent the entirety of her pregnancy here, and now we were all raising her baby. So, I decided to push the issue no further.

"I'm going to go down and check on dinner," I said, standing in the doorway of the guest bathroom.

Nodding, she blew bubble after bubble from her palms.

"Okay, and can you bring up the baby? I should properly feed him now."

I resisted the urge to sarcastically reply, *Yes, ma'am. Right away, ma'am. Anything you say, ma'am!*

I stepped lightly toward the kitchen for multiple reasons. First, if the baby had been sleeping, I didn't want to wake him with any sudden noises or movements. Second, I hoped to overhear the conversation between Peter and Elizabeth. My second reason felt more valid.

Elizabeth and Peter were very surreptitious. They spoke in hushed tones, only had conversations when they were alone, or waited until they thought neither Nica nor I was around.

I took a cautious step toward the kitchen, keeping my shoulders hidden behind the wall. The sound of boiling water filled the air. Elizabeth sat comfortably at the table, using her right foot to rock the bassinet.

"I know it must be the oddest thing to bring up now, but that birth was the strangest I've ever witnessed," she said with a nervous chuckle. Her tone was high-pitched and soft but projected enough for Peter to hear her over the sound of oil popping in the pan.

"What do you mean?" he asked.

"It's almost as though this baby birthed himself. I mean, it was the fastest, medication-free delivery I've ever seen. Her pregnancy felt… induced somehow—I don't know, honey. I—I can't even begin to explain it."

That's when I heard it. *Honey.*

"Come on now, we agreed—no pet names around the house," Peter replied, his tone slightly annoyed. The oil continued to sizzle in the frying pan. "And I'm sure I can understand if you explain it to me."

"The pregnancy was induced—no idea how. Maybe she and her husband had sex or something. She wasn't due until now."

I continued to listen, no longer interested in the details of the birth but more so in uncovering the depths of their relationship.

"…And the baby shows no signs of being premature. He is full-term but… not at-term. Am I making sense? I honestly shouldn't be because what I'm describing is almost impossible. And Peter, I fear for his overall development, but—but he's also surprisingly healthy, as strong as a horse. I will say this—the whole family seems strange. Based on what you've told me about the mother, oh my goodness, it's a wonder how you could have married into such dysfunction." She laughed.

"They aren't dysfunctional. Vernette really has a good heart. And her sister... I don't know, they're both just different," he defended.

"Different in size, maybe," she teased.

But Peter was not amused. I had been pestered about my weight so often that her comment barely fazed me. But what she said next nearly brought me to my knees.

"So, when are you going to tell her about us?" she pressed.

"Elizabeth, I can't do that," Peter quickly responded, as though he had anticipated the question.

"Peter, no. We had a deal!" Elizabeth snapped.

Just then, baby Jordan awoke, his cries echoing through the halls. A part of me was crying, too.

Immediately, Elizabeth cradled Jordan as Peter whispered, "See? Look what you've done. Now everyone will hear us. I am a Christian man, Beth, committing all types of sin. I never said anything about leaving my wife. I asked you to be here because we both know how dangerous childbirth can be for Black women. Having you here was the safest option."

"So, you used me?" she scoffed. "Okay, quiet down now, baby. You said once the baby was delivered, we would be together. You lied?"

I desperately wanted to hear more, but before I could, Veronica hollered from her upstairs quarters, having heard Jordan's cries.

"Vern, is everything all right?"

My heart sank. My cover had been blown.

Steeling myself for what I knew would be the ultimate confrontation, I stepped boldly into the kitchen. Both Elizabeth and Peter stood awkwardly as I snatched Jordan from her arms, wrapped him in his blankets, and walked him out of the room without another word.

"Say something!" I heard Elizabeth whisper.

"Vernette, can we talk?" Peter asked calmly.

"No!" I hollered, shielding the baby as I hurried up the stairs. Entering the guest bedroom, I immediately shut the door behind me, gasping as I carefully set Jordan down on the mattress.

Peter didn't chase after me.

Regardless, I had already made up my mind that I would forgive him. But, of course, I questioned myself—why should I, as a woman, be expected to just forgive and understand that a man will stray, whether in marriage or a relationship? My self-esteem was low. I didn't see him as the enemy, only as a man I couldn't imagine living without.

In the distance, I could hear them arguing. I focused on my breathing, watching as Veronica cooed and gently guided her left nipple between Jordan's lips.

I had to ask.

"Are you not going to ask me what just happened?" I said frantically.

Boldly, she responded, "No. I assume you're just going to confirm something I already knew."

I was too hurt to be curt, so I got straight to the point.

"That's his mistress. Elizabeth and Peter—they're sleeping together, Nica. He lied to me!" I couldn't stop shaking. I felt so deceived—so in love with a man, yet once again, history had managed to repeat itself.

Veronica, on the other hand, continued to play, laugh, and breastfeed her newborn as if nothing had happened.

"Hey, are you listening to me? That's his mistress!"

Knitting her eyebrows, she gestured for me to sit down.

I didn't want to listen—I just wanted to pack a bag and get away. Far away.

"Vern, I can explain everything, but you have to sit down," she said gently.

With my hands on my head, my eyes filling with tears, I paced back and forth, repeating, "What did you do? What did you do?"

How could I not have known my baby sister was involved in this? She always found a way to ruin my life!

"Have a seat, and I'm going to open the door, okay?"

I did as I was told, all the while resisting the urge to lash out.

After feeding Jordan, Veronica covered herself with a light gown and walked over to open the door. Baby Jordan lay fast asleep in her arms once again.

And then he entered.

"What the hell is going on?" I demanded, tears still in my eyes.

"Calm down. Peter spoke to me some time ago," Veronica replied. "He explained everything and… asked me to stay for a while. We didn't tell you because, well…"

Peter interrupted, "I didn't think you would be okay with it. Plus," he turned to Veronica, "she and David have agreed to let us raise Jordan while they travel and... see the world. Your sister really wants to do that, and I really want a child in the house," he said, his breath shaky.

I refused to believe it.

"You're both lying!" I screamed.

"Please, Vern, just listen. I know this sounds strange, but it's honestly a great idea. I need to live my life, and Peter's okay with it. David's mom has agreed to keep Ebony and Matthew, and, well, Jordan will stay here."

I was stunned. "You want us to raise a baby that isn't ours? Are you that desperate for a child? This baby will never call you Dad and will never call me Mom. He will know us as his aunt and uncle. Wait—wait a minute. So how do you explain the mistress?"

"I made a mistake. I was starting to loathe you and the fact that we hadn't had a baby yet, and I messed up. I should have ended things with Beth sooner, and I regret lying to you about who she was. But," he chuckled bitterly, "all of this sounded better when it was just an idea..."

I kept listening, but nothing was making sense.

"You want us to raise my sister's baby, pretending to be his parents for God knows how long? You expect me to forget that you cheated on me? And what about David? Why would he even agree to this? Your children deserve to be raised by their parents. Can you imagine if Mom and Dad did what you're doing to them, to us? Besides, Peter, am I really just not enough for you?" I was entirely disappointed. "You had an affair!"

My words tumbled out faster than I could control. How was I supposed to react? What would Jordan think? What were Peter and I supposed to tell him?

"Vern, you're overthinking this. We just thought it would be a good idea—something nice for both of us. To bring us closer together, to leave the past behind us."

Nice? I thought.

"Nice is allowing me to babysit once in a while. Nice is letting your children know who I am and the role I would play in their lives. Nice is not having a cheating husband. Nice is not finding out that my sister and my husband conspired behind my back to hand me a child out of pity. Neither of you knows what it means to be nice! I mean—what about his breast milk? Did none of you think this through?"

Silence.

"I just really need a vacation…" Veronica admitted, pouting her lips.

"You are disgustingly selfish." I sighed.

Silence.

"What do we do now?"

Finally, I had given in. Deep down, I had spent many long nights dreaming of how wonderful it would be to raise a child, and here I was, presented with the opportunity. Despite the way it had come about, Jordan had no role to play in their deceit and narcissism. So, I refused to punish him. I begged Veronica for the chance to hold him in my arms once again, as I had many times before. This time felt different, though. I watched baby Jordan in admiration as if I had birthed him myself. *How hard this must be for my sister to leave her child… with me,* I thought.

With no objection, she rose from her seat and placed him gently in my arms. Looking into his gray eyes, I simply melted.

Smiling from ear to ear as he gripped my index finger—just as he had done so many times before—I was so immersed in his love and warmth that I didn't notice Veronica gathering her belongings. Appalled, I asked, "Where on earth are you going?"

Silence.

"I love you, Vern," she said, beaming.

I watched as Nica and Peter exchanged a few words. He leaned over, grabbed her things, and walked her down the stairs. Nica came over to give me a hug, my body resisting. Kissing Jordan on his forehead, she threw her shawl over her shoulders and stepped confidently out of the room.

Once she was gone, I took a seat on the edge of the bed and placed Jordan in the center, my arm guarding him as I sang a short lullaby until he closed his eyes. Falling into a deep slumber, before I knew it, we were both fast asleep.

Despite having so many more questions for Peter— about his infidelity and about allowing my sister to abandon her newborn—I simply couldn't bring myself to engage in another argument. I needed rest—both figuratively and literally.

"When are we going to see him?"

The voice in my dreams haunted me, insidious and chilling. It carried the weight of death and malevolence. My body felt pinned to the mattress as I struggled to awaken. Trapped between life and death, the baby was crying.

Wake up, Vernette! Get up, Vernette!

I heard myself screaming, but my mouth remained closed. My body stiffened.

Dead—my first experience with sleep paralysis. A battle with demons.

"Make the world go round and round, our music we sing out loud, treading through gates, move through waters…"

Peter sang an old hymn, the rhythm off, but the words resounded through my soul.

Finally, I awakened.

As soon as my eyes opened, I felt completely exhausted. Jordan was no longer by my side, sending me into a panic. I ran down the stairs in a hurry, slamming into Peter, who was pouring milk onto his wrist to test the temperature of Jordan's bottle.

"Where is the baby?" I shouted.

Raising his hand to my face, he calmly said, "Please, lower your voice. Jordan is asleep, and I'm about to wake him for his feeding. Are you okay? You've been asleep for almost three days. I almost called the doctor."

He stretched his arms toward me, gently caressing my cheek as he felt my forehead. I let out a huge sigh. Something did feel off, as if something was feeding off of me, but our home was empty again…things felt…normal. I suddenly felt lightheaded, but to avoid any further discussion about myself, I changed the subject.

"We should probably go feed the baby."

Peter sighed, clearly unhappy with how I always avoided addressing my own issues, but he didn't push the matter.

"Why don't you feed him? I think he misses seeing your face."

Smiling, I moved with haste.

Peter turned back toward the kitchen—I assumed he was cooking. I wanted to ask what had happened to Elizabeth, but something told me not to. I decided to simply enjoy my new family.

To our surprise, after two weeks had passed with no word from either Veronica or David, Peter, Jordan, and I began to feel more and more like a true unit. Weeks turned into months, and we bought new clothes, toys, and a stroller, even building a brand-new crib together. We were laughing again whilst baby proofing the house, which was surely a good sign.

Jordan did the cutest things. He was growing into a handsome boy, always so happy. Things were undeniably pleasant… until one day…

"This is ridiculous, Veronica!"

The yelling could be heard from miles away.

Peter, Jordan, and I sat in the living room, watching cartoons while the baby pounded his toy trucks against the wooden floor. I refused to leave Jordan, so Peter went out to greet David at the front door.

"Where is my son?"

Hearing those words made my heart drop. But I didn't hear Nica.

"Jordan is fine," Peter said sternly.

I cradled the baby in my arms, listening as David stomped through my home, searching for his son. With no idea where Jordan could be, he turned back to Peter, who said little to nothing while being coerced into answering questions.

"This is kidnapping, you know that? My son is a baby, and it is in his best interest to be with his parents."

David didn't sound like himself. He was belligerent, shouting, banging on the walls. Finally, Jordan picked up on the commotion and started to cry. His cries led David straight to us.

The moment he saw my face, something inside him snapped. Before I knew it, he and Peter were wrestling in my living room.

Clutching Jordan tightly, I ran around toward the front door, intending to head upstairs, where I hoped we'd be safe. As I rushed forward, David struggled to break free from Peter's grip, yelling, "Get off me, man!"

I moved swiftly, hushing Jordan as we went.

Then, Nica appeared.

She stood by the front door, a gang of white police officers behind her.

I swallowed hard.

Finally, David and Peter emerged.

"That's my son, officer."

I stopped breathing.

Nica couldn't bring herself to look at me. She mouthed, *I am so sorry,* as the officers stepped inside my home. Her eyes dropped, her ponytail swaying in the wind, beautiful as always. She was dressed in a pair of olive-colored slacks and a red checkered, quarter-sleeve button-down, buttoned only midway, with the ends tied right above her waist—a tan wool coat hanging just over her shoulders.

Even as the officers pried Jordan from my arms, I couldn't take my eyes off her.

My heart ached.

Something came over me, and before I knew it, I was lashing out, screaming obscenities.

"You lying bitch! How could you do this to me? To him? David, ask your wife why her son has been here with my husband and me for the past four months! Ask her! Ask her!

Officer, what kind of parents leave their child somewhere else for four whole months? David, huh? Did you just now notice your son wasn't home? Is that why you're here now?"

As I let out my final cry, Peter began tugging on me, urging me to go back inside. The officers instructed me to quiet down while David stepped past us, grabbing Veronica by the waist as she cradled baby Jordan in her arms. The October winds were merciless against the neighbor's wind chimes.

Slamming the door behind them, I fell to my knees in agony.

Peter stood beside me, his arms folded. Tears welled in his eyes, but we remained in silence.

Nights came and went without a single word from anyone. The laughter, the crying—our home now felt empty. There were two rooms we no longer entered. The guest room we had redesigned for a child, once filled with toys, games, a crib, and wallpaper, now stood as a painful reminder. I could no longer bear to look at it. I begged Peter to close the door and never open it again.

We ate dinner in silence, stopped watching television together, and for eight weeks, we were both consumed by grief. We even skipped the holidays that year—no dinners, no gatherings, nothing.

Having Jordan made us realize how miserable we truly were without children of our own.

Doubts about Peter's past infidelity crept back into my mind. I found myself questioning everything.

We tried for months after that to conceive. I began tracking my ovulation schedule as best as I could—we didn't have all these fancy gadgets back then to help with that. Everything was done manually. But despite our efforts, we had no success.

At one point, I even remember giving Peter permission to have a child with someone else, and I would help him raise the baby. Unconventional, of course, but it was the only way I could ensure he wouldn't divorce me and run off with someone younger—or fertile. He quickly dismissed the idea.

We then discussed adoption, but as a middle-class African American family, it was not going to be easy, and no agency would consider us. They never said why out loud, but we knew.

Meanwhile, my blackouts were getting worse—I was losing days at a time. But after the doctor assured me I was fine, we assumed it was just hormones, especially since we were still trying for a baby. Maybe it was a symptom of pregnancy that left me feeling so exhausted all the time. But later, we would learn that wasn't the case either.

We never could put our finger on it.

By New Year's 1960, we had turned over a new leaf, and one day, while knitting and noticing the pewter ashtrays, I decided it was time to visit my parents. I hadn't seen them in so long, and after everything that had happened, I figured I could use the warm weather.

By the close of January, when the snow was at its heaviest, I packed my bags. Peter couldn't come with me due to work, but this did not worry me.

Our bond now seemed indestructible.

I began to trust him.

And he learned not to resent me for the family it seemed I could never give him.

I packed lightly—one suitcase and a handbag for the flight. Stepping outside, I moved past the little black gate, waiting by the curb for a checkered taxicab. When one finally approached, I hesitated. It already had passengers.

At first, I didn't recognize who was getting out of the vehicle.

Then it hit me.

I began to cry.

Matthew, now four years old.

Ebony, aged three.

And, of course, baby Jordan—a toddler.

Despite all the hatred I held for my sister, I couldn't stop myself. I ran forward, prying Jordan from her arms. He had grown even more.

Matthew, a rambunctious child, grabbed his small suitcase.

Ebony, wide-eyed and smiling, waddled toward the back of the cab as her mother instructed her to gather her things.

They were all there.

Everyone except David.

"Let's go, children. We have to move quickly," Nica said. "Get out of the road, Matthew, and please help your sister with her things."

"No," he snapped.

"No!" Ebony repeated.

I was so elated—so much so that I forgot my bags were still on the curb. I stood adjacent to the taxicab, holding Jordan in my arms. I loved listening to the children bicker and enjoyed watching Nica attempt to scold them.

"Let's go! Out of the street, I said!" she yelled.

I was so lost in my happiness that I didn't notice Nica calling my name.

"Vernette!"

I turned to see her standing there, holding Ebony in her arms. Matthew stood beside her, waiting for further instructions, dragging his leather-belted suitcase behind him. It hadn't dawned on me that they were handling luggage, so I didn't think to ask if they were planning on staying. All I cared about was that Jordan was back in my arms again.

At exactly 3:00 PM, the old grandfather clock tolled from the living room as we all made our way inside. I carried my bags and Jordan, while Veronica lugged in two belted cases. Ebony clutched her bear-decorated knapsack, and Matthew—who had an odd fascination with Popeye, as it was the only way to get him to eat spinach—dragged his suitcase behind him.

Once inside, everyone scattered across the house. Ebony struggled to climb the stairs, while Matthew made a mess in the kitchen, attempting to pour himself a glass of milk.

"This house is small, Mommy," he whined.

I didn't feel insulted; I understood his discomfort. My home was much cozier than my sister's, but it had been in our family for generations. That alone made it legendary—if not spacious.

"Mommy, Mommy! Come, I'll show you my room!" Ebony shouted from the top of the staircase.

Nica and I exchanged a look of curiosity. Jordan was fast asleep in my arms, and I had no intention of putting him down anytime soon. Before we could react, we heard the sound of running water.

With a leisurely gait, Nica sashayed up the stairs. I couldn't understand how she remained so composed while her children ran amok. And there were only two of them.

"Cartoons?" Matthew shouted.

I knew he was in my precious living room, the only place with a television. Upon entering, I nearly dropped Jordan from my arms. I gasped loudly.

Milk was spilled all over my kitchen counter—and worse, all over my expensive leather couch.

Placing Jordan meticulously on the dry section of the sofa, I turned to Matthew. "Go to the other room," I instructed, trying to keep my frustration at bay.

I hated yelling at him. He barely knew me and often referred to me as "Miss." To him, I was still a stranger. I wasn't prepared for this.

Just as I managed to restore some order downstairs, I heard Ebony's giggles echoing from upstairs.

"I'm going to get you! Come here, baby girl—Mommy's going to bite you!" Nica teased, laughter filling the upper level of my home.

Then I remembered the running water.

Seconds later, Nica appeared, carrying a naked Ebony in her arms.

"You gave her a bath?" I asked, hopelessly.

Before Nica could respond, Jordan let out a screech.

I spun around, my heart dropping—he had fallen from the couch.

I wanted to scream.

Fifteen minutes. That's all it had taken for my once peaceful home to descend into chaos.

"There are only two of us and three of them—they outnumber us, Vern. No need to get all worked up," Veronica said wittily.

I still couldn't understand why she was so calm. Something wasn't right.

I had been so consumed with cleaning up after Matthew and ensuring Jordan's safety that Nica and I hadn't had a moment to speak. I suggested we all sit in the living room, where the children could watch their favorite cartoons while she and I talked.

After a long pause, she agreed.

Finally, peace settled over the house. I closed my eyes and took a slow sip from a tall glass of water.

Nica stood with her back against the countertop, draped in an all-black linen jumpsuit, cinched at the waist with a pink Chanel belt. Her hands rested in her pockets, her expression unreadable.

"Why are you here? Haven't you caused me enough pain?"

She chuckled, her eyes glistening with their usual sparkle, and her dark, waist-length curls dancing around her face. Still, she looked ageless. Squinting, she licked her lips before responding.

"David and I are taking a vacation. We're going to visit Mommy and Daddy."

My right eyebrow raised almost instinctively. Feeling like the village idiot, I paused before responding.

"I—I—I was packed. I was going to visit Mom and Dad. D—D—Did he not tell you this? And besides, where is Lucinda to watch the kids?" I stuttered.

"Interestingly enough, Vern, Daddy suggested that you watch the kids because, honestly, he mentioned nothing about you going out there. He felt like this would be a good way for you and the children to develop some kind of bond," she said—lying. The dishonest look in her eyes, coupled with a cynical smile, told me as much. Her body swayed, and her arms swung like those of a child.

"Bond?" I questioned through tears. "What type of bond exactly is he referring to? Oh—oh, does he think that you should, um, I don't know, leave them with me out of pity? And then what? He can send his precinct next time to come pick them up. What do I look like? I have a life, I have a husband, I am no caretaker. I wish everyone would stop pretending to feel sorry for me because instead of helping, you're all making it worse. It's like everyone is taking pleasure in mocking my pain—bringing your kids here so I can look after them while you head off to parlay with Mommy and Daddy!"

My father knew how devastated Peter and I were after Jordan was taken. Heck, even my mother knew—she and I had begun speaking again shortly after that incident.

I couldn't help it. I was shouting, I was angry, I was emotional, and most of all, I was hurt.

"I get eighty-nine dollars from Peter a month, and that is more than generous. Are you leaving money? And how long will you be gone?"

I had settled down now, my tears dried as I realized Nica had absolutely nothing to say. We continued to stand in the kitchen. I motioned toward the sink, figuring I might as well begin preparing dinner.

Nica uncrossed her arms and whispered, "Vern, she's trying to take my kids."

My head snapped in her direction. Our eyes locked, but only for a second.

"You are the only chance they have to find the light and survive. I can't help them. I've tried staying away from them to protect them, and it's not enough."

I didn't believe her. I thought it was all lies—only because I hadn't had any blackouts or hallucinations recently. I had no reason to believe anything she was saying. The darkest part of our lives seemed to be over.

"Matthew—he is a firstborn, and that's who she's after right now. I don't believe in your G—G—Go—you know what I mean. So, Mommy said you can help them. Don't hate me, please."

As if in the blink of an eye, she tossed her scarf around her head. I asked no questions as she scurried down the hallway—not even so much as a goodbye—before disappearing out the front door.

Quivering, I whispered to myself, "What in God's name have they done to you?"

With no one to answer my question, I had to face the reality that I was now alone with three beautiful children, left to explain everything to my husband once he returned home. I paced, uncertain of how to react, what to do next, and completely doubtful of my ability to raise one child—let alone three.

These aren't ordinary children, I thought. *These children are gifts. How can I be sure of the right things to say?*

I wrestled with my thoughts, searching my mind for answers, but found nothing. I decided on the one thing I knew would never fail me—prayer. Taking a step toward my kitchen counter, I placed my hands atop the sink and closed my eyes.

"Father, please guide me," I whispered.

Moments later, I felt a sense of bravado. Without further hesitation, I marched into the living room. Turning off the television set, I stood before these three lovely children. Jordan swaying his legs, whilst he suckled on his thumb, Ebony stared at me with wide, searching eyes, and Matthew sighed over and over again. That's when I began.

"Children, your mother is going away for some time—" I hesitated, twirling my thumbs and batting my eyelashes profusely.

"Ma'am, Mommy is always leaving us," Matthew interrupted, his tone innocent.

"Mommy," Ebony said, fidgeting.

Although polite, I couldn't get past the fact that he called me *ma'am*. I was no *ma'am*. Granted, I was turning thirty-two that year, but I was still in my prime. Immediately, I called everyone to attention.

"Look, I am your Auntie Vern, okay? And that is how you will refer to me from now on. Is that understood?"

"What does *referra* mean?" Ebony asked, crossing her skinny legs. She was an articulate child.

"It means calling her and saying what she wanna be called as," Matthew snarled. Only halfway correct, but I giggled at their dialogue. It took me a moment to process that I was speaking to three individuals whose combined ages hadn't even reached double digits.

So, I rephrased. "Call me Auntie Vern, okay? Are you guys hungry?"

With hesitation, Ebony replied, "Ye-yes, Au-Aun-Auntie Vern."

Smiling, I felt accomplished.

They were warming up to me—slightly.

I didn't want to get ahead of myself, but that night, dinner was served. I prepared baked potatoes with baked chicken, salad, and corn on the cob.

Licking his fingers, Matthew was nothing short of delighted.

"What was that yella stuff? It was so good!" he said, smiling.

"Corn," I replied. "That's a good thing to eat," I added.

Feeling relieved, I instructed the children to head upstairs for a bath as the cold breeze began creeping through the house. The absence of Peter worried me as the clock now read 6:54 PM. With Jordan tucked safely on the sofa, I cleared away the dishes, scrubbing the pots, pans, plates, cups, and silverware before placing them on the counter to air dry.

Lifting Jordan, I began making my way up the stairs.

Noticing the guest room door was still locked, I felt unsettled until I overheard both Ebony and Matthew cackling—skinny-dipping in my bedroom bathtub. Stepping inside, I watched as water splashed from left to right, a big mess spilling onto the floor.

I felt exhausted, but I couldn't allow them to see me that way. If they had outnumbered Veronica and me before, this time was worse, and I had to keep a level head.

"No, no! Children, out of the tub—out now!"

Both Matthew and Ebony seemed perfectly comfortable bathing together, as if it were a routine they were both accustomed to. I couldn't understand the reason for my lack of patience; all I knew was that there was now an even bigger mess for me to clean, all while wondering why Peter had yet to return home.

A while later, after sorting through their luggage— including the suitcase Nica had pulled, which contained all of their things—and finishing bath time, I began instructing Matthew and Ebony on what to wear to bed when I heard the front door slam shut. Relief washed over me, but so did frustration—relieved that Peter was finally home to assist me, yet angry that he was this late. 7:47 PM. I had planned for the children to be in bed by eight, giving them just enough time to settle in. They couldn't sleep in the guest room because the door remained locked. Only Peter had the key.

Growing impatient, I sat upright on my mattress. Ebony and Matthew lay sprawled on Peter's side of the bed, while Jordan napped between my legs. I kept wondering why Peter hadn't made his way up the stairs yet. Fifteen minutes passed.

"Peter!" I called.

Straining to hear a response, I begged the children to stop bickering long enough for me to listen. Still nothing.

I refused to move—leaving Jordan alone while he slept beside two children, even if just for a moment, would be the cornerstone of neglect. So, I continued to wait.

Waiting.

Waiting.

Waiting.

Finally, the stairs began to creak.

I called again, this time my voice just above a whisper, as the children had begun to drift off to sleep, their noise fading into the silence of the house.

"Peter?"

At last, a response.

"Vernette?"

I trembled at the sound of his baritone—calmed yet uneasy.

"What in the world?" he exclaimed, striding into our bedroom, his face alight with a joy I hadn't expected.

Peter quickly gathered both Matthew and Ebony, stroking their sides and smiling. My presence became an afterthought—overshadowed, ignored. He offered me neither attention nor affection.

"So, how was your day?" I whispered.

No response. Just quiet. He kept smiling, ecstatic, his focus entirely on them.

I stretched over and placed my hand gently atop his arm. His stare burned through me.

Afraid to ask but needing to, I whispered again, "Should we open the guest rooms? The one downstairs and the one next to us?"

Silence.

"Peter!" I beckoned.

More silence.

Was he punishing me? Had I upset him somehow? I felt awkward, my mind racing through a list of things I might have done to make him angry. *Nothing.*

His dinner was in the oven.

The house was clean.

"Peter, honey, I know it seems as though I made an impromptu decision without consulting you, but I never meant to make you feel like your input isn't valued or considered."

I pleaded, consoled, and even let a few tears fall.

Completely mute, he now watched as the children slept. He placed his right hand atop Matthew's abdomen, feeling the slow rise and fall of his chest. Then, closing his eyes, he exhaled deeply—meditating.

"Do you wonder why you aren't taken seriously?" he finally said. His voice was calm but firm. "You take on others' responsibilities in addition to your own—for a manipulative sister and her husband, you once called a lover. What about your trip to see your parents? Why don't you ever prioritize your needs? We have plans and then suddenly—"

I stiffened.

"Your decisions no longer impact only you," he continued. "They affect me, too. And I can't even bring myself to ask what this is all about because, deep down, I already know. I will not get attached. I do not want to know why they are here or for how long. I will take it one day at a time, and I suggest you do the same."

With that, he pulled away.

The sound of keys jingling echoed from both upstairs and downstairs as he unlocked the guest rooms. Almost instantly, a pungent odor drifted up from the ground-floor bedroom, making its way to my nostrils. I didn't care to see the inside.

Instead, I lay back, lost in thought, replaying Peter's words over and over until sleep overtook me. My fingers lightly stroked Jordan's curls as he nestled against me. He bore a striking resemblance to a child of mixed heritage— Black yet with features reminiscent of Indian descent, his light brown complexion glowing under the dim light, his soft curls coiling under my touch.

The next morning, I begged Peter to have the bedrooms remodeled and redecorated—at least to the children's liking. He had many friends in the trade.

During breakfast, we asked them what colors they would prefer. Little did we know, décor, paint, and children do not mix.

"We want toys!"

"Toys are for babies, Ebony!" Matthew mocked.

"No, I want a dolly and some candy with rainbows on the walls."

"That's for girls!" he yelled.

"Okay, okay, kids. Once you've finished your omelets, you can both go into the living room to watch television," I said.

Jordan and I remained at the table, his sippy cup in my right hand as I continued to brainstorm ideas for their new bedrooms. Despite their stay possibly lasting only a week or two, I still wanted them to feel as comfortable as possible.

Green and yellow. The colors immediately came to mind as I listened to the television blaring, Peter upstairs preparing for another long day. *Green and yellow.* I repeated the words over and over in my mind. *Green and yellow.*

"Peter, green and yellow!" I bellowed.

Walking over to Jordan and me, Peter reached out his arms, instructing me to hand him over. Ecstatic that I had thought of neutral colors suitable for both Ebony and Matthew, I waited for a mutual response.

What I got instead was surprising.

"How are we funding this? I have no problem with the children staying here, but realistically, must we support them financially too? We live in a one-income home, and the mortgage may be rising in a few months. The ninety-three dollars we pay now is feasible, but that may change, Vern."

Peter was right. I felt completely embarrassed.

"You're right, honey. We can simply utilize the furniture we have now and make the best of it." I said it with confidence, though part of me wished I could do more.

Immediately after he left for the day, I made my way into the vacant bedrooms, determined to create a welcoming space despite our limitations. I cleaned, mopped, and swept, rearranging furniture upstairs and bringing some pieces downstairs. In the basement, I found old items that I brought up and refurbished, determined to make the best of what we had.

Before I knew it, three glorious months had passed. We celebrated Jordan's third birthday—my parents called, but neither Veronica nor David contacted him—followed by Thanksgiving and then Christmas.

By January 1961, we were still on a fixed mortgage, but Peter's salary would increase. He was covering numerous stories about the steady rise of the Civil Rights Movement and had even begun making trips to Montgomery, Alabama, where he met with Dr. Martin Luther King Jr. for exclusive interviews. Over the years, they had grown very close.

When *The Times* caught wind of Peter's plan to transition into freelancing, they quickly reeled him back in with enticing perks. They could not afford to lose access to his coverage of Dr. King, as breaking such news first was of utmost importance. With the bonuses and increased pay, I was able to afford new clothes, new furniture, and, of course, new toys for Ebony.

Peter also increased my allowance, allowing us to enjoy an extravagant holiday season. Communication between Peter and me was exceptional, strengthening our bond as we navigated the changes in our lives. His career continued to flourish, the children adjusted to our evolving lifestyle, and so, life was good.

Although I had sent multiple letters to our parents in Florida, I never received a response. No telegrams, no phone calls, no correspondence at all.

Radio silence.

Ebony often asked about Nica, while Matthew preferred to ask about his father. Jordan, however, was closest to Peter and me. Before I knew it, he had started calling me *Mum*. I never knew the right answers to give the children, so all I could do was discreetly change the subject.

I myself began to worry. *Where could Veronica and David be? Do they not miss their children? How could they have been gone for so long?*

Once spring came around, we had settled in nicely. I began preparing for Matthew to start first grade, which meant one less child to care for during the day. I could tell he was going to be a bright young man.

By the time Ebony turned five, we had already begun planning her lavish birthday party. She was quite the character—outspoken and full of life. We invited all of our neighbors to join us, and the celebration was filled with laughter, happiness, and, of course, gifts! I prepared a large meal, purchased plenty of finger foods, and even bought a jukebox for the living room, where her favorite tunes echoed through the speakers.

Many of Peter's friends attended, along with several of his coworkers. I met so many people that it became overwhelming to serve food, socialize, and keep an eye on the children all at once. Growing exhausted, I begged Peter to assist me. His friends did not approve. *A woman is supposed to cater, serve, and raise the children in front of her husband's peers.*

Peter refused to help. Instead, he sat back, socialized, and even stepped outside at one point to smoke a cigar on the stoop. Matthew, now six, sat atop his lap, swinging his tiny legs, wide-eyed at the conversation unfolding among nine grown men.

Meredith, the wife of a senior editor for the paper, noticed my struggles and kindly stepped in to help. She carried the finger foods, served champagne, and kept an eye on the children playing in the backyard. I appreciated her deeply.

As the evening wound down, I was finally able to rest. Before I knew it, I had fallen into a deep slumber, the children tucked away in their beds.

"Vernette! Vernette!"

I opened my eyes slowly, whimpering almost.

"Sweetheart, everyone is gone. I've cleaned the house, and the children are in bed."

This was why I loved this man.

Peter lifted me, guiding my right arm around his neck for support, and carried me through the living and dining rooms. The kitchen smelled of Pine-Sol, and the hall floors gleamed, polished to perfection. I kissed him gently, whispering, "I love you."

Because I absolutely did love him. Hell, I adored that man.

That night, I fell into a deep sleep, my pillow damp with drool.

Then, with little warning, the sound of crying pierced the silence, echoing through the halls.

I woke in horror.

Scrambling to my feet, I stumbled, barely able to catch my balance as I rushed downstairs. My heart pounded as I reached the foyer near Veronica's old bedroom—now Matthew's. The door was locked.

Immediately, I heard Matthew's loud, desperate cries. His voice cracked as he screamed, shouted, and whimpered.

"Help! Help me, Auntie!"

Completely shocked and overwhelmed with fear, I screamed for Peter, assuming he was tending to Ebony and Jordan, who had undoubtedly woken from all the commotion.

Try as I might, I was unable to unlock the door. It had been locked from the inside. I begged God to let me save my nephew. Something was hurting him, causing him unbearable pain as he continued to cry and plead. Thunderous noises erupted from the other side of the door—banging, rustling, and the violent thrusting of objects. It felt like the presence of a poltergeist.

The doorknob grew scorching hot, sizzling beneath my touch. I pounded on the door. *Boom, boom, boom.* The noise intensified, Matthew's screams growing stronger. *Boom, boom, boom, boom, boom!* My fists hammered against the wood until my knuckles bled. Sliding my hands down the door, I felt utterly defeated.

"Auntie Vern, I can't breathe!" Matthew's voice cracked, distorted with terror.

I threw my shoulder against the door, ramming it over and over until my arm throbbed with pain.

"Jesus Christ, Vern, this isn't your fight!" Peter shouted.

Jordan and Ebony stood atop the staircase, crying. I ran to them, cradling them helplessly as Matthew's screams echoed through the house. This wasn't a nightmare. Something evil was in that room, and my faith wasn't strong enough to fight it alone. I begged Peter to pray, to do something—anything—to save my nephew. He was just a child. What could they possibly want with him?

Minutes passed, yet the spirits did not relent.

Then—silence.

Matthew had stopped screaming. My heart pounded.

"Peter, we have to do something! Should we call the police? We have to get the door open!" I begged.

Peter ignored me, his voice rising in tongues as he prayed. I knew there was a reason this room had remained locked for so many years. I had hesitated to let Matthew sleep there, but I convinced myself he was old enough and needed the space. Now, regret consumed me. I felt like I had failed him.

Then—*creak*.

The bedroom door slowly opened.

Without thinking, I raced forward, but before I could step inside, an unseen force hurled me backward. I slammed into the staircase banister, a sharp cry escaping my lips.

Peter grabbed my collar, his voice firm. "This isn't your fight!"

I sobbed, feeling utterly powerless. The room was pitch black. Matthew was nowhere to be seen—only heard, whimpering atop his mattress.

I begged Peter to let me go in, but he refused.

"Show yourself!" he commanded, gripping the banister.

I was terrified. I had heard stories of demons invading homes, but I never thought I would experience it firsthand.

"Show yourself!" Peter bellowed again.

Still nothing.

The house fell eerily silent. Ebony clutched Jordan tightly, and I prayed she wouldn't drop him.

Then, I remembered Nica's warning before she left. *Bring them into the light.*

"Light!" I screamed. "Peter, light!"

Unsure of what to do, I ran to the living room, grabbing the cup of anointed oil that sat atop the television mantle. My hands trembled as I twisted the cap off, then I rushed back and flung the oil into the room, its drops glistening against the floorboards. Step by step, I moved forward, the oil guiding my way.

As I entered, my breath hitched.

Matthew sat upright on the bed, his body eerily still. A surge of goosebumps raced up my arms.

"Get out of there!" Peter yelled.

Ignoring him, I continued sprinkling the oil, a little at a time, moving cautiously toward Matthew. As I reached his bedside, my breath caught in my throat. A tall, dark shadow loomed over him, its mouth stretched impossibly wide, preparing to scream. Without hesitation, I flung the oil in its direction. A demonic shriek erupted through the room, and a faint light flickered along the wooden floorboards.

"Auntie! Auntie, help me, please!" Matthew cried.

I grabbed him as fast as I could, shoving him toward the doorway. He tumbled into the hallway just as the door slammed shut behind him—leaving me trapped inside.

Peter pounded on the other side. *Bang! Bang! Bang!* I couldn't see a thing. The room was pitch black. A crackling sound filled the air, the floorboards groaning beneath unseen weight. The presence was moving closer.

With the last bit of oil in my hand, I waited, my body trembling. My hands quivered so badly that drops of oil splashed onto the floor, illuminating faint, flickering spots wherever they landed. I began reciting the Lord's Prayer, repeating each line, my voice shaking. My eyes were clenched shut, but I *felt* it—hot breath against my neck.

This was real. This demon was in my home.

I didn't know what had been practiced in this room before, but with the door sealed, it had been confined.

I kept praying, gripping the remaining oil, preparing for one final attack. *Lord, see me through this.*

On the count of five, I thought. *One… two… three… four… FIVE!*

I hurled the oil.

For a brief, terrifying moment, the darkness peeled away, revealing a face.

It was Nica.

She was dead.

A bloodcurdling scream ripped from my throat, burning as it escaped.

The door suddenly burst open, and Peter grabbed me by the collar, yanking me out just as it slammed shut again. I collapsed onto the floor but immediately scrambled up, pounding on the door.

"She's trapped in there! Peter, we have to let her out!" I sobbed.

"That was not her, Vern."

I wept, my body shaking.

Ebony rushed forward, pounding on the door beside me. "Mommy! Mommy, are you in there?" she cried.

My heart shattered.

Matthew sat alone at the far end of the hallway, near the kitchen, rocking back and forth. He was completely still, his face pale, his eyes hollow. This poor boy was mortified.

I approached him gently, my steps careful. I didn't want to know what had happened to him in that room— I only wanted to hold his hand and assure him that everything would be okay.

We never spoke of that night again. The room was bolted shut, sealed away from our lives. That night, we all slept together in the master bedroom, the children nestled between us. Peter awoke every hour, checking the doors, ensuring nothing could reach us. I lay beside him, heart pounding, fear lingering like a shadow in my chest.

I was still terrified.

But a part of me was also *intrigued.*

Something was after my babies and I needed to know what it was.

FOUR YEARS LATER

I moved about the kitchen with practiced precision, our routine down to a science.

"I want to check your homework, Bones."

"Auntie Vern, why? I'm not failing anything, and my classes aren't hard."

"You're dumb, that's why," Matthew teased.

"Hey, hey, cut it out. No, the teacher stopped by yesterday, and she said she's a little concerned, okay? I just want to go over it, that's all."

"See? You're dumb," Matthew whispered.

"Auntie Vern, tell him to stop!" Bones began to sob.

The children were growing up beautifully and handsomely. Matthew was now ten, Ebony—whom we now called Bones—was almost nine, and Jordan, eight. Jordan had become my pride and joy, clinging to me like my better half, his soft, wide eyes capable of melting even the hardest of hearts.

"Okay, okay, you all need to start getting ready for school," I instructed both Matthew and Bones to gather their belongings, but not before placing their cutlery in the sink. "You guys know better—there aren't any housemaids here. Get those dishes up."

I snapped my neck slightly—a little bit of Bones had begun to rub off on me. Such a feisty one, that girl.

"Auntie Vern, you know I'm clean. It's Matthew who's filthy," she said, snapping her neck and rolling her eyes. "Jordan, you be good today, okay?" Always giving instructions like she was the adult around here.

"Leave me alone!" he snapped.

Breakfast in the mornings was always memorable and worthwhile. Their constant bickering and playful banter kept me cackling.

All the children attended the same school—within walking distance. Their classrooms were only a few doors apart, which was a relief. I always encouraged them to check on one another throughout the day.

At home, I spent my spare time studying. Although the memories from four years ago hadn't consumed me entirely, I remained determined to uncover what had plagued my family and how to prevent it from reaching the children—*my* children.

The kids shared the guest room on the second floor with Peter and me. He had been working on converting the den into a bedroom for Matthew, but with his increasing work-related travel, progress was slow.

Each of the children had their own hobbies— Matthew loved playing baseball with his friends in the small backyard, Ebony enjoyed singing to her dolls, and Jordan had taken a special interest in cooking. I wanted to nurture that passion, often allowing him to assist me in making dinner.

Dinnertime was always a special moment in our home. With Peter's unpredictable schedule, we valued the time we had together, never taking a moment for granted. We were making the best memories—ones I hoped would last a lifetime.

A few days later, on the afternoon of September 23, 1965, a knock on the door changed all of our lives.

The kids were old enough to walk home from school, and I was in the middle of knitting scarves for them when the sudden knocking on the door, followed by the doorbell ringing, caught me at an inopportune moment. Startled, I pricked my index finger with the knitting needle, letting out a sharp cry.

Immediately, I rose as blood began gushing from my fingertip. The doorbell continued to chime, the knocking intensified, and my finger throbbed with pain. I could see the shadowy figure of a woman standing just on the other side…

—

"Maybe we should take you to a hospital," Washington says.

"I don't need a hospital! It's called morning sickness!" Emily snaps. "Besides, you don't have a car here, and you're not driving my rental."

"You've been throwing up non-stop for days now," I say calmly.

"Auntie, please, just continue," Emily says as she sits upright. Her hands rest across her stomach, draped with a light purple towel. She shivers but insists I go on. Against my better judgment, I hear the words leave my lips—not because I am uncaring, but because I am triggered all over again by what's to come.

—

"NO!" I SHOUTED.

Veronica and David tussled with me outside on the stoop. I felt overpowered, defeated, and completely helpless. I shouted for the neighbors—a left hook to my ribs. I shouted for the police—a hand forced over my mouth. I shouted for anyone. The final blow—a spit to my face. Still, I remained adamant in my position to be the parent God had appointed me to be.

"Listen, Vernette, these are my damn kids!" Veronica yelled.

Jordan's face slowly came into view as the kids turned the corner onto our street, unaware of who these strangers were—attacking the only maternal figure he had grown to know. The look on his face gave me the strength to fight harder, to fight longer.

"No! No! How can you come back after all these years!? What the hell did you expect?"

Shockingly, Veronica responded, "We just needed some time, Vern."

I was confused—outright enraged by the fact that David and Veronica had been toying with my emotions, using me as they pleased. David had outwardly expressed his disdain for me time and time again, and yet, his children remained in my care with no word, no contact. Veronica was doing something to him. Though only a speculation, I wasn't far off—the look in his eyes always gave him away, making it apparent that he was under a spell.

"You abandoned them! You and David left for years. Peter and I have been the sole caretakers of these children! I sent letters, only to have them returned. How can you come back and simply take them? Jordan doesn't even know who you are!" I snapped—my voice ferocious. I no longer saw the woman I once called my sister. The person standing in front of me was now a complete stranger.

"Well, then, keep him. I want my other children," she spat, throwing her poncho across her right shoulder.

"Matthew will not come near you—he thinks you tried to hurt him!"

The expression she gave made me quiver.

Her eyes were menacing.

"Vernette, I asked you to protect them, not poison their minds against me! Do you want a family that badly, you sick woman?"

"Vernette. You haven't called me that since we were children."

Something was off.

She was standing here, but it wasn't her.

"Bring me the kids!"

I stood there weeping. Jordan's tender smile flashed before my eyes. I refused to put him through this any longer, and so, I surrendered.

The kids were making their way down the street—closer now. Matthew stopped walking—that was my cue. Pushing past Veronica and David, I ran to them, instructing everyone to stay behind me.

"Damn, they're big. Are you sure about this?" David whispered to Veronica, thinking I hadn't heard him.

Falling to my knees, I hugged them all, realizing I could no longer protect them. Fussing and crying, the children begged me not to let them go. But David insisted, promising them ice cream and presents once they got home.

Veronica watched in disgust as her children sobbed for me while she and her wicked husband came to tear my family apart. I couldn't bear to look her in the eyes.

David announced, "Sweetheart, don't move. I will carry them. Just be careful—you don't want to hurt the baby."

I shook my head slightly.

"You will never meet this child. Come, kids," she beckoned.

Matthew kicked at the rocks on the ground. Ebony sniffled. Both of them were coerced into the vehicle—only Jordan remained.

For a long time, I was not the same, even scratching my scalp so hard that it bled sometimes. I needed to go away—it was time. Once the dust had settled and Peter managed to accept the fact that my sister had abruptly removed the children from our care, we could mindlessly carry on with our lives. His state of mind was, *At least they are being cared for. Who better to do so than their parents?* But I was numb, which was not fair to Jordan.

Try as he might, Peter made several attempts to keep my mind occupied, but being a housewife in his absence began to feel like imprisonment—an inmate in my own home, stuck between mothering a young child and offering my nurturance to my husband—yet there was no one to care for me. I could do nothing but worry and ponder. My mind had become a jail I desperately wanted to escape from.

It was during this time, toward the later part of the year—the holidays—that we celebrated what was now called The New York Times Party. It was the only time I felt free from the perfunctory routine I called my life. Hosted by Peter and his colleagues, I was merely there to smile and serve. This had become a sort of tradition for us.

Once it was over, I packed in a fit of rage, gathering my blouses, shorts, and slippers. Jordan was ready to go, and although Peter had just passed out on the living room couch—exhausted—and our last guest for the evening had departed approximately two and a half hours earlier, our home was immaculate. I decided to catch an overnight flight out of New York. No one was informed of my departure or my intended arrival. I could not prepare my parents for my visit. I could not bear the sound of their voices, convincing me not to come. I did not believe my parents hated me, but I knew I was one child they could have lived without; without me, I believed my mother would have been far more attentive to Veronica, never allowing Grandma Martin the opportunity to bewitch her.

Jordan was so good on the flight, considering it was his first. He quietly read his books while I gazed over the ocean before drifting into a slumber. Veronica had not called or written, and I had no idea how she was doing. I dreamt happy dreams just before the rough landing at Orlando International Airport. We had arrived.

I allowed Jordan to stay seated as I shuffled past him to retrieve our baggage from the overhead compartment. A gentleman watching me struggle offered his assistance. He smelled of lilacs, which was odd for a man—a fine sign that I should not get too close. I blushed as he handed me both Jordan's and my carry-on luggage.

"Thank you," I said. "Come now, Jordan."

I decided to call my parents once we deboarded. There was no way they could deter me from coming now—we were already here.

Once outside the airport, I had not the slightest idea which direction to turn. I knew only the town they resided in, but nothing more. I felt foolish, flying all this way without so much as a clue as to where I was going, endangering both myself and a child. But I kept imagining their faces once they saw us.

I bellowed for a checkered taxi, which charged me a whole eight dollars to take us into Kissimmee. Although dark, the town was beautiful—palm trees everywhere. It was my first time in Florida, and I was impressed. A huge difference from city life, no doubt. Open roads, a cool breeze, and wonderful spring weather just before dawn.

"I need an address, ma'am."

I handed him a return envelope from a letter my father had sent me a while ago.

Upon our arrival at their home, I watched as both my mother and father stood outside, staring mindlessly into each car that passed, wondering if I was in one of them. I was so excited that they were excited.

Jordan and I crawled out of the backseat in front of a Victorian home located in a courtyard. The house was magnificent—large and beautifully decorated on the outside. Their landscaping was tidy. They were living in a predominantly white neighborhood. As a member of law enforcement, my father was respected far and wide.

Strangers to Jordan, he did not move quickly. Typically shy, I was not surprised at his reaction to my parents. They were unfamiliar to him, after all.

"Young boy, you are so fair and handsome! Vernette, my goodness, oh how I have missed you!" My mother squeezed me tight, smiling and laughing. I felt her love.

My father came over to hug me once he finished removing our luggage from the taxi. Instantly, I thought of Peter and how worried he must have been.

Hysterically, I said, "Mommy, can I call Peter?"

"Absolutely, dear. Did you tell him you were coming?"

I dared not tell her the truth.

Inside, his voice on the other end of the phone gave my body chills.

"Vernette?"

Gasping, I shouted, "Peter!" I was so ecstatic that I had not realized how selfish it had been to just... leave. "Peter, I am here in Florida with my parents." I felt overjoyed as we conversed. It had to be around 4 AM, and Peter sounded more awake than ever—but definitely not pleased.

"I have been up, worried sick about you, woman. Our young boy gone, you gone. Have you lost your mind? What were you thinking? I called the damn police, Vern, I thought—God, I thought something terrible happened. Your sister, her husband, those people are crazy, and I had no clue!" Peter was very angry, and for good reason. I had nothing to say. What could I say?

"I'm sorry. I-I just needed to get away for a little while. Um, my parents... I haven't seen them in God knows how long. Please don't be so upset, Peter."

Suddenly, I received the dial tone.

"Mummy!" Jordan cried.

Dropping the phone, I ran into the dining area, where I saw my father leaping him into the air. Jordan was not amused, his father's face hidden behind him.

"Daddy, I don't think he likes that very much."

Just as I walked in to grab Jordan, my father threw him to the ground, his head smashing against the tiled floor, causing him to whimper. Blood splattered about.

I turned to face him. "Jesus, Daddy, why did you do that?"

My heart sank. Turning to look up at my father, he remained at a standstill. His eyes blackened, his mouth widening, ripping his face apart. I couldn't move, and Jordan had now disappeared. I screamed for my mother, the room growing dark. I screeched and cried until I felt a hand around my neck. My hands were pinned to the ground. I felt my airways closing and my eyes widening, but I remained powerless to stop this demon—or whatever it was—from trying to kill me. I shook my head so hard that I gave myself a headache. My father's face drooped, his mouth still open. "Kill the beast," a voice echoed from his lagging tongue.

Reality.

I jumped up from my sleep, frantically searching for Jordan. Nothing else mattered to me—not even my own well-being. I found him sleeping peacefully in the bedroom next to mine. I stood, taking several deep breaths. I hadn't had a nightmare in so long. Why here? Why now? Why with my parents? I was so confused, and I wondered if nothing I dreamt happened, then maybe Peter still didn't know where I was. I stumbled into the hallway, where I found a phone. After several failed attempts to contact my husband, he simply would not answer. What was happening? I stood in a daze, dizzy for a moment. What if something had happened to him? I was about to pass out when I dialed again. Nothing.

I sat on the hallway floor in tears. At that moment, I had no idea what I was more upset about. Could it be the nightmare, or that my husband had no idea where I was?

My emotions were heightened.

"Sweetie, your mom loves the perfume!" That voice caused my body to quiver. Trembling, my eyes red from crying and my heart beating rapidly, I turned around to see Peter standing behind me with a breakfast tray. I gasped so hard and backed up, rubbing my temples. Disconcerted, I knew he felt it as he placed the tray atop the mantle. Falling to his knees, he grabbed hold of me.

"Sweetie, you have to talk to me." I touched his face, my brows knitted. Was he real? What was he doing here? I moved his face to look behind him. We were indeed at my parents' house. My eyes darted anxiously—I felt like a crazy person.

"Pe-Pe-Peter, what... um, what are you doing here?" His face pulled back, and he proceeded to lift me from the ground, carrying me into the bedroom, where he placed me on the bed.

"I'm going to call you a doctor." I didn't want a doctor. I wanted a response.

"No doctor. Tell me what happened, and what are you doing here?"

"Vernette, what in the hell are you talking about? We flew in last night." I struggled to remember. The lilac perfume, the man on the plane, the carry-on over his shoulder. It was him.

"Wait a minute. Did I black out or something? Or is everyone trying to drive me mad? Because last I checked, I left you sleeping in the living room after The Times Party. I don't understand how you're here. Physically here. And then last night—well, technically, this morning, before dawn—I called you, and you hung up on me because you were angry that I didn't tell you where I was going. So, did you just get in? Did you just get here? Peter, don't you dare lie to me!"

I was growing angrier with each word. I stood and began pacing. I felt something was off, something wasn't adding up.

"Is everything all right?" my mother asked, standing by the bedroom door.

Panicked, I said, "No, Peter is here, Mom," I scoffed. "I mean, when did he get here?" Peter and my mother exchanged a look of worry. I felt it was best to sit down, but I couldn't. Peter and my mother were always in cahoots.

"Daddy!" I ran down the stairs to find my father in the kitchen, letting his record play as he cooked some eggs. "Daddy, when did Peter get here?"

Laughing now, I decided to have a seat on the island stool. Rubbing my head, I felt a bit at ease watching him cook and dance. But that feeling quickly vanished as he stopped moving and turned his face to me, his eyebrows furrowed.

Peter and my mother then entered, holding Jordan by the hand.

"I don't know what's going on, but let's enjoy breakfast," Peter said, sounding slightly annoyed.

"No, I think it's best if we keep Jordan here and you take Vern upstairs so you guys can talk," my mother said.

Peter seemed reluctant to the idea. Across the counter, I noticed the small bottle of 3.5 oz lilac toilette perfume that I swear by. It was beginning to connect, and I had no further desire to explore the possibility that I had just experienced a blackout.

Drumming on the island countertop, I said, "No, no, I'm fine. Let's just enjoy breakfast." I was trying to remain positive. I was under attack, and this incident, like the one from four years ago, confirmed it for me. However, the morning was great. We laughed, ate, and reminisced. It was truly a great moment in time.

—

"What are you doing here, Elliott?" Emily whispers.

I am trying to take a nap and enjoy the summer breeze when the front door begins to creak open. I have come to learn that when this door creaks slowly enough, mischief is afoot.

"My aunt is sleeping. How did you even find me?"

"You have to come back to San Francisco. You have clients. Nathaniel Ramirez—Benner, Brown, and Motley, PLLC, out in New York, is requesting you. He and his wife, Alicia, have some serious money to invest." His tone shifts when he sees the disinterest on her face. "...And I came all this way because, baby, I haven't heard from you."

"Elliott, the last time we were together, you beat the shit out of me after I told you I might be pregnant."

"All right, and so you run away? You're a grown woman! I just asked you to take care of it. This doesn't look like an abortion clinic to me."

"You're such a fucking asshole! Please just leave."

"Look, I miss you, all right? Step outside."

"There's no way. I want you to leave," Emily insists.

"What is this? Some type of rehabilitation clinic for battered women? You've got a little bass in your voice," he chuckles.

"Don't mock me," Emily says.

I can tell she doesn't want him to leave, her voice laced with sadness. I eavesdrop, but not for long—the medicine makes me drowsy, my head falling and my eyes closing. However, I cannot rest peacefully without ensuring her safety.

"Elliott, you're going to cause a scene, and I don't want to wake my aunt. You're insulting me and being completely disrespectful. Just go."

"You think I traveled all this way just to go back home without you? Your mom is worried sick, and she keeps calling me! Nathan is one of my biggest clients, and I have to close this deal. My wife is starting to ask questions. This is getting way too messy. You need to come home."

"Messy, huh? The mistress disappears, and now everyone wants to worry. How cute—AHH!"

Emily's shriek for help gives me strength—Elliott grabs hold of her forearm.

"Get off her! Let her go, now!" I bellow, my chest tightening.

"Auntie! Oh my God, do you see what you're doing, Elliott? Just go!"

"Fine! Tell your mother to stop contacting me."

And just like that, he disappears into the night. I sit upright, waiting for Emily to make her way back over to the daybed. She walks into the kitchen, appearing as though she is searching for something—someone.

"I think he's still asleep," I say, referring to Washington. Emily drops her shoulders and makes her way over to me. Taking a seat, she bursts into tears.

"I am such a fool!" Face in palm, she becomes hysterical, sobbing and screaming, "He used me like I was nothing!"

I can do nothing but keep my head down, my poor ears ringing.

"Emily, dear, what happened?"

Taking a deep breath, she sits upright, crossing her legs.

"It's been almost six years. We were together. We were happy. Week-long vacations, brief trips, surprises, shopping excursions—anything I asked for, he gave it to me. Once my mother found out, she told me I had struck gold. Elliott is the first of his generation to own and operate a Fortune 500 company in San Francisco. Daily helicopter rides overlooking the city and, sometimes, journeys on private jets to small islands. When I met him, he was looking to hire a personal accountant and—ta-da!" She waves her hands as if to motion, *It was me.*

"What about his wife?" I ask.

Emily shrugs. "What about her? He doesn't love her—he's just stuck. They're in the public eye, and he's scrutinized for almost every little thing he does. His wife is the mayor's daughter, Anastasia Gallenport."

I close my eyes tightly as Emily continues.

"She's quite the humanitarian. I mean, she's loved by the city, catered to by the citizens of not only San Francisco but pretty much everywhere."

"I like me some Anna," I say, my head down. "She donated thousands of dollars to nonprofits to help us with healthcare and helped reconstruct it for the elderly. She's one of the reasons I can even afford my medication. And you're her husband's mistress." I emphasize the last part. "Years later, the Harringtons still find a way to be mischievous in their affairs, placing you all once again at the headline of some newspaper article. Tarnishing us further. If you get exposed, do you know what this would do to our family's history and reputation? As if there isn't already enough—"

"You don't think I know that? I have been begging Elliott for years to leave her so he and I can just live like normal people."

I sigh. "You're not understanding me, child. He's right. He cannot simply leave his wife—she is not a simple person. Their union is not modest. You will be exposed for what you're doing. You will be called a homewrecker, a whore, slandered to no end, and maybe even put out of work. This woman can do you harm without ever laying a finger atop your head!" I stress. "She is more loved than the Pope. The world calls her Anna-Agatha, for crying out loud."

"The world can call her whatever they want. I have a baby growing inside of me, and with or without anyone by my side, I am going to make a wonderful life for them. I have feelings. I am human too. I may not be able to spend millions of dollars on homeless shelters and Medicaid, but I am a wonderful person who just fell in love with an emotionally unavailable man."

"He doesn't want the baby."

"He doesn't have a choice."

I sigh. "Is that so? And what about Tippy? How does she fit into all of this?"

"He bought her a house, and pays all her bills—mine included. He takes care of us. Mother doesn't like him, but she doesn't want to ruin the good thing we have going. Once I realized I might be pregnant, I left."

"Did you really miss me, or did you just need a sanctuary? This wasn't about an article or my well-being. I knew something wasn't adding up. You asked me what happened to your grandmother—my sister—but had you read the article, you would have known. The questions would have been different."

Emily falls to her knees before me, her eyes welling with tears.

"Auntie, I know it looks so bad, but I promise you that's not why I'm here. I… I needed a break. The luxury, the hiding, the beatings… You say if the media finds out I'm a mistress, I'll be slandered. But what's worse? The slander from strangers or the slander from my own mother? I feel used, judged, and unappreciated. I can't have a normal life. What is luxury without love?"

"We all make our own choices."

—

I STRETCHED MY ARMS, yawning as Jordan snuggled comfortably beside me. Stepping out of bed, I made my way across the hall to the bathroom. I stood in front of the mirror, my own reflection startling me. I had come a long way with my weight—my face appeared slimmer, and my hair had grown longer.

After completing my morning routine, I returned to the bedroom, where Jordan was now sitting up in his pajamas, watching television. I figured Peter had gone downstairs to fetch us breakfast. I climbed back into bed, snuggling with Jordan as he enjoyed his black-and-white cartoon, *Dr. Wibbly*.

With no sign of Peter, I decided to head down to the kitchen. What I saw felt like déjà vu. My father stood hunched over the stove, scrambling eggs while music played softly from the record player. My mother came down moments later, pressing her lips against my cheek.

"Good morning, baby."

"Pumpkin, pass the spice, please," my dad said.

I handed him the black pepper and watched as he sprinkled some into the frying pan, careful to avoid the corners. I wanted so badly to ask the question that would surely get me institutionalized, but I held back. Instead, I turned and ran upstairs to sit with Jordan, who hadn't moved a muscle.

I grabbed his hands, waving them side to side as I sang along with *Dr. Wibbly*.

"Where is Pop-Pop, honey?" I eventually asked.

What he said next sent a surge of goosebumps up my arms.

"Pop-Pop's at home, Mummy," Jordan said, his voice soft and angelic.

Fear tightened in my chest. "Pop-Pop home?" I repeated, my voice barely above a whisper. "Do you mean Pop-Pop home in New York or home with us?"

I had lost him. Jordan was now chuckling, waving me away like I was nothing more than a distraction.

Knock, knock.

The sudden sound at the door made my heart quiver. Everything was making me paranoid.

"Vern, baby, it's me."

My mother's voice grounded me. I had been fearing for myself—fearing for my sanity. When I opened the door, she stepped inside, holding a breakfast tray. There was enough food on it to feed an army. There was no way Jordan and I could finish it on our own.

I asked if she would be joining us. She nodded in agreement. We sat on the edge of the bed, Jordan between us, nibbling on small bites of bacon.

"Mom, so how are things?"

"You asked me that yesterday," she said with a smile.

Running her fingers through my hair, she looked at me with sadness in her eyes before deciding to tell me the truth.

"We talked, you and I, for about four hours while your dad sat outside smoking a cigar with the neighbor. You told me about the house, the children, and what Veronica had done... You and I also planted five pots of the season's orchids while your dad and Jordan tossed a ball. After that, you insisted on helping me with dinner. You burned the peas a little, and I made lamb chops with baked beans and rice. Jordan fell asleep around seven, and you and I stayed up in the study talking about Peter. Yesterday morning and yesterday night."

I refused to eat. My appetite was gone.

"Mom, what is happening to me?" I asked, my eyes welling with tears.

"I know you're scared, baby," she said, her gaze dropping to the floor. "When I was a girl, I used to watch people come to my mother at all hours of the night, begging her to remove someone from their life or change something—make them successful, make them beautiful, heal a family member… or take one away. She did it, but not without taking something in return. A large part of me wanted my brother… gone." She paused, her voice heavy. "Did I ever think my Green Trees would end up like this? Of course not. But I prayed against her. I prayed hard. I prayed for you both, but maybe it wasn't enough. There are stages to it when you don't openly accept it right away. This one here is your last stage—something keeps changing, doesn't it?"

I interrupted, "Peter. Peter keeps changing."

I had so many questions, but I could tell she was growing uncomfortable.

"So why only in the mornings? How come I don't remember anything from yesterday? I keep blacking out—it's like I'm losing time. How do I stop it?"

"Vern, I didn't want to say anything because, honestly, I have no clue how to stop it."

I took a deep breath. "What's going to happen to me? Did this happen to Nica?" I began pacing. "Mom, you have to know something."

She hesitated. "Um, okay... Did you tell anyone you were coming here? Anyone at all?"

"No, I snuck out. Peter didn't know I was leaving." I stopped suddenly. "Wait a minute. Did we speak? Does he know where I am?"

A wave of anxiety hit me.

"Yes, you called him the moment you arrived."

"Okay, so we're getting somewhere. At least now I know what the reality is—and that is, Peter is, in fact, not here!"

She nodded. "That is correct."

But I still felt terrified, like nothing was truly adding up.

"How did you know something was off? Was I speaking to Peter—or at least thinking I was—at all yesterday?"

"No, that's not how it works. There are many ways to take a mind, and my mother knew all kinds of magic. This one seems gradual. I begged you to read your Bible, Vern. I begged."

"Forget the Bible, Mom. I wouldn't even know where to start with it. When will I see Peter again?"

"Tomorrow morning."

I sobbed. "Mommy, I feel like I'm going crazy."

I truly did. I felt drained, like I was fighting a monster I couldn't see. There was always something standing between me and true happiness.

My mother reached for my hands. "I think I know someone who can help. She's from the city and came down here for work a while back. Met her at the grocery."

About an hour and a half later, we arrived at a doctor's office—Dr. Lebons Psychiatry.

"Mother, what are you skimming?"

I was appalled and growing angry.

"Nothing," she said calmly. "The lady I'm sending you to is in the back nearest the basement. She works here, makes most of her money here, too. I don't think I need to explain why. She'll know you're coming."

"I'm coming? So, you're not going with me?"

"No."

"Mom, will I remember this tomorrow?"

She hesitated. "Maybe, maybe not."

Whatever it was—whatever Grandma Martin had done to me—it was frightening. Even at that moment, I couldn't tell if it was real or not.

—

Sitting on my porch, rocking my chair on this hot summer day, reminds me of the good ol' days—the days filled with laughter and commotion as the children frolic outside, climbing trees in search of new adventures and customers.

Owning a newly renovated cottage, bought from a terminally ill gentleman named Kansas Hendricks as a chance to start anew, means tearing away from the outside world just long enough to find ourselves, to rediscover a reason to love one another after everything we have been through.

—

I LET OUT A SHARP CRY.

My back ached, my arms trembled, and my feet were bare. Where was I? The entrance looked dark, almost non-existent. It was a wonder I had even found the place. My mother was long gone.

Talking to myself, I asked, "Am I dreaming?"

A voice responded, "No."

I turned toward the sound, but I couldn't see anyone. A touch against my cheek made me flinch.

"I have been waiting for you! My, oh my, you've grown."

The face I saw weakened me, and I lost my footing.

"You are so beautiful," she said as my eyes fluttered open.

Where are my shoes? I wondered.

"Your mother knows I do not allow shoes in my home."

"Home?"

The space smelled like a sewage-filled basement and looked nothing like a home. The stranger began lighting candles, one after another.

"How was your flight?" she asked.

"It was fine."

"The gentleman on the plane, Mr. Lilac… His name is Paul."

"Who are you?"

"I am a protector. Vernette, I know there are forces working against you. But there is no voodoo stronger than my God. We are a group of people who guide individuals like you back into your light."

Her Caribbean accent was spellbinding.

"You are special, and those who wish to do you harm will not succeed, my dear."

Finally, she turned to face me. She was a beautiful woman with mocha skin and shoulder-length dreadlocks. Her natural waves framed her full lips, and her hair smelled of sweet peppermint, just like Veronica's. In an instant, she disappeared.

"My child, tell me, what do you wish to know?"

I circled the room, my lips moving as I prepared to answer the question of a voice within the walls. I felt terrified. I felt alone, despite knowing I wasn't. And I felt foolish.

"I-I want to know what's happening to me," I said nervously, my hands fidgeting.

Her laugh was cynical.

"A loop to mad you, my dear—you have been touched by the dead. Paul was there to save you. There was a, uh, glitch, as one would call it. You see, I was there when Allery died. I watched with my own two eyes, and although our parents did not see eye to eye, a set of eyes was no longer a cause for worry. That is what set me on my path.

As a direct descendant, I am aware of those who are kind and pure of heart. That day when your grandmother walked you into the salon, I sat there, smelling your flesh and listening to your heartbeat—thump, thump, thump. It might as well have been outside your chest. You were so frightened, and from that moment, I knew you were the special one. I imagined Holly would protect you, but she did not. Could not, I should say.

God is sending His angels."

I was so confused—her voice was omniscient.

I tried to listen, grasping all that she had to say, but nothing made sense. She wasn't answering my question.

"What about this loop?"

"Ah, deh loop. We say the loop is to madden the mind. To set it on fire. Yet, your mind is like water—ease, peaceful, and flowing with only a small wave but no interruptions. No lifelong alterations. You are fine. Paul and the lilac, you cling close."

"What does that even mean?" I was growing agitated, shouting in circles. I had no shoes, the room smelled putrid, and I refused to believe that I had been thrown into a sewer only to receive less information from an expert than from my own mother.

"The loop is like the water. The wave comes, ride it out," she said.

"Dinner is ready!"

I could hear my mother shouting from the bottom of the stairs as I woke from my slumber. I had no recollection of how or when I had returned to my parents' home. My mind raced. I wanted to go back to Harlem.

Jordan's clothes were different from the day before—at least, the day I remembered. The bathroom door opened, and a wave of steam hit me from across the hall.

"Sweetie, I don't think I packed enough underwear," Peter said as he casually searched his suitcase for a fresh pair of boxers.

I wanted to scream.

I sat upright on the mattress, my eyes darting back and forth. I had no idea what to do or say. Peter continued his soliloquy. I was not there. Physically, I was, but mentally—I had gone.

"I said dinner is ready!" my mother cried again, this time from the middle of the stairs. Jordan ran down, tearing his eyes away from the television set.

"Be careful, kiddo!" Peter bellowed.

My husband was still a drowning sound—background noise I wished I could turn off.

"Vern? Vern!"

I dared not face him. Facing him would be like facing reality—the reality that I was losing my mind. I was ready to accept defeat.

"I, um, will meet you downstairs," I managed to say.

I whispered a quick prayer in my head, begging God that Peter would listen and continue without me.

I made it down to the kitchen, avoiding mirrors like the plague. I couldn't bear to see my reflection, believing that I, too, would only be an illusion. Everything was changing—my mind playing tricks on me, my body aching, the voices in my head growing louder, speaking faintly. As I entered the dining room, Peter caressed me from behind. I shuddered at his touch.

"Sweetie, please pass me that plate of mash," my mother requested.

Turning to face her silenced the malevolent sounds in my mind.

"Sure," I said.

"Vern, baby, we may have to get some recipes from your mother before we leave. I always knew she was quite the cook, but man, oh man—"

"Watch it, young boy! This here is my good pot of cooking. All right now."

They all laughed.

My father was quite the comedian when he wanted to be. I, however, felt awkward—like I was trapped in a twisted reality.

Something was off.

This nefarious plot plagued me, causing an obsession that grew by the minute.

"Vern, darling, can you help me over in the kitchen?"

After serving the men, my mother walked with me into the pantry, shutting the dining room doors behind her.

"You cannot let this win," she said.

Startled, I gasped. "Mom, oh my God, I didn't know if you were real or not. I'm so scared. Why is he here again?" I began to sob, my voice trembling uncontrollably. "Peter is here. He is here. He is in there, and we are out here, and Daddy, Jordan—they all see him. My God, you just gave him food, and he isn't even real. This is torture, Mommy."

I banged the kitchen sink, turning on the cold water and splashing it onto my face.

"I understand, I do. But, Vern, I need you to think. There are a few ways to slow this down, but you have to remember—when did she do this to you?"

I shuddered at the thought.

"Think!"

"I can't remember. I don't know!" I shouted.

"Think!" she screamed.

I thought long and hard, but as I searched my mind, I felt something scratching beneath my skin—scraping me, burning my flesh. My eyes rolled partially behind my head as if something within me was trying to escape. I wanted to peel the skin from my bones. One side of my mind urged me to do it, while the other fought to rationalize my thoughts.

"What if I just leave?" I whispered, ready to give up.

My mother shot me a look of contempt. "Then the loop wins, and whoever is causing you this pain will only continue. Confront it and put an end to this!"

"I don't know who to confront, Mommy. I have no idea!" I sobbed again, feeling helpless.

She was growing impatient. "When did she do this to you?"

I fought with my mind, the ticking clock growing louder as I stood still. Closing my eyes, I sent my thoughts back—years back.

"Nica," I said, opening my eyes. "A night at Nica's. I was asleep. She tried to strangle me."

Tranquilly, my mother said, "She came to work on you."

I let out a long sigh. "You knew?"

"I always knew. But this is not regular voodoo. This is not a fairytale. This is death. As a mother, I stand at a crossroads—I understand both the living and the dead. You have your light. I made sure of it before we left, your father and I. Learn the truth from your husband, Vernette. You need allies. There can be no secrets. Everything must come to light."

"So, you're not going to help me?" My heart pounded as fresh tears streamed down my face.

"I already did," she said, smiling.

The day went dark.

The next day, I decided to get serious. With only two days left, I had to figure something out. Peter was gone, and although he was absent physically, he remained a presence in my mind. I decided to call him. The sound of his voice on the other end sent my mind into an uproar.

"Hi, baby. I guess you're having a ball. I barely hear from you," he said. His voice sounded softer somehow—more pleasant.

"Peter, we need to talk."

Silence.

—

"So now you're saying Grandma Nica is some kind of witch? I don't believe in all this hoodoo, voodoo nonsense—superstitions and shit," Emily enters angrily.

Inebriated, she tumbles into the house, the evening sun casting long shadows around us.

"Aren't you pregnant?" Washington asks, his tone laced with disgust.

"Cheers! Yeah. But I'm killing this thing as soon as I touch back down in San Fran," Emily says happily. "I mean, everyone wants the kid dead anyway, so…"

She slurs her words, her voice, and movements resembling the whir of a vacuum. Watching her smile and drag her feet across the floorboards fills me with great worry.

"Washington, fetch her some water, will you, please?" I ask, though inside, I am raging with anger.

"Sit down, woman!" I motion for Emily to take a seat next to me, but she refuses.

"Now, why would I wanna do that? Right, Auntie? Everything you've said, everything you've talked about—" she cries, standing against the front door with her arms folded.

"Washington, you poor little thing. Did you leave him, or did he leave you? Things weren't as serious on his end, huh? Just a sad and pathetic faggot. You ain't here to do nothing good for nobody. These the type of stories you write—paranormal bullshit. I made some calls. But you don't know shit about what I'm going through or dealing with, okay? All you know is how to bend over and get fucked!"

"That is enough!" I shout, my chest tightening.

Washington comes running to my aid, the water he had intended for Emily now forced down my throat as I gasp for air.

"You think I feel good staying here and listening to your story while you make yourself sound like some kind of cherub? My grandmother is no witch! She loves us—all of us. Including you, Auntie. For a while, you were infatuated with her, and now she's some sorceress casting voodoo spells on you?

Oh, Washington, you flew all this way to listen to these lies? Readers must eat this shit up in that filthy city of yours?"

Washington has heard enough.

"Goddammit! You are a Harrington. They say the apples don't fall too far from the tree—well, here you are, a perfectly ripened apple. Listen, you insidious woman, understand that I and my sexuality are none of your business.

You were sleeping with a married man, and maybe the reason you're so defensive—why you wallow in your own self-pity—is because you've finally realized that you've been living a piteous life.

You may have the great job, the high-rise condo, and a rich lifestyle, but what is it all worth when you've remained nothing more than a secret?

You can call me names. Shit, you want to know all the facts? My husband's name is Derek Stoner. I left my wonderful husband and my wonderful life to come here. And no, it's not because the city I live in is some filthy metropolis or because I wanted to hear about ghosts. In fact, it's filled with people who are smart and passionate about their goals. We're fast-paced—not lying around fucking married men with nothing else better to do than plot how to get pregnant just for the chance to keep him!"

"Hey! Hey!" I say, thrusting my cup across the floor—the shattered glass jolting me as I place my hands over my face. My head throbs.

"Washington, please, don't get yourself so worked up. She's not in her right mind," I continue.

"You're siding with him—" Emily snaps.

"Juvenile," Washington interrupts.

"Stop it, both of you! Now!" I scream.

—

"PETER, IS THERE something you aren't telling me? I mean, can you tell me what happened the night of The Times Party? I was drinking, I know, but did I speak to anyone? Tell anyone anything? Am I missing something?"

Peter let out a long sigh. "Vern, please, can we not do this?"

"Peter, I know you're hiding something now. You have to tell me—you have no idea what I'm going through here."

"No?"

"No!"

—

Begging them both to take a seat is becoming increasingly strenuous. They are both stubborn, and I can feel my tremors worsening.

"Now you're calling me names? Funny how that works." Emily snipes, speaking ferociously to Washington.

"Ain't shit funny!"

Emily and Washington are now face-to-face, and for the first time since his arrival, I see the more flamboyant side of him. "If you do not remove yourself from my personal space—" Washington threatens, standing firm.

"What the hell you gonna do? Just because you take it from the back don't make you no woman!"

"Stop it, please!" My tremors intensify. This is a side of Emily I have never seen before.

—

"YOUR SISTER IS HAVING an affair with my boss. I thought it was over, I swear to you. Stoner is a good guy, okay? His wife doesn't know, and the night of the party, I saw you guys talking, so I figured I would join you because he was drunk, his wife was there, and I didn't want him telling you anything he'd regret. I am trying my best to keep things together, but ever since I met you and your family, my life just hasn't been the same. Then, when you just up and left, I thought maybe you had found out. I thought maybe he had told you and you were mad at me. It was a lot, I know—first the kids, and then that."

I could hear the pain in his voice. I was speechless.

"So you weren't angry with me? You—you were upset when I called you?..."

He wasn't mad at all.

"No, baby, I wasn't upset."

Was that all not real either? I questioned myself.

"So, that's how you recognized Veronica when she came to stay with us?"

"Yes," he admitted. "She caught me with Elizabeth once, around the time I caught her with Stoner. So, we just tried to…"

"Tried to what? Protect each other? In our home…just…" The tears seeped between my lips. There was no photo of David and Peter. She had lied. It was all a lie to cover…

"Is David even Jordan's father?" I asked.

"Oh, that—I—I swear, honey, I don't know. I can't say for sure, and I don't think she can either."

Silence.

"What now?" I asked, struggling to keep the phone to my ear.

"Vernette, baby, now we start over. We pretend like we know nothing about the Stoners or the pregnancy, and we just move forward. We don't have to let anyone else back into our lives. We have our family. We have one another."

As much as I wanted to believe Peter and agree with him, my heart simply wouldn't let me. I felt lied to, betrayed, used.

"How long?" I mustered up the words between my tears.

"How long what, baby?"

"How long has Nica been sleeping with your boss? I assume it's the same amount of time you were with Elizabeth."

That was the jealousy kicking in. I imagined her soft lips against his, her long hair flowing alongside his torso, her hands gliding across his pelvis, stroking his penis. I didn't think of Peter in that way, which frightened me.

"Sweetheart, that doesn't matter—"

"How long?" I shouted.

"Vernette, please, I am begging you now. It doesn't matter—"

"Well then! That explains it," I said calmly.

"Vern, let me explain…"

"No! You had years to explain! Years, and you let me go on thinking everything was okay, that things were fine. But things weren't fine. The Stoners aren't fine! Robert is sleeping with my sister, and poor Martha—she's such a good woman. She doesn't deserve that! Good God," I cried. "I didn't deserve that!" I shouted before hanging up.

At that moment, I realized that I had never truly dealt with Peter's infidelity. We had been thrust into parenthood, only to have it ripped from us, and we tried to fill that void with a baby of our own.

I broke down. It was like a wave of emotions attacking me from the very depths of my soul.

Peter would lose his job if the Stoners ended their marriage. We would be destitute.

Veronica was ruining my life.

It was clear to me now.

—

Washington and Emily finally settle down, but I can feel the rising tension.

"Robert Stoner? The New York Times? Nineteen sixty—" Washington inquires, almost bewildered. He turns, his hand atop his head.

"Yes," I say, confirming.

"So, is your sister the reason my husband's grandparents got divorced?" We both take a deep breath simultaneously. A long pause follows, and a feeling of dread falls upon me. I have no clue—now I believe the world is just as small as they say. I apologize profusely.

"I have more tequila. I left it on the porch," Emily says to him.

"I need a minute," Washington says as he proceeds out of the house onto the porch. Emily follows. I can hear them indistinctly.

"I think you need some tequila."

"I don't drink."

"Wouldn't it be funny?"

Silence.

"I am really not in the mood for your shenanigans," Washington replies.

"I mean, you're taking this really hard for a complete stranger. As I said, I made some phone calls, and as you said, the apple doesn't fall too far from the tree, and neither do the branches. Something about those Harringtons destroying people's lives, huh."

The next morning, waking up feels like death. I want to close my eyes and fall into an eternal slumber. I envy Nica for no longer having to feel pain, sadness, or suffering. She doesn't have to grow old. Washington has not yet awakened. Typically, he'd be downstairs serving up the best countryside cooking anyone has ever tasted.

Last night put things into perspective for me. Last night made me realize just how destructive my family really is.

"Morning, ma'am," the sound of Washington's baritone alarms me. Standing at the top of the stairs, I have no idea how to greet him. I remain silent. "There are no issues between us, Mrs. Vern. I still have a job to do."

"You can always erase the part I said last night, young man."

"Absolutely not! Unless, unless that's something you want. As I mentioned upon my arrival, if there is anything you want removed, I will abide." He makes his way downstairs.

"No, I mean, I am no longer impacted by it. I just didn't realize you would be so deeply hurt. I was more astonished by the coincidence of it all."

"Derek was raised by his grandmother. I have never met his actual parents. They left him when he was seven. Martha, I'm sure you've met her during her earlier days, is such a loving woman. Pure-hearted, selfless, and simply kind. Your days were before my time, but hearing of the infidelity struck a chord with me."

"I see." I do see. I completely agree with everything he says. Washington isn't lying about Martha. The thought that my sister could be responsible for prematurely ending a marriage sickens me. Even to this day. "Will you tell Derek?"

"I'll have no choice. Derek is by far my number one supporter. He'll read the book, he'll listen to the radio, and he'll find out. I'd rather have him hear it from me. His reaction is a risk I'm willing to take."

"Risk?"

"Good morning, beautiful people!" Emily makes her way down the stairs, interrupting Washington and me. We exchange a quick glance before I decide to stare a little longer.

TO BE CONTINUED…

Lisa K. Stephenson